Sarah Hilary's debut, *Someone Else's Skin*, won ~~~~~~~'s Crime Novel of the Year in 2015 and was a World Book Night selection for 2016. She has been chosen for the Richard & Judy Bookclub, and is the author of six novels featuring DI Marnie Rome and DS Noah Jake. She lives in Bath.

Praise for *Never Be Broken*:

'Deeply contemporary, painfully real, heartbreakingly good'   **Mick Herron**

'[A] searing perceptive novel'   *Observer*

'Sarah Hilary is going to be up there with the likes of Ruth Rendell, PD James and Val McDermid, as a game changer of British crime fiction'   *Crime Review*

'Addictive, chilling and beautifully written. The timely story pulls you in deep'   **Will Dean**

'The Marnie Rome stories are clever and sharp, but they also have the most incredibly emotional depth and clarity. I adored it'   **Joanna Cannon**

'Tough, tender, absolutely terrifying'   **Erin Kelly**

'A satisfyingly complex mystery'   *Mail On Sunday*

Praise for *Come and Find Me*:

'Complicated, nuanced and psychologically rich. So assured and beguiling. I am lost in admiration at her imagination and skill'   **Sabine Durrant**

'A ten~~~~~~~~~~~~~~~~~~~~~~~~~~~~~~~~t breakneck speed ~~~~~~~~~~~~~~~~~~~~~~~~~~~~~~~*ndependent*

SARAH HILARY
NEVER BE BROKEN

HEADLINE

First published in 2019 by
HEADLINE PUBLISHING GROUP

First published in paperback in 2020 by
HEADLINE PUBLISHING GROUP

1

Cataloguing in Publication Data is available from the British Library

B format ISBN 978 1 4722 4902 9

Typeset in Meridien by Palimpsest Book Production Ltd, Falkirk, Stirlingshire

Printed and bound in Great Britain by Clays Ltd, Elcograf S.p.A.

HEADLINE PUBLISHING GROUP
An Hachette UK Company
Carmelite House
50 Victoria Embankment
London EC4Y 0DZ

www.headline.co.uk
www.hachette.co.uk

To Pretana Morgan, and all the other mothers.

Now

The car alarm was still shrieking when Marnie reached the crime scene.

'Can't we shut that off?' She'd heard it from two streets away, a giddy note of outrage under London's morning soundtrack, making her want to turn her own car around and head the other way. But here she was, doing her job, with a police crime-scene officer so young she looked around for a grown-up. 'Surely we can shut it off?'

It was hard enough being this close to the wreckage – twisted metal, bloodied broken glass – without the sickening wail from inside the vehicle.

'The sensor's bust.' The young PCSO wiped at his mouth. 'Believe me, we've tried.'

Marnie turned away to rest her eyes, waiting for the pain in her chest to ease, or at least to blunt a little. She was finding it hard to breathe. Her throat was pinched tight with panic, and with guilt. Guilt rode with her most days, but panic was a new companion. She was unused

1

to its temperament, the hiccupy whispering in her ear: *Are we there yet? Are we done?*

Behind her, cars crawled two lanes deep, the morning's rush hour reduced to horns and hand signals. White noise reached from the ring road, whiplashing when it hit the tailback. The dregs of the sound slipped around the sides of Erskine Tower to find her.

She didn't look at the tower; she didn't need to. It was there at the periphery of her vision, would be there if she walked a quarter of a mile in any direction. Three hundred and thirty feet of municipal sixties high-rise, a crude concrete finger flipping off the rest of west London. From street level, the block was gaunt, its shadow a chilly welt running up the road from the low-lying bohemia of Notting Hill before striking out for Ealing, queen of London's suburbs. You wouldn't want to be here after dark, but at 8 a.m., the neighbourhood was hung-over, abandoned. Flanked by that rarest of London landmarks: unmetered parking spaces, a greater abomination in the eyes of city planners than the ugly high-rise itself.

This morning, empty flags of sky hung either side of Erskine Tower. Smoke was seeping from a window at the very top, so far away it looked like a cloud unravelling. If she stood very still and held her breath in her chest, it was a day like any other.

Rain spotted her face. One of those arbitrary handfuls that falls on a dry day, smelling of rust and copper. Unless it was the smell of blood from the ruined bonnet of the car. Her skin recoiled. She took a step back, away.

The PCSO warned, 'Mind your feet, ma'am.'

She looked down to see Noah Jake's shirt twisted in the gutter.

Are we there yet? Are we done?

Noah's shirt. She recognised the blue cotton, its smooth

weave stained by the same blood that was running from the bonnet to pool under the car's front tyre. The shrill of the alarm drowned out the smaller sounds of brittle chips of glass falling from the wreckage. An Audi, Noah had taken it from the police station less than an hour ago. She hadn't looked up when he'd said he was heading out; only nodded with her eyes on the morning's paperwork. She hadn't said, 'Good luck,' or, 'Take care,' or anything at all. He'd gone without a glance from her, or a word.

'What a mess.' The PCSO sucked air between his teeth.

Marnie lifted a hand to brush the rain from her face, holding it there for a long moment to block out the drunken lurch of the tower. Seeing through the bars of her fingers all the ways in which the morning's chaos had altered everything.

1

Forty-eight hours earlier

'Is Detective Sergeant Jake around?'

'Who's asking?' DS Ron Carling spun in his chair, bending his brow at the newcomer. He'd become protective of Noah in the last ten weeks, a contingency neither man could've foreseen when they first began working together two years ago.

Watching from the window of her office, Marnie saw the visitor smile.

'Karie Matthews.' The woman held out a hand. 'Dr Matthews.'

Ron rose to shake her hand, losing a little of his gate-keeper gruffness. Karie Matthews was small even in her heels, wearing a dark grey dress under a bright grey jacket tailored to her slight frame. Her fair hair was cropped short, shot through with silver. Her eyes, deep-set and expressive as a dancer's, fixed on Ron's face, giving him her full attention. Marnie saw him soften, fighting his first instinct to protect Noah, because that was what you did when your mate was being subjected to occupational health and welfare counselling. No one on the team would deny that Noah needed support, as anyone in his circumstances would, but few believed it was best provided by a stranger, someone from outside the team.

'He'll be in a bit later,' Ron was saying. 'Detective Inspector Rome's around, if you need her?'

Karie Matthews said, 'It's always a pleasure to talk with DI Rome.'

Marnie couldn't fault the woman's manner or her charm, but she opened the door to her office reluctantly, as if inviting a viper inside. It wasn't Karie's fault, she knew. It was the memory of her own time with Occupational Health and Welfare, seven years ago. She'd resisted the referral by her line manager, OCU Commander Tim Welland, just as Noah was resisting Marnie's referral now. She had to hope that Karie, like Lexie seven years ago, would keep faith with the task until Noah was able to benefit from it.

Noah Jake was speaking with his brother, Sol. More precisely, he was arguing with Sol. As kids, he'd rarely lost an argument to his little brother. But that had been down to Sol's habit of losing interest and walking away, rather than Noah's persuasive skills. It was different now. Now Sol was the one seeking him out to argue, about everything. Noah's clothes, his breakfast choices, how he spent his evenings. He wouldn't have minded, but it was ten weeks since Sol had died. Noah was arguing with a ghost.

'Seriously, bruv. That tie with that suit?'

'What's wrong with this tie?' Noah asked the question in spite of the promise he'd made to himself last night that he would stop rising to Sol's bait. 'Exactly?'

'Just you look like an undertaker.'

Noah met his dead brother's eyes in the mirror. 'You're obsessed with funerals.'

'Yeah?' Sol picked at his teeth with his thumbnail, a habit he'd had as a kid. 'You're the one dressing like an undertaker.' He slouched into the wall, his pink hoody a blast of carnival music in the bedroom Noah shared with Dan, who was taking a shower and couldn't hear the argument over Noah's sartorial choices.

He set the tie aside. 'So I'm hoping to see Mum at the weekend.'

Sol stiffened, then shook his head. 'Not cool. I'm not up for that.'

'She's on her own, and the last time she was on her own—'

'Not like that.' Sol cut him short. 'It's not like that.'

'Well, what is it like?' Noah hadn't seen his mum in days.

'She's got new friends.' Sol pulled a face. 'Talks with them all the time, just like Dad said. And you know what? It's your fault.' He pointed both fingers at Noah, accusingly. 'Your. Fault.'

'How is it my fault?'

'You had to buy her that computer. Showing off, flashing your cash. I mean, what were you *t'inking*?' Jabbing his fingers at his temples. 'What was going through your head?'

As someone who'd been conversing with a ghost for the last ten weeks, Noah wasn't sure he could give a convincing answer to questions concerning the contents of his head.

'Dad said she doesn't get out much at the moment.' He reached for a different tie. 'The computer's so she can keep in touch, do her shopping online, that sort of thing.'

'Oh, she does her shopping online.' Sol burst out laughing. 'That and everything else.'

Noah's fingers chilled. 'Her new friends . . . they're online friends?'

'Online *freaks* is what they are.' Anger altered Sol's voice. 'Online mind-screwing *freaks*.'

'And Mum chats with them?'

'All the time. Dad *said*, remember?' Sol collapsed onto the bed, hiding his face in the crook of his elbow. 'So, yeah. If you want to go round, you're on your own. Not cool, not coming.'

Noah looked down at his brother, processing what Sol had said. Or rather what his subconscious was trying to tell him through the medium of Sol's ghost. Imagining their mum, Rosa, with an internet addiction on top of everything else. 'Is she taking anything right now?'

Pills, he meant. Sometimes the pills helped. But often they made it worse.

'Yeah.' Sol's voice was muffled by his arm. 'Some herbal shit one of her new mates came up with. Dad says it's just vitamins, can't do her any harm. Well, you heard him saying it. Except I've not seen her this weird in years. She's never been right, but this's *wrong*. Spending all her shit on water and batteries, and Dad pretending that's okay, that's normal? Bullshit.'

'Water and batteries?' Noah echoed.

Dad had told him about this, he must've done. How else would his subconscious know the words to put into Sol's mouth? But Noah couldn't remember the conversation. It made him wonder what else he'd forgotten from the ten weeks since he'd lost his brother.

'And tinned crap,' Sol was saying. 'House's a disaster zone, you should see it. *Your* room? Wall-to-wall water, for when it stops coming out of taps. Whole world's going to shit, that's her thing now.' He laughed, unhappily. 'She's given up the brushes. No more cleaning, no more nothing. *Boom*. Apocalypse, that's her new thing.'

'She's stockpiling food and water.' Noah's eyes throbbed. 'Is that what you're saying? Dad said . . . And her new friends, they're encouraging this?'

'They're all doing it, bruv. Latest craze. Latest *boom*.' Sol kicked a foot at the bed. 'Fucking *preppers*, innit?'

Noah and Marnie had dealt with a case involving preppers, two years ago. He'd witnessed their paranoia and fear first-hand. He'd never imagined his mum would fall prey to it, despite knowing how fragile she was. And it was all so much worse since—

'Noah?' Dan was towelling his hair, barefoot in jeans and a T-shirt. 'Were you on the phone?'

Noah shook his head. 'Just . . .'

'Thought I heard voices.' Dan scrubbed at his head with the towel.

Noah glanced at the empty bed, its covers pulled smooth. No Sol, not even the shape of him there. Because his brother was dead. Sol was dead. There was only the neat space where Noah lay all night blinking at the ceiling, waiting for the morning so he could dress and leave the house. Bury himself in work, so deep he couldn't hear Sol speaking to him, picking a fight over the route he'd taken to the police station, or the theory he had about the case they were working. Sol would've argued with DI Rome had Noah let him. He didn't, holding his brother at arm's length for moments like this one, when Dan returned from the shower with his hair wet, eyes dark with worry for Noah and the way he was dealing with his grief – or not dealing with it.

'This tie.' Noah held up the one Sol had criticised. 'It goes with the suit, right?'

Dan slung the wet towel around his neck and crossed the room, taking the tie from Noah's hand and running it under the collar of his shirt before knotting it. They were so close, Noah could see the razor burn on Dan's jaw. He leaned in to test its smoothness with his lips, tasting shaving foam, catching the warmth of Dan's skin, wishing he could steal a little for himself. He was numb with cold, pricked by goose bumps from his brother's ghost.

'Don't go to work today.' Dan curled his palm around the back of Noah's neck, pulling him close. 'Stay home. Let me—'

'Don't tempt me.' Noah straightened, smiling.

'Why not?' Dan's elbow was hard and spare in his hand. 'You said yourself DI Rome wanted you to rest.'

'So we'd be resting?'

But Dan shook his head at Noah's smile. 'Afterwards, sure. It's what you need.'

'I need to work.' His brother's pink hoody was in the doorway, heading down the stairs to the street. He couldn't let Sol out there on his own, it wasn't safe. 'See you tonight. I'll cook, okay?'

'How is he?' Karie Matthews folded her hands in her lap, considering Marnie's question. 'Relying on work to see him through this. Resenting time away from work, resisting the counselling. So far so typical.' Her smile wore a frown. 'How is he here?'

'The same. Conscientious, clever, compassionate. The best detective I've worked with.' Marnie met the woman's gaze. 'Is he working too hard? Yes, but he always has. Do I have serious concerns about his welfare? No, but neither am I complacent. We're meeting regularly, and he's talking with me. Not as much as I'd like, or you would like, but enough for me to believe it's progress.'

'These cases you're working on. Are they affecting him, do you think?' Karie had averted her gaze from the evidence boards in the incident room. All those young faces, eyes burning black and white. It was hard to look at them. Harder still when a new face was added, which was happening all too often as the investigations dug deeper.

'Of course. But no more than they would've done two months ago. It's affecting us all.'

'He's worked on tougher cases,' Karie agreed. 'Dead brothers. Vigilantism. The personal attack two years ago that left him with broken ribs.'

Marnie waited for a question.

'He's been through a great deal. I'm not trying to make a special case for him . . .' Karie cut herself short, shaking her head. 'Or perhaps I am. I like him a little too much, that's the truth of it. I admire his courage, and his commitment. And I worry for him. Professional distance only gets us so far in this line of work.'

'I understand. I feel the same. He's an exceptional detective, but more than that, he's a good man. Perhaps if it wasn't so rare . . .'

They shared a sad smile.

'He needs to work,' Marnie said. 'It would feel too much like punishment for him to be signed off. Of course I'd do that if it became necessary. Nothing's worth risking his recovery. If it comes to that, he wouldn't want to jeopardise the integrity of the investigation. He might resist it, and resent it, but he'd understand. He wants these prosecutions as badly as the rest of us, maybe more.'

She'd seen Noah studying the evidence boards, meeting those stares head-on, refusing to look away. Frank Reece and the others. He had committed their names to memory, and their faces. They were haunting his dreams, driving his days. Children, many recruited from care homes, picked up and held in debt bondage. Exploited, or simply killed. Used to run guns or drugs across county lines, passed like gifts between gangs. London's lost.

'Modern-day slavery,' Karie said softly. 'That's what they're saying. I listened to a radio programme; the extent of it sounds horrific. Frightening.'

It was how most people first learned of the plight of these children – from the comfort of their kitchens or cars, in a sanitised radio broadcast. Not by looking into the faces of the exploited kids, or listening to their interviews. Those torturous hours of silence and denials, misery and anger.

'And gangs,' Karie was saying. 'When that's how Sol died.'

How Sol had lived, too. Marnie didn't need to remind Dr Matthews of that fact.

'Given the circumstances of Sol's arrest, and his death . . .' Karie shook her head. 'And now Noah's working on cases directly linked to gangs and knife crime.'

Sol had died in a prison yard, bleeding from a stomach wound.

'If we could pick our cases . . .' Marnie said. 'But we can't. And if we kept Noah away from crimes involving gangs or knives, he wouldn't be working more than a case or two a year. This is London.' She paused. 'But I'm staying close to him. We're talking, and I'm being careful, watching for signs of post-traumatic stress. It's in no one's interests to break him.'

Sol was waiting in the street with a look of disgust for Noah's tie. He twitched the pink hood of his jacket over his head, falling into step with his brother. 'I knew that kid, Frank Reece. Frankie.' He sniffed, wiping his nose with the back of his hand. 'He was a nice kid.'

Noah didn't speak, seeing Frank's face grinning at him from the evidence board at the station. Fifteen years old, so good-looking it hurt. Shiny brown eyes, shiny white teeth. Happy.

'That's no way to die.' Sol turned his face away, reaching to pull a leaf from the hedge they were passing. 'No way.'

Frank had died in broad daylight outside a corner shop in Tottenham where he'd stopped to buy a Capri Sun. He'd pushed the plastic straw into the drink and sucked a mouthful before he was approached by a boy of seventeen, who stabbed him twice in the heart.

Sol turned the leaf in his fingers before letting it go. 'Better than the stomach, though.'

Noah shut his eyes, instructing his subconscious to dial down the morbidity. It wasn't even 10 a.m. and he had a day's work to get through, not forgetting a session with Dr Matthews.

'Love you, bruv.' Sol sloped sideways, peeling away, raising a hand behind his hooded head.

It worked like that sometimes: an instruction to his subconscious and Sol was gone. But it didn't always work. Less and less, in fact, as the weeks went by. Noah had thought the opposite would be true, that his brother's ghost would fade as the days passed, each day taking him a step further from the last time he saw Sol, the last time they spoke.

A taxi slid up to the kerb, disgorging a man in a Burberry trench coat who gave a hostile stare as he shouldered past. Noah checked his watch before patting his pockets for his Oyster card. He'd told no one, not even Dan, but he'd grown claustrophobic in the weeks since Sol died. Hated being below ground, even in a car park or underpass. Taking the Tube was his way of dealing with the pressure that crowded his chest, stuffing his head with black puffs of panic.

Thanks to Dr Matthews, he was well versed in grounding techniques, which he practised in rotation each morning while travelling to work, avoiding rush hour by forty minutes (his concession to the fear) after telling Marnie he was finding it hard to navigate the crowds. He couldn't lie to her, and he didn't want to. She wouldn't in any case have believed him, knowing how deep the damage went. His kid brother killed in a prison yard, after being put away on a drugs charge. Noah's arrest. Noah's choice. Guilt had dug a pit at his feet into which every day he was tempted to fall. But there was too much work to be done. Other young men, lost as Sol had been. Running with gangs, in bondage to men like Shafi Ellis, who'd pulled the makeshift knife in the prison yard. Sol didn't die like Frank Reece, whose heart was stopped by a single blow. His death was messy and slow, bleeding from a wound that shouldn't have killed him had the response been quicker, had the men in the yard not walked on by, mouths shut, eyes averted.

The tiled wall of the Tube station slanted the sun into Noah's eyes. He looked around for Sol, catching a flash of pink, but it was a kid's rucksack not his brother's hoody. The back of his neck tightened, his skin nagging. If he was going down, he'd have liked Sol with him.

The bump of bodies, shrill smell of the rails, sticky black rubber of the escalator rail. He watched the posters as they went past, screens lit and flickering. Acoustics shut his inner ear as he stepped off the escalator, stopped short by a man whose wheeled suitcase refused to roll the right way. Burned-wood aftershave, irritation bristling up the line of people pushing forward to find a way around the blockage. White mouth of the tunnel, black rails running away, black smell to match.

You can do this.

That flash of pink again – the kid's rucksack – his subconscious fully occupied with surviving the next thirteen minutes; no room for Sol. People pushing for the carriage doors, *move down inside the car*, full gamut of armpits and coffee breath. He found a space and held it, slipping his wrist through the strap above his head, meeting a woman's eye by accident and smiling as he looked away, trying to be non-threatening, but a black man was always threatening, or a man of any description if he met your eye at the wrong moment. *Damn*. He was becoming paranoid, on top of everything else.

His phone pulsed in his pocket. The first of the day's messages from Dan, making him smile. He propped his head against his raised arm, relaxing into the sway and pitch of the train. He could do this. He'd ridden the Tube since he was a kid, knew all its moves. You just had to find its rhythm, like dancing. He'd go out with Dan tonight. The two of them and a hundred others in a club, music and lights, no room to think. But first, the day's work.

Frank and Sabri, Clarke and Naomi, and the others. The boys and girls on the evidence board who'd once ridden the Tube to school or with friends, who'd known its moves and caught its rhythm as Noah was doing now. Suliat and Ashley. Kids who'd been afraid to smile at strangers or just because the roof was so low and all the tunnels too narrow, swallowing up the light like a snake.

'Dr Matthews was here,' Ron Carling said. 'You just missed her.'

'Oops,' Noah offered. He slipped into the seat opposite. 'Any news from Frank's family?'

'They're releasing his name to the press today. And there's a new kid.' Ron nodded across the room. 'Last ten minutes.'

Noah stopped what he was doing and stood, crossing to the board where the faces were waiting. Ashley with his head cocked, a careful crop of stubble on his chin. Suliat with her big smile, eyes half shut, a yellow wall of flowers behind her. Frank's white teeth. Clarke's blue baseball hat. The new face was white, a girl turning to greet the camera, green parka hiding her neck.

'Raphaela Belsham.' Ron came to stand at Noah's shoulder. 'Thirteen years old.'

'Stabbed?'

'Shot. Drive-by. Muswell Hill.'

Noah leaned in, meeting Raphaela's eyes. 'Her family are well-off?'

'Yes. But I'd love to know how you got that from this.'

'She's wearing a Moncler.' Noah pointed to the distinctive diamond pattern on the collar of the girl's parka. 'They retail for over a grand. And Muswell Hill? Not your typical spot for drive-bys.'

'Nowhere's off limits.' Ron scratched the back of his head. 'Isn't that the new guideline? Gangs getting everywhere. Forget the postcode lottery, it's all county lines and two fingers to the CCTV.'

'Raphaela's on CCTV?'

'Yep. A dozen witnesses, too. We'll be cross-eyed by the end of it.'

Noah put a hand on the board, just below the girl's face. 'Is DI Rome at the scene?'

Ron shook his head. 'Ferguson wants anyone above DS staying wide. Too much fodder for the press pack, she says. They'll be jumping up and down over this latest one.'

'Then it's you and me.'

'Debbie and Oz.' Ron sounded glum. 'We're on phones and paperwork.'

'Detective Chief Superintendent Ferguson doesn't want a black face on the ground?' Noah straightened. 'I thought that was meant to play well for the cameras.'

'The cameras love you. Everyone loves you. But all it needs is one journo who's done his or her homework . . .' Ron shrugged an apology.

One journalist linking Noah Jake to Solomon Jake, whose face belonged on this or any other wall recording victims of violent crime in the capital.

'DCS Ferguson can't keep me locked up in here forever,' Noah said. 'Unless she wants an outrageous overtime invoice from Dr Matthews.' He turned it into a joke because Ron was looking angry. 'Hey, it's okay. I don't need a bodyguard, though. She should let you out, at least.'

'And leave you with Oz the plod?' Ron put a big hand on Noah's shoulder and squeezed it. 'I wouldn't do that, mate.'

Noah returned to his desk. Funny, the things that made him want to weep. He'd yet to shed a tear over Sol, but Ron's clumsy kindness had the bridge of his nose burning. He opened his emails, working in silence for a while. Then he got up and walked back to the boards, taking out his phone so he could capture this latest face: Raphaela Belsham in her expensive parka, wild hair tied in a topknot. He caught Ron's eyes on him and gestured towards the door. Ron answered with a nod. Comfort break; that was normal, that was allowed.

The station corridor was furred with sound. Raised voices from the front desk, the hiss of fluorescent lighting, phones ringing around the clock. Familiar, safe. In the lavatory, Noah washed his hands and then his face, after first flipping his tie over his shoulder.

'Still doesn't go with the suit.' Sol leaned against the nearest stall, pink hood down, eyes bright.

'I'm working,' Noah said over the running of the taps. 'Can we do this later?'

'Whatever, bruv. But don't go weeping over that old pagan.'

'Pagan?' Noah shook water from his hands, reaching for a sheet of paper to dry his face. 'We're speaking patois now?'

'Two-faced, s'all I'm saying. Hated you when you started here.'

'Ron? He didn't hate me. He just didn't know me.'

'*Riiight.*' Sol drew the word out. 'Because up close you're irresistible.'

'I do all right.' Noah threw the screwed-up ball of paper at the bin. 'Obviously I'll do better once I get my shit together and stop talking to you.'

'Don't do that. Least not while you're working this case. I can help. Know the gang Frankie Reece was running with, maybe even the lot who gunned down your new girl.'

Noah stopped what he was doing. He gripped the lip of the sink and leaned into the mirror to meet his brother's eyes. 'Tell me how that helps me. Just tell me what good it does? Even if you knew them, even if you *ran* with them. What good is that to me?'

Sol fell silent for a beat before he said, 'You found yourself a gang. Same as me.'

'That was years ago.' Noah took a step back. 'We were little kids. And I got out.'

'Not talking about when we were kids. Talking *now*. You got your bass lady and that old pagan pretending to be your friend, streets you're stamping – what endz you got? All of Greater London. Hustling the brothers, coming at us all hours, coming at our fam. Protect and serve but you're all up in our faces, trying to boss our postcode. Metropolitan Po-leece. *That's* your gang.'

It was a great speech. Noah wondered how long his subconscious had been bottling it up. And what else it had in store for him. Since Sol's death, all bets were off. He couldn't count on a good night's sleep, couldn't even use the urinal without a running commentary from his brother's ghost.

'The difference being we're trying to stop the violence. The knives, the guns.'

'Keep telling yourself that, bruv.' Sol stepped backwards into the stall, kicking the door shut, raising his voice on the repetition: 'Keep tellin' it!'

Marnie caught a lift back to the station with DS Harry Kennedy. They'd been attending a meeting at one of the many police and crime committees that had sprung up across Greater London in response to the spread of violence in the capital. Harry's boss, like Marnie's, insisted they stay away from crime scenes but also insisted they show their faces to those with tough questions for London's mayor and the MPS. Not that Marnie and Harry were required or indeed allowed to voice opinions on behalf of the Metropolitan Police. Such opinions were pre-recorded in parsimonious reports for which the facts had been diced so thinly it was tricky to fish them from the soup of platitudes and promises. DCS Lorna Ferguson had decided Marnie was the right face to put before the committees, and it seemed Harry's commander at Trident felt the same way about him. So here they were, the Met's poster pairing, at the beck and call of bureaucrats when they could and should have been on the front line looking for those responsible for the murder and exploitation of so many of the city's young people.

'This isn't why I joined the police . . .' Each morning, Marnie swallowed the speech she'd prepared for Lorna Ferguson, and did as she was told. Each night, she went home with a sour taste in her mouth, her gut churning with empty gestures, face aching from the expression of studied concern she wore for the cameras. Not that she wasn't concerned, for London and its young people, her team. *Noah*. But she was angry, too. At the wasted lives, the apathy. The averted faces, people crawling inside their phones to fight on Twitter or else to virtue-signal, refusing to look at what was happening in their city. Anger didn't play well for the cameras, however. Studied concern was the look they were after.

Returning them from this latest committee, Harry switched off the car's ignition and put his head against the seat rest. 'When is it acceptable for a sound bite to involve actual biting? Because I'm *this* close to sinking my teeth into something. A journalist, possibly. Or an MP.'

'Wouldn't play well,' Marnie reminded him. 'For the cameras.'

'Sod the cameras.' Harry rubbed both hands at his face, rolling his neck. 'Sorry, not very poster-police.' He pulled down the visor's mirror, baring his teeth at his reflection. 'I may need a new smile soon; this one's got all sorts of cracks in it.'

'Looks good to me.' Marnie opened the passenger door. 'Let's get some real work done.'

As he locked the pool car, Harry asked, 'How's Noah?'

'He's getting through it.' She searched for the words with which to appease Harry's nagging sense of guilt without diminishing Noah's struggle. 'It's tough, but he says work's helping.'

'He didn't take much time off. I wondered about that.'

'He doesn't blame you for what happened.'

'Doesn't he?' Harry looked unhappy. 'I do. I should have joined the dots faster. I knew Sol was part of the gang we were watching. I'd even asked Noah if Sol could be persuaded to give evidence against them. Then the firearms charges . . . I told myself I was doing Noah a favour by keeping him in the loop, but I missed the main angle. Shafi Ellis had a gang-activity flag. He was all over our matrix, back when we still believed in it. If I'd joined the dots the way I'm supposed to, Ellis wouldn't have been within sixty feet of Sol.'

'Congratulations on the promotion,' Marnie said solemnly. 'I didn't realise you were a prison governor now. That's the only way you'd be able to control which prisoners were put where and with whom, isn't it? Harry, you need to let it go. Noah doesn't blame you, no one does. And guilt will eat you up when there's too much else to do. Trident needs you. Hell, *I* need you. I can't hack this poster-police gig on my own.'

He accepted this, smiling in response to her smile.

'See?' she told him. 'No cracks for the cameras. We can do this, DS Kennedy.'

'As long as they let us near the real work often enough.'

'That's why I'd better get going. DCS Ferguson doesn't like to be kept waiting.'

On his way back to the incident room, Noah checked his phone for messages. Dan had texted, but there was nothing from Mum or Dad. Noah hadn't needed his subconscious to alert him to the state his mum was in. She'd suffered all her life with mental illness. At its least vicious, it made her obsessively tidy, always clearing and cleaning. He hadn't seen her at its worst for a long time.

'Noah? Hey . . .'

Harry Kennedy was in the corridor. DS Kennedy, Trident's ascendant star.

'Hey.' Noah nodded a greeting, hoping his face didn't betray him. Harry didn't deserve the blame for what had gone down at the prison, or no more of the blame than Noah himself deserved. They'd each put a man into HMP Pentonville, but only Noah had arrested his own brother. 'How's it going?'

'It never stops.' Harry's blue eyes darkened. 'How're things here?'

'The same. Someone new this morning. Raphaela Belsham. Thirteen years old.'

'The drive-by shooting in Muswell Hill? I saw the flag.'

'One of yours, you think?'

One of Trident's, Noah meant. Gangs were Harry's bread and butter. Pursuing intelligence, targeting offenders, responding to incidents. Weapons raids, amnesties, arrests.

'One of ours,' Harry agreed. 'Looks like.'

Noah nodded, ignoring the pink stain on the wall behind Harry's head. Sol was glaring with such savagery it was hard to believe that Harry couldn't feel the force of it. Noah might have been the one who put his own brother away, but it was Harry who'd jailed Sol's murderer, Shafi Ellis. Noah's subconscious was having a hard time coming to terms with that.

'Are you looking for Marnie?' he asked.

Harry shook his head. 'I gave her a lift, thought I'd show my face.' He scratched at his right cheek. 'Noah . . . we're good, yes? I mean, nothing's good. I get that. But you and me . . .?'

'Fuck that,' Sol said. 'Suck yuh madda, rasshole.'

'We're good.' Noah nodded.

Harry looked relieved. He held out his hand, and Noah took it.

'I'll see you around. Take care.'

'You too.'

Noah watched Harry moving down the stairs, shoulders sloped, hips loose. Heading back to his post at Trident, an integral part of the team responsible for making London safer for its citizens. Noah's compatriot, his brother in arms.

Sol leaned over the rail and shouted after Harry, 'Rain a fall, rasshole!' He straightened and met Noah's eyes, repeating the words softly. 'Rain a fall.'

2

Marnie hadn't exaggerated Lorna Ferguson's dislike of being kept waiting. The woman was tapping her polished nails on the desk when Marnie stepped into her office.

'Ma'am.'

'You took your time. I thought the committee had its tea break an hour ago.' Ferguson scowled. 'I say *tea*. We all know their beverage of choice is the tears of police officers brewed in the bitter reprisals of career politicians. I trust you and DS Kennedy gave them short shrift.'

'Service with a smile.' Marnie sat in the chair facing her. 'Although Harry's worried about his teeth.'

'Dishy DS Kennedy? All he's got to worry about is which journalist'll make a pass at him this week. He's a handsome bugger. Doesn't seem to know it either, which is a bonus.' Lorna toyed with her necklace, the links of which were shaped like tiny lozenges of bullion. Every inch of her was glossy, from the heels of her Louboutins to the retouched roots of her hair. 'I've been asked whether the pair of you are keeping it professional.' She arched her tinted eyebrows. 'I pointed that weasel in the direction of his local news-agent's, suggested he satisfy his curiosity on the top shelf.'

'A journalist asked you that – whether we're keeping it professional?'

'Don't look so fiery. It's their job to stir the pot, never mind how thin the slop. With the media scraping its news from the bottom of Twitter's muck bucket, it's small wonder we're experiencing a drop in standards of crime reporting. Knives and guns and gangs aren't exactly Instagram fodder. The way they see it, you and DS Kennedy are a bit of nice-looking light relief.'

'Wonderful,' Marnie said drily. 'Perhaps I should be handing out my favourite recipes, too. Or photographs of kittens.'

'Whatever keeps the faeccs wide of our collective fan. Harry's boss feels the same, for whatever that's worth. It's not just you on dolly duty.'

'What a relief.'

Lorna clicked her tongue. 'Any sharper and you'll cut yourself, lady.'

'Well it's not as if we need every pair of hands working these murder cases, is it? I'm sure Raphaela Belsham's family will understand. And Frank Reece's family.'

'Oh cheer up. I'm shipping you out to Muswell Hill. How does that sound?'

It sounds, Marnie thought, as if someone's decided that the death of a white girl in a nice part of town matters more than that of a black boy from a sink estate.

'I'd like to take Noah with me.'

'Take DS Pembroke.' Lorna glanced down at her paperwork. 'He needs the experience.'

'Yes, he does,' Marnie agreed. 'Which is why I prefer to take Noah.'

Raphaela's parents would be in shock, grieving. They might be angry, or numb, or scared. It was unlikely they'd be ready to answer questions about their daughter's life, but inevitable that they'd have questions about her death. Above all else, they'd be in need of sympathy and respect. Noah would know how to handle all of that, and he'd do it instinctively.

'Look, I don't doubt DS Jake's the man for the job. And I know you're keeping a close eye on his fitness for work.' Lorna uncapped her fountain pen, then recapped it. 'That's not the issue here. It's the Belshams, Guy and Lynne. He's an investment banker, she's a florist. Raphaela went to a good school, they lived in a good area, she was a good girl. Their only child. I'm sure you can see where this's headed. Their good girl didn't go looking for trouble, it came for her.' She thumbed a speck of mascara from her right eye. 'She's not on the Met's gangs violence matrix, but all the same there's a GA flag on the crime report. Gang-activity-related because the *car* threw a flag, because the toerag driving it *is* on our matrix. To say Mr Belsham is unhappy about this is an understatement.'

'He's unhappy about the gang-activity-related nature of his daughter's death?'

'Let's say he sees it as an added insult, a smear on his girl's good name.'

'She died less than six hours ago. Isn't it a little soon to be worrying what people are going to make of the manner of her death?'

Lorna looked surprised. 'Usually you're the one reminding me we can't judge people on their first reaction to terrible news. Matilda Reece laughed when we told her about Frank's death, but it was you who set me straight there. Shock does funny things to people, that's what you said. And you were right. I expect that poor woman wept for a week once she'd started. We can allow Mr Belsham his irrational fear of shame, or whatever label we want to put on it.'

'I'm assuming it's a little more than that, since you're so reluctant to let Noah near him.'

They were stepping around the reason, the word. It made Marnie's skin crawl. Was she sorry for Guy Belsham's loss? Of course she was. But so would Noah be sorry.

'How's it going to look,' she asked, 'that I stayed away after Frank's murder, and Suliat Drake's, and Ashley Benjamin's, only to visit Raphaela's parents in their good area with its good school? Aren't you concerned what the media will make of that? I thought we were trying to avoid giving them any fresh excuse to drag out the "white-wash" headline?'

'We're not the only ones investigating these killings. Your dishy DS Kennedy is working all hours to find Frank Reece's killer, and Trident's hardly slacking over the others. But look. Guy Belsham may very well be a racist.' Lorna shook herself upright, distaste written across her face. 'There, I've said it. You're thinking I'm reluctant to dispatch DS Jake in case the grieving father can't keep his bigotry to himself. Well, maybe he can, maybe he can't. Who knows what state you'll find him in? What we do know is it's a miracle no bright spark on Twitter's put two and two together and figured we've a grieving detective on our team whose brother was stabbed to death by a former gang nominal. To use the official jargon.'

'As I told Dr Matthews, we can't keep Noah away from every case involving knives or gangs,' Marnie argued. 'Not unless you're intending to second him to a desk job. He's the best detective on my team, and I want to be able to use him. I *need* to use him. He solves cases, and he gets results. If we're to make progress with these debt bondage cases, with the exploitation of young kids, with *murders* . . . You need Noah working cases like this. With me, with

DS Pembroke, as part of the team, not sidelined because we're scared word will get out about Sol.'

Lorna bristled at that. 'It's DS Jake I'm protecting. He's been through enough lately, wouldn't you say? And community relations aren't likely to be improved by the revelation that one of our own put his brother behind bars, where he was – what's that word they use? – *splashed*. No.' She shook her head, inspecting the glossy tips of her nails. 'I want him wide of the front line for a while longer. It's not as if he's magically scaling this wall of silence all on his own.'

The wall of silence had been a running joke since it was first cited by the Met's commissioner in response to rising crime and falling detection rates. No one wanted to talk to the police, least of all those in the communities most affected by violence, where it might be argued a dialogue would do most good.

'None of us can achieve anything on our own,' Marnie pointed out. 'We're a team. I need my best players. Let me take Noah to Muswell Hill, and to Tottenham to meet Matilda Reece. I need him in play. *We* need him.'

'Oh very well.' Lorna tugged at an earring that matched her necklace, miniature gold bullion. 'It's been a long week and I'm not about to get aerated over deployment, not while we've a crime wave on our hands. But watch out for the weasels, and keep me posted. I'll work on some tactical PR for when it's needed.'

Back in the incident room, Noah was on the phone. Marnie gestured for him to come to her office when the call ended. Ron followed her with his eyes, Colin Pitcher looking up from his computer, where he was chasing requests for CCTV footage. She smiled at the pair of them. The team was tighter than ever since Sol's death.

Noah neatened his tie as he entered her office, looking for a second like a nervous job applicant.

'I'm headed out to Muswell Hill.' She smiled at him. 'I'd like you with me.'

He hesitated. 'Raphaela Belsham's family?'

'Yes. But I'm hoping we can make time to go to Tottenham to see Matilda Reece.'

'Frank's mum.' He looked relieved, as if he'd shared Marnie's misgivings about the special treatment, real or perceived, for the Belshams. 'Are Debbie and Oz still in Muswell Hill?'

'Organising door-to-door, yes. But we'll be the ones who speak with her parents.'

'Are we taking a car, or . . .?'

'A car.' Marnie nodded.

Noah hid his relief better this time, but she'd guessed how hard it was for him to travel by Tube. For the longest time she'd considered him an open book. Now, he seemed stitched shut. Pain was such a secret thing, more personal than any other emotion. You'd fight to keep it close, protect it from other people's curiosity, even those who might lessen it. Especially those. Hadn't she half exiled herself from Ed Belloc, whom she loved? Pain made you selfish, and secretive. She couldn't wrestle Noah's pain from him; no one could. He had to learn how to put it down. It was her hardest lesson after her parents died. She wished for a swifter peace for Noah.

Together they went down to the station car park, where the pool cars were waiting, beetled by rain. Noah headed towards the Audi they typically took, but Marnie shook her head. 'It's Harry's today. He's driving out to Walthamstow.'

Noah nodded, his face turned towards the sound of kids squabbling in the street. Marnie had told Harry that no one blamed him for Sol's death. Noah certainly didn't, that was what she'd said. But she saw the tension in his shoulders, and knew it was for Harry.

'How's Dan?' she asked.

'He's good, thanks.' Noah turned towards her. 'How's Ed?'

'The same.'

They shared a smile, climbing into the car. Marnie fired the engine and the radio belched into life to the pungent strains of a rock ballad from DS Pembroke's preferred playlist.

Noah jabbed a button, turning the sound off. 'Oz really needs to get out more.'

'Or less.' Marnie waited for him to fasten his seat belt. When he didn't, she said, 'Safety first?'

He dragged the belt across his shoulder, shutting it with a snap. In the past, he'd been the one who prompted her. *Safety first*, a shared joke between them. The car smelled aggressively of Oz's aftershave, the olfactory equivalent of his musical taste.

'You know Lynx used to be called Ego.' Noah opened his window. 'They advertised it with the slogan, "The Ego man's guide to getting laid". It's sold as Axe in most countries.'

'I'm getting flashbacks from *The Shining*.' Marnie turned the car towards Muswell Hill.

'*Here's Johnny* . . .' Noah's attention strayed to his phone. He straightened in the passenger seat. 'Do we know much about Raphaela Belsham?'

'Only that she was thirteen, attending a local school. A good one, I'm told. Dad's an investment banker. Mum's a florist. He's not too happy about the idea of this being gang-related.'

'Do we have any evidence that it was?'

'The shooter's car is registered to a Terrance Malig. He's served time for firearms offences, and he's on Trident's matrix. We know the matrix is problematic, has been for months.' Discredited was the word the press used to describe Trident's matrix for tracking those with gang connections. 'We might argue that of course Malig is on it, and of course Raphaela isn't. But right now, her death is looking like a targeted hit.'

'A targeted hit on a thirteen-year-old? A schoolgirl.'

'That's how it appears, at least on the matrix. Her dad's not happy about it.'

Noah nodded. 'Bad enough to lose her, without her death becoming just another statistic.'

They'd stopped at traffic lights. Marnie glanced across at him.

'Can you imagine seeing your child's face on that wall?' Noah was watching the knot of people at the bus stop. 'Or part of the collage of faces the papers like to print? I'd be unhappy too.'

She gripped the wheel, watching her knuckles whiten. Lorna Ferguson had wanted him kept wide of this case, but Noah's first instinct was better than Marnie's had been. He knew exactly what brand of sympathy Guy Belsham needed, understanding how the man's shame was tied to his pain.

'Her face will stand out, at least.' Noah rubbed his thumb at his phone screen. 'Matilda Reece says she's afraid no one will be able to see Frank because of all the other young black faces.'

'She's organising a vigil.' Marnie took the left turn after the lights. 'DCS Ferguson wants us to make sure she understands how that might go. We can't rule out far-right demonstrators, or rent-a-mob. We'll need a police presence, Ferguson thinks.'

The car filled with shadow as they passed under Erskine Tower. Blight on the landscape or brutalist masterpiece, depending on your perspective. Flags of washing hung from the balconies, beige and white and the sudden Rio pink of a beach towel.

'In case the vigil turns into another murder?' Noah craned his neck to watch the tower. 'She's right to be cautious. Are we supposed to advise Frank's mum to cancel it? Because I don't see how we can do that without a public order notice.'

'It won't come to that. Matilda's respected, and loved.'

'Frank was loved. It didn't stop him getting killed.' Noah withdrew his gaze from the high-rise, glancing at Marnie. 'Sorry, that sounded a lot less confrontational in my head.'

'Don't apologise. You're right. Frank *was* loved. It's why his mum wants the vigil, so his friends can pay their respects. And she wants to speak about knife crime, to appeal directly to the young kids carrying weapons. She's hoping to make a difference.'

'She needs Frank's death to have meant something.' Noah nodded. 'Of course she does.'

The Belshams' house stood back from the road, behind a garden of gravel and flint. A bay window faced the street, half shuttered, hiding the room inside. The house had been newly whitewashed, dazzlingly pale between its red-brick neighbours. A snub-nosed white Mercedes was parked in the space allocated for residents only. Marnie glimpsed a skylight, and wondered whether the attic conversion was Raphaela's room. These houses sold for well over a million, despite their modest size; an attic conversion added tens of thousands to the value. She knocked on the front door, then stepped back to stand shoulder to shoulder with Noah.

Hardwood floors echoed with heavy footfall before a broadly built man answered the door, in pinstriped shirt-sleeves and navy trousers, a Samsung phone wedged to his ear.

'The police are here,' he said to the caller. 'Yes, I know. Well, we'll see.' He fastened the left cuff of his shirt, shoulder raised to prop the phone. 'I doubt it. Ha! Quite.' Face tanned, brown hair thickly waved. His nose had been broken, but not recently. Flat eyes, a shade paler than his hair, scanned Marnie and Noah, then the street behind. 'You'll be the first to know,' he told the caller. He dropped his shoulder, catching the Samsung in his hand. He didn't step back, or make any gesture for them to enter the house. They waited while he fastened his other cuff and pocketed the phone before finally looking at them.

'DI Rome, is it?' He used the same voice he'd used on the phone, brisk and confident.

'Mr Belsham.' Marnie wondered who'd given him her name. 'This is Detective Sergeant Jake.'

Guy Belsham flicked his stare past her for a second, then nodded at their feet. 'Shoes off, if you don't mind.' He turned and called into the house, 'Lynne! The police are here.' From behind, his work shirt was sharply creased, as if taken new from the packet. Beneath the navy trousers he wore skinny red socks. He had the build of a rugby player at the end of a final season, the small of his back padded with muscle and a first layer of fat. 'Lynne!'

He blocked Marnie and Noah's way so they had to stand with him, an audience of three as Raphaela's mother came down the stairs. She wore a cream and brown dress patterned with links like the ones Lorna Ferguson wore around her neck. The dress was a wraparound, silky, clinging. A sexy dress, but she didn't look sexy. She was too thin, gym-bodied, her calves roped with muscle. Her feet were bare. She was massaging her wrists one after the other, her fingers shiny with hand cream, strawberry-blonde hair pulled into a thin ponytail. Her face shone like her fingers. As she came closer, Marnie recognised the medicinal scent of emollient cream: white paraffin and lanolin. Her face was tanned like her husband's. Her green eyes were red-rimmed from crying. She held her hands away from her body, as if afraid of getting the emollient on her dress.

Her eyes went to Marnie and then Noah before twitching back to her husband. 'Hello.'

'Kitchen's best for this, yes?' His phone rang and he answered it, turning his back as Lynne led the way to the rear of the house. 'Guy Belsham . . .'

The route went through an open-plan room, its fireplace filled with a spectacular display of flowers – fluted lilies, smouldering bronze chrysanthemums – an elegant and unmissable reminder that Lynne Belsham was a florist. The expensive herringbone hardwood floor was spread with pale rugs. Pale sofas, pale chairs, a white radiator cabinet, glass table holding three clear vases of tight-lipped white tulips. The kind of room where you'd be afraid to sit in case you left a mark. Impossible to imagine relaxing here, but perhaps the Belshams managed this trick. A widescreen television occupied one wall, its trail of wires the only untidy thing in sight.

Lynne led them through to another living space, where grey flannel sofas stood either side of a hammered copper drum table, a smaller television mounted on the wall above alongside ugly artwork, surely chosen as an invest-ment: a blocky black and white figure, her dress made of yellow chevrons, her eyes two bruised plums. From recessed shelves, white orchids spidered the walls.

Finally they reached the kitchen. Marnie had to wonder

whether Guy had insisted on this room because it neces-
sitated walking through the other two, stamped as they
were with proof of his income and taste. The kitchen had
a feature radiator – six vertical white pipes running up one
wall – and a butcher's-block table with mismatched chairs.
More flowers, artfully arranged to look wild and unaffected,
spilled from a bowl in the centre of the table. Low windows
looked out onto a surprisingly scruffy garden: a straggle of
lawn, sagging football net, beer-garden benches. It was a
relief to look at the garden, as if the Belshams' tidiness
ended at the back of the house. For the first time, Marnie
could picture a child living here, catch at the girl's ghost.
Raphaela kicking a ball into the net, or lolling on her
stomach on the neglected grass. Running indoors for a cold
drink from the shuttle-sized fridge with an ice dispenser in
its door. The slam of the fridge shutting, slap of her feet
on the quarry-tiled floor, ice clashing in her glass . . .

Lynne drew out a ladder-backed chair and sat at the
table, still massaging the emollient cream into her hands.
Up close, Marnie could see the scaly patches she was
treating, red at her wrists and hairline where the skin was
drawn taut.

Noah took the chair next to Marnie, their backs to the
window.

Guy had his phone in his hand when he entered the
kitchen. His eyes scanned the seating plan before he took
a chair at the head of the table. 'Where're we up to?' He
looked at Marnie.

'I'd like to begin by saying how very sorry we are for
your loss—'

'Let's take the platitudes as read, shall we?' He cut her
off with a sweep of his hand. 'We need to hear about
progress. We've a lot to organise, as you'll appreciate.
Time is precious.'

'Raffa was precious.' Lynne didn't speak across her husband or as if she were correcting him. Rather she was appending his statement, or translating it for Marnie and Noah: *What my husband means*, she was saying. She touched the tips of her fingers to her ponytail. 'She was precious.'

Guy nodded his agreement. 'So if we could hear what progress you've made. This nonsense about her being the target of a gang, for example. You've corrected that, I assume?'

'It was never our intention to suggest Raphaela was involved in a gang,' Marnie said. 'But we know the car was driven by a man with a history of gang-related violence.'

'Drugs too, no doubt.' Guy shot a look at Noah. 'He drives past, opens fire. This happens in broad daylight, two streets away! She wasn't out late, wasn't drinking. She'd gone for a coffee at Carluccio's, for God's sake.'

Noah said, 'It's a horrible shock.'

'A fucking outrage,' Guy's jaw popped, 'is what it is.'

The wild-flower bouquet shivered in the centre of the table, ox-eye daisies dropping their petals onto the scrubbed butcher's block.

'We've lost her,' Lynne translated. 'Our little girl.' She clenched at her left wrist. 'Raffa.'

Guy stared at her for a second before he looked away, blinking hard. His anger bumped in the room like the fridge as it hit a cooling cycle. *Thump-thump-thump.*

Noah said, 'There's no reason to believe Raphaela was deliberately targeted, but we need to rule it out in order to concentrate our efforts. I'm sorry, I know how painful this is—'

'Lost a child, have you?' Guy reached for his phone, as if willing a call to come through, a distraction from this conversation, some better way to be kept busy.

'We're sorry,' Noah said. 'We know it must feel intrusive, especially at this time. But there is a process, and we do need to follow it.'

'It's outrageous. Questions about gangs, about guns. As if she was mixed up in some sort of *galdem*, or whatever the hell the slang is. She's thirteen, for God's sake. She . . . was thirteen.'

'Our little girl.' Lynne pressed her fingers to the table then took them away, leaving a set of dark marks from the grease on her hands. 'Our Raffa.' Her pain was palpable, her eyes like the bad art in the other room, bruised deep in her face.

'This is too soon,' Marnie said. 'We understand. But we want to find whoever did this and take them off the streets.'

'Like he took her off the streets? She was in the gutter!' Guy balled his fists. 'She bled out in the gutter like an animal!'

'My Raffa.' Lynne held the edge of the butcher's block, her face straining towards Marnie as if Marnie could make this stop, undo everything from the last six hours. 'Please. *Please* . . .'

'She hadn't any dodgy friends!' Her husband swept a hand at the room. 'I'd have known about it, we both would. She didn't like being out, hated the dark, hated noise. She had her headphones on. Noise-cancelling three-hundred-quid headphones. That's how much she hated being on the streets, even round here where it's supposed to be safe. Studying, that's what she liked. The library, school, interviewing people for a project – it was all *safe*. I made sure of it.' His chest worked. He threw his stare around the room before fixing on Noah. 'She didn't wear make-up, or provocative clothes. She hated all that, said it was fake. Disgusting, that's the word she used. Hated boys, stupid jumped-up little posers.' He stared at Noah, nostrils flared for a fight. 'As for *gangs* . . . that's the most ludicrous part of this entire circus.'

Marnie stood. Guy's stare snapped to her.

'Mrs Belsham. May we see her room?'

Lynne nodded. 'Please,' she said again.

Noah put back his chair. Guy stood in the same moment. He was shorter than Noah by half a foot, but wider by twice that measure. His face was knuckled, ugly. He was looking for a place to put his anger and his grief. It was too much for him. He didn't know what to do with it. Marnie could see it struggling under his skin, twisting his expression this way and that. Rage, and loss.

Noah saw it too. 'I can wait in the car,' he offered.

But Marnie said, 'It'll be quicker with two of us.' She smiled at Lynne. 'We don't want to take up more of your time than we need to.'

'We understand.' Raffa's mother looked towards Noah, not quite meeting his eyes. 'It's like you said, a horrible shock. Too soon. We're still . . . We haven't taken it in. We can't.' She smoothed her hands at her dress, then stopped, rubbing at her fingers in dismay. 'Her room's at the top of the house. I'll take you.'

Her husband was in the doorway with his shoulders squared, but he moved aside when Lynne looked at him. 'You'd better stay by the phone,' she said. 'There might be an important call.'

Marnie caught the man's heat as she passed, tinder-dry and explosive. She waited until Noah was out of the kitchen before nodding for him to go ahead of her, following Lynne up the stairs. She didn't trust Guy not to come after them, after Noah. She was surprised at how quickly he'd acquiesced to his wife's suggestion that he stay by the phone, but perhaps his temper was always this short. In which case Lynne must have stockpiled strategies for defusing it. Had she needed to shield Raffa from his temper, the way she'd helped Marnie to shield Noah?

They climbed two flights of carpeted stairs – glimpses of bedrooms furnished as palely as the rooms downstairs, quilted headboards, silvery scatter cushions, funereal flowers – before reaching a pair of adjacent doors on the top floor of the house:

'Raffa's bathroom.' Lynne touched the first door. 'Do you need to see?'

'Yes, please.'

The bathroom was narrow, white-tiled, with a shower, toilet and sink. It smelled of damp towels and strawberry shampoo. A red rubber duck sat on top of the cistern. Lynne scooped a green towel from the floor and shook it out, hanging it from the rail beside the door, saying, 'She showered before she went out this morning. Her hair wasn't dry. She hates hairdryers, but she ties it up.' She raised her hands to the crown of her head. 'Here . . .' She caught sight of herself in the mirror, blinking as if at a stranger, her eyes swerving away.

Dark hair clogged the shower grid, staticky strands clinging to the tiles. It was hard to accept that the girl who'd used this bathroom so recently was gone. Dead.

'May we see her bedroom?' Marnie asked.

'Yes.' Lynne pulled the damp towel straight, clenching its hem in her hand before letting go.

Raffa's bedroom was big, brimming with blue from the skylight, the slope of its ceiling strung with fairy lights. The wrought-iron bed frame was also strung with lights, its quilt stitched with silver stars. A white wardrobe and dressing table stood at the tallest part of the room. Shallow bookcases had been built into the perimeter of the eaves, each shelf packed with books and CDs, dolls and trinkets. The mess was reassuring, like the garden. Marnie had been afraid this room would be as colourless as the ones downstairs. There was a stab or two at adulthood – a film poster for *Léon*, another for *Rancid Aluminium* – but most of the mess was old toys. Stuffed animals, a jumbled pot of chewed felt-tip pens, a wooden mobile of painted birds. A child's room.

Lynne moved past Marnie and Noah, to the bed. She stood with one hand on the iron frame, her eyes searching the room. 'What is it you hope to find? I never know what the police are looking for in cases like this. Something to say she deserved it, a reason she was gunned down?' Her face gritted. 'She wasn't in the wrong place at the wrong time. That's what they'll say, I expect. You see it in the headlines all the time. But she was in the *right* place. She went for coffee there every morning. It was him – *he* was in the wrong place.'

'We think so,' Marnie agreed. 'But we need to follow the procedure that's in place. We'll be careful and respectful.' She waited until the woman was looking at her. 'I give you my word.'

'Her dad doesn't mean to be so aggressive. He's struggling.'

'We understand.'

Noah said again, 'It's a horrible shock. A horrible loss.'

'Thank you.' Lynne looked at him, gratefully. 'For understanding. Can I be in here while you're searching?' She didn't wait for an answer, sitting on the foot of the bed, holding onto its frame.

She was guarding it, Marnie realised. Not guiltily or obstructively, but because it held the shape of her daughter. Raffa's head was in the pillow, the tangle of her legs in the covers.

'I'm sorry,' she said gently. 'We do need to look every-where.'

'I'll wait downstairs.' Lynne stood, walking on stiff legs to the door.

Marnie took two pairs of crime-scene gloves from her pocket, handing one pair to Noah. 'Help me?'

They lifted the mattress and searched the spot where Lynne had been sitting. It made Marnie feel grubby, but it needed to be done. There was nothing but the edge of the sheet tucked under the bed's frame. They lowered the mattress, searching the rest of the bed as lightly as possible, both of them wanting to preserve Raffa's shape in the covers. It was the hardest part, but it was nothing compared to what the Belshams were facing. One day, probably not soon, Lynne would need to strip her daughter's bed, wash the strawberry scent of her from the sheets and pillowcases, put it all away.

Noah said, 'I'll take this side, shall I?'

Dividing the space, they searched the wardrobe and dressing table before starting on the bookshelves. Marnie sorted through the tangle of chargers plugged into the wall: phone, iPad and iPod, laptop. None of the electronics were in the room.

'She had her phone and iPod with her.' Noah straightened, rolling his neck before squatting to search the rest of the shelves. 'We'll have to ask about the laptop and iPad.'

'I'll do that.' Marnie moved a snow globe back into its original position.

'She could draw.' Noah was looking through sketchpads. 'These are good.'

Marnie watched the white flakes settle in the globe before moving on with her share of the search. The attic was well insulated. None of the day's chill had found its

41

way inside. She could hear the stutter of traffic stopping and starting in the street below. Clouds moved across the skylight, thinning to show a rinsed-white sun. A blackbird was sounding. Not singing – the pitch was too high. Warning of a cat, perhaps.

'Look at this.' Noah held up his cupped hand. He'd found a piece of bubblegum stuck to the underside of a shelf. 'Her thumbprint's in it.'

The print was precise, whorled into the hardened pink pellet. Marnie could see Raffa blowing a bubble that burst against her lips before wadding the gum with her teeth, licking her thumb and forefinger to transfer it from her mouth to the shelf. Pressing it into place, smiling as she did so, her own small rebellion against the pallid perfection of the house. She saw the Belshams' daughter clearly, and it pulled at her heart. From Noah's face, it moved him the same way.

'What did you make of Guy?' she asked.

'He's hurting. Angry, of course.' Noah took a book from the shelves, riffling its pages. 'He knows more about gangs than he'd like us to think. *Galdem*. That's not in common usage. Either he's been researching online, or he's heard it somewhere.'

'What does it mean?'

'A group of girls. Not necessarily a gang, but it's an odd word for him to know.' Noah reached to the rear of the shelf. He drew back a closed fist. 'And then . . .' He moved to the centre of the room, where he could straighten to his full height, head brushing the bright string of lights. 'Then there's this.' He opened his fist. Gleaming in his gloved palm, snub-nosed, copper-coloured . . .

A bullet.

3

'Bag it,' Marnie said.

She crouched beside the shelf where he'd found the bullet, shining her phone's torch into the recess. Noah watched her remove the books, stacking them on the floor. Her hand was smaller than his, able to reach behind the shelf to the slim gap where it met the wall.

He bagged the bullet, feeling its heat in his hand as he waited for Marnie to complete her search. A single bullet. It might almost have been a gimmick – a lipstick or a cigarette lighter – but it was real. And it was here in the bedroom of Guy and Lynne's dead daughter. Terrance Malig had fired four bullets into Raphaela Belsham, hitting her chest, stomach, shoulder and back before dropping her into the gutter. Noah had watched the CCTV footage, seen the cruel dance the gunfire forced her to perform. He kept his palm cupped around the bullet, so hot he half expected it to start sweating inside the evidence bag.

'Nothing.' Marnie straightened and stood. 'But we should get a specialist team in here.' She looked at the bag in Noah's hand. 'Do you think it's real?'

'Yes.'

A voice drifted up through the house: Guy on the phone again.

'We'll have to tell him,' Marnie said. 'And Lynne.'

Noah felt a familiar lurch of sympathy. 'Do you want me to make the call?'

'To the firearms team? Yes. I'll talk with her parents.' She glanced around the room, her eyes snagging on the bed where Raffa's mum had stood guard. 'Let's get it over with.'

Downstairs, Guy ended his call, pointing the phone at Marnie. 'Are you done?'

'Mr Belsham, can we talk? In the kitchen, if you prefer.'

He stood his ground, face darkening. 'You've not found anything; you can't have.'

His wife came through from the sitting room, pulling a brown cardigan around her shoulders, peering up at Marnie and Noah. They stayed on the stairs. Guy was occupying too much of the hallway, his aggression elbowing the narrow space. Noah could smell it in the air, seared like meat.

'I'm afraid we did find something,' Marnie said in her level way.

'What?' His jaw jutted. 'What did you find? We've a right to know.'

'We need to bring in a specialist team. For firearms detection.'

Guy stared at her, then swung his gaze at Noah. 'Show me what you found.'

Marnie retrieved the man's attention by holding up the evidence bag. 'A bullet.'

It froze him, but only for a second. 'Who found it? Which one of you? You?' Jabbing a finger at Marnie. 'Or him?' Jabbing his whole hand at Noah.

'Mr Belsham. I'd like you to step back, please. And try to calm down.'

Raffa's mum stayed in the doorway to the sitting room, her face blind with horror.

'Don't patronise me!' Guy surged forward, rage ripping across his face. 'We should've had a lawyer here, I knew it. I wanted a lawyer. I'm supposed to be the type who trusts the police, but this? *Him*, finding a bullet in my girl's bedroom?' His nostrils flared at Noah. 'Guaranteed he put it there himself! Or the pair of you did. You don't want her to be blameless; why would you? Far better if she *was* part of some gang. Your statistics are a shambles. Protect and serve, what a fucking joke! You're a disgrace, you know that? The *police*! You couldn't police a pigsty. Coming in here, telling lies about my girl!' He came closer, eyes on Noah, blazing with hate.

'Mr Belsham.' Marnie put herself between them, holding up a hand. 'Step back. Now.'

Noah couldn't see her eyes, but Guy could. It brought him to a standstill.

'Listen to me,' she said. 'You're upset, and you're angry. But not at us. We're here to find the people who did this. You can help. Your wife needs you to help.'

'I want *him* out of my house.' He worked his jaw to get rid of the adrenalin, or to produce more. Rage was the only thing keeping him from tears. 'Get him out.'

'DS Jake, could you make the call to the specialist search team?'

'I'll make it from the car.' Noah didn't want to stay in the house when it was upsetting Raffa's dad so acutely. But nor did he want to leave Marnie alone with the man in his current mood. 'If you'd prefer?'

'That's a good idea, thanks.' She didn't turn to smile at

him, giving Guy her full attention. It was what the man needed. That and Noah's exit from his house.

'And get a warrant while you're at it!' Belsham flung at him as he passed the man in the hall.

'We don't need a warrant.' Marnie spoke coolly. 'You gave us your permission to search Raffa's room.'

Noah slowed, in case Guy's anger boiled over at her.

'We said you could see it, not conduct some forensic free-for-all!'

'The permission you gave covered both eventualities. If you prefer, we could expedite a warrant. But that would necessitate me arresting you for obstruction. Which I don't want to do, as you have enough on your plate.'

'It's *your* plate you should be worrying about. And his.' Jerking his head at Noah. 'There's no way Raffa had a bullet in her room. She was thirteen years old! You saw it up there, she's got teddy bears on her bed, for pity's sake.' His voice cracked finally, as if his fury had baked it dry. 'She was a *child*!'

Marnie came down the final two stairs to stand at his side. 'Let's go into the kitchen.'

Noah knew who he had to call. It was Trident's Active Series Linked Team; it was Harry Kennedy. He sat in the car with his phone in his hand until Sol joined him, lolling in the back seat, hands deep in the pockets of his pink hoody. 'This's how come you're in the wrong gang. That old racist in there giving you shit.'

'He's a grieving father.'

'Saying you planted a bullet. Saying it because you're black, not because you're police. You'll always be a gangster to men like him. Mi ah bad man.'

He dialled the number. 'Harry, it's Noah.'

'You talking to that shotta?' Sol demanded. 'That murderer?'

'We're in Muswell Hill,' Noah told Harry. 'With the Belshams.'

Sol was singing in the back seat: 'Here comes the hotstepper, *murderer*. I'm the lyrical gangster, *murderer* . . .'

'Cascade Avenue, yes. We found a bullet in her bedroom.'

Kicking the back of Noah's seat. 'Excuse me mister officer, *murderer* . . .'

'We need a forensic team . . . Yes, that's what we thought.'

'Still love you like that, *murderer*.'

'No, she's inside. Talking with the parents . . . Will do. Thanks, Harry.' He rang off.

Sol leaned forward, the sharp scent of his skin making Noah shut his eyes in protest, because it shouldn't be this real. Sol shouldn't be this real.

He whispered into the back of Noah's neck: 'Excuse me mister officer.'

'Stop it. *Please.* I get it. I have a guilty conscience. A guilty subconscious. But it needs to stop. Sol, please. I need you to stop.'

His brother was silent for a beat before propping his chin on the seat by Noah's shoulder. 'She had a bullet, though. That's dark. That's not dolls and fairy lights.'

'No, it's not.'

'No no we don't die. Yes we multiply.' Sol was singing again, but solemnly. 'Cut to fade is me. Fade to cut is she . . .'

'Next time, can we have some Beyoncé? Something I can dance to?'

'You going back in there?' Sol nodded towards the Belshams' house.

'Not unless I'm needed.' Marnie was better on her own. She'd known what to say to bring Guy back from the brink of his temper. Noah couldn't help. He could only make it worse.

'She's worried about you, bruv. Your bass lady. Sees the darkness, sees the steppa.'

'There is no steppa. I'm a detective.'

'Yeah? You didn't detect shit when it came to me.'

'Actually, Sol,' Noah met his brother's eyes in the rear-view mirror, 'I detected you were in trouble. When I arrested you, that was me trying to get you out of it.'

'By putting me in *prison*. Yeah. Thanks.'

Noah's phone chimed: Dr Matthews.

'Better take that,' Sol said, peering at the screen. 'You need her.'

'Thanks, yes. I figured that much out for myself . . . DS Jake.'

'Noah, good morning.' Karie had a great voice, low and melodic. Under other circumstances, he could've listened to it all day. 'We have an appointment at midday. I'm checking you're still able to make it.'

'I'll certainly try. But I'm with the parents of a child killed in a drive-by shooting this morning.'

'I'm sorry to hear that. Is DI Rome with you? I know she'd prefer you to keep our appointment if you can.'

'Yes, she's here. Look, can I call you back? I'll try and make the appointment, but I'll let you know either way. Sorry to be abrupt. I know you'll understand. Thanks.'

He ended the call, meeting his brother's eyes in the mirror until Sol looked away, watching the traffic trail past the Belshams' house. It could have been worse, he decided. Sol could've been blowing kisses for Karie, or fake-hugging himself. Was there hope for his subconscious after all?

'Always hope, bruv.' Sol grinned into the mirror. 'You going out tonight?'

'Why, d'you want to come?'

'You and Dan, dancing? Sure.' Sol slunk down in the seat, dragging the pink hood over his head. 'Better than being left at home, dying of boredom.' He laughed, kicking the back of Noah's seat. 'Dying of boredom . . . That's gotta be the best way to go.'

Marnie came out of the Belshams' house alone. Guy and Lynne had stayed inside with this new knowledge about their murdered child. Hidden behind her books, behind the snow globes and soft toys. A bullet. Worst of all, it was a possible motive for her murder, hard evidence that this might not have been a random killing. Their child might have been deliberately targeted.

Noah climbed from the car, seeing the sky lying along the roof of the house, touching the window of Raffa's room. 'I've spoken with Harry. He's organising the forensic team.'

'Good.' Marnie nodded at the car. 'I'll give you a lift to Dr Matthews.'

'She called, in fact.' It was on the tip of his tongue to lie that Karie had cancelled their session. But Sol was watching from across the street, cocking his head to hear what his big brother was about to say. 'She'll understand if I can't make it today.'

'You can make it.' Marnie put her bag on the back seat. 'We'll just have to postpone our visit to Matilda Reece.'

Noah nodded, climbing back into the car. Sol was sitting on the wall in front of the Belshams' house, swinging his feet. He raised a hand to wave them off, mouthing something Noah couldn't hear. He watched in the wing mirror until Sol was a pink smudge no bigger than the pellet of gum pressed to Raffa's shelf, still shiny from her saliva, holding the delicate whorls of her thumbprint.

'What did they say about her laptop and the iPad?' he asked Marnie.

'The iPad's a family one. They were happy for me to take it, for Colin to run checks.'

'And the laptop?'

'The laptop is lost.' Marnie's tone was dry. 'A month ago. Stolen, Raffa said. At school.'

That sounded suspicious. In the light of the bullet, everything was going to sound suspicious.

'They didn't report it to the police?' Noah asked.

'Guy wanted to. The school asked for the chance to search for it. Raffa had a reputation for losing things that later turned up. Her gym kit, textbooks, a pencil case.'

'But the laptop hasn't turned up . . . She definitely said it was stolen and not lost?'

'I got the impression she'd been given a final warning.' Marnie waited for a cyclist to pass. 'Not everything she lost turned up again. Guy replaced her phone charger for a third time last month. She might've been hoping to avoid trouble at home by saying the laptop was stolen.'

'But the school didn't report it to the police? So they thought she'd lost it, like the chargers.'

'*If* the chargers were lost. Yes.'

'You think they were stolen?' Noah watched her, seeing the frown in her eyes. 'No . . . You think Raffa sold them. Maybe the laptop too.' He paused. 'Bullets aren't cheap.'

'I don't want to jump to conclusions, but no. Bullets aren't cheap. We need to search the house, and the garden. We can't pretend this was a random shooting, not now.'

Karie Matthews didn't cross her legs or brush her hair behind her ears. She didn't touch her clothes or her neck, sitting with her hands loose along the arms of her chair, unmoving. She made it look effortless, although it wasn't. It was hard to sit without moving, resisting the itches and tics of your own body. The hardest trick was ignoring your instinct to mirror the other person's body language. Spies were taught to do exactly that. Psychopaths didn't need teaching, since mirroring was in their nature. Karie was the opposite of a psychopath – whatever that might be – but she wasn't far from being a spy. And here was Noah's paranoia kicking in, right on cue.

'How have you been?' she asked.

'Good, thanks. Busy.' Too busy for this.

She waited. She could wait hours, Noah knew. But so could he. And maintain eye contact while he waited, since this was what she wanted. She wanted more than eye contact, of course.

'I thought perhaps we could talk a little about your childhood today. How does that sound?'

'Honestly? It's not relevant.'

She waited, nothing on her face but patient enquiry and a light dusting of mineral powder to bring out her cheekbones. Not that they needed bringing out. She wore Marc Jacobs' Rain, a clean water scent with a hint of orchid underneath. Her dress was a restful shade of grey, her heels low, ankles trim. Everything about her was understated. Carefully, extravagantly understated.

'How's everything else?' she asked when the silence grew too large to ignore. 'The sleeping, for instance?'

'Better since I started running again.' Physical exhaustion, like a wet sandbag applied to the back of his skull, guaranteed sleep. Whether it would be dream-free was another matter. Noah ran when he needed to take Sol away from Dan or Marnie, or anyone else that mattered.

Karie considered the reasonableness of his response.

Then she did what she'd been doing since the start of their sessions together. She tried to make Noah twitch.

'You lost your brother.' Her voice was feather-soft. 'You lost Sol.'

As if Noah needed reminding of this, as if he might've forgotten in the thrill of compassionate leave that his brother was in the ground. Sol bled out in a prison yard after being stabbed with a piece of melted plastic. A slow death under a blue sky, no one taking any notice, no one to hold him or comfort him. Alone and afraid.

'Yeah, bruv.' Sol paced behind Karie's chair, picking at his teeth. 'Chuut.'

Truth.

Silence didn't work with Dr Matthews. Noah sat it out, then said, 'Yes.'

'It's natural you're grieving. I'm not trying to take that away from you. But I'd like to make it a little easier to navigate. The grief, and the guilt.'

Guilt and grief. It sounded like the start of a list of good reasons for Noah to be going off the rails. He preferred the reaction of Ron Carling back at the station: *Aw, shit. Shit, mate, I'm sorry.*

'That old pagan,' Sol sneered. 'Give it up.'

'Disabling responses,' Karie was saying in her gentle way, 'are perfectly natural. Leaving aside what you went through ten weeks ago, your work brings you into contact with trauma on a frequent basis. Is that fair to say?'

'It's my job. It's what I was trained for.'

'Well, we've talked about this.' She spoke simply, spacing her words. 'You were attacked two years ago. And we've talked about vicarious trauma. Your work exposes you to it, constantly. That's not going to change. What can change is your method for coping with it. This is where I hope to be of help, with your cooperation, of course.'

Noah wished he'd brought his running shoes. After this, he'd need to run three miles just to get the bile out of his system. 'Great,' he said. 'Let's talk about coping methods.'

'Did you think any more about the poetry, or painting?'

She wanted Noah to extend the therapy in new directions. Creativity counselling, she called it. The kind of bollocks that made Ron roll his eyes.

'I have a CD,' Noah offered. 'Arvo Pärt, *Spiegel im Spiegel*.' He didn't mention that a member of the public had found the CD on the bus and handed it in at the station.

'That's a good start. Let me know how you get on. *Spiegel im Spiegel*, mirror in mirror . . . Pärt's influence was Gregorian chants, and bells. Some people find its resonance spiritual.'

Noah resolved never to listen to the CD. Sol was bent double with laughter behind Karie's chair, his pink hoody like a polluted sunset. A welcome reminder that whatever else he'd lost, Noah still had his sense of humour, more or less intact.

'Oh, Noah.' Karie put her hands in her hair.

It was so out of character, he held his breath for a second. 'I'm sorry. Are you okay?'

'Not really.' She dropped her hands into her lap, then swept them outwards as if she didn't know what else to do with them. 'I'm supposed to be good at this.' She gave a bittersweet smile. 'Very unprofessional of me to mention that, but there it is. I'm supposed to be good. I'm not helping you at all, though, am I? In fact I'm starting to worry that I'm making it worse.'

'You couldn't make it worse.' It was the first honest thing he'd said to her. It made Sol stiffen, looking a warning at his brother.

'I talk to him.' Noah smiled at Karie. 'Every day.

Sometimes every hour. I talk to Sol, my dead brother. It doesn't help. I thought it might, back at the beginning. But it doesn't, and I have work to do. Work that needs doing. I need to be able to do it.'

Sol stood at Karie's shoulder, his dark eyes on his brother, accusing. Noah looked away, at the calendar above the desk. He tried to retrieve his anger, feeling naked without it. The calendar was a promotional gift from a pharmaceutical company, whose stylised logo was printed beneath a photo of Welsh mountains in the rain. Anger made sense, the only thing that did. How much was Karie paid for these sessions, from the Met's health insurance scheme or whoever bore the cost of counselling? The longer it took to fix Noah, the more Marc Jacobs she could buy. Maybe she'd like to start with Noah's great-grandmother, work her way from there. By the time they reached the present day, her curiosity might be satisfied. Then again, it might not. He heard Sol murmur approvingly from behind her chair.

'You talk with Sol every day.' She was prompting more of the confession, wanting a foothold in the stonewall of his silence. A way in.

But Noah wasn't ready to give up Sol to her scrutiny, or anyone else's. It was no one's business how often he spoke with his brother, or what they said. It was private, like his pain.

Against the rules, to stay silent. Karie was waiting, her face poised on the edge of patience. Noah had to give her something, even if it was none of her business. 'You wanted to talk about my family? My dad works in a garage. He's a mechanic, can fix anything. Mum was a researcher for a while. They're cool.'

She processed this in silence. One rule for her, another for him. He wished she wasn't trying to help him, that this was just about money for her. He wished he had a proper excuse to hate her. If she'd been bad at her job, he could've filed a complaint about her incompetence. She might ask, 'How do your cool parents feel about your career choice? It killed your brother, didn't it? I bet they weren't too cool about that.' And he'd sit in stunned silence, not wanting to share anything with her, least of all the fact of his brother standing behind her chair with his shit-eating grin strung from ear to ear, daring Noah to point at him and say, 'This's Sol. This's my dead brother. He won't leave me alone, not even for a minute, not ever.' And then maybe she'd stroke the sleeve of her jacket thoughtfully and ask, 'What about your other choices? In bed.'

Noah would mirror Sol's grin for all he was worth. 'They're happy for me. It's what families do, isn't it? Be happy for you, as long as *you're* happy.'

'And you, Noah?' She'd press the point, scrabbling for his pain with her unpainted fingernails. 'Are you happy?'

He could walk out then. He'd have grounds. He could stand and nod for Sol, who'd come around her chair like a puppy with a grenade in its teeth. And Noah could pause at the door if he felt like it, and say something like, 'I'm super, thanks for asking,' and she'd have to sit and take it because otherwise she wouldn't get paid, and it was all about the money because she didn't care about Noah, why would she? Except she did. He saw it in her face, as if somehow his pain had spilled over, slipping across the desk like smoke and getting into her eyes.

'This's bullshit.' Sol put his hands on the back of her chair, pink hoody looming behind Karie's head. 'You wanting to weep over this skinny witch? You got *work* to do. Bullets to trace.'

55

'I'm sorry.' Noah climbed to his feet. 'I'm not concentrating very well this session. I really need to get back to work. Back to the station.'

'Of course.' Karie nodded. 'I understand.'

Sol stepped back as she stood but stayed close, shutting his eyes and smiling. It was starting to freak Noah out, the way his subconscious relished stuff he'd never even noticed before, like the scent of a woman's hair, her perfume like earth after rain, just a hint of orchid underneath.

West Brompton was smug, millionaires' houses cold-shouldering the marginally more affordable 'luxury conversions', which in reality were dim basements or rehabilitated squats. The Troubadour café offered coffee priced according to the wealth of its doorstep clientele. Noah's dad had been a regular at the Troubadour in the seventies. Sol had hung out there whenever he could beg, borrow or con the cash for an omelette. He fell into step as Noah neared the café, but didn't speak, as if his mind was on other things. As if *Sol's* mind was on other things – possibly the maddest thought Noah had ever allowed into his head. He dug out his phone and speed-dialled Marnie, hoping she'd ask him to come to the station. Filing, he'd happily do filing for an hour or two. Anything to be back at work, being useful. Sol hated the station, and rarely showed his face there unless it was to surprise Noah when he was using the urinals or grabbing a gasp of fresh air.

'Aren't you meant to be in counselling?' Marnie asked.

'I'm done. Headed back your way.'

'Good session?'

'Great. I know we need to speak with Raffa's friends about her missing laptop, but what about those interviews her dad mentioned? For a project, he said. Somewhere safe: "I made sure of it." What was he getting at, do you think?'

'I looked into it. The project was with residents at Erskine Tower. The school was sending small groups of students with a teacher in tow, to ask questions about what it was like growing up in London in the 1950s. They were talking with pensioners, in other words.'

'Erskine Tower,' Noah repeated. If he walked north, he'd see it looming over west London like a pockmarked chimney stack. His parents' house was on the way, a five-minute detour. You could see the tower from his old bedroom.

'That shithole,' Sol said, as if he'd solved the case, 'is how come the bullets.'

He might be right. Stranger things had happened. Were happening.

'Pensioners,' Noah said to Marnie. 'I don't suppose the bullet could've been a souvenir from an old warhorse?'

'I had the same thought. But it's a live bullet, Harry's team confirmed it. And Harry says there's a connection between Erskine Tower and firearms.'

'Yeah.' Sol laughed. 'Like how come the whole shithole's full of guns and bullets.'

'I can be at Erskine Tower in twenty minutes,' Noah told Marnie. 'Hammersmith and City Line will take me most of the way.'

'All right. Let me clear a couple of things and I'll meet you over there. That'll give you time to get some lunch . . . Noah? Get some lunch.'

He didn't knock on the door of his parents' house, knowing he'd get no answer. It'd been years since Mum had answered the door to anyone. Instead he used his key, taking care not to make too much or too little noise, following the rules he and Sol had grown up with. Silence had a sound, Mum said, that set her teeth on edge. Too much of it could make her shout, sometimes yell.

'Mum?' He stood in the hallway, listening for where she was in the house. 'It's Noah.'

She didn't answer, but she was upstairs. Years of experience had taught him that. Sol hung back, shaking his head at Noah, who shut the front door and turned away from his brother. The house smelled of cardboard, and something sharp that hurt his teeth and gums. He climbed the stairs, avoiding the steps that creaked, going to the bathroom first, expecting to be dazzled by the gleam of her cleaning. The bathroom wasn't dirty, but nor was it frantically clean. Rosa-clean, so bright you could see your face in the tiles. A bucket of brushes and scouring pads sat in the bath like a child waiting to be washed. But she hadn't washed the bath, or the sink. She'd left the job half done. Noah's jaw ached where he was clenching it. He headed for the front bedroom.

'Mum, it's Noah.'

His parents' bedroom was empty, curtains drawn against the day. The bed was made but didn't look slept in, its covers hotel-tight. An alarm clock blinked, red digits giving 12:00 repeatedly, waiting to be reset. How long had it been like that? He'd called Dad less than a week ago, when Sol first alerted him to their mum's decline. He'd listened to the upbeat assessment of her health – 'She's fine, boy, she's doing good' – knowing it would take a catastrophe to shake Dad's blind faith in her ability to dance to the cliff edge of sanity without falling.

'Mum, it's Noah.' The house threw his name back at him. Odd acoustics, like being underwater. He went to the front of the house – his bedroom, until he moved out.

'Don't,' Sol warned from the doorway. He stood with

his back to Noah, his ear to the door of the room, shoulders taut inside the pink hoody.

Noah shut his eyes for a second, until his brother moved aside. He put his hand on the door, its old paint so familiar, chipped in places, patched in others. The door had two narrow glass panels that'd been painted over so many times you'd never know there was glass underneath. Unless you grew up here, seeing the house scuff and shadow, helping your dad to touch it up, make it good as new again. Noah could smell the tins of thick white paint. He could feel the smooth varnished wood of the brushes, and hear the spongy squeak of a roller on the walls.

'Mum, it's Noah.' He opened the door and stepped into his old room.

His face stared at him from all sides. Stretched like a ghoul's, all eyes and open mouth, forehead bulging as he stepped forward, chin disappearing as he stopped dead. The room was wall-to-wall water. In plastic barrels, the kind that fed drinking fountains in schools and hospitals. Blue-tinted, balanced one on top of the other from floor to ceiling, only stopping to leave space for the door to open. No bed or bookcase. Nothing but the barrels. Forty, maybe fifty in total. The floor groaned with the weight. This was Dad's version of Mum 'doing good'. He must've helped her stack the barrels, unless whoever delivered them did the job.

No wonder Sol was freaking out. 'Yeah, bruv . . .' He said it on a long sigh, broken.

Sometimes Noah forgot it was Sol who'd stayed in the house after he moved out. Dad was working all hours. Just Sol and Mum in here back then. Sol and . . . this.

'Mum! It's Noah.' He reached the back bedroom in four short strides.

The house had always been small, but it'd shrunk since he was last here. Boxes everywhere, even on the landing, like dodging an assault course. Some of them hadn't been opened. He recognised the logo on a couple, the same one he and Ron had seen on a website selling long-life food to people afraid the world was coming to an end: *Preparing for the best possible survival in the worst imaginable world.*

Light was wedged under the door to the back bedroom. Dim and shallow, the sort that made you squint, made your eyes ache. The quiet from inside was oppressive. Since the funeral, Mum had been stockpiling silence, as if she anticipated a steep rise in demand should the effort of talking become too much for the three of them. Noah and Dad, and her.

He opened the door. 'Mum?'

At the window, a blackout blind was drawn, fastened with string to a bolt in the sill. The light came from the monitor where Rosa was sitting, her face so close to the screen it painted her skin the colour of wet chalk. Headphones gripped either side of her head, straightening her hair. Babble on the screen, words and boxes, babble in her ears to match. Noah could hear it, thinned out by the headphones. Her fingers fretted at the keyboard. She couldn't hear him. She couldn't see him either, her attention eaten by the screen. He moved close enough to make out what she was reading. Instructions for salting meat, ads for multipacks of iodised salt, slabs of highlighted text: *Egyptians evaporated seawater from the Mediterranean and used salt as a valuable part of mummification.* Crates to either side of the desk were filled with food cans, batteries, loo roll, plastic sheeting, cleaning products. It was almost a relief to see the cleaning products, something familiar in this new madness. Pills, too.

In foil strips and plastic tubs. Pills were normal. Plastic sheeting wasn't.

He touched a hand to her shoulder, getting a tiny shock of static. 'Mum.'

She looked up, worry making a mask of her face. 'Noah? What's happened?'

'Nothing. I came by to see you.' He held his breath, braced for her hate. She'd said she never wanted to set eyes on him again, that he wasn't to put a foot back inside this house.

But she reached for his hand, turning it over to check for dirt or damage before pressing it to her face. He could feel her checkbone; she'd lost so much weight. 'My brave boy.' Her eyes strayed back to the screen. 'Are you safe?'

'I'm fine. I'm good. Mum—'

'No,' she said fiercely, 'are you *safe*?' The screen stole the colour from her eyes, made her stare achromatic. 'Tell me.'

'I'm safe, Mum.'

'Where's your brother?'

All her attention was on the screen. No wonder Sol had cursed him for bringing the laptop into their home. Noah knew how easily she latched onto new anxieties. New addictions. The internet was the worst gift he could've given.

'Sol's staying with me for a while. He's safe, too.'

'He should come back here. You both should.'

'Where would I sleep?' Noah tried a joke: 'I don't fancy the waterbed.'

She pulled away from him, hunching closer to the screen. 'Tell your brother to come home. He needs to stop running around, settle down. He doesn't know how dangerous the world can be.'

'I'll look out for him.' Noah's throat ached. 'You know I will.'

*   *   *

61

He made a mug of tea before he left the house. There was no fresh milk in the fridge, only long-life cartons. No fresh food, either. Just tins and more tins. When did she last eat a proper meal, and what was the long-life diet doing to her health? He wished he could invite her for supper with him and Dan, but he knew she wouldn't leave the house. He could cook for her here if he shopped first, or bring a takeaway. A takeaway was probably best, since the next time he came she might remember and send him out of the house, screaming Sol's name. Noah wished he wasn't so grateful for this reprieve. It meant she'd lost ten weeks. Forgotten that her younger son was dead, forgotten his funeral and the friends who'd rallied round. Fallen into the internet's grasp. There was nothing in any of that to be grateful about.

He boiled the kettle, dunked the tea bag, added a little long-life milk. Sol watched him the whole time, but neither of them spoke. There was no bread in the house, only biscuits. Noah put three on a saucer and carried them upstairs with the tea, setting the mug and saucer at Mum's elbow. She didn't take her eyes from the screen – fifteen flat inches where dust clung like fungus.

'Love you, Mum.' He bent to kiss her head, not knowing the next time she'd let him do that.

Sol stayed in the house when he went, standing at the upstairs window. Somehow he'd fitted himself past the barrels in Noah's bedroom, pink hoody swimming with the water's reflection. He raised a hand to his brother, and Noah raised his in return. A salute of solidarity, born of years of navigating Mum's illness. Years and years of not knowing when silence would become a sound she couldn't stand, another thing that set her teeth on edge until the only way she could stop it was to shout and scream and beat her hands against her legs until they bruised.

His phone pulsed in his pocket. 'DS Jake.'

'Noah, it's Harry Kennedy. I'm at Erskine Tower. Marnie says you're on your way over here?'

'Yes. Give me ten minutes.'

'I'll meet you outside.' Harry named the precise location. 'The press are here, a protest about stop and search. We don't want you running into it.'

We. As if he and Marnie were the team now, making decisions together, deciding what was best for Noah. He clenched the phone until his hand hurt. 'I'll see you there.'

'That motherfucker.' Sol lengthened his stride to match Noah's. 'How much longer you putting up with that?'

'I thought you were staying with Mum.' He kept the phone at his ear, speaking into it although Harry's call had ended. He didn't want to be caught talking to himself in the street; his day had enough drama in it without that. 'I wish you'd stayed with her.'

'And miss this next bit? Shit, no. I'm with you, bruv. Don't wanna miss it when you finally lose it with that motherfucker.'

'What happened to you wasn't Harry's fault.'

'You don't believe that,' Sol said slyly. 'Or we wouldn't be having this conversation.'

It was impossible to argue with this logic.

'I'm not going to lose it with him, in either case. What good would that do?'

'Might get me off your back.' Sol kicked at the pavement, raising dust.

Noah could smell the Tube on his hoody, and cigarettes, and weed. Underneath everything else, he could smell laundry detergent, the kind he and Dan used at home. He'd washed Sol's hoody, he remembered, about six weeks before he'd arrested his brother. Twelve weeks before Sol was stabbed. The hoody wasn't in the belongings the prison had returned. Noah didn't know where it was. But he could smell the detergent he'd used, his hands remembering how it felt as he pulled it into shape, damp from the washing machine, to dry on a plastic coat hanger over the bath.

'How are you so real?' he whispered into the phone. '*How?* Am I losing my mind?'

Sol looked sideways at him and laughed.

4

Erskine Tower throbbed with bodies, skinny and fat, short and tall. In jeans and T-shirts, dresses and headscarves. And hoodies, lots of hoodies. Sol peeled off as soon as Noah arrived, pressing into the crowd of protesters as if he'd found his tribe.

Placards jostled above the protesters' heads, spray-painted with a loud mash-up of slogans and obscenities accusing the police of violating civil rights, and worse. Many of the placards carried abuse aimed at the Met. And Parliament, of course, but Parliament didn't catch nearly enough of the flack. The abuse felt personal, brutish. *Fuck the police!* It was directed at Noah and Marnie, and at Harry Kennedy.

The crowd were chanting and surging, stomping together in what the press would call a well-orchestrated protest. Many of the faces were black. The police presence wasn't helping. A young black officer about Sol's age was taking a lot of the abuse. Noah didn't know the officer's name, but he recognised his face from protests around the capital, black faces still rare enough to stand out above the uniform. The young officer was an easy target for the crowd's rage, his face flinching behind the riot shield. *Oreo, choc ice, blood clot, bag o wire* – Noah had heard every insult. And it was getting worse, racism coming from all sides, a gleeful free-for-all sealed with a loving kiss by Brexit.

He looked for Harry. There by the side of the tower, out of range of the protest, standing with Marnie, her red head close to Harry's dark one. Too close. Noah had known she liked the man ever since Harry took a knife to the gut and nearly died.

'Not nearly enough.' Sol was back, carrying a placard that read: *Police THIS!!* and some other words that Noah chose to ignore.

'Nice,' he said. 'Understated, but articulate.'

Sol nodded towards Harry and Marnie. 'Him moving in on your bass lady.'

'It's called teamwork.' Noah started walking in the direction of Sol's stare. 'You might want to sit this round out. I need to work.'

'Mi gaan.' Sol strolled back to the crowd, swirling his placard and chanting with the rest.

Marnie knew from the twinge in Harry's eyes that Noah was approaching.

'Hey.' He greeted her and Harry with a nod. 'Is this a coincidence?' He glanced back at the protesters, eyes scanning the crowd. 'Raffa coming here, and now this.'

'We think so,' Marnie said. 'We're going to talk with Eric Martineau. He's the pensioner she was interviewing for the school project.'

'How's the search going at the Belshams' place?'

'Slowly,' Harry answered. 'So far, nothing beyond the bullet you found. But we've the garden to get through yet. And the rest of the house.'

Noah turned to Marnie. 'How's Guy taking it?'

'About as well as you'd expect.'

The protest hit a new pitch, the crowd bouncing on its toes, placards slapping the air. Marnie watched Noah's stare move across the crowd as if searching for someone he knew. 'Lift's out of order,' she said. 'We'll have to take the stairs.'

Noah nodded. 'I could use the exercise.'

Harry said the same, and the three of them went through the side entrance into Erskine Tower.

The block was chilly, a tongue of cold licking at Marnie's neck and wrists. It smelled of cooking fat and washing and the cheap bleach used to mask everything else. The noise of the protest was cut off by the doors, the building better soundproofed than she'd expected.

'Are they protesting anything in particular,' Noah asked, 'or just putting in practice?'

'A couple of kids from here were searched two days ago,' Harry said. 'From a family with a history of possession. Drugs and knives.'

'Arrests?'

'Not this time.'

'Black?' It was unlike Noah to be so direct.

Harry turned on the stairwell to look at him. 'Yes.'

Noah's face was open, his body language the opposite of confrontational. 'Drugs and knives,' he echoed. 'But not guns.'

'Not that family.' Harry shook his head. 'But Trident's made four arrests for firearms here in the last six months. We know it's a hot spot.'

They climbed the stairs in silence. Eric Martineau lived on the nineteenth floor. Each turn in the stairwell brought a fresh blast of graffiti, bright colours, bold words.

'So we think the bullet from Raffa's house might've come from here?' Noah asked next.

'It's a strong possibility,' Harry said. 'We'll know more after the forensic tests.'

'But we don't think it came from Eric. He's not a suspect, is he?'

They turned a corner and a shaft of sun struck their eyes, coming through the stairwell window like a missile. Harry's profile was grim against the light. 'I wouldn't rule anything out.'

'Pensioners dealing in firearms and ammunition . . .' Marnie shielded her eyes. 'It's happened before. Eric Martineau doesn't have a criminal record, not even a parking fine—'

'But we're assuming the worst.' Noah nodded. 'That makes sense.'

'I hope we're not making any assumptions. Mr Martineau may be able to tell us whether Raffa had dealings with anyone else in here. One thing that struck me – the phone chargers and laptop went missing during the time she was coming here.' Marnie spoke to Harry: 'Noah and I have a theory she may've sold them, but there's no evidence at this stage.'

'Worth looking into,' Harry agreed. 'We know drugs and weapons have been traded out of these flats. Once an address gets a reputation for any sort of trade, it tends to attract more.'

They turned another corner in the stairwell, the sun striking their eyes afresh. Noah showed no sign of slowing, taking the stairs easily. He was keeping fit, running before and after work.

'It's this floor.'

He had climbed too far, jogging down to join her. Harry held the door for the three of them, letting it swing shut when they were in the corridor. Chipped paintwork, the ghost of old graffiti, a carpet that managed to look scabrous and wet at the same time. The low ceiling had been fitted with a new sprinkler system, badly painted around the wounds left by the work. All the doors were the same shade of brown; only the locks differed, depending on how often or violently they'd been changed. The council was repossessing homes at an alarming rate. How many of the people living here felt secure enough to call it home? Even those who were born here, raising families, paying rent without fail – even these families were being moved out. The corridor felt uneasy, electric with the sense of eyes watching through the peepholes in closed doors. Marnie's chest tightened reflexively.

Eric Martineau had a chain on his door. He peered over it at her badge before sliding the chain free. 'Come along. Quickly, please. Before too many of my neighbours decide I'm a police informant.' His eyes twinkled, but there was a serious underscore to his words. He ushered them inside, closing the door and sliding the chain back into place. 'Through here, if you would.' Spreading an arm in the direction of a living room that faced the front of the tower.

He was the wiry side of thin, carrying himself very upright, as if at any given moment he might be called upon to snap into a salute. His head was baldly freckled, his face lined by laughter. Eyebrows bristled along the bony ridge of his forehead, a trim moustache performing the same trick on his top lip. It made his face look lively, mischievous. His eyes were hazel, their lids nearly lashless. Only the generous size of his nose and ears betrayed his age – in his late seventies, but quick on his feet. Sprightly was the word that came into Marnie's mind as she watched him cross the room to make way for his visitors. She could smell his breakfast of smoked haddock and toast.

Across the west-facing wall, a sliding glass door had

been propped open by a mouldy copy of the Yellow Pages. The sound of the protest drifted up, buoyed by traffic and a police helicopter that churned the sky as it swept past. Beyond the window was a shallow balcony where Eric had opened a sunlounger next to a crate of beer. Along the length of the balcony wall, a sunken trench of soil had been planted with purple heather and pink hyacinths. It was an unexpectedly sunny spot, the kind most Londoners coveted.

'I'll leave the window open,' Eric said, 'if you don't mind. Helps to air things out.'

The sitting room had been furnished in the sixties with yellow walls, a faux fireplace, built-in cupboards. A flame-coloured tufted rug was spread across the floor. A sofa and two armchairs upholstered in dark green were positioned in a right angle facing the fireplace. The television was free-standing on a wheeled base, almost an antique in this day and age. On the wall above, mounted on a matching pair of brackets, was a ceremonial sword in a polished scabbard, from the neck of which hung an elaborate crimson tassel.

Eric said, 'Oh dear. I should've shoved that under the bed before I let you in, shouldn't I?' He stepped close to the wall, pulling the cuff of his cardigan over his hand to polish the scabbard. 'It's for show, really. But it sends the wrong message to a certain kind of person.' He winked at Harry and Noah, then shook his head. 'I have the paperwork for it somewhere . . .'

'Mr Martineau.' Marnie caught his attention with a smile. 'May we sit down? We'd like to talk with you about Raphaela Belsham.'

'Little Raffa?' His eyes brightened, then clouded. 'What's she been up to?'

'May we sit?'

'Of course.' He nodded, spreading his arms at the room's seating plan.

Harry and Eric took the armchairs, while Marnie and Noah sat together on the sofa.

'Three of you.' Eric hitched at the knees of his trousers as he sat. 'That can't be good.' The trousers were putty-coloured, immaculate creases down the front of each leg. His shirt was brushed cotton chequered in red, his cardigan khaki, darned at the elbows. Every item of clothing was clean and pressed. It was a long time since he'd been in the army, but it had stayed with him, in his bearing and the care he took of himself and his surroundings. All the dust had been swept from the surfaces in the room.

'DS Jake and I are with the Metropolitan Police. DS Kennedy works with Trident.'

'That's gangs.' Eric inclined his head at Harry. 'You're in the right place. We've got 'em coming out of our ears round here.' His eyebrows twitched into a frown. 'But what's all this to do with my little Raffa?'

'When did you last see her?' Marnie asked.

'Thursday last week. She always comes on Thursdays.'

Today was Monday.

'I'm afraid there was a firearms incident, earlier today.'

'No, no.' Eric cut her off by raising both hands, palms out in a gesture part-surrender, part-protection. He ducked his head away from her. '*No.*'

'I'm afraid Raffa died of her injuries shortly after eight o'clock this morning.'

He kept his hands raised, crossing them at the wrist, his palms hiding his face. He was visibly shaking, even the lobes of his ears.

'Mr Martineau, I'm sorry to be bringing such bad news. Is there anyone I can call? A friend, or a neighbour perhaps?'

That drew a breathless laugh from him, devoid of humour. 'You'll be interviewing most of them! Or DS Kennedy will.' He lowered his hands, taking hold of the arms of the chair. When he had his emotions under control, he raised his head and met Marnie's gaze, his eyes wet with tears. 'That little girl . . . She was a *child*. Who does such a thing, whoever does such a thing?'

'That's what we need to find out. We need to know as much as possible about the kind of girl Raffa was. The friends she had, people she might have met.'

'Here, you mean.' His stare was shrewd. 'It wasn't an accident, then.'

'We don't know yet. We're piecing it together.'

'Drive-by, they said on the news. I heard it.' He nodded towards the kitchen, where the smell of haddock was strongest. 'I'd the radio on. Drive-by shooting in Muswell Hill, never thought for a minute it might be her, although I knew she lived out that way with her mum and dad.'

'She talked to you?' Noah leaned forward. 'About her home, her family?'

'She didn't draw breath from the second she was through the door. I made a joke about it, said wasn't I the one supposed to be doing the talking?' His eyes misted. 'But I loved listening to her rattle on. It was . . . peaceful. Even when what she was saying wasn't so nice to hear.'

'What did she say that wasn't nice to hear?' Noah asked.

Eric appraised him. 'You're from a close family? Jamaican, yes? I knew a couple in the army. Bravest men I ever met, and both from close families. Wish I could say the same about Raffa. But modern families are another kettle of fish.' He blinked, eyebrows beetling. 'She'd a hard time getting her dad to listen. Mum too, from what I could gather. Not that she was complaining as such, just nattering. No different to what her friends were going through, from the way she said it. Except they all had boyfriends to confide in.'

'Raffa didn't have a boyfriend?'

'No time for it, that's what she told me. Boys were boring, that was it. And she didn't think much of their personal hygiene habits, either.' He twinkled briefly, before turning sad again. 'Little Raffa, it's not right. It's *indecent*. A child like that, shot on the street? These knives are bad enough, a fresh stabbing every other day.'

'You said I'd be interviewing your neighbours.' It was Harry's turn to sit forward. 'Were you being cynical, or is there something I should know?'

'You came through that crowd.' Eric looked at him. 'Protesting police brutality, or whatever they're calling it this week. Well, you keep arresting residents! Found a cache of knives on the floor below mine a fortnight back.' He frowned. 'It was on the tip of my tongue to tell Mr Peters to call off the project. Bringing the kiddies in here with all this going on.'

'Mr Peters?'

'Raffa's teacher. Big chap, you can't miss him. Sweaty handshake.' Eric examined his own hands. 'Nice enough fellow, but a bit wet, kept insisting it was good for his students to see the real world, as if his school's in some fantasy realm, like those games Raffa liked to play.' He fanned his fingers, shakily. 'Card games, princesses and goblins. She said it made her unpopular at school, so she kept her pack hidden. Showed it to me, though.'

'Did she leave anything with you the last time she visited?' Marnie asked. 'Last Thursday?'

He shook his head. 'Just a packet of biscuits. She'd started bringing ginger nuts after I said they were my favourites.' His voice cracked. 'It must've been an accident, surely? Who shoots a child like that? A sweet girl, no trouble to anyone. A *good* girl.'

Guy Belsham had described his daughter in the same words: a good girl.

'It must've been an accident,' Eric insisted.

'It may have been. But we found something that suggests otherwise.' Marnie paused, aware of Noah and Harry watching as she was for Eric's reaction. 'In her home. Ammunition.'

'Ammu— Bullets, you mean?' His eyebrows rose so high they formed a fringe. 'In her home?'

'Hidden. In her bedroom.'

Eric whistled through his teeth. Then he shook his head. 'A child like that? *Bullets?* It makes no sense.'

'But if she was a girl living here,' Noah said. 'In Erskine Tower. One of your neighbours' kids, let's say. Would that make sense?'

'More sense than Raffa! And nothing to do with the neighbourhood, lad, though I see where you're coming from. No, this's about Raffa herself. She didn't know one end of a gun from the other. Swords, now!' He nodded to the ceremonial scabbard. 'She wanted to hear the story about that. It fitted with her princesses and goblins. Swords and sorcery, that's what she called it. Not guns, though. Never guns.'

'Could she have met someone when she was visiting you?' Harry asked. 'You said you were concerned about her coming through here with all the arrests taking place.'

'Always with Neville Peters in tow.' Eric frowned.

'*Was* Mr Peters always with her?' Marnie asked.

'That was the plan, the way it was supposed to work. They were just kids, after all. I was asked to fill out a stack of paperwork. Safeguarding policies, they said. We must've passed their checks, me and Meg Horton and

Elsie Weeks, all of us in the study. What it was like growing up round here in the 1950s. You want to be able to say they'd recognise the place, that it wasn't so different to now. But we can hardly say that, can we? With all these knives about, and guns.'

Marnie waited a beat. 'How many teachers came with the students?'

'Just Mr Peters that I saw. He sat in, the first couple of times. Then once he was satisfied with how it was going, he'd rotate. His word. He'd get us settled, then rotate between the other flats.'

'So sometimes you and Raffa chatted alone. Did she ever arrive or leave on her own?'

'Not officially. But yes, once she got to know me.' Eric nodded, his big ears wobbling. 'You're thinking the whole set-up was wrong. Kiddies coming in and out in their smart uniforms, bags full of expensive phones and computers and whatnot.'

'Did Raffa bring a phone and laptop with her?' Noah asked.

'They all did. Stood out a short mile, too.' He looked tired suddenly, and ten years older. 'I wish I'd said something. Something that *meant* something.'

The flat felt crowded, too many people in its shallow sitting room. Eric was shrinking in the chair, his eyes moist, freckles amplified. He looked under siege in his own home. Noah noticed it and stood, saying, 'May I see your balcony?'

Eric nodded, and Noah crossed the room, sliding the glass door to step out onto the balcony, with its sunlounger and its dizzying view to the crowd below.

Marnie said, 'What is the story with the sword? The one Raffa liked to hear.'

'Oh nothing very exciting. I hiked it round when I was

with the Rifles, then paid a tidy sum to keep it on discharge. The usual thing.' He wiped at his eyes. 'But she liked to hear it, said it was romantic. As if war's ever that. Mind, I'm not saying she was any more naïve than the rest, just that she saw the world from a different angle. Keen eyes. And bags of curiosity, which isn't so usual these days, not with young ones. She took photos,' nodding at the sword, 'and researched the Rifles. Taught me things I'd never known, or else I'd forgotten. I'll miss her. I really will.' He held onto the chair as he climbed to his feet. 'We'll have a cup of tea, shall we? And a biscuit for the lad out there,' nodding towards Noah. 'He looks like he could use one.'

Harry met Marnie's eye. 'I'll lend a hand.' He went with Eric towards the kitchen.

Marnie stood, glancing around the sitting room, imagining how it must've looked to Raffa Belsham in her nice uniform from her neat home where she struggled to connect to her parents. The tufted rug alone had more colour than the whole of the Belshams' house. And Eric was a listener, attentive. Marnie could see his eyes twinkling at Raffa, pleased with her curiosity, happy to let her rattle on until Mr Peters returned. Or didn't. What happened when Neville Peters didn't arrive to collect her from Eric's flat? Did she make her own way down the flights of stairs, or in the lift? Did she meet any of the residents? With her keen eyes and her curiosity, did she *find* the bullet, was that possible? Stooping to collect it from the floor of the lift or in the stairwell, hiding it in her hand, pocketing it to take home. Marnie studied the sword on the wall. How would a girl like Raffa feel if she found a bullet? Scared, or brave?

She joined Noah on the balcony, where the air was brisk and fresh, too high to carry more than a whisper of

London's traffic fumes. He was standing with his hands in his pockets, watching the crowd below. The purple heather and pink hyacinths clashed with the dinginess of the concrete, a startling stripe of colour running along the balcony's narrow ledge.

'Harry's helping Eric make tea.'

'Are we going to search the flat for bullets? That's why Harry's here, isn't it? To find out whether Eric's as upright as he seems. Whether he might have an arsenal under the bed.'

'It's a team effort,' Marnie said cautiously. 'Are you okay?'

'Sorry.' He reeled in his gaze from the crowd. 'Too much soul-searching with Dr Matthews. It's good to be at work.'

'Even with Harry in tow?'

'I'm . . . Sorry, really.' Noah gripped the back of his neck in the crook of his hand, a new hollow under his cheekbone. 'I got up the wrong side this morning. I'll shake it off.'

'Don't apologise,' she told him. 'But I need to know when this is too hard for you. Some days it will be too hard, and that's okay. If you need to take a day? Take a day.'

'Thanks . . . Can you imagine Raffa here?' Noah looked back into Eric's sitting room. 'I can't.'

'In this flat? Yes. But not in the stairwell, or not on her own. What was the school thinking?'

'I'm surprised her dad didn't challenge them. Or refuse to give his permission. He said it was safe, that he'd made sure of that. How? What did he mean?'

'Perhaps the school made a big deal of the chaperon, Neville Peters. We should speak with him, and the other students who came here.'

Noah was quiet for a moment. Then he said, 'Are we

focusing too much on this place as the source of the problem? It has a bad reputation, I accept that. But Trident's found firearms in plenty of nice neighbourhoods, including the Belshams'.'

'That's true. But we have to start somewhere. And we know Raffa was in and out of these flats in the last few weeks.'

Noah accepted this with a nod. His eyes were back on the crowd.

'Tea.' Marnie touched a hand to his elbow. 'Come on.'

Eric Martineau made a strong pot of tea. While they drank it, Harry asked a handful of questions about Erskine Tower, Eric's neighbours, the gangs he'd come across. Not so long ago it would've been unusual to quiz a man of Eric's generation about the gangs of young men and women living in his immediate vicinity. But it would have been stranger not to speak of them now.

'There's a bright lad one floor down from me. Felix Amos. Used to run errands; you could trust him with a fiver to pop to the shops and pick up a carton of milk or a bit of fish. But he turned thirteen last month and I've already seen him with the twins.' Eric tipped his teacup at Harry. 'You know the pair. Robert and Tyrone. The Bellamy boys.'

'We know them.' Harry nodded.

'They're the reason for that noise out there.' Eric glanced towards the terrace. 'That crowd. Your lot keep arresting them, but you can't blink before they're back out again. It's why you won't find anyone turning witness round here. No one believes a conviction'll stick. Pair of clever blighters. Young Felix is bright as a button, so of course they want him. There's not a lad or lass round here who isn't being sized up by the Bellamys. No need to bother with the careers officer at school when you can get a job for life here on your doorstep.' He sipped at his tea. 'I'm tolerated because they've a grudging respect for old buggers with war medals. Same as Elsie, who was a midwife and knows their grans. I'll give them that – they respect their elders. It's the young ones I worry about. Hard enough growing up round here without that sort of temptation. I expect Felix'll think he's doing very nicely for himself. They look after their new recruits, for a while at least. Posh clothes, plenty of cash. He was a scruffy beggar when I first met him. Thin as a rail.' His eyes went to Noah. 'Nice with it. Now he hasn't the time of day for the likes of me.'

'Could Raffa have met Felix here?' Harry asked. 'Or the Bellamy boys?'

'It's possible, I suppose.' Eric looked glum.

'Did she change at all in the time she was coming here?' Noah wrapped his lean fingers around his cup of tea. 'Anything to suggest she was straying towards the same sort of trouble as Felix?'

'She was quiet this last time.' Eric frowned. 'Unusual for her, so I remarked on it. She brushed it off, something about her dad not letting her do something or go somewhere. Nothing that made me worry.' He dropped his eyes to his tea. 'I *should* have worried. Maybe if I had . . .'

'Mr Martineau,' Marnie said. 'Forgive the blunt question, but if you had to guess where a girl like Raffa got her hands on a bullet, what would be your best bet?'

'Mine?' His eyebrows met over the bridge of his big nose. 'Same as yours.' He set down his tea and spread his arms. 'Here. On my own doorstep. It grieves me to say it, but I'm living in a jungle. Not just the tower, the whole square mile. You can't walk three steps in any direction without seeing a syringe or one of those little drug bags, or laughing-gas pellets. She educated me about those, did Raffa. She knew what was what, and not because she was mixed up in it. Because she was curious, about the whole world.' His voice broke again. 'That's what we've lost. That's what they killed. Gunning her down in the street . . .' He shut his eyes tight against the image. 'You'll find them, I'm sure of that. Arrest them, take them off the streets. But for how long? Until the next time, the next child. Another protest about stop and search, about civil liberties.' He kept his eyes shut, as if afraid to open them. 'People get scared, that's when they're dangerous. I've seen it in young Felix; maybe I missed it in Raffa. That fear that makes you do stupid things, like carrying a knife or a gun . . . Fear makes the whole lot of us into fools.'

When they'd climbed to Eric's flat, the stairwell had been deserted. But as they went back down, it was nineteen floors of echoing footfall and catcalls. A steady trickle of protesters taking a break from placard-waving, pumped full of adrenalin, coming inside to grab a drink or a snack, or to compare notes with their neighbours on how the protest was going.

Harry glanced across at Marnie, then down to where Noah was taking the stairs with his spine loose, the palm of one hand skimming the rail. The noise rising from the stairwell didn't slow him, or alter his body language. If anything, he appeared in a hurry to meet it head-on. Two boys led the pack, aged fourteen or fifteen, both white, their feet slapping the steps. They jerked their chins at Noah, a compatriot welcome, before they spied Marnie and Harry behind him. A double-take, seeing Noah's suit, his clean lines, their stares hardening towards hostility.

'You under arrest then?' one asked.

Noah kept moving, his hand skimming the rail. Harry and Marnie followed, but the boys jockeyed for position on the stairs, getting between them and Noah.

'Blad, you better be under arrest.'

They were just kids, but they were tracking Noah down towards the sound of older voices. And they knew it, their courage rising with each turn in the stairwell.

'I'm talking to you, blad.'

'We're talking to you!'

'Hey,' Harry said. 'Which one of you's Mario?'

The kids swivelled to stare at him.

'One of you's Mario, right? Mario Durate. Is it you?' He pointed at the more vocal of the two. 'It's you. I'm right, aren't I?'

'It's not me, man.' The boy looked confused and wary.

'Yeah, it is you. I recognise your face. Mario Durate.'

'It's not me.' But he pulled back from following Noah, grabbing at his friend to go with him past Harry and Marnie, up the stairs instead of down.

'Who's Mario Durate?' Marnie asked, when the boys were out of earshot.

'No idea. I guess they didn't want to be recognised.' Harry caught up with Noah. 'There's another staircase on the other side. We can cut across from this floor.'

Noah didn't stop moving. 'It's fine.' He sounded distant, distracted. 'They're just kids.'

The crowd parted around them, busy with their own chatter. A couple of placards bumped against the steps, but no one singled out Noah. Harry and Marnie might have been invisible for all the notice they were paid.

Outside, the air was sharp. Wind blustered litter about their feet, but the protesters were straggling now, their day's work done.

'We should head to the school,' Marnie said. 'Speak

with Mr Peters, and Raffa's friends. Eric said she educated him about drugs. Perhaps her knowledge wasn't as academic as he imagines.'

Harry nodded. 'I'll call you when the team's finished with the search at her house.'

'Thanks.'

They started walking to the side road where they'd parked the pool car, Noah two strides ahead of Harry and Marnie.

'I'll give you a lift to the station,' she called to him. 'Or home, if you'd like.'

He turned to look at her. 'The school, you said.'

'I'd forgotten the time.' She checked her watch. 'We might catch a couple of the teachers, but the students will have gone home by now. It's after four.'

'Frankie Reece, then. His mum's in Tottenham, that's not far.'

Marnie wondered when Noah had started calling Frank 'Frankie'. Matilda Reece only ever called her son Frank. 'We should do that, yes. But let's check in at the station first. I'm hoping Colin will have news for us about the car. And Terrance Malig—'

Her phone buzzed as she was saying the man's name. 'DI Rome.'

Ron Carling said, 'The toerag driving the car. Malig. We've got him.'

'At the station?'

'At the morgue.'

Marnie stopped, aware of Harry's eyes on her. Noah's too. 'How did he die?'

'Drove his car under a truck on the M4. Not much left of the car, or him.'

'Who's over there?'

'Harry's lot. Malig's lighting the gangs matrix like Las Vegas on steroids.'

Harry's phone was ringing. Noah's too.

'All right,' Marnie said. 'We're on our way back. Keep us posted.'

5

Noah had lost Sol. He hadn't seen his brother since Erskine Tower, where Sol had blended into the crowd of protesters with his placard. *Police THIS!!* was the last Noah had seen of him. He hadn't expected Sol to catch a lift with him in Marnie's car, and was grateful when his brother stayed wide of Harry. But by the time he was done for the day, leaving the station in his running gear, he was missing Sol, ready for his company on the run home. Not that Sol ever ran with him, as such. Yet he managed to keep up, even on those occasions when Noah put effort into shaking him off. Tonight, he wanted Sol at his side, found himself slowing to give his brother the chance to catch up. Crazy. He was losing his mind, no question.

'Sol?' He put in his Bluetooth so passers-by were spared any overarching concern for his sanity. 'What's up?'

Nothing. Just the pounding of his own feet on the pavement and the punchier sound of car horns in the adjacent street. He thought of Raffa Belsham walking home from Carluccio's with her coffee, jaywalking because that was what you did in London, never imagining a car could be bringing death, a spray of bullets from a wound-down window. People jaywalked all over London, the more so when you were on your own patch, familiar with the sequence of red lights, crossing spaces. Raffa died on her own patch, what Sol would've called her *endz*.

'That's right, isn't it? Endz. Her patch. Sol?'

He slowed to listen to the pattern of cars and bikes, trying to imagine a world of danger in those everyday sounds. Chances were at least one of the cars he could hear was being driven by someone with a knife or a gun. Death had come to London in a big way over the last two years, redrawing the city's lines. The Met was under mounting pressure to make the streets safer, but the task was gargantuan, unlike anything Noah had been trained for. 'This isn't New York City,' he'd been told in training. 'We police by cooperation, as peaceably as possible.' But that was before the crime rate rocketed, challenging NYC for its crooked crown. The Met was playing catch-up, with Trident in tow. Everything was different now.

'Sol? If you're sulking, that's fine. But I thought we were going out tonight? You, me and Dan. Dancing, remember? Better than being home alone, that's what you said.'

The pounding of his feet, beating of his heart, stop-start of London's rush hour.

Otherwise, nothing.

Dan was home, cooking risotto. For the first time, Noah wanted to tell him about Sol. The way his brother hung around, how they talked together. How real Sol was. But he couldn't. He was afraid that as soon as he shared the secret Sol would be gone for good, and he wasn't ready for that, not yet. He wasn't ready to give up his brother's ghost.

'Let's go out.' He leaned into the kitchen counter, rubbing the run from his face with the crook of his elbow. 'After supper, which smells great, by the way.'

'In that case,' Dan turned from the stove, scooping his fair hair from his blue eyes, 'you may snog the chef. And dance with him, later.'

'Hold that thought . . .'

Noah headed for the shower, wanting to wash off his day. Not just the run – the tower block, his mum's bedroom, Karie Matthews. He wanted to be clean. Properly, squeakily clean.

When he wiped the mist from the mirror after the shower, he expected to find Sol's face there, just behind his shoulder. But it was his own eyes that stared back at him, searching.

Where the hell are you?

He retraced his steps, trying to work out exactly when his subconscious had decided to take Sol out of play. When he went inside the tower? Why should that've altered anything? He was used to Sol staying wide of the station. Focusing on his work was generally a good tactic for avoiding whatever pathology gave rise to the hallucinations – auditory, visual, olfactory, tactile – of his brother's ghost. But he was alone now, far from work, and Sol was silent. Staying away. Should he be grateful for the reprieve? Surely it was a good thing that his conscious mind had the upper hand for a change, even if he couldn't pinpoint any good reason for this being the case. He pulled on jeans and a T-shirt before reaching for his phone. The call went straight to voicemail.

'Dad. It's Noah. I saw Mum today.' He sat on the edge of the bed, pillows at his back. 'She's not doing great. I'm worried about her, want to help. Will you buzz me?' He ended the call.

After a while, he realised he was praying. Not for Mum. For his brother. And not praying that Sol was at rest, or at peace. He was praying for his brother to be behind him, for the scent of cigarettes, weed and washing powder on the pillows when he and Dan slept. Missing his brother was a physical pain, as if he'd swallowed a stone and it had lodged at the base of his throat. Everything hurt. Sitting here holding the phone, his fingers throbbing as if he'd cut them, tendons tight and burning from the run.

'Supper's ready.' Dan was in the doorway, wearing a smile to mask his concern.

Noah stood, pocketing his phone. 'Great. Thanks for cooking.' He reached for Dan's elbow, pulling him close, filling both hands with the shape of Dan's head.

This is real, hold onto this, don't fuck it up with your loss, your rage.

'Noah . . .' Dan smiled into his neck. 'Come and eat.'

He went, not looking back at the empty bed, concentrating on Dan's hip moving next to his, the two of them in synch. In the kitchen, he uncorked a bottle of wine while Dan served the risotto.

'I was at Erskine Tower earlier.' He knew Dan loved the place. Brutalist architecture was his idea of beauty: purpose and design working together. 'Thought of you.'

'For the protest?' Dan set their plates on the table, watching as Noah poured the wine. 'I saw it on the news.'

'We were interviewing a pensioner on the nineteenth floor. You should've seen the view he had from the balcony. Sunlounger, beer, even a bit of garden up there.'

'An original resident? That's pretty rare, isn't it?'

'A dying breed.' Noah didn't want the conversation to be bleak. 'He was great. A warhorse, but a gentleman. Old-school.'

'Sounds like your day wasn't too bad.'

Noah set the wine bottle down on the table. 'How was yours?'

'I heard a horny story, if you'd like me to share it.' Dan looked glad of the light mood. 'Involves a rhino and a banker.'

'You're a maniac, Noys.'

Dan laughed. 'So I'm working on this art installation at ZSL.'

'London Zoo?' Noah squeezed lime over his plate. 'Yep, with you so far.'

'And they're bringing in this rhino from Blair Drummond safari park. A cow rhino. In a crate. From Scotland.'

'Where does the banker come in?'

'I'm getting to him. Stay with the rhino.' Dan loaded his fork with rice. 'She weighs a ton. Literally. They had a crate specially made. Covered her eyes so she wouldn't get scared, hosed her down at intervals to keep her cool during the journey.'

'Wait. What's the rhino's name?'

'Glad you asked. Bella.'

'Bella, the cow rhino.' Noah topped up their glasses. 'Go on, you lunatic.'

'When the shipment reaches the zoo, Bella won't come out of her crate. Not for nearly an hour. The banker's getting agitated because he's the sponsor. He's paying for the shipment and he wants Bella on show, there's money in it. A lot of money. She's his new poster pet. What's more, he's hoping for a calf. Or a crash.'

'Wait – what?'

'That's what they call a group of rhinos. A crash. In the end, Bella decides to take a look at her new home.' Dan sipped at his wine, savouring the punchline. 'She comes out at full charge, turns a circle and prangs the side of the truck. *Six* times. No one liked to get in her way. The truck's a total write-off and the banker's in bits.'

'A toast,' Noah proposed gravely. 'Bella.'

They chinked glasses.

'Okay, so I cheated when I called it horny. Cow rhinos don't have horns. But you should've seen the banker. *Actual* tears.'

'Is Bella going to make it onto his posters?'

'Oh I expect so,' Dan said cheerfully. 'He's invested too much to pull out now. Can you believe *he* told *me* a joke about bankers? While he was retrieving his machismo.'

'A good joke?'

'An old joke. What's the difference between a banker and a pigeon? A pigeon can still make a deposit on a Porsche . . .'

'That's so old it's pre-decimal.' Noah ate a forkful of risotto. 'This is perfect, thanks. Christ, I was hungry.'

Dan looked relieved, but not entirely fooled. 'How was the rest of your day?'

Dr Matthews, he meant.

Noah shook his head. 'The rest of the day is this,' reaching for his wine, 'and dancing. If you're up for that.'

'Always.' Dan let go of the residual tension. 'Although I warn you, I'm rusty. How long's it been since we went out?'

'Too long.' Noah smiled. 'Let's make a night of it.'

'Christ,' Dan said, his eyes kindling. '*I'm* hungry.'

Ed answered the door in his oldest board shorts and Jurassic Park T-shirt. 'Hey . . .'

'Hey yourself.' Marnie held up the four-pack of Peroni, and the Chinese takeaway. 'I hope you're not busy.'

His face lit up. 'Come in.'

The living room was a familiar jumble of books and

DVDs, a couple of work folders on the sofa. Ed moved the work out of the way, saying, 'I'll bring a bottle opener, and plates.'

'No need for plates. I have chopsticks. Oh, and a new magnet for the fridge.'

The magnet was a black rectangle bearing the legend *Nihilism*. Underneath, in a smaller typeface: *There's nothing. Like it.*

Ed laughed out loud. 'Perfect.'

They ate from the foil dishes, sitting on the sofa together. The silence was comfortable. Marnie leaned into it, letting go of her day. She'd missed this – Ed and his shambolic flat so solidly soundproofed with clutter. London's night-life might have been miles away. Her own flat, where she'd been living for the past ten weeks, was larger and better located. An estate agent would have no hesitation valuing it over Ed's, but they'd be wrong. *This* was a home.

'How're things?' Ed sucked rice from the back of his fingers. 'How's Noah?'

'Keeping busy. You know how it is.'

'You're worried about him.'

'I am.' She reached for her Peroni. 'I wish he'd talk. But he's locked tight. I can't get in.'

Ed didn't repeat any of the popular platitudes. He didn't say, 'Give him time,' or 'It's a process,' the latter being Lorna Ferguson's favourite. Instead, he ate another mouthful of fried rice, giving Marnie space to keep speaking, cushioning the silence more comfortably. All day she'd carried a black wad of pain behind her eyes, as if someone had stuffed the front of her skull with wire wool. Here in Ed's flat, she felt the pain lifting, clearing the clouds from her head. She drank another mouthful of Peroni, drawing up her bare feet to sit cross-legged on the sofa.

'Thank you, for this.'

'No need . . . D'you want me to give Noah a call? As a friend, not a professional.'

'Yes.' She realised that was exactly what she wanted. 'Please.'

Ed nodded, licking his knuckles. He stopped when he saw her eyes on him. 'What?'

'Fried rice isn't meant to be sexy, Belloc.'

'Tell that to my stomach.' His eyes brightened. 'Damn, I've missed you.'

'How much?' She put the foil trays aside, freeing the space between them. 'Show me.'

The music in the club was loud and pink, an onslaught of solidarity, arms waving, hips swivelling, everything moving. Noah caught the rhythm from a street away, the pavement beating time until he was part of it, past the bouncer in his ironic string vest, through the swing doors and into the music.

Everything was music, moving. The throb of it rose through the soles of his feet to his fingers. His thighs tightened to the slide of it, Dan's hips in his hands, his head thrown back, lips neon-painted under the lights. Mirror balls bouncing their reflections to a thousand pieces, skin singing along to the tune, Beyoncé at last, his skull sucked empty by it, *thank-God-thank-God-thank-God*.

Someone else's hands on his hips, Dan's eyes flashing a warning to match the strobe light, blue as fire, and it was a cliché, it was all such a cliché, but Noah didn't care as long as it kept his head empty, as long as all he was feeling was the music and Dan, and the bodies all about them. He'd missed this. This feeling of being a part of something so fierce, a happiness so hard-won. He'd told himself he'd outgrown it, too old to be clubbing until the small hours. But he hoped he never outgrew it, because this was where he'd found himself. He'd been lost, and he'd found himself in the hot light running up the walls and across the floor, orange and blue. His head began to hurt, burning behind his eyes, but it was all good. He felt good, didn't want it to stop.

Dan danced closer as the track changed, doing that thing with his eyes that should've been illegal. Outraging public decency. Noah reached for him, pulling Dan's arms around his neck until there was nothing between them but clean cotton and sweating skin. 'I love you.'

'What?'

'I love you!' He shouted it, catching the eye of the couple dancing beside them.

Both men grinned, one blew kisses.

Dan leaned in, possessively. 'Excuse me mister officer . . .'

Noah didn't freeze, not right away. He was too mesmerised by Dan's eyes. But then he said, 'What did you call me?' drawing back a fraction.

'I meant detective. Excuse me mister detective.'

Sol's voice: 'Still love you like that, *murderer*.'

Noah looked past Dan's shoulder into the pulse of bodies broken up by the light. For a second it looked like a special effect from a horror movie – the strobe like a blade flashing, splashing bodies, slicing heads and torsos, arms and legs. He turned his hips, taking Dan with him, circling so he could search the room. *There*. A flash of pink, but it was just the light hitting someone's tattoo. Not a hoody. Not Sol. The track switched to a slow one, and he stayed in Dan's arms, dancing. Circling, searching. But Sol wasn't here. Sol wasn't anywhere.

They left the club after 1 a.m., street lights making the pair of them blink.

Noah propped Dan to a wall. 'I'll find us a cab.' He walked to the end of the road, seeing London lit up, no time for sleep. Traffic came in a stream, no cabs with their lights on. He took out his phone, contemplated the Uber app, closed it down. A cab would come, and it was good to stand this short distance from Dan, with London alight around him.

'Fuck off back home!' Women's voices, daggered heels flinting at the pavement. A hen party, holding one another upright. 'Fuck off home, you dirty perverts!'

The abuse was directed at a couple of Asian boys who'd come out of the same nightclub where he and Dan had been dancing. They turned away from the hen party, sticking to the well-lit side of the street. Noah watched the women, alert for an escalation in the abuse, but they were too drunk to give chase to the boys, laughing as they stumbled up the street, one woman trailing a tattered bridal veil. He saw Dan watching and raised a hand to let him know he was okay, turning back to scan the traffic again. Pressure was building in his chest. He put his hand across his mouth as if he might be sick, or in case he might howl. Right here in the street. Fall to his knees and howl like an animal for his brother, and his city.

Raffa Belsham died in the gutter. Like Frank Reece, but it was Raffa he was seeing, so vividly. Curls knotted on the crown of her head, stories of princesses and goblins, her thin child's legs, coffee running into the road. Her eyes blinking at her own blood, the pavement sticky under her cheek. Surprise spreading to pain in her chest and shoulder, the small of her back. People screaming when she wanted them to be quiet, because it was too loud to lie like this. Die like this. It was too loud on a quiet morning with the smell of car tyres scratching her nose, black rubber screeching, something shining at the edge of her eye, rolling free from her body, squashed to a brass button like the ones on Mr Martineau's old uniform. Call me Eric. Tea and ginger biscuits, the sword on the wall so romantic. Screaming on the street. Much later, the sound of the sirens, but she was sleepy by then. Too tired to stay awake and see who the sirens were bringing, or to squeeze the hand that was holding hers, begging her to stay.

6

Neville Peters was a large man, just as Eric Martineau had said. Topping six foot and broad at the shoulder, spreading to fat from the chest down, knees turned inwards under his own weight. He offered a hand the size and colour of an uncooked chicken. 'Mr Peters. Neville.'

'I'm Detective Inspector Rome. This is Detective Sergeant Jake.'

'You're here about Raffa Belsham.' Neville shook her hand then reached for Noah's. 'Such a terrible thing, the whole school's in shock.'

'Is there somewhere quiet we can talk?'

He led them to a room where science equipment was housed, glass flasks and test tubes in wooden racks, a plastic crate filled with safety goggles. The air was sulphurous. Neville wheeled forward two chairs, taking a third for himself. 'Apologies, but the classrooms are all taken for mock exams. Raffa would've been sitting hers today.' He sighed as he settled his bulk in the chair. 'All that hard work she put in . . .' He stroked at the straggle of beard at his chin. His hair was grizzled and greying, although he was only in his early forties, no older than

Guy Belsham. Brown eyes buried in the weight of his face, thread veins across his cheeks, running in thin red rivers to his jaw. A kindly face, or capable of kindness. Eric had called him a 'nice enough fellow, but a bit wet'.

'Did she lose much of the work when her laptop went missing?' Marnie asked.

The question made Neville shift in his seat. 'It was all backed up, fortunately.'

'But the laptop hasn't been found, is that correct?'

'That is correct.' He linked his fingers in his lap. An old burn mark speckled the back of his left hand, as if he'd misjudged a chemical experiment. 'I'm afraid.'

'What's your theory?' Noah asked. 'Was it stolen?'

'No . . .' He moved his head from side to side, slowly. 'No, I can't say that. Raffa had a knack for losing things. I wondered if she'd left it on the bus, perhaps.'

'She took the bus to school?'

Neville looked between Marnie and Noah as if he needed to fix his attention on one of them but couldn't decide which. 'I was thinking of the bus we took to the tower block.'

'You think she left the laptop on that bus,' Noah said. 'And that it wasn't handed in.'

'Apparently not.' He blinked at them.

'She had a knack for losing things,' Marnie said. 'What else had she lost?'

'Phone chargers, I believe. And a phone. Textbooks on a couple of occasions.' He gave a pained smile. 'Never the cheap ones.'

'And all this was . . . carelessness?'

'She'd have been the first to admit that.' He nodded towards the racks of flasks and test tubes. 'It happened a lot in here. Breakages and so forth. But she was a sweet girl, always terribly upset when anything like that happened.'

The door to the room slapped open. 'Sir!'

A boy of Raffa's age with bleached hair and bad skin, school tie knotted at a jaunty angle, skinny black jeans passing for uniform, one hip cocked against the door to keep it open.

'Not now.' Neville spun his chair, speaking sternly. 'This is a meeting.'

The boy glanced at Marnie and Noah without interest. 'Laters, sir?'

'Later,' Neville agreed. 'Close the door.'

The boy did as he was told.

'Sweet,' Marnie said.

Neville started. 'I'm sorry?'

'You were saying Raffa was a sweet girl.'

'Ah. Perhaps sweet is the wrong word. She could be headstrong, emotional. Some of the staff found her hard work, but she was generous and kind. Mr Martineau had nothing but praise for her.'

'This is Eric Martineau, at Erskine Tower?'

'He was very taken with her, and she with him. They struck it off straight away. Some of the students grumbled about the project, but she saw beyond the grim exterior.' He sat upright, warming to the theme. 'She was an idealist. You'd be surprised how rare that is amongst our young people.'

'In what way?' Noah wasn't smiling, watching the man's every move.

'She felt injustice very keenly. When her friends complained about the smell in the flats or remarked on the police vehicles we often saw outside, it was Raffa who stood up for the residents, saying how brave they were to live in a place like that. Especially the children. We saw rather too much of them whenever we went there. Hanging around in the stairwells, or outside, in gangs.'

He made a conscious effort not to look at Noah. 'Never in school, sadly.'

'You weren't worried about the safety of your students?' Marnie asked.

'We took proper precautions.' His mouth marshalled a defensive line. 'And we consulted with the parents, of course. The project wasn't compulsory. But most agreed it was a good thing for students to see a place like Erskine Tower. We can't keep them wrapped in cotton wool.'

'Raffa's parents agreed with that?'

'Mr Belsham wanted a personal assurance that the students would be escorted to the venue and back.' His face flushed when he mentioned Guy. 'A number of these social science project venues were offered to students, and he wasn't too happy about Raffa's choice. I imagine he'd heard a little too much about the tower block from the tabloids. Caution is his watchword, you might say.'

'So the project is running at other venues apart from Erskine Tower?'

'We narrowed it down once we had final numbers for those interested in participating. But Raffa was set on the tower block right from the start. I believe she saw its potential.'

'Unlike her father, who only saw its threat. Is that what you're saying?'

'He certainly didn't share his daughter's enthusiasm.'

'He wanted a personal assurance that the students would be escorted at all times?'

Neville nodded. 'Caution being, as I say, his watchword.'

How had Guy made his demand for this assurance? Here at the school, in a meeting full of other parents? Or in one of his many phone calls, asking for Neville Peters by name, spelling out what he wanted, ticking it off his to-do list for the day.

'How did Raffa get on with her dad?' Marnie asked. 'An idealist, you said.'

The question put Neville on his guard. 'I think . . . well enough. Yes.'

'The school wasn't aware of any problems,' Noah said, 'at home?'

'Not to my knowledge. Her father has a robust work ethic, set a high standard for Raffa, but that's true of most of the parents here. They work hard to get their children into the school, and they expect the children to do the same in return.'

'You said the staff found her hard work,' Noah said. 'Do you think her dad felt the same?'

'I've no reason for thinking that, but it's possible.' Neville picked at his left ear. 'Two robust personalities . . . It's possible.'

'How many students took part in the project?'

'Eight in total. A small group, but that's ideal in many ways. We only had a handful of participants at the flats, so a small group of students was preferable.'

'And staff stayed with the students during the time they spent there?'

'Mr Martineau and the others were vetted, very carefully.' Neville had his tells under tight control, as if he'd anticipated questions about his role as escort. 'Of course.'

'That wasn't our question,' Noah said. 'Were the students ever left alone in the flats?'

'I'm not sure what you're driving at . . .'

'Eight students took part in the project. Did eight members of staff go with them on the bus?'

'Well, no. That would hardly have been practical.'

'So there were times when the students were alone in the flats. When Raffa was alone.'

'Not alone.' Neville spoke patiently, as if Noah had

missed the point. 'With the vetted adults. Mr Martineau and the others.'

'And Mr Belsham agreed to that?' Marnie showed surprise. 'He understood there would be occasions when his daughter would be unaccompanied inside Erskine Tower.'

'You're confusing the issue, with respect.' Neville ran a thumb inside the tight collar of his shirt. 'I'm not sure how it's relevant, in any case. She didn't come to any harm at the flats, did she? And she enjoyed her time there, hugely. What happened was appalling and nonsensical. But it happened in Muswell Hill, not Erskine Tower.'

'You're not aware,' Noah said, 'of any connection between her murder and Erskine Tower?'

Marnie's team was aware of a connection, since the news had broken of Terrance Malig's death.

'No.' Neville looked at Noah, then at Marnie. 'I mean . . . Is there a connection?'

'Any *possible* connection,' Noah amended. 'How about that?'

It was interesting to observe Neville's mounting discomfort. Either he was well aware of a connection between Terrance Malig and the tower where he had left Raffa unaccompanied, or else he was feeling guilty about his failure to keep her safe. Noah's direct questions, and the unequivocal way in which he asked them, brought the man close to squirming.

'You mean its reputation,' he said at last. 'Those flats are . . . But the students were visiting pensioners, people we'd vetted. We undertook a thorough risk assessment, of course.'

The school was oddly silent, no bells sounding or feet running in the corridors. The mock exams explained some of the silence, but Marnie wondered about the discipline here. The school had a decent reputation for grades, but the latest Ofsted inspection had downgraded its status from Outstanding to Inadequate, citing the need for greater trust between staff and students.

'Why did you choose Erskine Tower in particular?' she asked. 'There are pensioners living nearer to the school. In nicer parts of town, to coin a phrase.'

'They see those sorts of people every day.' Neville linked his fingers back in his lap. 'If this was just about interviewing pensioners, they could have asked questions of their grandparents. No, it was about experiencing real London, getting beyond their comfort zones.'

'It certainly took Raffa Belsham beyond hers.'

'If I may . . .' Neville blinked at Noah. 'That's an outrageous remark, unspeakably callous. I was very fond of Raffa, we all were. Her death is a tragedy. An atrocity. But I fail to see how it can be blamed on the project she enjoyed so much.'

The tension in the room was electric, as it had been in Muswell Hill when Noah's presence alone was enough to provoke Guy Belsham. This was different, Noah deliberately provoking Neville Peters in a bid to make the man drop his mask and tell them the whole truth. Because he was hiding something, and perhaps it was nothing relevant – he'd slipped outside to smoke a cigarette, or to take a break from shepherding the students – but perhaps it was more than that.

Marnie said, 'Let's return to the missing laptop. You believe it may've been left on the bus?'

'Possibly. Although in that case we'd have hoped for it to be handed in, which it wasn't.'

'And the phone chargers, and textbooks. Were those also lost on the same bus?'

'No, I don't believe so.' Neville frowned.

'But the chargers and laptop were lost *after* the project got under way, is that correct?'

'I'd have to check the records to be sure.'

'We checked.' Marnie ghosted a smile. 'And it's correct. Earlier items Raffa mislaid, such as her gym kit and a pencil case, turned up again. It's only those items lost after she began visiting Erskine Tower that haven't yet been recovered.'

'Ah.' Neville examined his hands, rubbing at the old chemical burn. 'Well, I must admit I hadn't made that connection. If it *is* a connection and not just a coincidence.'

'Raffa's reputation for losing things came in handy,' Noah said. 'No one looking too closely at what went missing or why.'

Neville turned to Marnie. 'I'm beginning to feel a little badgered.' His smile was ghastly. 'Should I be requesting a solicitor? Only this line of questioning seems somewhat . . . belligerent.'

'We're investigating the death of a child,' Marnie reminded him. 'You would expect us to be thorough. Especially as you were so fond of Raffa.'

'Of course, but I find your colleague's approach unnecessarily antagonistic. Am I a suspect? I can't imagine how, since I don't own a firearm of any description, but I feel I should be asking the question all the same. This is becoming very uncomfortable.'

'Questions are good.' Noah leaned away from the man, looking around the room. 'It's why we ask so many.' He brought his gaze back to Neville's face. 'And murder investigations aren't meant to be comfortable, for anyone.'

Marnie said, 'Were you aware of any friends Raffa made inside Erskine Tower?'

The question surprised Neville. He retrieved his attention. 'Friends?'

'You said she stood up for the children living there, remarked on their courage. Did she have anyone particular in mind when she said that?'

'It was intended as a general observation. As I say, she was an idealist.'

'You don't need to be an idealist to sympathise with the kids in Erskine Tower, you just need a pulse and a pair of eyes.' Noah got to his feet, moving around the room. He picked up a conical flask then set it down, ringing a tune from the test tubes with a flick of his fingers. 'You didn't sympathise with those kids?'

'I wasn't there for that.' Neville creaked in his seat as he followed Noah's progress. 'Please don't touch those – they're sterilised.'

Noah put his hands in his pockets, turning on his heel to face the man. 'You don't own a gun of any description. How about knives? D'you have any of those?'

This was an alien version of Noah, hard and careless. A caricature of the tough detective, and it was getting results; Neville was increasingly agitated. He was hiding something. Marnie and Noah had seen too many witnesses not to recognise guilt when it was sitting in the same room. And they didn't have time to tread carefully around this man's finer feelings.

'Eric Martineau has a massive sword on his wall,' Noah said. 'How about you?'

'Of course I don't own any knives!' His face was brick red with indignation. 'I'm a teacher!'

Noah met Marnie's eyes. She gave him a nod, unseen by Neville.

'What about bullets?' Noah asked.

'Do I have any *bullets*! What kind of question is that?'

'Raffa had a bullet. Hidden in her bedroom.'

'She . . . What?' His face collapsed in confusion. *'Raffa?'*

103

'Had a bullet.' Noah nodded. 'Hidden in her bedroom.'

'You'll understand the need for uncomfortable questions,' Marnie said. 'In the light of this.'

'Yes, of course.' Neville nodded so vigorously his whole body shook. 'Of *course*. And you think she got this bullet from Erskine Tower? Someone she met there, perhaps?' He wetted his lips, straining forward. 'I wish I could help, I really do. But I don't see that she had *time* to make acquaintances, not of that kind. There may've been windows of opportunity when she was making her way back down to join the others after talking with Eric, but nothing of the kind you're imagining.'

'Might her friends be able to help? The other students who were working on the project?'

'It's possible, but doubtful. She wasn't part of a group, not like that.'

'She didn't have friends?'

'She wasn't a loner,' Neville said quickly, as if they might be drawing dangerous conclusions from Raffa's isolation, the words 'school shooter' unspoken but loud in the room. 'Just not part of the peer group. That's not so unusual.'

'She was a sweet girl,' Noah said. 'You stand by that?'

'Yes, I do.' It was the first time he'd answered vehemently, without a second's hesitation. 'One of the best I've taught.' He gripped the arms of his chair. 'What happened to her is a stain on this city. A *stain*.'

Since Raffa's friends were finishing their exams in the designated classrooms, Marnie and Noah stepped outside into the school grounds, in need of fresh air. The school stood at their backs, its stony Georgian exterior a good disguise for the ordinariness inside. Seen from this angle, it looked elegant, a lofty guarantee of money well spent.

'He's hiding something,' Noah said. 'Did you see how relieved he was when we started talking about the bullet instead of the laptop? Most people would've been appalled at the idea of a child with a bullet in her bedroom, but not Neville. He was just glad of the change of subject.'

Marnie watched a group of kids playing hockey in the field to their left. 'Eric said he had sweaty hands, but I didn't notice it just now, did you?'

'Not sweaty,' Noah agreed.

'Not here on his home turf.' Marnie watched the kids. 'Just at the tower.'

'The flats made him nervous?' Noah followed her line of thought. 'In that case, why leave the kids alone? Because it's obvious he did that. He didn't want to admit it, but he left Raffa alone.'

'Unless he wasn't nervous for her. Just nervous for himself.'

'Getting up to no good, you think? He didn't like the questions about the missing laptop.'

They looked at one another until Noah broke eye contact, glancing across at the field. 'Anything on the iPad we took from the house?'

'Nothing. Colin ran thorough checks. We can return it to the Belshams, and give them the news about Terrance Malig.'

'A truck on the M4.' Noah frowned. 'How did the crash happen, do we know yet?'

'Malig was speeding, CCTV confirmed that much. Firearms forensics found a handgun in the car. Ballistics are checking if it's a match to the murder weapon, but that's what we expect to find.'

'And the team at her house? Did they turn up anything?'

'Nothing in the house or garden. Harry's going over the paperwork, and Trident are questioning Malig's known associates, including those in Erskine Tower. Since we now know he was linked to an arrest made there three months ago.' Marnie looked up at the colonnaded facade. 'Damn, I hate schools, they bring me out in a cold sweat. The chemicals in that room . . .' She shuddered.

'You weren't a good student?' Noah was smiling.

'The worst. I didn't want to learn, that was the problem. Headstrong and emotional doesn't begin to cover it.'

'Neville liked Raffa.' Noah shielded his eyes against the flare from the building's windows. 'I believed that much of what he said. And the bullet came as a surprise. A welcome change of subject, but a surprise.'

Marnie nodded. 'Let's see if her friends agree.'

Raffa's friends numbered three. Two girls with long blonde hair, fingernails painted gunmetal grey. And the boy in skinny jeans who'd interrupted their meeting in the science room, and who answered to the name of Byron Jeffries. The girls were Katie Lloyd and Georgia Hamilton. They didn't look pleased to be giving up their break time to the police.

'It's dead wrong,' Georgia said. 'What happened to her. But we should be in counselling, not doing this. It was random, you know? It was *London*.'

'Right, like how're we supposed to know anything?' Katie said. 'She didn't even live near us.'

'It's sick, though.' Byron was laconic. 'She was like the youngest of all of us. It's sick what happened. You need to sort it out.'

'That's what we're hoping to do,' Noah told him.

'The streets, though.' He picked at an oozing yellow spot on his chin, the least Byronic teenager Marnie had seen in a long time. 'That's what I'm saying. You need to sort out the streets.'

'Yeah,' Katie agreed.

She was echoed by Georgia. 'Yeah.'

Both girls were earnestly downplaying their middle-class accents, an effort somewhat undermined by the Tiffany charm bracelets rattling on their wrists.

'You're all part of the project over at Erskine Tower,' Noah said. 'How's that going?'

Their teacher, Miss Robbins, bristled to attention. She'd agreed to the students speaking with Marnie and Noah, but of course she had to be present, for safeguarding reasons.

'It's okay, I guess.' Katie smoothed her hair. 'Raffa loved it.' She pulled a sad face. 'I'm hoping like the school will put on a memorial, you know? Display all her drawings and stuff.'

'I bought a scented candle,' Georgia said, without any hint of irony.

'Me too. I hope, like, tons of people turn up?' Katie flicked her hair across her shoulder. 'Even though she didn't have that many friends. Everyone should come. It's so sad.'

'Except that would be hypocritical.' Byron kicked his feet out in front of him. He'd somehow worked his hands into the pockets of his skinny jeans, a feat that tested the laws of physics to their limit. 'She'd hate that.'

'She liked the project at Erskine Tower. Why was that?'

Byron considered Noah, tonguing the inside of his cheek. 'Said she felt at home there.'

Katie and Georgia erupted into discord: 'No way! You're such a bad liar, By. She liked talking to that old grandad, but that was *it*. No *way* did she say she felt at home there. You're just stirring it, you're such a *stirrer*.'

Byron heard them out, then said, 'Ask her. Oh, wait. We can't.' He wriggled a hand free from his jeans to wipe at his nose.

'That's not a nice sentiment, Byron.' Miss Robbins looked pained. 'We're all very upset by what's happened.'

'Yes, *miss*!' The girls leaned closer to one another, glaring at Byron.

'I wasn't dissing her.' He scratched at his chin, the shadow of chipped black polish on his nails. 'I liked her. She didn't give a shit about any of us, did her own thing. She was cool.'

The girls fell silent, wrinkling their noses at him as if he were a family pet who'd performed an unexpected and lewd new trick. Miss Robbins caught Marnie's eye with a look of apology.

Noah said, 'She didn't have many friends here. Did she make any at Erskine Tower?'

'You're *obsessed* with those flats.' Georgia rolled her eyes. 'Like, I get it. They're nasty, my mum didn't want me going there, loads of mums didn't. But Elsie was *funny*. She made me laugh, you know? I took her cupcakes.' She pouted, pleased with herself. 'She'd never had one before.'

'Raffa loved her old grandad,' Katie put in. 'Like, she *loved* him.'

'She was cool.' Byron rubbed at his eyes. 'She wasn't scared either, didn't care how nasty the flats were. She liked exploring stuff, loved it.' When he dropped his fist to his lap, his eyes were red. 'She was cool.'

As soon as she saw the tears, Katie started sobbing. Georgia put her arms around her quickly.

Byron watched them, his face hardening. 'You didn't even like her.'

A wail came from the girls. 'We *did*!'

Miss Robbins rose from her seat. 'I think perhaps that's enough for now.'

'They didn't.' Byron shrugged. 'No one did. Not enough,

anyway. She was lonely, that's what she said. Didn't matter where she went or who she was with, she was always lonely.'

Back in the car, Marnie checked her phone messages. 'Early post-mortem results. No trace of drugs or alcohol in Raffa's blood.'

'That's something,' Noah said. 'Although I'm not sure it brings us any closer to understanding what was going on at Erskine Tower.'

'If there was anything going on.' Marnie fired the engine, pulling out of the school's visitor parking space. 'Perhaps those kids are right, and we're obsessed with the flats.'

'Ammunition's been found there.' Noah reached for his seat belt. 'Harry confirmed that. And there's the connection to Malig. So was Raffa running with the wrong crowd, about to be recruited by a gang? If she met the Bellamy boys, they might've liked the look of her, or the other kids. I'd put money on Byron doing weed at the weekends. The Bellamys could've seen a whole new market opening up, pampered kids with pocket money to spare . . .' His stare strayed to the streets. 'Or she was just lonely, as Byron said.'

'We should let her parents know.' Marnie slowed in the traffic. 'About the post-mortem.'

'You can drop me at the station,' Noah offered. 'Guy won't want me back in his house.'

'Guy doesn't get to choose.'

Noah accepted this in silence. He propped his head to the window, still searching the street, his gaze restless. 'Sol's post-mortem made my dad cry. He held it together for the funeral, and afterwards. But the post-mortem made him cry. No drink or drugs in Sol either. I think Dad would've preferred it if they'd found something. Anything, to take the edge off.'

Marnie didn't speak, seeing his profile soften at the memory.

'He told me once that Sol was trouble since before he was born. But to lose him like that . . . So *unnecessary*, that's the word he used. If the prison had been watching him the way they were supposed to, or the other inmates hadn't walked away, or if he'd called for help. Dad couldn't bear the thought of Sol knowing he was dying, with no one to help him.' Noah reached a thumb to wipe a mark from the car's window. 'He didn't call out to anyone; I wish I could make sense of that. He can't have known he was dying, that's what I told Dad. He can't have known or he'd have called for help. But I could be wrong. I was wrong about a lot of things when it came to Sol.'

Marnie waited for him to say more. When he didn't, she touched a hand to his elbow. 'I could drop you at the station, spare you another dose of Guy Belsham at least.'

'Guy doesn't get to choose,' Noah reminded her. 'And neither do I.'

In Muswell Hill, the snub-nosed Merc was parked outside the Belshams' house, its bonnet spotted by leaves from the plane trees that flanked the avenue. Marnie had to search for a space in the adjoining street, walking with Noah to the flint garden that led to the Belshams' front door.

Guy answered in the same suit and tie he'd worn on the morning of his daughter's death, a phone in his hand but not at his ear. He'd aged, new lines on his face, and he'd cut himself shaving, a bloodied nick on the under-side of his jaw. He turned his head towards Noah, but kept his stare on Marnie. 'You're back. Should I be grateful?'

It was an odd greeting for a grieving father, but Marnie hadn't expected a warmer one. 'May we come in?'

'For what, exactly? I'm trying to get some work done. And Lynne's sleeping.'

'We've had the preliminary results from Raffa's postmortem.'

'So you've come with fresh accusations.' His face clouded bitterly. 'What is it this time? Drugs, drink?' His chin jutted at Noah. *'Bullets?'*

Marnie hadn't expected warmth, but she'd hoped Guy would be calmer at this second meeting. She'd even hoped he might show remorse for his earlier antagonism towards Noah, but it seemed the opposite was true. He was angrier than he'd been during their first encounter. She wondered whether he'd left any room in his rage for his wife's grief. And whether he was aware of the extent to which his hostility was open to misinterpretation. Anger was an inevitable part of grief, but this level of aggression was atypical. Some would have taken it as evidence of a guilty conscience. A couple walking their dog paused to listen to the doorstep conversation, alerted by Guy's raised voice.

'You've been at the school.' He pointed a finger at Marnie. 'Asking about my family. Did you think I wouldn't get to hear about that? Trying to dig up dirt to let yourselves off the hook, hoping to stir the turd in my direction. Well, two can play at that game.' He jabbed the flat of his hand towards Noah. 'Detective Sergeant Jake should be on compassionate leave, shouldn't he?'

Noah stood very still. Marnie saw the ends of his fingers twitch.

'Mr Belsham, do you really want to have this conversation in public?' She nodded towards the pavement.

'Because we don't. We came here to give you important information about your daughter's death. We could've made a phone call, but we felt this was a more considerate approach.'

'Considerate,' he echoed. 'After you pulled that stunt with the bullet? I've had your people digging up my lawn, looking through my wife's knickers, whole house turned upside down. For what? Because your boy there *found a bullet* in my girl's bedroom.' He drew air quotes around the offending section of the statement. 'Your DS, whose brother was stabbed in a gangland killing.'

'Mr Belsham, I'm going to stop you right there and give you a formal warning—'

'No, you're going to listen to *my* formal warning.' He clenched his teeth. 'Get the fuck off my property. Take your snivelling apology or whatever you're bringing to my door and *piss off*. I'll wait for the coroner's report, thanks very much. Because I *knew* my daughter. She had no drugs or alcohol in her system, of course she hadn't. No bullets in her bedroom either. And no reason to die two days ago out there on streets you're meant to be policing.

'The pair of you shouldn't even be *on* the streets.' His stare was red on Marnie's face. 'You with a brother behind bars for murdering your parents. And him! His brother in a gang – stabbed to death by a gang – and you have the fucking nerve to bring him here when my girl was slaughtered by the same sort of scum? Someone you let loose with a weapon, who's only off the streets now because he drove the wrong way up the motorway. It beggars belief! Not one of you's fit for purpose. If I went about my job the way you lot do, I'd be bankrupt six times over.' He grabbed the door frame, knuckles grey with pressure. 'My girl's dead and not one of you could do your job right if your own life depended on it. Not one of you! So piss off before I do what I've been wanting to do since we first met and put my fist through something.' He was staring at Noah as he said it. 'My fucking fist.'

He took a step back, slamming the door with such force the pavement jumped under their feet.

Marnie said, 'Let's go. Come on.' She was furious with Belsham for the words he'd flung at Noah, shaking with anger of her own.

Noah walked at her side in silence, back to the car.

When they reached it, she said, 'You didn't deserve that. I'm sorry. I'd have stayed wide if I'd known how much worse he'd be the second time around.'

Noah shook his head. 'He's right, though.' His mouth wrenched. 'Isn't he? We're failing. This isn't our city any longer. It belongs to them, Terrance Malig and the Bellamys. We've lost control. We failed Raffa, and the others. Frankie and his mum. We're failing. I'd call it fair comment.'

'Get into the car,' Marnie instructed. 'And listen to me.'

She waited until he was seated alongside her, the car doors closed. 'Guy Belsham is *wrong*. He's in pain, lashing out, looking for someone to blame. But he is wrong. Noah, look at me.'

He looked, nodding blindly through a hot glaze of tears.

'You and I are doing a job hardly anyone wants to do, and we're doing it well. It's a harder job than we signed up for, and getting tougher every day, but we're not cutting out. We're not quitting, because we don't do that. We're *needed*. Most people know it. Guy Belsham knows it, he just can't see past his own pain right now. This is our city, and we're its police. As for you – you're the best detective I've worked with. Bar none. You have courage, compassion and commitment. I asked for you to work this case because I knew you'd give it a hundred per cent.' She drew a breath. 'Not because I couldn't stand being stuck in an enclosed space with Oz Pembroke's aftershave and taste in music, although obviously that was a secondary consideration.'

Noah laughed, pressing the heels of both hands to his eyes. 'Great pep talk, seriously.' He dropped his hands, meeting her gaze with a look of gratitude. 'I'm . . . tired. It's been a long couple of days.'

'You're no use to me if you're burned out. Then I'll *have* to put up with Pembroke and his rock ballads. You wouldn't do that to me. Reckless endangerment, at the very least.'

'I wouldn't do that.' Noah smiled. 'I'm taking care, I promise.'

'That's all I needed to hear.' She held his stare a moment longer, searching his face for a chink in this new armour. 'Keep me posted. And buckle up. Safety first, remember?'

No one was home. Noah climbed the stairs hoping to hear Dan's music, or Sol's. But the flat was empty. Dan was working late, he remembered. As for his brother, there was no trace of Sol anywhere. Not sprawled on the sofa, or sleeping on the bed. Not standing at Noah's shoulder as he washed his hands at the basin. If this was 'getting well' – if this was progress – he wanted to be ill again. He needed his brother here with him.

He called out, 'Sol?' but heard only silence, underscored by traffic. Guy Belsham's words rang in his skull, despite Marnie's pep talk in the car. The city felt huge and hostile.

'Sol. Please . . .'

The weight of his loss brought him to his knees, as if he'd been struck down.

He kneeled on the bathroom floor, head bowed, chest heaving with sobs. But still no tears came, as if the act of weeping would wash away what little remained of Sol's ghost. He stayed kneeling, the thunder of blood in his ears, waiting for his tears. Waiting for Sol.

7

Marnie was woken by a text from Harry Kennedy: *No prints on the bullet. Can that be right?*

It was 5.03 a.m., too early for puzzles. She wondered what had woken Harry, or whether he hadn't slept. Ed stirred at her side. She leaned to kiss his shoulder before slipping out of bed, pulling on a T-shirt and knickers, taking the phone into the sitting room.

'Harry? When did the forensics come in?'

'Officially, not yet. I called in a favour . . . Wait, did I wake you? Shit, I've just seen the time.'

'No prints on the bullet?' She spoke softly, not wanting to wake Ed. 'Are they sure?'

'As sure as they can be without rerunning the tests.' She could hear a sleepless night in Harry's voice. 'They've confirmed it's a match for ammo we found in Erskine Tower six weeks ago – a weapons cache when we were searching for the knife that killed Frank Reece. The Bellamy brothers are our chief suspects, but they're too good at covering their tracks, keep themselves clean by using kids. And none of the kids will name them, no matter how much trouble they're in.'

'Do you have a name from an arrest warrant?'

'No arrests yet. We found the ammo in an empty flat on the twelfth floor. Fingerprints all over it, though. Which makes me wonder about this bullet. If Raffa found it, would she have wiped it?'

'I can't think why.' Marnie sat cross-legged on the sofa. 'There's nothing to link her bullet to Terrance Malig? What about the gun found in his car?'

'They're still running tests. But from his pole position on the gangs matrix, Malig's your killer. Why he went after Raffa is another matter . . .' Harry broke off.

She heard the sound of a paging system, doors swinging open and shut. 'Are you in hospital?'

'For Mum, yes. She's okay. They're looking after her.'

Marnie knew Harry's mum had been hospitalised ten weeks ago, after months of increasing confusion was diagnosed as dementia.

'Sorry to wake you,' he said. 'I thought it was later. Explains why the favour I just called in didn't go down too well either.'

'You'll be forgiven,' Marnie told him, 'if we solve this case. No prints on the bullet . . . I don't have a good feeling about that.'

'Me neither. I'd better go. I'll call you as soon as I hear from ballistics about Malig's gun.'

'Thanks. Take care, Harry.'

'You too.'

Marnie cleaned the phone screen on the hem of her shirt, glancing up to find Ed in his board shorts, bedhead curls in his eyes. 'Damn. This's your T-shirt, isn't it?'

'Looks better on you.' Ed gave her a sleepy smile. 'Coffee?'

*   *   *

Noah was at the station. He wasn't the first to arrive.

'Shit, mate. You look like death warmed over.' Ron winked at him. 'Coffee?'

'Thanks, but I'm heading out.'

'This early?' Ron glanced towards Marnie's office. 'Where?'

'I'm hoping for a head start on the traffic. Back to Erskine Tower, I think we missed something.'

Noah didn't say it was Sol he missed, but it was at the tower that he'd last seen his brother. And that was where Raffa had spent time with Eric, whose neighbours were being arrested for possessing knives and guns. He couldn't shake the feeling it was where they'd find the answers in this case.

'Is the boss going with you?' Ron asked.

Noah shook his head. 'I'll let her know what I'm thinking.'

Marnie was on the phone, working through the morning's paperwork. She didn't look up when he said he was heading out, just nodded, her attention on the call.

He had his pick of the pool cars and chose the Audi, dropping his jacket into the back and his rucksack onto the passenger seat, checking the fuel level. Harry Kennedy had been the last to drive the car. Noah didn't need to adjust the seat because he and Harry were the same height. He adjusted it anyway, putting it back a fraction then moving it forward into its original position, adjusting the mirror in the same way, avoiding his reflection.

Cheating the traffic had been a great idea. So great, everyone else'd had it first. Between the station and the tower block, cars were crawling two lanes deep. The delay gave Noah time to think. It was either that or listen to Oz's playlist. He'd slept badly, but he'd fixed that with coffee. Last night's panic had receded. He could convince himself he was working the case, not going AWOL in search of his brother's phantom. Sol had helped him sort his thoughts into order about Frank Reece, and what the bullet in Raffa's bedroom said about her home life. Was it any different to the way he traditionally worked a case with Marnie, the pair of them taking roles, play-acting through the evidence to make sense of it?

Sol was his dead brother, but he was more than that. He was the better part of him. His remorse, his conscience. Making him question his decisions, like the one to join the police when all his friends were headed in the opposite direction. Setting himself up for failure, you could say. Institutional racism was a fact of life, certainly of the life he'd chosen. Yet he was on the same side as Trident, with its discredited gangs matrix, its stop-and-search policy. Those kids in the stairwell at Erskine Tower had wanted Noah to be under arrest because the alternative was treachery, that was how they saw it. It was how Sol had seen it. His big brother, the sell-out. Traitor. Noah had picked this path – this straight and narrow – and what if that's why Sol had run so hard with the gang? To prove he wasn't the same, sending a message to their childhood friends, demonstrating his solidarity in whatever way they asked of him. Without his big brother in the Met, he might've settled down, content to smoke a little weed, look after their mum. God knows she needed that.

He pulled into a rare space at the foot of Erskine Tower, parking the Audi snug to the kerb. Further up the road, they were fitting new meters, but the yellow lines had yet to reach this end.

The tower loomed over him, dropping its long shadow through the Audi's windscreen into his lap. This was the back of the block, no balconies, just windows, most of which were shut. He sat forward, craning to see the flats, counting to the nineteenth floor and Eric's kitchen.

That was when he saw it.

The open window catching the sun, firing it back into his eyes. Making him blink, doubting what he saw. Seconds later, there was no doubt. But by then, it was too late to do anything other than watch.

8

The car alarm was still shrieking when Marnie reached the crime scene.

'Can't we shut that off?' She'd heard it from two streets away, a giddy note of outrage under London's morning soundtrack. 'Surely we can shut it off?' It was hard enough being this close to the wreckage without the sickening wail from inside the vehicle.

The Audi was unrecognisable, a welter of twisted metal and bloodied broken glass. She could hear it dripping, chips breaking free, falling to the gutter. As if it was still happening, and she was watching in slow motion as the morning's chaos unfolded.

Noah's shirt was twisted like the metal, bloody like the bits of broken glass. She crouched and looked into the wreckage, seeing his jacket on the back seat. The Audi held the crude shape of the accident, its bonnet like a hand cupped deep around the damage. *This is what happened*, it was telling her. *Here is the point of impact, the heart of your crime scene.*

Another fragment of glass fell free.

The Audi's alarm kept shrieking, the way the woman

at Carluccio's had shrieked as Raffa lay dying in the street, gunned down. No bullets here, no drive-by shooting. Just the bonnet of the car creaking and whispering as the metal held onto its savage shape of death.

'Who was the first on scene?' Marnie wished it'd been her, that Noah hadn't been alone.

The PCSO said, 'DS Prowse, ma'am.'

'And where is he now?'

'Kilburn, ma'am.'

She turned away from the car and looked up at Erskine Tower, shielding her eyes against the sun and the smoke. Such a small fire in the scheme of things, but smoke had filled the flat fast. It hadn't spread, thankfully. Neighbours raised the alarm. No one panicked, which was a miracle in itself. Someone grabbed an extinguisher and used it as a battering ram to get inside before spraying foam over the fire. Too late in one vital respect, but it could've been much worse.

Marnie looked to where the fire engines were parked. Four, because tower-block fires were frightening. A news crew was setting up. This could so easily have been another devastating disaster. Gangs were forgotten for the moment. Yesterday's protesters, some of them at least, were heroes for having fought the blaze. Marnie could do nothing inside the flat until the fire investigation team declared it safe. Immediate neighbours had been evacuated, were striding about speaking on their phones, foil blankets flapping at their backs like superhero cloaks. No one looked scared or in shock. But no one else had been this close to the Audi, its alarm acting as an unofficial part of the police cordon, keeping people away.

Her phone played the station's tune. 'DI Rome.'

'How bad is it?' Lorna Ferguson demanded grimly.

'It's bad.' She began walking away from the wreckage

of the car, needing its noise out of her head. 'I'm going to Kilburn. DS Prowse there was first on scene.'

'Do you know him?'

'By name.'

'He's going to handle it sensitively?' Lorna said. 'Or is that a daft question?'

'We'll find out.'

'Kilburn's where they took him, is it?'

'Yes.' Marnie glanced back at the ruined car. 'That's where they took him.'

9

'Your rucksack.' DS Prowse put it on the table. 'It took some damage coming out of the Audi.'

'Thanks.' Noah set it on the floor next to the shock blanket. The heat in the station was oppressive. Hard to see what damage had been done to his rucksack; he could make out its shape at his feet, but not much more than that. It was like looking through steam, or smoke.

'Tea or coffee?'

'Whichever's easiest.' He didn't want a drink but he needed a moment to himself, to get his thoughts in order. A chance for his vision to clear, and his hearing.

Prowse went to the door, calling into the corridor, 'Baz, get's a couple of coffees?' He came back, lowering his bulk into a chair. 'Shouldn't be long.' He was built like an outhouse, and bald. No hair or eyebrows, no lashes. Freckles gritted the dome of his head. 'You're with DI Rome's lot.' He flipped his tie across his shoulder. 'How's Tim Welland faring these days?'

'Okay, I think.' Noah tried a smile, hoping it looked less gruesome than it felt. He knew what DS Prowse was thinking. He was thinking Noah would make a great witness because he was a detective with DI Rome's lot; he'd help wrap this up quickly. Prowse was going to be disappointed. Noah couldn't get a fix on the man's face, let alone the events of the last two hours. He rubbed at his ribs, where the skin felt too tight, and hot.

'That hurting you?' Prowse frowned, nodding his head towards Noah's ribcage. 'You saw a paramedic. No injuries, just shock, that's the version I was told.'

'Scar tissue.' Noah stopped rubbing. 'It itches sometimes, that's all. I'm fine.'

'Hazard of the job. I got this,' showing a dent on his forearm, 'from a crackhead who'd got his hands on one of our riot shields.'

Prowse waited for a corresponding confidence from Noah, or perhaps he was just remembering his encounter with the crackhead, before he turned his attention to a file of notes: Noah's initial statement taken at the scene while a paramedic checked him over, three more moving around the bonnet of the car, trying to make sense of what they were seeing.

A door thumped in the corridor.

Noah flinched, tasting metal in his mouth. Tasting the Audi, and bitter smoke that'd uncurled like a claw in the sky above the tower. He bit the inside of his cheek to stop the taste flooding his mouth. The interview room squirmed around him. He had to fight the urge to put his head on the table, or between his knees.

It was less than two hours since he'd said goodbye to Marnie and headed out in the pool car, hoping to find answers, or Sol. Congratulating himself on getting a free parking space, forgetting nothing was free in London, always a price to be paid. His palms sweated, wet with the weight of what had happened. As if he could have caught her. Saved her.

Dark hair hanging from the bonnet of the Audi, pale legs at the wrong angle, ruined. A girl, a young girl. Her hair like a curtain across her face.

'All right, take it slowly,' the paramedic had said. 'We've got you. Can you tell me your name?'

He'd sat in the back of the ambulance with a shock blanket round his shoulders, listening to the noise of her being removed from the car. No matter what they did, its alarm wouldn't stop, stuffing his head with its shriek until he wanted to cover his ears and shout. In his T-shirt, because he'd taken off his shirt to try and stop the blood gouting from her throat.

'Lucky it wasn't yesterday afternoon,' Prowse was saying. 'That crowd of protesters. We could've been looking at multiple casualties.'

Noah nodded, grateful the man wasn't asking his questions before the coffee arrived. He was afraid of what he'd say if he opened his mouth while it was full of the flavour of her death, her dying. He shivered, despite the heat in the room.

'Here.' Prowse stood and reached for the shock blanket. It crackled like a live thing. He put it around Noah's shoulders, resting a big hand there for a second. 'Take your time. I'll fetch us some water, and chase up the coffee.'

'Thanks.' He sat tight, concentrating on the sheet of paper on the table, his witness statement. He needed to get the facts right. He rolled his neck vigilantly to one side and then the other, wishing the lights weren't so bright. The foil blanket crackled on his back.

Prowse returned with a bottle of mineral water. He broke the seal, placing the cap on the table, and handed the bottle to Noah, standing beside him as if he needed to be sure Noah wouldn't pitch from the chair to the floor.

Prowse smelled of marker pens and fried eggs, yellow and black. Noah's sense of taste was working overtime, as if he was seeing the world through his tongue. His vision, adjusting to the shock, gave him the interview room in two dimensions, pixelating Prowse's freckled head and hands as he moved the sheet of paper to the centre of the table. Someone said, 'Witness statement,' but it didn't sound like Prowse. Was there somebody else in the room? He was afraid to turn his head and look.

'I'm not sure what I saw,' he managed. 'Smoke, and what must've been fire.'

'One thing we need to clear up.' Prowse uncapped a pen. 'Was your vehicle moving?'

Noah shook his head. He saw the Audi, its bonnet an impromptu grave. Had he hit her with a moving car – if she'd run out into the road, say – there'd have been an inquest into his driving. He could have been charged with involuntary manslaughter. They'd have taken fibre samples from the Audi's seats to be sure of his story. The fibres would confirm if he was driving at the moment of impact, whether he'd made an emergency stop and at what speed. But she hadn't run. She'd fallen, from the sky.

'Vehicle was stationary.' Prowse made a note of this. 'Just something we have to get straight. So you'd parked up and got out of the car. That's when she hit.'

She hit. Noah felt it in the roof of his mouth, her impact. It was the worst thing he'd ever felt. The chair hurt. He shifted, trying to get comfortable. Chances were he'd be here for hours. 'Yes.'

Somewhere in the station, he could hear a tap dripping, hitting a metal sink.

'Lucky you got out of the car when you did.' Prowse sucked at his teeth. 'Erskine Tower . . . You were there to interview someone? About this drive-by shooting.'

'We were there yesterday, talking with . . . Eric Martineau.' He had to scrabble for the man's name. 'But I wanted to ask a couple more questions.'

'After sleeping on it.' Prowse nodded. 'Makes sense.' He referred to his phone. 'Fire crew confirms a blaze in her kitchen. Looks like it cut off her only safe exit.' He lifted his eyes, their whites poached with pink. 'Is that how it looked to you?'

'I . . . saw the smoke.' He'd doubted what he was seeing, imagining chem trails, a plane flying too low.

'What else?'

'Light.' A yellow flash. 'It could've been the fire, or the window being pushed wide.'

'Then what?'

A doll at the window, bending forwards. Not a doll. His fingers twitching for his phone, too late. His feet stuck to the pavement, everything slowing for a second.

'I saw her at the window. She was leaning out.'

'You saw her leaning out of the window.'

His gaze had locked to her as it would to any distant point, such as the path of a plane or a first star. It was how the human eye operated in crude terms, always trying to find its focus. He didn't say this to Prowse. To Prowse he said, 'Yes.'

'Twenty-eight floors between her and the ground. I'm guessing she was shouting for help.'

'No. At least I didn't hear anything.'

Not even traffic. As if London had switched itself off, two minutes' silence to observe the girl leaning from the window, smoke rearing blackly behind her.

'Hardly surprising you didn't hear anything at that distance,' Prowse was saying. 'The wind probably drowned it out.'

'There wasn't any wind.' No leaves coming down from

the trees that morning. He'd stood at the kitchen window with Dan's arms around him, his breath warm at the back of Noah's neck. How long ago was that? Less than three hours. He couldn't believe it. 'She wasn't shouting,' he told Prowse. 'And she wasn't waving.'

She'd made no sound, he was sure of it. He could see her, so precisely. More precisely than he could see this interview room, or DS Prowse's freckled face. Her arms at her sides, head lifted, eyes dead ahead. She looked like a doll, a mannequin, someone's idea of a prank. Then she folded at the waist and tipped forwards, over the edge of the window.

Turning somersaults. Five, six times. He was counting, as if it were important. Seven, eight. Turning. He lost count. Forwards, backwards. Not always falling – the air played with her, sucking her down, batting her up. Then it got bored, and she was coming fast, ripping a scar from the sky, hurtling towards him. No time to flinch or blink or shout . . .

'She wasn't waving,' Prowse repeated.

Noah swallowed. His throat felt bruised. 'No.'

'You didn't hear any sound from her, coming down?'

'Nothing.'

Until the slam of her into the Audi, its shock wave rippling the skin of his face, the thud lodging in the roof of his mouth and at the top of his throat, in the small bones of his ears. The seismic, blood-altering shock of her. His feet rocking on the pavement, tipping him towards her. Catching his balance clumsily, the breath fisting at the top of his lungs.

'She wasn't shouting,' he told Prowse. 'She wasn't doing anything other than falling.'

The dry sound of glass splintering. Then a lesser noise as pieces of the Audi's windscreen started to fall, hitting the kerb. The car alarm took a second, as if it too was shocked, its world altered. The thud of her was a solid block of sound trapped in Noah's hands, changing their shape, making him stagger, ham-fisted.

'She landed right in front of you. You were feet away. That's correct, isn't it?'

'Yes.' Noah put his hands under the lip of the table.

'No smoke coming from her clothes?' Prowse referred back to the notes. 'Burns? You didn't see anything like that.'

'I don't think she was burned, but I'm not sure. It was hard to look at her.'

He'd made a mistake in the split second after she landed. He'd thought she was a boy, that he was looking at a boy. Her torso was stretched flat by the angle of impact, blue jeans pulled down at her hips, yellow T-shirt rucked up around her neck. He'd blinked, seen her exposed navel, the black trail of her hair. Then he'd put his hand up in protest to block the awful sight of her. And that felt wrong, like a betrayal. As if he was denying the ugly fact of her death to protect himself from it.

A scratch of voices in the police station corridor: 'I told him we beat that horse to glue bloody weeks ago.' Laughter.

Noah adjusted his focus on Prowse's face.

'So you think – what?' Prowse put his hand to his nose and sneezed into it. 'That it was suicide? Because she wasn't shouting for help.'

'I don't know what to think.'

Prowse inspected the contents of his hand, taking a tissue from his pocket. 'Let's go back to the start. Something made you look up.' He scrubbed at his palm. 'Was that smoke, or fire?'

'I can't be sure. The window opening? It could've been fire, or the light reflecting off the glass.'

Prowse balled the tissue in his fist, referring to the notes taken at the scene. 'That's when you saw her jump.'

'I . . . watched her fall.'

'Okay, this is important. *I saw her jump*. That's what you said at the scene.'

Empirically, he wanted to say, *empirically I saw her jump*.

'You see, this's the thing.' Prowse scratched at his head. 'The fire was put out quickly, everyone attests to that. So we're left with why she didn't wait. Most people, they'd head for the bathroom and wet a towel, shove it against the door to keep the smoke out. Hope for the best, at least to begin with. But she jumped almost as soon as the fire got under way. That's a bit weird, don't you think?'

'Fire's frightening, especially if you're living in a tower block.'

'True.' Prowse dropped the ball of tissue onto the table. He sat forward, the chair creaking under him. 'If it'd been bigger, we'd reckon the blaze drove her to the window, maybe threw her out. An explosion can do that, and a couple of her neighbours are saying they heard a small explosion, like a gas ring blowing maybe. But you're the only witness on the ground.' He looked at Noah, fleshy eyelids giving him a sphinx's stare. 'I've dealt with fires before, not just lethal ones. Insurance jobs, arson. I went on a course. They do love to send us on a course, don't they? It's all in the physics, that's what they taught us. Ignition, propulsion, acceleration. But there has to be a decent fire in the first place. For us to be thinking it threw her.'

'So that leaves . . . suicide?'

'Or she panicked. Like you say, fire's frightening.' Prowse framed his hands into a square. 'What I'm getting at is *when* she started to exit the flat, either under her own volition or otherwise. If we can isolate that moment, we can start to figure out how and why it happened.'

Ignition. Propulsion. Acceleration. A doll in a yellow T-shirt, blue jeans. Not a doll.

'I wish I could be clearer about what I saw. It happened so fast.'

'Ten seconds. That's how long they reckon it took her to fall from the flat to the Audi.'

Ten seconds. Had it been that long?

Prowse picked grit from his bald eyelids and looked at it before flicking it away with his thumb. 'You didn't see anyone else in the vicinity, immediately after it happened?'

'I didn't look.' Her dying had taken up everything, three hundred and sixty degrees, panoramic. He wasn't a detective in that moment. He was a pair of eyes and ears, and a mouth filled with the violence of her death. 'I was trying to help her, and then I was calling an ambulance.'

'Mind if I take a look at your phone?' Prowse's palm was padded, shreds of tissue sticking to it.

Noah surrendered the phone, watching as the man thumbed through its contents. He could taste glass now, the iron flavour of ice cubes, or a shattered windscreen.

'Thanks.' Prowse returned the phone with his fingerprints greased across it.

A young PC brought coffee in two polystyrene cups. 'Her dad's here,' he told Prowse. 'And a bereavement counsellor. Luke Corey.'

Noah drank a scalding mouthful of coffee, forcing his throat to swallow.

'Bereavement counsellor?' Prowse raised the skin where his eyebrows should've been. 'Bit slick off the mark. What sort of commission's he on?'

'He was counselling her family. Brother died a few years back.'

'Her brother died?' Prowse glanced towards Noah.

For a second, he thought the man knew about Sol. But it was the idea of suicide; Prowse was reconsidering that in the light of this news. Because grief did strange things to people.

'From injuries in Afghanistan. He was on foot patrol.'

'Aw, shit.' Prowse climbed to his feet, rubbing both hands over his face. 'Unhappy families.'

The words, and the heavy way he said them, made Noah queasy. Dan would smile when he got home, and ask, 'How was your day?' and Noah would have to avoid the question, because how could he describe this? The polystyrene cup of coffee that failed to rid his mouth of the Audi's taste. The strip lighting in the station, its scent of sweat and carpeting. Prowse's bald face creased with enquiry, the weight of his hand on Noah's shoulder. The wreckage they'd cut his rucksack from, the Audi a crime scene now. Empty white sky scarred by her falling. The small bloody huddle of her shadow, unmoving at his side.

When DS Prowse returned from speaking with the dead girl's father, his face was heavier than ever. He nodded at Noah. 'We'll get the statement run off for you to sign. I'm not sure about this idea of suicide. Her leaning out of the window, her jumping . . . Her dad's in a bad enough way as it is. Too early for verdicts in any case. Just stick to the facts of what you saw.'

Noah had been sticking to the facts from the start. Suicide hadn't been his idea. He didn't point this out. As he was signing the transcript of his statement, his phone buzzed.

Prowse nodded at him to take the call.

'Noah?' It was Marnie, her voice at its steadiest. 'I'm on my way. Sit tight.'

'Yes.' He kept the phone in his hand, seeing his face blurred by Prowse's fingerprints, then . . .

The hang of dark hair hiding her face, its ends lying in the gutter. He'd forgotten to tell Prowse about that, an omission in his statement. He should've said how he'd wanted to lift her hair clear of the dirt and leaves, but he hadn't because he knew he mustn't touch the body until the police came. As if the police were other people, nothing to do with him.

10

Marnie waited in the corridor of Kilburn police station for DS Prowse and Noah. She considered putting a call through to Karie Matthews, but decided against it. She needed to see for herself how Noah was coping. Ed had promised to be in touch, so she texted to say she needed to speak with him before he made contact with Noah. This new death altered everything.

Like any police station, Kilburn had faces pinned to its corridor wall, active cases and those growing cold. Marnie recognised some but not all of them. Dozens of faces, taken from family snapshots. The words printed underneath didn't belong to the smiles. *Beaten, burned, raped, missing.* This job they did – she feared for Noah. And for Colin, who spent his days searching CCTV for final glimpses of those killed or missing. Where was the time to process and grieve? To the press, Matilda Reece had said, 'Blessed are the hearts that bend; they shall never be broken,' but this new death had come so soon after Raffa's murder. They were lectured regularly about the dangers of compassion fatigue and moral damage. Dangers that were never far away, snapping at their heels as they went about their work. It shouldn't have been possible to look at a wall like this without feeling pain of some description, but Marnie could do that. And it frightened her.

A door opened at the head of the corridor, letting through a barrel-chested man with a bald head. He was carrying Noah's rucksack, his running gear.

'DS Prowse. You're DI Rome.' He offered a bear's paw for her to shake. 'Your boy's just coming. He's popped to the bathroom.'

'You've got what you need, for now?'

'Yes.' He put Noah's rucksack on the floor. 'Very helpful. And lucky. If he'd stayed in the car . . .' He pulled at his top lip.

'Do we have her name yet?'

'Samantha Haile. She was twenty-three, living alone up there. I need to speak with her dad. Terrible thing – he lost his son a couple of years back. Samantha's brother. Now this.'

'That's very hard. Does DS Jake know?'

'About the brother?' Prowse nodded. 'He was there when I was told. Seems to back up his first impression that it was suicide.'

'He said that?' Marnie was surprised. It was unlike Noah to share such a charged first impression of a crime scene.

'Backtracked a bit in there.' Prowse nodded towards the interview room. 'But at the scene, yes. Said she jumped. Good job he got out when he did; wouldn't have given much for his chances otherwise.' He pre-empted her next question: 'Paramedics looked him over at the scene. Shock, but no physical injuries. He's good to go. We'll stay in touch, compare notes and so on. For now, I'll let you get him home. I'm going to spend some time with the dad and then we'll get inside her flat, see what's what.'

'We're investigating another death with a link to Erskine

Tower. Raphaela Belsham. If you uncover any connection between her and Samantha Haile, I'd be grateful for the heads-up.'

'No problem.'

'Thanks.' Marnie picked up the rucksack as DS Prowse walked back down the corridor.

The door swung open a second time and Noah came through it, moving as if his whole body hurt. He was wearing a white T-shirt and grey suit trousers. When he drew close, Marnie saw goose bumps on his bare arms. She unzipped his rucksack, searching inside.

'I think there's a connection to Raffa.' Noah's voice was odd, as if the smoke had somehow got into his lungs. 'Apart from that place, I mean. The tower. I think there's a connection.'

'Put this on.' Marnie held up the hoody from his running kit.

'Prowse says her dad's here, and that her brother died.' Noah took the hoody but didn't put it on. His eyes were fierce with focus. 'In Afghanistan, a soldier. That's guns, bullets. Maybe Raffa met her at the flats. Sam Haile.' He shivered.

Marnie helped him with the hoody. 'Let's get you home.'

'I'm okay.' He seemed surprised, double-taking to look at her. 'They checked me over at the scene.' His voice jerked. 'Because of her blood on me.'

'You're shivering.' She zipped the front of the hoody, leaving her hand on his breastbone for a moment. 'Will Dan be home?'

'He's working.' Noah's eyes strayed to the wall of faces. *Beaten, burned, raped, missing.* 'Later, though. He'll be home later.'

'Come on.' Marnie picked up the rucksack. 'Let's get you out of here.'

*   *   *

Noah looked at the car, then away from it, at the road where traffic was running into the centre of town. Marnie didn't want to force him into the car, but nor did she want him collapsing in the street, which looked more likely with every passing moment.

'Can you give me a minute?' He sat in the passenger seat but kept the door open, his feet on the pavement. 'Just a minute, to catch my breath.' He managed a smile, to reassure her.

She nodded and left him, walking a short distance to make a call. 'Ed. I'm with Noah. He witnessed a death, possibly a suicide, a young girl. I only saw the aftermath but it was bad, far worse than usual. And Noah was right where it happened. I'm taking him home, I don't want him on his own. I'll try and get hold of Dan, but—'

'I'll be there,' Ed said without hesitation. 'Text me the address. Go, be with him.'

'Thank you.' She ended the call, turning to face the car.

Noah was in the passenger seat with the door shut, his seat belt fastened. Just for a second, she thought he was laughing, relief washing across his face, but it must have been a trick of the light, because the next moment his face was smooth in the way only shock could smooth it, wiping out all expression as if his face had forgotten what it was for or how it worked.

From a distance of three blocks, the shadow of Erskine Tower fingered the collar of her shirt. She got into the car, firing the ignition. 'Okay?'

'Hmm.' Noah moved his mouth into a smile. 'Sorry about the Audi, stupid of me to take it.' He sounded better, more like himself.

But Marnie was on her guard against this latest trauma.

'You left your jacket in the car. I'll see if we can get it back once the PCSOs are done.'

Noah nodded. He rolled his neck away from her, watching the wing mirror as if someone was tailing them, or else sitting in the back seat of the car. He held onto the smile.

'You wanted to go back there,' Marnie said. 'That's what Ron told me after you left this morning. Back to Erskine Tower. There was something you thought we'd missed?'

'Graffiti,' Noah said after a second. 'In the stairwell. When we were coming down after seeing Eric. It wasn't the right time to stop and look, but there was a name. Princess something, and a symbol written very small. In pink felt-tip pen, by the look of it.' He scratched his cheek. 'After what Eric said about how much Raffa liked princesses, I thought it was worth a look.'

'Yes,' Marnie agreed. 'If she was leaving a mark there, it might mean she felt a connection to the flats, something more than a school project.'

Had the two girls met in the tower? Samantha Haile, who was twenty-three and living alone, grieving for her brother. Raffa, a visitor, thirteen years old. An idealist, her teacher had said.

'I'm taking you home.' Marnie waited at traffic lights, looking across at Noah. 'I'll keep in touch with DS Prowse in case he has follow-up questions, but you should catch some rest.'

Noah didn't argue, his eyes on the wing mirror. After a bit he said, 'The impact undressed her. Sam. That was the most shocking part. Not the worst part, I don't mean that. But none of her clothes were in the proper places. She had no shoes and her feet were . . . Just a second, I thought she was a kid.' He rubbed at his face. 'She looked Raffa's age. Thirteen, maybe fourteen. Just a kid. I'm sorry.

That's . . . I'm okay, really. Talking too much, I know. But that's the shock. I'm okay.'

'I'm taking you home,' Marnie repeated. She reached a hand to his wrist. It was icy cold.

'The weirdest thing's what happened to my eyes back there.' Noah spread his fingers and studied them. 'I couldn't see properly. Only pieces. The tips of her toes, ends of her hair. Everything in the middle was bleached out. But I got this feeling I was *meant* to be there, to see her fall. Not that I was in the wrong place at the wrong time but that she wanted it to happen the way it did.' He moved his mouth painfully. 'Not a random thing. I know it's nonsense, but it felt as if she wanted someone to witness what was happening, and she chose me.' He shook himself. 'Okay, now I sound like a lunatic, never mind an egotist. I'd better go home, you're right. Let me sleep it off.'

As if he could do that. Sleep and not dream. Wake and be better.

Marnie couldn't imagine how it'd felt to watch Samantha Haile falling, to feel the sickening thud as she landed. 'I've asked Ed to pay you a visit, I hope that's okay.'

'Sure.' Noah moved his head, eyes on the wing mirror again. 'It'll be good to see him.'

She hesitated, watching the traffic up ahead. 'You said you saw a connection between Raffa and Samantha. We don't need to talk about it now, but I'd like your thoughts on that.'

'It's the tower,' Noah said. 'Both of them died because of that place. I can't put my finger on it, not quite, but there's something. When she was falling, I nearly had it.' He crooked his head as if listening to music or a phone. 'I'll try and figure it out.'

Marnie wondered whether he was hearing the car alarm. It was inside her head, and Noah had witnessed far worse. The rattle of blood in the girl's throat, the tortured sound of the metal reshaping itself around her. 'I want you to get some rest,' she instructed. 'Real rest.'

'You need me working the case.' Noah shook his head. 'The team's stretched enough as it is.'

'I need you, but not like this.' She kept the emotion out of her voice. 'I want you fully operational. You found the bullet, and you spotted this graffiti that Harry and I both missed. You're the best detective I have, and I need you fit and well. Not running on empty.'

Noah didn't answer. She had the feeling he was listening, but not to her. 'I'll get some rest,' he said at last. 'But I want to be on this case. Raffa, and Samantha. And Frankie Reece, I want to be on his case. Suliat Drake. Ashley Benjamin. I know they're Trident's, but I want to be helping.' He drew a breath. 'Everyone this city's torn up and spat out. That's how I'm going to get better. That's my *counselling*.'

'I'll let Dr Matthews know.'

He laughed at her dry tone. 'Okay, I apologise for the impassioned speech. But I don't need the kid-glove treatment. I'll jump through the hoops, you know I will. But I'm not made of glass.'

No, Marnie thought. Right now you're made of guilt and grief. Glass would be better, tougher.

She said, 'I'm visiting Stephen at the weekend.'

'You're—'

'It's the anniversary of their deaths. Mum and Dad's murders. Seven years.' She held the wheel lightly, as if it hardly mattered. 'I always visit him on the anniversary, against everyone's advice. Beware the abyss, and so on. Good advice, for the most part.'

'How is he?' Noah asked. 'It's not long since he came out of hospital. Acute . . . what was it?'

'Acute respiratory distress syndrome. Smoke inhalation. He's made a full recovery, or as full as it can be. He's been warned of possible long-term effects. Physical weakness, fatigue. An increased risk of pneumonia and sepsis.'

'But he's back in prison.' Noah frowned. 'Is that safe?'

To a stranger listening in, their conversation would have sounded like a concerned discussion about a friend or loved one, not a twenty-one-year-old convicted of double murder.

'It's safer for everyone else. I think that's how the reasoning goes.'

'And you're visiting him. On the anniversary of their deaths.'

The lights ahead turned green. She switched up a gear. 'One last time, yes.'

'Last? You mean . . .'

'I'm going to stop.' She checked the mirrors. 'I want to be able to grieve for them and I've realised I can't do that while I'm asking questions about their deaths. In fact I'm pretty sure the questions are my way of avoiding it . . . It works, it really does. But it's time. I want the peace, the space to be able to grieve for them. Properly, finally. Does that make sense?'

'Yes.' Noah bent his head for a second, then lifted it and looked at her. 'Can you forgive him?' He moved a hand. 'Sorry, you don't have to answer that.'

'No, it's a good question.' She signalled left. 'Ask me again after the weekend.'

'And you'll keep me in the loop,' he insisted. 'About Raffa. About Sam Haile.'

'Of course.'

'That speech was for you, bruv.' Sol dropped onto the sofa in his old spot. 'The peace of grieving . . . She wants you to give me up.' He shut his eyes. 'Everyone always wants you to give me up.'

'Where were you?' Noah sat facing his brother. 'I lost you yesterday, at the flats. That's the reason I went back, the reason I saw her.'

Sam Haile. He couldn't get the images out of his head. Smoke uncurling like a claw, the doll bending forward from the window. Then the gathering weight of her speeding through the sky, the shock wave as she slammed into the car, pavement rocking under his feet . . .

'You need a beer.' Sol opened one eye. 'And to stop thinking so hard. You think so hard it makes *my* head hurt.'

Noah had been afraid to get into Marnie's car. Afraid of his reaction to the smell of the seats, the sound of the engine. He'd sat with his feet in the road, asking for a minute before they set off. When Marnie walked away to make a phone call, he told himself to get a grip. Ignore the taste of Sam's death in his mouth. Be a detective. He was a *detective*. Then—

'That coffee, though. That tasted worse, yeah?' Sol was in the backseat of Marnie's car, making Noah laugh out loud in relief, not caring how close to hysteria he sounded. His brother was back.

Sol stayed with him the whole way home, commenting from the back seat as Marnie spoke about Ed, and Sam Haile. He only fell silent when she started talking about Stephen.

From the sofa now, Sol said, 'We going to talk about that shithole? Erskine Tower. I spent the night there while you were skanking with Dan.'

'You said you'd come out with us. Why didn't you?'

'Easy nuh.' Sol kicked back, hands deep in the pockets of his hoody. 'Bring the beers.'

Noah climbed to his feet, aware of pain tugging in his chest. It was two years since the ribs were broken, but they still ached from time to time. Some of it, he was sure, was psychosomatic. Though didn't they say it was the spine not the ribs that stored the memory of pain?

'Too much t'inking, bredda!' Sol shouted from the sofa. 'No enuff beer!'

Noah opened the fridge, leaning into its chill, needing to shake off the heat from the police station, DS Prowse's head like a boiled egg, the scalding polystyrene coffee . . .

The buzzer sounded from downstairs.

He checked the security cam, seeing Ed Belloc standing in the street. Marnie had said he'd call round. Noah considered him a friend, but Ed was also a victim support officer. He buzzed him into the building, telling Sol, 'I need the sofa.'

His brother looked pained, but he rolled to his feet and walked towards the bedroom.

'Sol,' Noah called after him, 'stay put. I want to speak with you later.' Crazy. But having his dead brother's ghost around felt like the only thing keeping him sane.

He let Ed into the flat and onto the sofa.

'I won't stay.' Ed was wearing beaten-up jeans and an old shirt under a blue jumper. His work clothes. 'Unless you're okay with that.'

Noah handed him one of the cold beers. 'Unless you're driving?'

'Oyster card.' Ed took the beer. 'Thanks.'

'Give me a minute?'

Noah walked to the bedroom, needing to know Sol hadn't done his vanishing trick. His brother was lying on the bed, hoody up, eyes shut. Noah went to the bathroom and washed his hands, avoiding his reflection because he knew it couldn't be good.

In the sitting room, Ed was taking the caps off their beer bottles. He looked up as Noah returned, smiling through his fringe of brown curls. Noah realised he'd got out of the habit of trusting men like Ed, whose job it was to help people like Noah. Victims. It was Karie's job too, but Ed was better at it, unthreatening, open. None of which meant Noah wanted to talk to him about Sol. But he could talk about Raffa, and the young woman who'd died in front of him three hours ago.

'Samantha Haile.' He sat facing Ed. 'That's why you're here.' He linked his fingers around the beer bottle. 'I'm glad I have a name for her. It matters, more than you'd think.'

'It must've been awful, being so close to what happened. To her.'

'She was just a blur. Hair and skin . . .' Noah stopped. He shouldn't have used that word. *Skin*. It sounded ugly, voyeuristic. He needed to stick to the facts if he was going to do this.

'You don't need to,' Ed said lightly. 'I'm not here to make things harder. We can talk about anything, or nothing. I can shut up and we can drink beer.'

'No, I want to talk about it, about her. It matters too much. When she was falling, it was . . . I don't know how to describe it. But I need to, need it straight in my head.'

What did you see? Prowse had asked, and he'd said, *I'm not sure. I'm not sure what I saw.*

But here he was, unpicking it, frame by frame, from his memory, for Ed's inspection. 'When she hit the car . . .' He rubbed condensation from the dimpled glass of the bottle. 'The whole road jarred. I felt this . . . rippling, heard the car creaking. The alarm didn't go off right away. I don't know why, but it didn't. There was this long second of silence when I should've been moving, but I wasn't.' His fingers felt bloodless. He looked at the bottle, realising he wasn't going to drink it, that he didn't want to. It was just something to hold onto while he told his story. 'I was less than three feet away. The impact . . . Her clothes were caught up in the car.' He glanced away, a voyeur again. 'It was hard to believe she was in one piece. Her knees were buried in the bonnet. I could see her toes. She was face down, her head hanging over the side.' He shut his eyes. 'Her hair was in the gutter.'

Ed didn't speak, staying very still, his body angled towards Noah. He made it easy to talk, too easy. Noah told himself to be careful. If he strayed towards the subject of Sol, he might not come back. He rolled the slim neck of the bottle between his fingers. 'It's all in the statement I gave DS Prowse. There's nothing new. No facts, anyway.'

'That's okay. I'm not here for facts.'

'I know, but thanks. I need to do this. Sooner the better, too. There's too much work on for me to spend time being . . . like this.'

'Being like this is what makes you a good detective.'

'In touch with my feelings? Empathising with the victims? Yes, usually. But this feels like too much empathy.' He leavened it with a smile. 'Too much empathy is a thing, right?'

'Probably. But you can't help how much you care. You want to solve this case, and all the others. Sam Haile, Frank Reece, Raffa Belsham. They matter to you.' Ed had learned their names.

'I used to think so,' Noah agreed. 'Now I'm not so sure. Results are what matter. Oh I don't mean Ferguson's solve rate, or official statistics. I mean making it better, safer. Getting the guns and knives off the streets, stopping kids like Raffa and Frank from dying just because they're crossing the road. Trident's going after Frank's killer, I hope they get him. But I don't know why she died. Raffa, or Sam Haile for that matter. Two senseless deaths . . . Except we're here to try and make sense of it. That's why I signed up for this, because too much of what I was seeing made no sense. But it's getting worse, not better. And I'm not sure how it helps that I feel it all too much. If that's even what I'm doing.'

'Too much t'inking, bredda!'

Sol, from the bedroom. Or inside his head. Sol was inside his head.

'Sorry,' Noah said. 'I'm getting maudlin.'

Ed leaned forward, setting his bottle on the floor. Like Noah, he wasn't drinking. The beer was a prop, a way of making sense of this madness. Two grown men talking about the futility of death.

'I saw Ayana Mirza yesterday,' Ed said. 'She asked me to remember her to you. Not that you need reminding, but that's how she put it. "Remember me to DS Jake, to Noah." She's just one of the people whose lives are safer, thanks to you.'

'How is she?' Noah had nothing but admiration for Ayana, who'd survived the worst abuse and refused to let it stop her or change her. He and Marnie had worked on her case, at one time fearing the worst for Ayana's chances, but they'd underestimated her survival skills, and her resolve.

'She has a new name, a new life. She's studying law.' Ed moved his mouth into a smile. 'And she's grieving. For her mother. Her brothers.'

Grieving for her tormentors. The brothers who'd blinded her, the mother who'd sanctioned it. Was that the secret of Ayana's strength? Finding forgiveness for those who'd sinned against her?

'She said, "My mother's not a wicked woman, she's unhappy. I want her helped, not punished." It was hard to hear her talking like that.' Ed rubbed a hand through his hair. 'By going into witness protection, she's severed all ties. The only time she'll see her family again is in a courtroom, and it's breaking her heart. But she's determined to move on.'

'She deserves a new chance. And she'll make a great lawyer.'

'Won't she?' Ed's eyes shone in agreement. 'She'll do good. That matters so much right now.'

Noah could hear the bubbles bursting in their beer. And his brother listening from the next room, ears pricked for Noah's new betrayal. He could do it, lean forward and tell Ed, 'I'm seeing Sol. Everywhere. He's so real, I can smell him. I go looking for him when he vanishes. I tell him to stay put when I find him. He's in the bedroom back there waiting until you've gone so I can talk to him. I want to talk to him, I don't care how mad it gets. It's the only thing keeping me from going off the rails.' Ed would listen without judgement; maybe he'd even find words to make it better. If anyone could do that, it'd be Ed. But then what? Sol would leave. Noah knew his brother. He'd go because Noah had given him away, again. It'd been hard enough in the club, frantic at his loss, at the thought of never seeing Sol again. It was too soon. He'd tell Ed – and Marnie too – but not yet. He needed Sol here with him.

'Marnie's visiting Stephen at the weekend. For the last time, she said.'

Ed nodded. 'It's been a long time coming.'

'Can she forgive him, d'you think?'

'I hope so.' Ed reached for the bottle on the floor, hiding his eyes for a second. 'For her sake.'

'Does he deserve that? Not just for the murders. He was fourteen then, and I know she's decided it wasn't entirely his fault, because of the abuse back home when he was a little kid. But all the times since then, when he's baited her about their deaths. This sick game he's been playing, making her doubt everything, turning her parents into strangers, wrecking her chances of recovery. He's the worst kind of psychopath. Does he deserve her forgiveness? I'm not sure he does.'

Ed heard him out, his eyes flickering with fellow feeling, as if he'd asked the same questions himself. He must hate Stephen for the harm he'd done to Marnie over the years. 'I don't know,' he said in reply. 'You're right, on all points. He's made her life hell for the last seven years, but it's not as simple as forgiveness for Stephen. She needs to forgive herself, that's how she put it when we spoke about this last visit. She needs to forgive herself for her failures as a daughter and a detective. Stephen was living in her house for eight years before he killed them. She never suspected a thing. I don't believe she failed them, of course I don't. But she's been carrying that burden of guilt for years. She's ready to put it down, and that's all that matters. The forgiveness isn't for him, it's for her. So she can do what Ayana's doing and move forward. Make peace with her past.'

Noah listened in silence to the speech, knowing it was intended to resonate. It *did* resonate. But he wasn't ready to tie his guilt to Marnie's, or her story to his. He felt a short flare of anger at Ed for working this foothold into his grief. It was *his* grief. His guilt, his pain. No one else's. He wasn't ready to give it up, any more than he was ready to remove his brother from the bed in the other room, where he lay with his eyes shut, pink hoody on the pillow that belonged to Dan.

Ron Carling was waiting when Marnie returned to the station. 'Where's Noah?' he asked.

'I dropped him home. Ed's there. What's the news here?'

'No new stabbings. And zero drive-bys. We're ahead.'

This was how they judged a good day now, one that began without violent death.

'I need you to make contact with DS Prowse over at Kilburn. Noah thinks there may be a link between Raffa and the young woman who fell from the flats, Samantha Haile.'

'Not very likely, is it?' Ron frowned. 'I mean, I can see Noah might be thinking those flats are cursed. But a shooting in Muswell Hill and a tower-block fire? They're hardly the same thing.'

'Even so. Ask DS Prowse if we can be kept up to speed with the investigation into Sam Haile's death. He'll understand why.'

'And if it's not a suspicious death? We'll have a job convincing the boss it's worth adding to our workload, especially if Lenny Prowse's on the case already. He's a top bloke, drinking buddy.'

'Good. You handle Prowse. I'll tackle DCS Ferguson. If there's no connection and no suspicious circumstances around this latest death, frankly that will be a relief. But Noah needs whatever answers we can get for him.' The Audi's alarm was echoing in her head. 'I didn't see her die, I didn't even see her body. But it was one of the worst crime scenes I've attended. And Noah was right there. He's going to need answers.'

Talking to Ed helped, more than Noah would've thought possible. When it was time for Ed to leave, Noah opted to go with him, instead of heading for the bedroom where Sol was waiting.

'I could use some fresh air. And I need to check in with

my mum, do a bit of shopping for her. Since I'm under orders not to go back into work today.'

'If you're sure.' Ed didn't press him, but he stayed at Noah's side until they reached the supermarket close to where Noah's parents lived.

'I'm fine from here.' Noah held out his hand and Ed took it. 'It was good to see you.'

'Any time, Noah. Take care of yourself.'

'I will.' He meant it in that moment, with Ed's fingers warm around his. It was easy to make promises to Ed.

In the supermarket, he bought eggs and fish, rice and bread. Red peppers, spring onions, fresh parsley. He'd steam the fish and stuff the red peppers. The meal would be ready in half an hour. He'd eat with Mum at the table where they always ate, leave some food in the fridge for Dad. He added fruit juice to the shopping trolley, and a bottle of rum. Mum loved her rum.

In his parents' road, signs of regeneration were everywhere. It was one of the area's smarter streets if estate agents were to be believed. Queen Anne gables ghosted the upper storeys of a handful of houses, their listed status an expensive responsibility resented by those blessed enough to live there. The house next to his parents' was in the process of having its face lifted, windows framed by scaffolding, a breeze swelling the plastic sheeting. It was months since he'd seen workmen on site. In all likelihood, the project had been abandoned.

'Mum?' The house felt empty, but he knew it wasn't. Leaves had blown into the hall, where they'd been allowed to sit, loudly announcing Rosa's neglect. Ten weeks ago, the hall had smelled of fresh flowers and furniture polish. Noah felt the press of silence from the abandoned house next door, and wondered if his parents felt it too. Surely it was too heavy to ignore, a warning coming through the walls of what lay in store if they failed to mend the fractures in their family.

Mum was standing in the sitting room, staring at a trio of cushions on the sofa.

'There you are.' Noah put down the shopping. 'I'm going to cook us lunch.'

She thumped a cushion with her palm. Picked it up, tried a different configuration. 'These looked good in the shop.' Her voice was hoarse with disuse.

'I like them,' Noah said.

It wasn't the cushions, it was the sofa. A family sofa, big enough for four, it hadn't been used in months. The seats showed straight lines from the last time she'd brushed it. She reached for a vase of dying roses, her thin fingers arranging the stems. The pain in Noah's chest was like trying not to breathe underwater. He blinked in a bid to reset his brain, seeing her falling towards him, turning somersaults, trailing smoke. Samantha Haile. He stretched his spine, leaving the shopping bags at his feet. He'd been stooping since the morning, as if carrying her corpse, searching for a place to put it down. He'd left pieces where he could – at the police station in DS Prowse's safe keeping, with Marnie, and Ed – but the greater part was with him. And he'd brought it to his mum's house, brought the body of a dead girl here. The thought was clammy, shot through with shame, as if he'd been caught trying to hide her corpse in the family home.

Mum sucked at the pad of her thumb where the thorn had scratched. In profile, her face was fragile, cheek bracketed by the curl of her unwashed hair. Noah saw the Audi flaying her alive, Sam Haile. Was she conscious when she hit the car? What was the last thing she saw? Did she see him standing there, empty-handed, open-mouthed?

'Steamed fish and stuffed peppers. For lunch.'

Mum nodded but didn't reply, moving past him towards the stairs. He heard her climbing to the back bedroom, shutting the door, shuffling across to the corner where the laptop waited.

'Sol?' Noah looked around the sitting room, seeing its silence. 'I don't suppose you're here?'

Nothing. Dad's empty slippers on the floor. Noah would cook the meal, but it wouldn't make a difference. The house wouldn't yield to anything he did, as if it was contaminated by the emptiness from next door. Or from upstairs, where Mum was hunched over the computer, staring at the dim reflection of her own face, more like a ghost than Sol.

He steamed the fish, stuffed the peppers with brown rice and spring onions. Laid the table and ate with Rosa, who smiled through him to the wall, where family photos were framed – the four of them together, Noah in his new uniform, Sol breaking into a big grin. As kids, on a beach.

'Do you see him too?' he asked, knowing she wouldn't answer because she wasn't here, not really. She was on the beach in the photo, or worse, before the beach, back when she was sick. When Sol was away at school camp, and Noah was ten. Building a fire with Dad in the garden, hearing breaking glass in the bathroom. He was glad Sol was away, then and now, because he couldn't stand his brother to see their mum in so much pain.

Marnie messaged to check in, and he messaged back: *All good. What news of the fire?*

No news, not yet. He did the washing-up, covering the extra food with foil and placing it at the back of the fridge.

He wrote a message, leaving it propped where Dad would see it, against the bottle of rum: *Call me.*

'You're back early,' Dan said. 'How was your day?'

'Not good,' Noah admitted. 'I saw someone die this morning. She fell, or jumped. From Erskine Tower. She landed on my car.'

'Jesus.' Dan reached for him, the blue of his eyes turning black with shock.

'There was a fire in her flat. She may've jumped because it was the only way out. She was on the twenty-eighth floor.' He gripped back at Dan's fingers. 'I've seen dead bodies before, of course I have. But this was the first time I'd seen someone die like that. So . . . close. And so horribly.'

There was no relief in telling Dan. The weight across his shoulders didn't lessen. He'd brought her corpse back here, where there was no safe place to put it down. Nowhere that wasn't already taken up with their own worry. 'Sorry, that's . . . It happened.'

Dan drew him close, kissing the side of his face. 'I'm so sorry.'

'I'm okay. I've seen worse things.' Not true. Nothing he'd seen was like her lying on his car, dying. 'I'm okay.'

'What was her name?' Dan asked. 'Do you know?'

'Samantha Haile,' Noah answered. 'She was Sam.'

Marnie parked at one of the new meters close to the foot of Erskine Tower. The wreckage of the Audi had been towed, taken for forensics. Broken windscreen glittered in the gutter, bloodstains too. Police tape trembled in the breeze reaching around the tower. She'd changed at the station into running gear and a zipped jersey, hiding her red hair under a black beanie. She didn't want to risk being recognised as the detective who'd questioned Eric

Martineau. She stood in the spot where Noah had stood watching Sam fall. The tower's boxy windows shredded the body of the building. Seen from this angle, it could've been a cardboard construct, hollow.

It was hard to single out the flat from which she'd fallen. Marnie searched until she found the blackened window. Had the flat faced south like Eric's, Sam could have sheltered on the balcony as her neighbours fought the blaze. But the flats on this side had no balconies, their windows opening into dead space. The window looked small, shut tight by the fire investigation team. They'd declared the scene safe almost immediately, allowing DS Prowse and his team to search for the clues they needed to make sense of her death. Nothing, yet.

Marnie walked to the side entrance, following the route she'd taken with Harry and Noah two days ago. She could smell the smoke inside the building, even this far from the flat and ten hours after the blaze was out. Smoke, like water, went everywhere. Finding its way through the pores in brickwork and plasterwork, burying its scent into the fabric of a building. It raised the spectre of a far worse fire in a high-rise some distance from here. Sam's flat faced towards that site; she'd have seen its skeleton every time she went to the window, a daily reminder of what fire could do. She'd have heard the stories they'd all heard, on the news and online. The trapped families, the speed with which the flames ate through the tower, no time to escape, no chance for fire crews to rescue those on the top floors. Was that why she jumped? Because she saw that black ruin from the window she'd opened to escape the smoke in her own small home? A split second of panic that changed everything.

Marnie climbed the stairs, reading the graffiti as she went, retracing their route from yesterday. Most of the graffiti was gang legends, some of it recognisable from the Trident paperwork that crossed her desk. She couldn't find any writing in pink felt-tip. A name, Noah had said. Princess something, and a symbol. She kept climbing, reaching the nineteenth floor, where they'd stopped to speak with Eric. The smell of smoke was stronger here. She could climb another nine floors, see the fire damage for herself. But she wasn't here for that. It was DS Prowse's case. She turned and began walking down, keeping to the right as Noah had yesterday, her hand skimming the rail like his, her eyes scanning the walls for the graffiti he'd seen.

A door slammed open above her. She tensed, but kept moving. Two girls came past at speed, spurred boots jangling on the stairs. They were not much older than Raffa, wearing leggings and hoodies, hair knotted high on their heads, hands lost in pockets. They didn't speak, just barrelled past, in a hurry to be out of the building. Marnie kept to the right, scanning the walls. *There.* Pink writing, small. How had she missed it? She slowed her speed, didn't stop until the girls were gone. Then she took out her phone and crouched to photograph the graffiti.

Princess + Flea. Written in a child's cursive hand. Underneath was a drawing of what looked like a bolt of lightning inside an earplug. She adjusted the angle to allow for the bad light, and took more photos, expanding each image to be sure she'd captured the detail.

Princess + Flea. Eric had said Raffa was obsessed with princesses. If she wrote this, was she 'Princess'? In which case, who was Flea? And why a bolt of lightning in an earplug?

Marnie straightened, feeling the skin clench at her neck.

Not an earplug. A *bullet.* And not a bolt of lightning. *Flames.*

If Raffa was responsible for this graffiti, or even if she wasn't, here was a connection between the dead girls. Bullets and fire. Raffa Belsham, gunned down in the street. Sam Haile, escaping a fire in her flat. Two deaths within twenty-four hours. She could hear Lorna Ferguson scoffing, 'You're getting that from this? Princess plus Flea?' Regardless, Marnie felt it. A connection, the kind that broke cases. Raffa and Sam. Bullets and fire. Noah was right. The deaths were linked.

11

Sol was at the breakfast table, reading the headlines on Noah's laptop. He glanced up when his brother came into the kitchen. 'You need to see this shit.'

Noah leaned close enough to read the headline – *New tower-block tragedy prompts fresh calls for fire safety investigation* – aware of Sol's watchful gaze, wondering what tricks his subconscious had in mind for him this morning.

'"Fresh calls have been made for a full investigation into fire safety at Erskine Tower after a young woman died trying to escape a blaze in her flat on the thirtieth floor."' Sol scoffed. 'That's shit; for starters, it was the twenty-eighth floor. "Residents say another fire is 'almost inevitable' unless improvements are made to the tower." Can you believe these geniuses?'

Noah poured himself a cup of coffee from the press Dan had left on the counter. He'd offered to stay home but Noah had persuaded him to go into work, saying, 'One of us needs to be in gainful employment.' He carried the coffee to the table, sitting at Sol's side to read the full story.

Erskine Tower, the piece continued, *has been widely condemned as one of the least desirable places to live in west London, thanks to antisocial behaviour and a high crime rate. Following the award of Grade II listed building status in 2008, an attempt was made to regenerate the area. Its failure was blamed on budget cuts and lack of investor interest, although this may be changing . . .*

'Grade II listed *bullshit*,' Sol said.

Enthusiasts claim the tower's gritty image gives it cult status. Erected in 1965 in what architects term the brutalist style, it was the scene of gangland violence throughout the 1960s and 70s, and was recently the subject of a police investigation into people-trafficking for the sex trade.

'Shithole. Didn't I tell you?'

Yesterday, the tower became notorious for another reason, after the tragic death of twenty-three-year-old Samantha Haile, a promising law student. Her death is a double blow for her family, coming after the loss in 2014 of her brother, Dylan, a decorated lance corporal serving with the 4th Battalion The Rifles. He was one of the last British servicemen to die in Afghanistan before the withdrawal of troops there in October 2014.

The photo showed a young man in dress uniform with his arm around his sister. The sun was in her eyes. She wasn't smiling, her hair held off her face by a chequered scarf tied like a keffiyeh. An oval face, clear-eyed and straight-nosed, it belonged on a Russian triptych. Hard to imagine that face inside Erskine Tower, whose allure existed solely in the minds of those who weren't required to live there. Couldn't she have found a better place, student digs or a flat share?

'Unless she liked it . . .' Sol clicked his teeth with his thumbnail. 'Not the cult status. The mood. *Violence*. You felt it.'

'I did, but that's a leap.' Noah rolled his neck, holding it in the crook of his hand. He drank a mouthful of coffee, studying the picture of Dylan Haile with his arm around Sam. He scrolled through the recent news, stopping when he reached Raffa's face to read the outraged reports of her shooting, demands for the Mayor of London to take responsibility for the capital's collapse into violence, calls for the Home Secretary to step in. A glowing reference to Guy Belsham's property portfolio and Lynne's florist business, approval for their life choices. A perfect family ripped apart by the evil chaos spilling over from the less savoury side of the city.

'Bull-*shit*,' Sol said.

Propping his elbows on the counter, Noah picked up his phone and speed-dialled Marnie. 'I'm coming into work. You have work for me, right?'

'How are you?'

'I'm good. I need to be doing something.'

'Ferguson wants you home for forty-eight hours.'

To avoid accusations of managerial incompetence. Because traumatised police officers had been headline news all summer. Noah scrolled down the new article, seeing a smiling Guy Belsham shaking the hand of an investor. 'I'm going mad here.'

'Read a book,' Marnie advised. 'Break out a box set.'

'I'd rather be working.'

Why didn't I look away? When she was falling. Why didn't I just look away?

He could see the tips of her toes so clearly, the dark heart of the scene eviscerated. That was shock, he knew, his brain doing its best to censor what he'd seen. But he hadn't looked away. He'd told Marnie it felt as if Sam chose him as her witness, landing not on his car but on his back, a weight he would carry until he had answers for exactly how and why she died. His brother's ghost was ten times lighter, easier to carry.

'And Raffa,' Sol said. 'Don't forget her. And the brothers and sisters on the wall. Just because they didn't choose you doesn't mean they're not yours. Same as Sam, same as Raffa.'

'Noah?' Marnie was still on the line. 'I'm not saying you can come into work, but I do have something for you to think about.'

Sol cocked his head at his brother as if he too wanted to be given something useful to do. But work was likely to send Sol into hiding – was that why Noah was so keen to get back to it?

'Anything,' he told Marnie.

'You were right about the graffiti. I went back, took photos. I'll send them across. Take a look and see what you think; you saw the sketchpads in her room. I'm waiting for the full post-mortem results on both Raffa and Terrance Malig. I should warn you, Ferguson's keen to wind it down since Malig's dead and we've no other suspects for the shooting.' Marnie paused. 'Guy wants the case closed, too. No lingering suspicion over the bullet. His daughter exonerated.'

'A senseless death,' Noah murmured.

Sol laughed, without humour.

'Yes. But there's another thing,' Marnie said. 'The bullet was clean. No fingerprints.'

'It was wiped? Okay that's . . . odd.'

'Isn't it? Unless Raffa was in the habit of polishing it.'

'She'd have kept it in a pouch if that was the case,' Noah said, 'or a box.'

'I thought the same thing. I've asked forensics for the full report from the house, but they didn't turn up anything else. Just the bullet. And Guy, who was so

161

unhappy about Raffa choosing Erskine Tower for her school project, wants all this to be over.'

Noah traced a circle on the counter with his thumb, thinking about what this meant. He scrolled back to the photo of Raffa's dad smiling, shaking hands with the property investor. A Russian, the report said. 'Send me the graffiti. I'll see what I can find.'

'Thanks. But Noah? Take it easy. Try and get some rest. That's your priority for the day.'

Sol sat forward when the call ended. 'Show me the tags.'

Noah forwarded Marnie's phone images to his email, opening them on the laptop.

'Princess plus Flea.' Sol squinted, sounding disappointed. 'More bullshit.'

Noah could see his brother's hoody reflected in the monitor, a good match for the pink felt-tip pen on the wall. Was it Raffa's writing? He'd seen it in her sketchpads, the notes she'd made under her artwork, different versions of her signature. Had she drawn this symbol?

'Fire and bullets. That shithole summed up.'

'I'm not seeing the bullet . . .'

Sol leaned in and pointed. 'Bad gyal.' Raffa, he meant. Not the good girl her father imagined. Bad.

'It's just a picture,' Noah said slowly. 'It doesn't mean she was starting fires, or firing bullets. She was a child.'

'Remember you at thirteen.' Sol grinned. 'Looking out for me. You could *move*!'

At thirteen, Noah had spent weeks as the lookout for the gang Sol was running with. He'd stayed outside the flats they robbed, ready to raise the alarm if the police came.

'That's who you are, bruv. *Fast*. I was proud, telling everyone that's my brother.'

'I'm not proud of who I was. But I grew out of it.'

'Grew into this.' Sol poked at Noah's police ID disgustedly. 'Your new family.'

'Are you going to help me?' Noah got up to fetch a refill of coffee. 'Only I could use a hand. Fresh eyes, and all that.'

'You should eat.' Sol pushed his hands back into his pockets. 'One of us needs to.'

'I haven't heard from Dad.' Noah took an apple from the fruit bowl, weighing it in his palm. 'D'you reckon he's okay?'

Sol shrugged, his eyes avoiding Noah's. 'Sure.'

'We always worry about Mum, never about him. But he loved you too.'

Sol lapsed into silence. Noah stood studying him. Every part of him: the broad hunch of his shoulders, the sprawl of his legs under the table. The shape of his skull, his long eyelids, the smooth dent above his upper lip. 'We all loved you,' he said softly. 'We all miss you.'

Sol scratched at his cheek, one foot kicking under the table.

'I wish . . .' Noah gathered a breath, 'that I'd spent as much time with you when you were alive. Just hanging out like this, talking. I wish I'd done that.'

'Doing it now, tho.' Tapping his foot at the floor.

'You know what I mean. Sol, I'm sorry. Truly. I let you down. Broke Mum's heart, and Dad's. And I think I've broken my own heart. I know I've broken my head.'

'So call the doctor. Call *Karie*.' Sol sounded angry, a new development. 'Don't be talking to me about it.'

Noah leaned back into the counter, crossing his legs at the ankle. 'I'm worried about Dad. And Mum, if he's not going home as much as he needs to.'

'You're worried about everything,' Sol complained.

'Thought we were looking at Princess and her flea?' He snapped his fingers at the laptop. 'Know what fleas do? They *jump*. This's the shit you should be thinking about, not whether Dad's paying attention to how far Mum's gone off the rails.'

'Fleas jump . . . You mean Sam Haile?' Noah was distracted by the symbol onscreen. 'Raffa is the princess, so Sam is the flea?'

'If she knew something 'bout Raffa's death, she had to die. You saw that smoke behind her, big like that. Could've been more than smoke; could've been *Bellamys*. Robert, or Tyrone.'

Sam at the window, smoke rearing blackly behind her.

'Her neighbours,' Noah said. 'They broke the door down to rescue her from the fire.'

'Yeah, or to make sure it killed her. One way or another.'

'It's a stretch.' Noah studied the graffiti Marnie had photographed in the stairwell. 'Even if Raffa drew this.'

'You saw her sketchpads,' Sol argued.

'There was nothing like this in there. The writing, perhaps, but not the symbol.'

'Fire and bullets.' Sol tipped his chair onto its hind legs. 'You'd be thinking you dreamed it, but for your bass lady's photos.' He'd dialled down the patois, as if Noah's subconscious was cutting him slack after what'd happened yesterday. 'You'd be thinking you imagined it.'

'It might have occurred to me,' Noah admitted drily. 'Given everything else that's going on.'

'I'm right here, blad.' Sol looked affronted. 'Right here.'

'Don't call me *blad*. You sound like those kids on the stairs.'

'Baby gangsters.' Sol hooted a laugh. 'Keepin' it real.'

Noah clicked away from Marnie's photos of the graffiti,

pulling up an image of Erskine Tower from the news website where Sam Haile's face was unsmiling next to her brother's, the sun in her eyes. He shut his own eyes, smelling smoke, seeing the sky filled with her falling.

'I need to be back there.' He said it quietly, to himself.

But Sol was up and ready. 'Let's go.'

Marnie was having a hard time convincing Lorna Ferguson that the investigation into Raffa Belsham's murder, far from being over, was just getting started.

'We found a bullet in her bedroom, wiped clean. Trident's made a number of arrests for firearms found in Erskine Tower, where we know she was part of this school project. Mr Peters, her teacher, admits there were times when she could have made contact with people other than Eric Martineau. She went there eight times in the last six weeks.'

'All right.' Lorna held up a hand, reinforced by gold rings. 'Let's say Mr Belsham's little cherub was talking to the wrong people and she found a bullet in the stairwell or nicked it from a dodgy mate she made . . . Where does that lead us? The firearms were seized, arrests were made. Malig is dead. We've had confirmation this morning that the gun retrieved from his vehicle is a match for the murder weapon. Fran Lennox found plenty of evidence he was under the influence at the time of his death: class A drugs in his blood, not to mention alcohol. Whether he gunned her down by accident or on purpose because he's a trigger-happy toerag, he's *dead*. He had the decency to put himself head first under a garbage truck, where it could be said he belongs. No more drive-by shootings, one less scumbag to keep under surveillance. Now *I* call that a result. What's more, Guy Belsham calls it a result. He's stopped threatening to escalate this to his mates in the Home Office and the mayor's office, and anywhere else he has friends who might make trouble for us. It's a result.'

'And if more bullets are out there?' Marnie asked. 'Because someone in Erskine Tower is handing them to schoolchildren? We can't ignore that possibility.'

'Right now? Yes, we can. We have to. We've killers enough, unsolved crimes piling up on a daily basis. One bullet in a child's bedroom doesn't get priority. It can't.'

'A dead child's bedroom.'

'Precisely!' Lorna flushed. 'Look, I'm not saying it makes me happy. I'd rather there were no bloody bullets in any bedrooms, certainly not ones belonging to children. But we have to prioritise. We haven't found the scumbag who killed Frank Reece yet, or any of the other kids on that board I'm sick of looking at because it gives me indigestion on a good day, nightmares the rest of the time. We need to get killers off the streets; that's our number one priority. Terrance Malig is off the streets. We know he killed Raffa Belsham. Maybe in time we'll figure out why, but it is *not* the focus of this team for the foreseeable future. If her parents were pushing for it, perhaps. But they want the case closed. They want the chance to grieve, to bury their child and move on. And we have enough work to do. Have I made myself clear?'

Practically see-through, Marnie thought.

'At least let me stay in touch with Trident about the firearms arrests. Raffa wasn't the only child going in there on a regular basis. And we know these gangs love new faces. It's happened to others from good homes. She wouldn't be the first thirteen-year-old tricked into smuggling.'

'A bullet at a time? That's not smuggling, it's not even pickpocketing. Chances are she picked it up off the ground and kept it as a souvenir. I'd be surprised if she even knew what it was.'

'She was thirteen, not three. And she hid it.' Raffa's secret: lethal ammunition in the attic of her parents' perfect house. 'That suggests she knew exactly what it was. We also need to consider the possibility that she wasn't the one who put it there.' She paused, wanting to stress her next words. 'There were no fingerprints on the bullet. Someone wiped it clean. This is a child who didn't pick up her wet towels from the bathroom floor. And Guy—'

'Stop right there,' Lorna warned her. 'If this's headed where I think it is.'

Marnie stood her ground. 'Guy Belsham is the angriest man I've met in a long time. Not just grieving. *Raging*. If there's guilt in the mix, it would explain that level of fury.'

'Or he's guilty because he's working long hours and wasn't home enough, didn't see the danger signs. Failed to keep her safe. You know better than to try and rationalise a parent's grief.'

'He used a gang word: *galdem*. And he went digging into my personal life, and Noah's. How does he have time for that, apart from anything else? He made it personal. Why did he do that?'

'You don't like him. I sympathise. I've had an earful of his complaints myself, and a warning to tread carefully. He's thick as thieves with the commissioner, for one thing.'

'Should that matter? This is a murder investigation. A child was murdered.'

'His child. And her killer's dead.'

'The shooter's dead. That isn't necessarily the same thing.'

They eyed one another.

Marnie said, 'The bullet is in evidence. It was wiped clean.'

'One bullet.' Lorna held up a finger. 'When we take how many guns off the street every week? And more keep coming. Not to mention the knives and swords and machetes. Police tasers, that's the latest haul. Our own bloody tasers, if you please. Ten dozen of them in some housewife's shed in Southwark. Whichever way we slice this, one bullet isn't impressing anyone. Even if the PM's name was engraved on it. No. We bag it, write it up, and move on. That doesn't mean we leave avenues unexplored; just that we prioritise given our stretched resources. Understood?' Lorna dusted the shoulders of her scarlet shirt. 'How's DS Jake?'

'He's resting, as you requested. A victim support officer saw him yesterday.'

'*Your* victim support officer?'

'Ed Belloc saw him, yes. He says Noah's bearing up remarkably well.'

'If it were me,' inspecting her French manicure, 'I'd be starting to think I was cursed. Unless it's that bloody tower that's cursed. Lenny Prowse says the fire team ruled out arson. She was a smoker, Sam Haile. Cigarettes on her bedside table. Cannabis in the wardrobe. Oh, and a home-made crack pipe, with all the trimmings.' She nodded at Marnie's surprise. 'Yes, you might like to keep that to yourself for now. I doubt DS Jake'll be much cheered by the thought he witnessed a drug-induced suicide. God knows what she imagined was chasing her. A two-headed fire-breathing dragon, most likely. She wasn't the innocent little thing the papers have her down as, that's for certain. Lenny Prowse'll fill you in. I'll leave you to bring DS Jake up to speed when you feel the moment's right. Let's let him rest for a while longer.'

Marnie agreed to this plan, because Lorna was right. Noah wouldn't be any happier to learn Sam Haile had been an addict. And in the light of that revelation, it looked less likely that she'd had dealings with Raffa Belsham. Marnie had been able to imagine a promising young law student making friends with an idealistic schoolgirl she'd met by chance in the stairwell of Erskine Tower. But add drugs to the mix and the picture fractured, sending the dead girls in opposite directions. Especially since Raffa's post-mortem had ruled out drug or alcohol abuse.

'You're off to HMP Cloverton this weekend, I take it? I signed the paperwork.'

'Thank you.'

'You might help me out here.' Lorna cocked her head. 'How did my predecessor handle these visits? I can't imagine he thought it the best use of your time.'

'It's my own time. Ma'am.'

'No need to get starchy.' She tapped her nails on the desk, making a long study of Marnie's face. 'I'm looking out for you, like it or not. Stephen Keele's a nasty psychopath from where I'm sitting. And you're a credit to the force, not to mention my star player. That entitles me to a certain degree of scepticism, some might say outright cynicism.'

'I do know what I'm doing.'

Marnie hadn't minded telling Noah and Ed that she intended this visit to Stephen to be her last, but she didn't want to repeat it to DCS Ferguson. She'd come to enjoy having a colleague who didn't know all the facts of her private life. And she could imagine Lorna making short work of any shared confidence, pointing out the flaws in Marnie's logic, that sort of thing.

'Oh I'm sure you know what you're doing. No flies on either one of us, come to that. But here's a funny story.'

169

Lorna reached a hand for her phone, unlocking it. She tapped at the glass before holding the screen for Marnie to see a photo of a shaggy brown dog with a dirty white fringe, its expression mournful and devoted. 'Tamsin. I inherited the name, in case you're wondering. I've tried Tammy, and Tam, but she'll only answer to Tamsin.' She tilted her head at the phone. 'I'd gone to the kennel to get myself a chocolate labradoodle. Oh, you should've seen her. Proper little madam, longest lashes I ever saw. Beautiful manners, and her brain wasn't half bad either. True chocolate, Australian.

'I'd fallen for the hype – adapts well to apartment living, limited drooling, low prey drive. I'd all the paperwork signed, passed my home visit with flying colours, bought the lead and the dog bed. I was raring to go.' She stroked the sleeve of her blouse. 'I swear they design those kennels on purpose, so you've to walk past the strays to reach the pedigrees. Who should be sitting in a cage looking like she's not eaten in a week, stinking to high heaven and drooling for Britain? My Tamsin. She gives me the big eyes.' She looked fondly at the photo on her phone. 'I say hello, because I don't want to come off as unfriendly. She sheds hair all over my hand, flashes her rotten teeth and gums, rolls over so I get the full picture. There's not a bit of her that isn't mangy. Head to toe, she's a vet's bill. But I fell, hook, line and sinker. She's been with me six weeks now. You should see the state of my carpets.'

Marnie gave a sympathetic smile.

But Lorna shook her head. 'This isn't a story about how I was taken in, if that's what you're thinking. Tamsin's not my Stephen Keele. But we all have a blind spot, even you and I. Nothing we can do about it, other than know we have it. Tamsin's for keeps. I steer her wide of strangers, pay the vet's bills and pray she doesn't break a tooth on the posh toys I bought for my labradoodle.'

'Fewer bills with Stephen.' Marnie wanted to meet the woman halfway. 'Although I suppose as tax-payers we're bearing the brunt of his prison costs.'

'No walkies, at least. Not since his little outing to intensive care.' Lorna put her phone away. 'Give my best to that crooked Irish charmer Aidan Duffy if you see him.'

Aidan had been Stephen's cellmate two months ago, at the time of the fire that had hospitalised him. Marnie and Aidan had an on-off working relationship. *On* when Marnie needed an inside track at the prison. *Off* when Aidan pushed his luck and tried to get privileges.

'I doubt I'll see him. He's being moved to a Cat C prison. Day release pending.'

'His lad'll be pleased about that. Finn, is it?'

'Yes.' Marnie had kept in touch with ten-year-old Finn Duffy since his rescue from a vigilante. She had a soft spot for Aidan's son that had nothing to do with his father. Finn was simply the bravest boy she'd met. 'He's looking forward to it.'

'There's one happy family at least,' Lorna said. 'No matter how crooked.'

Like Ron Carling, Lorna measured success differently in the wake of London's rise in violent crime. A day without murder was a good day. A ten-year-old with only one parent in prison, day release pending, was a happy family. Where did that leave the Belshams? Or Matilda Reece, whose son had been stabbed a street from his home? Where did it leave Sam Haile's father, with both of his children dead? Or Noah, with his brother gone and his parents struggling to forgive him?

'Say hello to Tamsin from me.' Marnie stood, offering a smile.

Lorna nodded back at her. 'Say goodbye to Stephen.'

Noah had lost Sol en route to Erskine Tower, finding him again on the corner of the street that ran past Kilburn police station. The sun was out, but Sol's hoody was up. He was kicking his feet against the brickwork and watching the traffic, balefully.

'Took your time,' he complained when Noah approached.

'Yes.' Noah fitted his Bluetooth, protection against looking like a madman. 'I was trying to remain in the realm of reality a little longer.'

'Fuck that.' Sol jumped from the wall, falling into step at his side. 'Where we going?'

'You know where we're going. Erskine Tower.'

'In *here*.' Sol screwed a finger to his temple. 'Where we going in here?'

'Guy Belsham doesn't want to know where the bullet came from. Doesn't that strike you as odd? He's her dad, but he doesn't want to know the full facts about her death.'

'It's murder. You go digging under that, you're burying more than your kid.'

'Meaning he has something to hide?'

'You're looking too deep.' Sol swivelled to make space on the pavement for a couple of kids in headphones and football shirts. 'Like always.' He shook down his hood. 'Dad didn't want to know the full facts, did he? Mum didn't want to know.'

This was a new development, his subconscious switching up a gear. Sol had never spoken about his own death before, and on the rare occasions Noah introduced the theme, he'd shut it down.

172

'That's because we knew the facts. We had the murderer, and the weapon.'

'Same as him. *Guy*. Only his murderer's under a truck. Mine's still strutting.'

'Shafi Ellis is getting a life sentence,' Noah said. 'I'll see to that.'

'And the other rasshole – the one your bass lady loves?'

'Harry Kennedy didn't kill you. We've been through this.'

'Yeah, but you're still hearing me. We're still talking.'

He had a point. Until his subconscious stopped putting words in Sol's mouth, Noah couldn't claim to have forgiven Harry. 'Marnie's not in love with him, you're wrong about that.'

Sol made a kissing noise, walking a pace or two ahead so he could wrap his arms around his hoody, pantomiming an embrace. Noah swallowed a sigh. Setting aside the matter of his dead brother's ghost, the street had the look of flypaper, sticky with traffic and litter. A peeling billboard poster announced that the Olympics were coming to London in two years, as if conspiring to undermine Noah's grip on reality, his ability to differentiate between *been and gone* and *here and now*.

'We have the murderer, the weapon and a motive. Shafi Ellis and his shank. His vendetta for the gang you gave up. Guy Belsham doesn't have any motive for the man who killed his daughter. So why's he so keen to close the case?'

Unless it was a simple question of prejudice. Terrance Malig was black, and Guy believed all black men were violent, even those who'd elected to join the police force.

'Don't dig the dead.' Sol shrugged. 'Hard enough to stay upright without you do that.'

Don't dig the dead. It was an expression Noah hadn't

heard in years. It meant let sleeping dogs lie, don't look too closely at what's past. Tread lightly over that ground. He could smell potatoes baking in the garden at home, Dad at his side. Then the sound of glass smashing in the bathroom . . .

Sol pulled his hood back over his head. 'Don't dig the dead, blad.'

He was right. Noah had work to do, no time to be dredging up his family's past. Hard enough, right now, to remain in the present.

Sol peeled off when they reached the tower, just as he had yesterday. Leaving Noah to count the shiny new parking meters, one after another, until he reached the scars on the road where the Audi had been towed. Someone had thrown sand over the patches of oil and blood, making a small beach in the gutter, littered with chips of windscreen. He waited until his breathing was normal, then turned to face the flats, raising a hand to shield his eyes. The sun was firing all the windows on the west-facing wall of the tower. From this angle it looked like a lie. An impossible feat of engineering, too narrow to be so tall, not solid enough to support its own structure. His phone played the theme tune from *The Sweeney*.

'Just checking in.' It was Ron at the station. 'The boss says you're catching some rest.'

'That's right.' Noah squinted up at the tower block. 'How's it going there?'

'Lenny Prowse called, from Kilburn. Fire investigation's saying it was accidental. Shoddy wiring in the new kitchen. They've not put in the paperwork yet, but it doesn't look like arson. They're letting her dad collect her stuff, and they wouldn't do that if there were any suspicious circumstances. I thought you'd want to know.'

'Yes. Thanks.'

'There's something else.' Ron lowered his voice. 'Drugs in her bedroom. Cannabis and cocaine. And a crack pipe, the clean kind. Gauzes, chopsticks for getting shot of build-up. The works.'

A serious addiction, that was what Ron was saying. Sam Haile, promising law student, had been an addict. Noah shut his eyes, struggling to recalibrate the image in his head of the girl who'd died on the spot where he was standing.

'You there?' Ron asked.

'Yes. Thanks, I appreciate it.'

'Okay, only you didn't hear it from me. It's not a secret, but you're on sick leave so . . .'

'Sure. I didn't hear it from you.' He opened his eyes on the patch of sand at his feet. 'So what're they thinking, that she was high?'

'They're looking into that, yeah. I'll let you know what Lenny says after the autopsy.'

'Thanks.'

'No problem. Take care, mate.' Ron rang off.

'You all right?'

Noah turned his head so quickly he saw spots. A young white woman was peering at him from the pavement. Blunt cheekbones under wide-set eyes, the fag end of a fake tan making her skin look jaundiced. Blonde dreadlocks, a silver nose-ring, orange crop top exposing her navel, ankle-length red skirt. She looked twenty, maybe twenty-three. Sam Haile's age. Noah had his fist filled with his house keys, as if she might've been about to attack him. His heart was slamming in his chest. Roadworks added a distant soundtrack, the grinding pound of metal on metal.

'Seriously,' she said, 'you all right? You look like you're gonna puke.'

He nodded and twisted sideways, the morning's coffee slicking hotly out of him. No retching, no effort required on his part. He just opened his mouth and out it came, spattering as it hit the gutter.

She skipped backwards. 'Shit!'

'Sorry . . .' He straightened, wiping his mouth. 'I'm sorry.' His teeth were shut tight, ears popping under the pressure. He bent and spat in the gutter, one hand on the nearest parking meter for support. The tower shuddered above him.

When he looked up, she was still standing there. She put her eyes over him, her expression shrewd, nose wrinkled. Deciding what? That he was drunk? An addict, like Sam Haile.

'Want me to call someone?' There was a phone in her hand, bubble-gum-pink cover. She wore a lot of rings on her fingers, and on both thumbs. Silver rings, some set with green stones.

Noah shook his head. 'I'm all right. Thanks.' His eyes were damp, his skin sticky, but there was nothing left in him to bring up.

'Want to come for a cup of tea?' She looked past him, towards Erskine Tower.

Noah glanced down, seeing her bare feet, beaded flip-flops fraying between her toes. What was she offering him? Drugs? Sex?

'You were here yesterday, weren't you?' Her face was fidgety, unsettled. 'I saw you, with the police. Answering their questions. I'm on the same floor. She was my neighbour. Sammy. Sam.'

He nodded, ashamed of his suspicion. She wasn't offering anything other than normal human sympathy. She had a shoulder bag stitched with flowers and a carrier bag from the Spar, weighted with what looked like a carton of milk, another of lemonade.

She spread her hands in a dazzle of rings. 'You can come up, if you want.'

The lift had been fixed since yesterday, saving them both the long climb up the stairs. A notice was glued to the doors, warning it wasn't to be used in the event of a fire. Someone had written *Justice for Grenfell* across the notice. When the doors opened on the twenty-eighth floor, the smell of smoke and fire was sickening.

'Come on.' She led Noah to a brown door, taking a set of keys from her shoulder bag.

He followed her inside the flat, telling himself this wasn't a police matter, and anyway, he was on sick leave. He half expected Sol to have something to say about that, but his brother was staying away, as he always seemed to when Noah came to Erskine Tower. He should try and figure out the reason for that, see if his subconscious would cooperate with an interrogation.

Sam's neighbour went to the kitchen at the back of the flat. 'I'm Terri.' She nodded the name over her shoulder as she filled a kettle at the sink.

Noah stayed in the doorway, equidistant between the living room and the counter where she was making tea. The kitchen's low-slung ceiling was tiled in polystyrene, discoloured above the cooker and window. Jars of sauce and jam, Marmite and mustard were pushed to the back of the counter, together with a colourful collection of mugs, battered boxes of tea bags, a crusty bag of sugar. On the shallow windowsill, an empty jam jar held a wilting sunflower. Behind him, the living room looked out onto a balcony like the one where Eric had set a sunlounger.

'Have you lived here long?'

'Three years. It's a dump, but better than the dump where they wanted to put me.'

Social housing explained the municipal furniture: sagging sofa, chipped table, flat-pack bookcase erected against the wall. She'd filled its shelves with photos and pieces of cheap pottery, lumpy paperweights, little wooden bowls. The clutter made the space feel homely, despite the polluting stink of the fire.

'Biscuit?' Terri reached for the shelf above the counter, where cereal boxes shared space with a jumble of tins. Her outstretched arm was blotchy with the fading fake tan.

'No, thanks.' Noah watched her, still wondering what she wanted. She shouldn't have invited him up here, that wasn't safe. No matter how harmless or nauseous he looked. And he shouldn't have come. 'I read about the fire safety investigation. Will they move you out, d'you think?'

She took a carton of milk from the fridge, sniffed it, then poured a measure into their mugs. 'They'd better not. There's no fire hazard, anyway. No worse than anywhere else.'

'But what happened . . . there *was* a fire.'

In Sam's new kitchen, Ron had said, shoddy wiring. Noah looked at the electrical sockets above Terri's oven, measuring the distance to the door and then to the window, wondering about the layout of the flat. What was in Terri's bedroom? Cannabis and a crack pipe? He couldn't reconcile that evidence with the pictures in his head of Sam trapped dying in the bonnet of his car. But it wasn't hard to imagine what DS Prowse was thinking, and DCS Ferguson too. *Death of a drug addict* was an easy headline to police, especially round here.

Terri saw him looking. 'My flat's built the other way round. A fire starts here, I can make it out okay. Her flat's back to front. All the flats that side are back to front.'

'You're not worried?' Noah took the mug of tea from her hand. 'Thank you.'

'I'm worried I'll lose my job and miss a payment on my rent, get chucked out of here. That I'll turn up to work with the smell of this dump in my clothes and they'll think I'm using.' She bared her teeth in a grin. Patchy enamel, thinning in places. 'Stinks, doesn't it? Like a dog died. Not to mention the weed that they sell like sweets to anyone with cash enough to spare.' She eyed him as she picked up her own mug. 'Makes a change to smell fire.'

She was right, the whole building reeked. Noah tried to picture Sam Haile, sister of a war hero, housed in one of these boxes. Living under low stained ceilings, antisocial behaviour on her doorstep. A place hated even by traffic wardens. 'Did you know her? Samantha. Sammy, you said.'

'A bit. Not much.' Terri shrugged. 'I've got a balcony. Want to see?'

The balcony was a good match for Eric Martineau's. Three feet deep and eight wide, with a curved wall of concrete hiding the view until you leaned over. Then you saw parked cars, potholed tarmac, a greasy straggle of grass. Further away, the chimneys of Battersea Power Station crowned the Thames, the river looping like a belt between bridges; London, crammed and climbing, crawling in all directions.

'I'm one of the lucky ones.' Terri sipped tea. 'They don't get balconies on the other side.' She looked down at the cars. 'I guess she could've stayed out here if she'd had a balcony. Until the fire crew came, I mean. With ladders or whatever.'

Would she have done that? Samantha Haile. Stood and waved from the balcony for help? Or climbed to its blunt concrete lip and jumped?

'Balcony's all I've got going for me, that and the new kitchen they keep promising. They've started on the other side. She must've got hers right before it happened.' Terri cradled the mug in her hands. 'I never saw it. The fire, her falling . . . I was out late on Sunday night, didn't get back here until it was all over. That's when I saw you, getting hassled by the police. Pigs.' She made a face. 'They'd taken her away by then. I never saw her.' She bit on her bottom lip. 'But a couple of times since? I *have* seen her.'

'I'm sorry?' Noah blinked.

She released her lip. 'I read about it in the papers, so I know what happened. But like . . . this morning, yeah? I'm walking to work, not even near here, and I see her falling from that window. Like a kind of . . . vision.'

'A hallucination?'

'Yeah, maybe. You're the only one I've told. Weird, right? I mean, I don't even know you.' She glanced away. 'I guess I thought anyone who knew me'd think I was going crazy.'

Noah searched for something to say. 'Blind people have hallucinations.'

'Yeah?' It was her turn to blink. 'When they can't even see? Where'd you hear about that?'

'They think the optic nerve in the eye carries a ghost image to the brain. The memory of something they saw before they went blind.'

'I'm not going blind, am I?' She was joking.

He smiled. 'I shouldn't think so.'

'Good, because I didn't even see it happen. Not like you. You got a good look at her.' Terri stared past him, at the cars parked below. '*You* should be the one seeing ghosts, not me.'

* * *

The corridor outside her flat was freshly painted, a rash of graffiti just visible under the white topcoat. 'See you then,' she said.

'Can I give you my number?' Noah asked. 'In case you think of anything else about Sam?'

It was what he'd have asked if he was on duty. He half expected Terri to say no, but she shrugged and held out her hand. 'Sure.'

She trusted him, he realised, for the same reason Guy Belsham did not. Because he was black.

He wrote the number on the back of her hand. 'Thanks for the tea.'

She went inside the flat, closing the door. As he walked towards the lift, a voice called from the far end of the corridor, 'Hold it, would you?'

Noah turned. The man was fair-haired, shouldering a brown nylon rucksack. He waved a hand and called again, 'Hold the lift?'

'Sure,' Noah called back.

'Won't be a minute.' The man disappeared in the direction of the flats without balconies, the side of the building where Sam had lived.

Noah pressed the button to summon the lift. His mouth tasted of tea, and bile. He should've asked Terri if she had mints, or mouthwash. She'd talked to him so easily, would've talked more if he'd let her, or led her. Making a face when she mentioned the police, accusing them of hassling him. *Pigs*. Not imagining he might belong that side of the line, summing him up by his skin colour. He knew what Sol would say about that: 'Wrong side of the law, blad.'

The lift hadn't responded by the time the man with the rucksack reappeared. He was with a second man, middle-aged, carrying a cardboard box with *Bananas* written up the side. He held the box to his chest, both arms underneath as if he feared the bottom would fall through. The crown of his head was bald, but thick hair lifted in a grey hood from the rear of his skull. His tan suit was too short in the leg, his black shoes newly polished. His companion with the rucksack was Noah's age, dressed in beige chinos and a blue sweater over a white polo shirt. Freshly shaven, with crisp fair hair brushed back from his forehead. Good-looking in a clean-cut, boy-scout way. He made a point of standing between Noah and the man with the box. The three of them waited for the lift as it laboured its way up from the ground floor.

'We've not met.' The younger man smiled at Noah. 'But you're DS Jake, yes?'

Noah froze. 'I'm sorry, you are . . .?'

'Luke Corey.' He held out his hand until Noah shook it. 'I saw you at Kilburn police station yesterday. We didn't get the chance to say hello.' He shrugged the rucksack higher on his shoulder. 'This is Howard Haile. Howie, this is DS Jake. He gave the witness statement to the police.'

Sam's dad moved his head away from Noah. Had he been told about the witness statement, the suspicion of suicide? Noah had stuck to the facts, just as DS Prowse had said, but the implication was there in black and white, the idea that Sam might've jumped. For some, the stigma of suicide was worse than murder.

Noah held out his hand. 'Mr Haile. I'm so sorry for your loss.'

If he hadn't known better, he'd have thought Howard was blind. His stare took in nothing, neither Noah's outstretched hand nor his attempt at a smile. He wetted his lips and looked away, clasping the *Bananas* box to his chest. He had a neglected physique, flabby in places, thin in others. He hadn't shaved in a couple of days, stubble sanding his jaw. He lifted a knee to support the box from beneath, before taking it back into his arms. What was inside? Books, clothes, letters. Chopsticks, gauzes. A crack pipe. Did he know that version of his daughter? Had he ever known that version?

'Please let me help you with that, Howie.' Luke held out his hands.

Noah studied him. A bereavement counsellor, Prowse had said. He'd been counselling the family after Dylan Haile's death. But that was five years ago. Had he become a friend? Or had they needed five years of counselling, still coming to terms with their loss when this fresh tragedy struck.

'Please, Howie. Let me help.'

Howard cut his eyes at Luke the way he'd cut them at Noah, unseeingly. He didn't want either man's help. Luke who'd supported his family through their grief for his son. Noah who'd witnessed the death of his daughter. He clung to the box of belongings as if it was the one thing stopping him from pushing Luke, or punching Noah.

'I'll take the stairs,' Noah said.

He waited in the stairwell until he heard the lift carrying the two men to the ground floor. Then he followed the curve in the corridor that led to Sam's flat. A fire and safety notice was pinned there, but there was no one guarding the door, which was the same as the others in the corridor except for the scuff marks around the lock, wood splintered where it'd been forced. The corridor's ceiling was punched full of smoke detectors, but no sprinklers had been fitted. No evidence of smoke damage in the corridor, just the pungent smell of the fire. It would take months for that smell to fade. Noah shut his eyes, resisting the urge to rub at the scar tissue on his ribs.

'I hoped I'd find you here.'

He turned, his heart hammering for the second time that day.

Luke Corey had followed him. He must've doubled back, like Noah. Alone, empty-handed. 'I'm sorry about Howie. He didn't mean to be rude.' He glanced at the door to Sam's flat. 'I have a key. Do you want to see inside?'

Noah shook his head. 'No.'

Luke scratched the end of his nose. 'I think you do.' He unlocked the door. 'It's why you're here. You need to see. I was the same.' He pushed the door wide with one arm, looking back at Noah with his head cocked. 'Come on, it's okay. I get it. Better if you see.'

12

Marnie was on her way out of the station when Oz Pembroke stopped her. 'New arrest, incoming. Thought you might want to take a look. Picked him up in Hackney, but his home address's Gilborne Road. That means Erskine Tower.'

'The charge?'

'Possession. Bit of weed, bit of crack.' Oz stuck his hands in his pockets. 'Oh, and he had a blade, but that's a given.'

'Name?'

'Felix Amos. We're waiting for an appropriate adult.'

'How old?'

Oz yawned. 'Thirteen, pushing forty.'

Raffa's age, and with Sam Haile's drugs of choice on his person. Hadn't Eric mentioned a boy called Felix who was straying from the straight and narrow in the direction of the Bellamy brothers?

Marnie removed her coat. 'Was he dealing?'

'He says not.' Oz clicked his knuckles, bouncing on the soles of his shoes, two of his less noisome habits. 'But he had it all in nifty little bags, so I'd call that a good guess.'

'Let's take a look.'

She went with Oz to the interview room where Felix Amos was awaiting his appropriate adult. He was a skinny kid, like so many they took off the streets, narrow shoulders under a grey Nike sweatshirt, matching jogging pants, scruffy trainers. African Caribbean, according to the paperwork. His face was pointed, with big eyes that swept the room like lasers, hair buzz-cut at the sides, dreadlocked on top. Small ears, a button nose, chapped lips. His skin was shockingly clear and smooth; Marnie knew grown women who'd kill for a complexion like his. He tucked his chin down when Oz came into the room, then shot a look past him at Marnie.

'This your boss then?' A child's voice, but deep. 'Knew you was too thick to do this on your own, Gucci.' The bravado was well practised, his head cocking to one side, top lip lifting to show crooked white teeth. The *Gucci* was aimed at Oz Pembroke's wristwatch, which Oz wore under the sleeve of his shirt and suit. Felix had a magpie's eyes, and expensive tastes. He sat bonelessly in the plastic chair, as if it was the best seat in the house. 'You'd better be his boss.'

'I'm Detective Inspector Rome. Would you like a drink of water, or tea?'

'Or squash? Or milk?' He cocked his head further. 'Piss off.'

'You'll get a crick in your neck,' Oz warned.

'Better than a finger up my arse.' Felix showed him one, the middle finger. 'Bet you love that, don't you, Gucci? Stop and search, that's your thing. Bend and cough. Bet your girlfriend gets it right up there when you're screwing, the dirty cow.'

Oz clicked his knuckles. 'Your mum and dad must be proud.'

'My dad's dead.' Felix balled his fists and mimed

weeping. 'Boo-hoo. Means you'd better be careful, or my social'll have you in court. I'm a vulnerable person, at risk.'

'At risk of being sent down,' Oz agreed. 'That knife'll get you six months for starters.'

'DS Pembroke, could you bring us a couple of bottles of water?'

'Yeah, Gucci, earn your keep.' His eyes moved smoothly to Marnie as soon as Oz left the room. 'You should put that fat bastard on a diet.'

Eric had said this boy used to run errands – *You could trust him with a fiver to pop to the shops and pick up a carton of milk or a bit of fish* – back before the Bellamys began showing an interest in him. But Eric also said the Bellamys looked after their new recruits, at least to begin with: *Posh clothes, plenty of cash. He was a scruffy beggar when I first met him. Thin as a rail.* Felix was painfully skinny, and scruffy. Did that mean the Bellamys had dropped him? Bright as a button, Eric had said, but here he was, under arrest for possession.

'Who's your appropriate adult, Felix?'

'Shit knows.'

'Your social worker? Or your mum?'

He laughed. 'Yeah, my mum. That'll be it. She'll be here any minute now, can't miss her. Face like a factory recall.' He wiped a finger under his nose. 'She wouldn't come if I was on fire.'

'Who looks after you? At home. You live in Erskine Tower, that's right, isn't it?'

'We look out for each other.' He twisted his arms together, fingers facing outwards, showcasing his bony wrists. 'One big happy family.'

'With knives,' Marnie amended. 'And crack cocaine.'

His face sharpened. 'That's illegal.' He pointed a finger

at her. 'You can't ask questions, can't give me shit until my social gets here. You think I don't know the rules?'

'Oh I'm sure you're intimately acquainted with the rules. This isn't your first time inside a police station, or your first arrest.' Marnie drew out a chair and sat facing him. 'Who else is at home, or is it just you and your mum?'

'And whoever she's shagging this week.' He dropped his head to his shoulder, studying her shoes. 'You were on your way home. Why'd you stop for me? Sex life a bit shit, is it?'

'You were on your own in Hackney when you were arrested. Is someone waiting for you?'

'Like who?' He yawned. Crooked teeth, but good; no fillings, or none that she could see.

'Whoever you're dealing drugs for. It'd explain why you're not in a hurry to get out of here. I can't imagine whoever it is will be too pleased to find you've run off with his product.'

'I'm not dealing.' Felix pulled one foot onto the chair, holding it by its skinny ankle. 'That would be bad. Wrong.' Widening his eyes at her. 'I'm just looking after it for a mate.'

'Which mate?'

'Can't remember. Got so many.' He flashed her a grin. She thought: You're just a kid. A silly, swaggering kid. 'And the knife? Does that belong to the same mate?'

'Blade's mine.' He pulled at the fraying laces on his trainers. 'It was a present.'

From this, Marnie deduced the knife was within the legal limit. A penknife, probably. But you could kill someone with a penknife. She knew a man who'd killed a gang rival with the part of a Swiss Army penknife designed to remove stones from the hooves of horses.

'Tell me about Erskine Tower. Home. It's been a bit busy round there just lately.'

'You'd know.' He bored of the laces and rolled his neck. 'You lot can't keep away from the place. You should just burn it all down, that'd sort it out.'

'There was a fire at the flats yesterday, in fact. But perhaps you were already in Hackney.'

'Yeah?' The tips of his fingers flexed. 'Which floor?'

'Twenty-eighth.'

'Yeah?' He tongued his teeth, pulling at his upper lip. He was paying attention now, but he didn't want to give her the satisfaction of knowing it.

'One fatality,' Marnie said.

He chewed the skin from his lip slowly, as if he were eating a sweet.

'Samantha Haile. Did you know her?'

'No.' But his eyes said *yes*. He wasn't scared, not quite, but he was unsettled.

Oz chose that moment to return with the bottled water. It gave Felix the chance to recover some of his earlier audacity. 'Took your time. Lots of stairs, were there?'

'His social worker's on her way.' Oz put the bottles on the table. 'Traffic's bad, though.'

'Your arse causing a tailback?' Felix juggled the bottle between his hands. 'You can piss off again, Gucci. I'm having a nice chat with your boss 'bout your wanker's cramp.'

Oz clicked his knuckles and the kid laughed, nodding. 'Yeah, that.'

'Thanks for the water.' Marnie smiled at Oz, letting him know she had this. Felix wouldn't talk while he was in the room, and she needed him to talk.

When Oz was gone, she asked, 'Which floor do you live on, Felix?'

'Any floor I can find,' he fired back. But he was frowning now. He set the bottle back on the table. 'Did she burn? Is that how she died? You said there was a fire.'

'Yes. It started in her kitchen. But she didn't burn. She jumped.'

'She . . .' His eyes shocked wide for a second.

'From the twenty-eighth floor.' She felt a twinge of guilt because he was only a kid. 'That's how she died. Are you sure you didn't know her?'

He shook his head, pointing his eyes away, across the room. He looked narrower than ever, as if he was trying to fold himself into the chair, disappear.

'We think she must have been high. Sam Haile. We know she smoked dope, and crack.'

'Everyone smokes. Have you seen the state of that place?' Felix reached for his laces again, looping his fingers through them unseeingly. Marnie caught a glimpse of the boy who used to run errands for his elderly neighbour. 'Did she make a mess? When she landed?'

'She fell from the twenty-eighth floor. So yes. Did you sell her crack cocaine?'

'Fuck off.' He twisted at the laces, tying his fingers in a knot. 'No.'

'But everyone smokes. Where do they get it? From your mate?'

He rolled his eyes. 'It's London, fuck's sake.'

'And you've just been arrested for possession. Of the drug Sam was smoking before she fell twenty-eight floors from the tower block where you live.' Marnie broke the seal on her bottle of water. 'I'm not a big believer in coincidence. And my boss doesn't believe in it at all. She'll be expecting me to pin this on you. Too good a chance to pass up.'

'That's corruption.' He stared at her. 'Police stitch-up. You're mental, telling me this shit.'

'While it's just the two of us.' She drank a mouthful of water. 'Before your social worker gets here, and we conduct a formal interview. We're just having a chat, isn't that what you said?'

She felt sorry for him, but she knew exactly how far sympathy would get her. Any hint of softness and he'd exploit it while at the same time despising her for it. She couldn't help him unless he trusted her. And kids like this didn't trust adults who tried too hard to help them.

'I didn't sell shit to her, okay? I didn't know her, don't know half the bastards in that dump. Why'd you think I was over in Hackney?'

'You have to go home sometime. When you do, you'll be able to smell the smoke in the building. It stinks.'

'It always stinks.'

'Not like this.'

He stared at her a moment longer. 'Your sex life really *is* shit if this's how you get your kicks. Stitching up kids for arson they didn't do, *dealing* they didn't do—'

'Who said anything about arson?' She lowered her bottle, looking at him as if he'd given her a whole new idea. 'Arson would make it murder.'

'I didn't fucking do it!' His lips were red where he'd bitten them. 'Not the fire, not the crack, *none* of it, okay?'

'But you knew Samantha Haile.'

He shook his head, shutting his mouth as if he'd realised he couldn't say anything that wouldn't dig him deeper into trouble. What was it Eric had said? *People get scared, that's when they're dangerous. I've seen it in young Felix.*

Marnie leaned towards the boy. 'Felix . . . I'm not interested in arresting kids. Not when I know they're working for adults who deserve to be in jail. *Those* are the people I want. Not you.'

He stared at her, still knotting his fingers through the laces of his cheap trainers.

'Okay.' She stood. 'I'll wait for your social worker, and we can start the interview properly. Do you want a sandwich? Or a Kit Kat?'

He shook his head, watching her leave the room.

In the corridor, Oz was on his phone. He ended the call when he saw Marnie.

'Where's the knife,' she asked. 'And the drugs we found on him?'

Oz took her to the store, showing her the evidence bags. A lightweight non-lockable pocket knife with a two-and-a-half-inch blade. The drugs were in six small resealable plastic bags. The kind favoured by dealers, and often found littering parks, and pavements outside nightclubs. Each bag had something stamped on it. Marnie moved under the light. She took out her phone, scrolling through her recent photos until she found the one she wanted.

Oz was at her shoulder. 'Found something?'

'Something,' she agreed.

On each of the bags was a stylised logo of a bullet with a flame inside. The same as the one drawn in pink felt-tip pen in the stairwell at Erskine Tower. By Raffa Belsham, or so they believed. Had Raffa copied the logo from the deal bags, or did it go deeper than that?

'Stupid to say he's holding these for a mate.' Oz picked up one of the bags. 'Doesn't he know we can have him for intent to supply? You'd think his *mate* would've trained him what to say. These dealers are getting sloppy. That little shit reckons we can't touch him. He's probably right, too.'

'He's a child,' Marnie said. 'Let's not forget that.'

She walked to her office, dialling Noah's number. The call went straight to voicemail.

'The graffiti,' she said. 'Did it ring any bells? Only it's turned up again. On deal bags found on a thirteen-year-old from Erskine Tower. Eric's neighbour Felix Amos. I'm starting to think you're right about that connection.'

Back in the interview room, Felix was sitting with his feet pulled up, arms wrapped around his knees. She watched him through the window in the door, seeing him practise expressions for his social worker. Innocence, fear, bravado. He wiped his face with the crook of his elbow and started again. Innocence, fear . . .

She opened the door. 'Hey, Flea.'

His head snapped towards her, eyes wide with recognition.

'That's you, right? Flea. Your nickname. So tell me. Who's Princess?'

13

Noah followed Luke Corey into the fire-damaged flat where Sam Haile had lived. It was the same shallow box as Terri's, its ceiling brought lower by a curling tide of ruined tiles. The order of the rooms was reversed just as Terri had described, the bedroom separated from the front door by a kitchen, one corner of which was a misshapen mess of melted plastic units. Such a small patch of damage, but it had killed her.

Noah couldn't believe the police had allowed Howard inside the flat so soon after the fire. Even if they'd ruled out arson, found Sam's wardrobe full of drugs, it was too soon to say there was nothing suspicious here. He couldn't help comparing the way they were handling this death with the care being taken in Muswell Hill – the Belshams' house searched, their garden dug up. Here in Erskine Tower it was just another day, another death, and that didn't feel right.

'Soot gets on everything.' Luke bypassed the kitchen for the bathroom, washing his hands in the small sink, watching Noah in the mirror bolted to the wall. He dried his hands on a handkerchief pulled from his sleeve, showing off the watch fastened at his wrist. 'Present from a mum whose son died on a swimming trip.' He touched the watch face fondly. 'I didn't want to take it, but she insisted. Poor Jeanie. She's battling back for the sake of her other kids. It's all you can do, isn't it?'

Noah stood aside to let him pass, the skin bristling on his neck. He didn't know why, but he disliked Luke, intensely. Perhaps it was the man's job, so similar to Karie Matthews'. He watched Luke move through the main living space to stand beside the window where Sam had jumped. 'Down there's where you parked, isn't it?' His voice was light and sympathetic.

Noah didn't speak. His nose was pinching shut, making it hard to get enough air into his lungs. He should've stayed outside. What was he doing here? What was he thinking, coming into a dead girl's flat as if he had to see or had to know . . . *something*. He'd no business being here. It could compromise the investigation, put paid to any prosecution. He must be out of his mind.

'A thing like this can feel very personal,' Luke murmured. 'Howie said she went with her mum and dad to the hospital where they took Dylan, after they flew him home to the UK. That must've been horrendous. He was burned in an explosion, poor guy. His tank was shelled, can you imagine? Half his face gone, Howie said, almost nothing left. The smell was the worst part, as if he was still burning . . . Samantha saw that. No wonder she was scared of fire.' He looked back towards the damage in the kitchen. He was a shade under Noah's height, with a similar build. He ran, or swam, or played squash. It was hard to picture him sitting with a book. 'I failed her. I was there to help, after Dylan. It's what I do, and I've been at it a long time, so it stings that I couldn't do anything.'

Why did it sound as if he cared more about this personal failure than he did about Sam's death, or Howard's loss?

'I should've been able to help,' he repeated.

'Sometimes you just can't.'

'D'you have kids?' Luke's eyes fixed on him, brimming with curiosity.

Noah shook his head.

'Samantha was twenty-three, but she seemed younger.' He frowned at the smoke damage around them. 'She was sad, but I don't believe she was suicidal.'

Noah tested the dryness in his mouth, waiting for the spike of nausea to retract. He could see her hair spilling into the gutter. He needed Luke to stop speaking. Needed to leave this flat, take the stairs back down to the street, breathe fresh air. Find Sol.

'Her dad believes it was a tragic accident,' Luke said.

'Of course it was tragic.'

'But you think it might've been suicide. That's what you put in your statement.' His stare grubbed at Noah's face. 'You didn't use that word, but you couldn't rule it out . . . D'you mind if I ask if you're an only child?'

'Yes.' *Yes I do mind*, Noah meant.

But Luke misunderstood him. 'Me too. It was different for Samantha. She had her big brother to look up to, and to *live* up to. Have you ever attended a military funeral? It's an amazing spectacle, uniforms, salutes. There'll be nothing like that for her.' He pinched the bridge of his nose as if conscious of his body language and how it might be made to compensate for the sterile way in which he was describing the violent deaths of two young people. 'I'm helping Howie organise her funeral. He's insisting no flowers, won't even let me organise a wreath. It's his choice, of course, but it feels wrong. Lonely, somehow. At the very least she should have flowers.'

Noah had been thinking of sending flowers. He wouldn't now. How was Howard able to bear Luke's solicitation? The man wielded his sympathy like a blunt axe.

'Hard to believe we're a stone's throw from Notting Hill, where the celebs live. London's all layers, I guess.' Luke touched a thumb to the window. 'What did you look like to her all the way down there? I expect the police wanted to know what she looked like to you. "Was she shouting, waving. Did she jump?"' He leaned closer to the window, his profile etched with emotion suddenly, as if he'd drawn lines down it with a marker pen. 'The cars either side of yours were soft-tops. Did you know that? The free parking attracts all sorts. Maybe she was hoping to land on one of those other cars. Or maybe she didn't think about the landing at all. I expect that's nearer the truth.'

He straightened, adjusting the rucksack at his shoulder. 'Have you tried to breathe when it gets really hot? Jeanie's an asthmatic. She struggles on hot days. I can't imagine how she'd cope in a fire, when the air's burning and you can't breathe.' His eyes were wet. 'There's no choice when it gets that bad. There's just whatever it takes; you do whatever it takes.'

It sounded as if he was trying to talk himself into believing in Sam's tragic death. A death born of panic or fear, but not despair. Did he believe suicide was a sin? Plenty of people did.

'I'm sorry.' He came away from the window. 'This isn't very professional. I'm just struggling to understand how it happened. You saw it, the only one who did.' He stopped, eyeing Noah with interest. 'Are you okay? Hey . . .' His face changed again, alert with concern. 'Look, come back outside. I didn't mean to upset you.' He put out a hand. 'Come outside, okay?'

'I'm all right.' Noah stepped out of range of the man's hand, moving towards the flat's front door. 'It's the smell in here, that's all.'

'I should've thought.' Luke held the door open. 'I'm sorry.'

When they were in the corridor, he locked the flat, returning the key to his pocket. Then he unzipped the rucksack and held out a bottle of mineral water. 'Here.'

Noah wanted to refuse, but he was suddenly very thirsty. 'Thanks.' He uncapped the bottle, taking a mouthful before handing it back.

'Maybe Howie shouldn't have taken her to the hospital to see Dylan like that.' Luke stashed the bottle in his rucksack. 'She was never the same afterwards. I was afraid she was drinking, or worse. I wanted to protect her from her mum and dad's grieving for Dylan. When a family closes ranks, it's so hard. I see it all the time. Grief can be a contagion, or an addiction. Poor Howie's had a double dose of it.' He rubbed at his forehead with the back of his hand. 'And Patsy, Samantha's mum. She's been knocked sideways.' The diver's watch was scarred across its face. Had it really belonged to Jeanie's son who'd died on the swimming trip? No, she wouldn't have given away her son's watch, not even to the man who helped her recover from his loss.

'My boss keeps telling me I shouldn't go into this expecting to make things better.' Luke rolled his shoulders stiffly. 'No one can do that for someone who's lost a child. But you have to *hope* you can. I really thought I was doing good for Howie and Patsy. And Samantha too. She wouldn't let me do much, just little things like shopping or changing a fuse, taking photos when she wanted to sell something on eBay, nothing that amounted to real help. I failed them. Now Howie won't even let me carry her things to his car. I expect he'd like to tell me he's had all the counselling he can take, but he doesn't want to be rude.'

He twisted a smile from the hurt on his face. 'I used to work for the lost property department on the London Underground, before I took up counselling full-time. You wouldn't believe the things people leave behind on trains. Artificial limbs, livestock . . . A jar of bull's sperm once, left by a student at agricultural college. I was able to hand it over when he came asking for it.' He looked wistful for a second. It took ten years from his face. 'That was a good job, somewhere I was helpful.'

How much of Luke was defined by this determination to make a difference? Some people needed to help others, to the point where they failed to function otherwise. A pathology, of sorts. What was it doing to Luke's self-esteem to be unable to help the Hailes in their hour of need?

'Listen to me, a jar of bull's sperm!' He gave an embarrassed laugh. 'If only you could hand over someone's peace of mind as easily after they've lost a loved one. You have to try, though. You can't leave them alone with that sort of grief. It's a *pit*. Once you fall in, you can't climb back out. Not easily, sometimes never.' He touched his watch. 'You have to be like Jeanie and move on. If you let grief take over, there's no room left for the living.'

He was right, Noah knew he was right. It made him dislike the man even more intensely.

'Can I tell you something?' The light in the corridor mugged the colour from Luke's gaze, turning it black and white. 'Something personal, a thing I always tell the people I work with. It helps to hear it.' He didn't give Noah the chance to object. 'Lily and Pearl, my twin sisters, were stillborn.'

'I'm . . . sorry.' Noah's neck clenched. 'But I don't think—'

'It's okay. It was years ago. But my mum couldn't let go of her unhappiness, not for the longest time. Even now, she lets it take over everything else.' He thinned his mouth. 'I had to tiptoe through my childhood, respecting the silence in the house, navigating this . . . *glut* of grief. Even in the garden, where she planted rosemary and white roses. I wasn't allowed to play there. It was a shrine. The whole house was a shrine, to her loss.'

Noah needed him to stop speaking. He didn't understand why Luke had singled him out for this confidence, this confession. He didn't want to hear it. He had enough to carry without this.

'It was terrible, of course. I'd have loved them as much as she did, my big sisters. But she wouldn't let me near her grief.' Luke gave a soft laugh, sad. 'I had the box room even when I was a teenager, because their nursery wasn't to be touched. She'd sit in there for hours. It was a big room, mostly empty. She was so unhappy she made herself ill with it. And there was nothing I could do to make it better.' He drew a breath and held onto it for a long moment. 'No one should go through that. Not parents, not the kids left behind. It's why I wanted to help Samantha so much.'

Noah didn't speak, imagining the woman's suffering. Mrs Corey, Luke's mother, sitting in the empty bedroom, kneeling to plant rosemary in the garden. Then he thought of his own mother, huddled in the darkness at the back of their house, walled in with the tins and barrels of water.

'You tried to help her, too.' Luke hitched the rucksack

at his shoulder. 'Samantha. I'm glad you were there. That she had someone watching over her, at the end.'

It was a strange thing to say, arcane almost. Everything about Luke was oddly old-fashioned, off-centre. As if he were acting a part in an amateur dramatics performance of a superficial play about compassion. Nothing about him felt honest or real. For a second, Noah wondered whether Luke might be a figment of his imagination. Sol's supporting cast. He was saved from further speculation by his phone alerting him to a missed call from Marnie. He dialled voicemail: a message about Felix Amos being found with deal bags bearing the logo from the stairwell. Bullets and fire. Marnie was beginning to believe in a connection between Sam and Raffa.

'I need to go.' He pocketed his phone, straightened to face Luke.

'Of course. By the way, Howie doesn't blame you. I know he was frosty before. He and Patsy are in shock, but you mustn't think they're bearing a grudge because of the statement you made. You had to say what you saw, they understand that.'

It sounded like sympathy, but it felt like a reprimand. Luke was very good at that, saying one thing while meaning another. The lift wheezed below them, cables creaking inside the shaft.

'Thanks for letting me see the flat.'

'It helped, didn't it? Just a little.'

'Yes.' He watched Luke's boy-scout face contort with a smile.

'Glad I was able to help someone.' Luke put out his hand. 'Take care.'

'Thanks, I will. You too.'

*   *   *

Back home, Noah dropped his keys into the bowl on the hall table. He wanted a shower to get rid of the stink of smoke, and to brush his teeth free from the taste of tea and melted ceiling tiles.

Dan wasn't home yet, no bike in the rack downstairs, so he called out: 'Sol?'

'Sofa, blad.'

Sprawled against the cushions, pink hood up, bottom lip turned out.

'What's up?'

'*Hours*. You were gone hours.'

'You could've come with me.' Noah put his hands in his pockets, amused by the sulky look his subconscious had pinned on his brother's face. 'That's within the remit, isn't it? Of a haunting or hallucination, or whatever this is. Have visions, will travel.'

'You lost me,' Sol complained.

'What happened to the patois?'

'*You* happened. Company you keep. Street kids, white gyal with dreads. White boy with blonde pants taking you in her home, feeding you shit about sorrow.'

'It *was* shit, wasn't it?' Noah sat down facing his brother. 'That wasn't just me.'

'Wearing a dead boy's watch like a trophy? That's *sick*, man.'

'He's a bereavement counsellor. So it might be my natural prejudice playing up.'

Sol kicked a foot at the floor. 'Got to go with your gut, though.'

'I'm not so sure,' Noah said. 'My gut put you on this sofa, in my head. I'm not convinced it's up to the job just now.' He heard the bump of bike tyres on the stairs, and stood. 'Dan's home.'

'Take me clubbing, then.' Sol's lower lip stayed out. 'Like you used to.'

'I'm tired, Sol. I need a night in.'

Dan's key was in the lock. There was a moment when Noah's eyes were locked to Sol's and he was afraid his brother wouldn't leave. That Dan would come into the room and see the pair of them locked in this insanely stubborn struggle. He didn't know whether it would be a relief that Dan knew, or the final straw. An image in his head, unwelcome: Karie Matthews armed with official paperwork, *Detained under the Mental Health Act.*

'I'm home.' Dan wheeled his bike into the hall. 'Rack's knackered again so the bike's out here, sorry. Try not to trip over it.'

Sol rolled sideways and stood, his hands in his hoody pockets. 'Walk good.'

Goodbye, in patois.

Noah said, 'Take care, Sol,' so softly only he could hear the words.

The traffic was a nightmare, despite the fact that Marnie left the station long past rush hour. Her evening was shot to pieces, so it was just as well Ed was away for the night, called to an emergency at a refuge in Essex. Roads were closed due to an accident, a vehicle on fire, lives lost. She listened to the news on the radio as she sat in the tailback. For once the city's gun and knife violence wasn't headline news. Some days – most days, lately – the reports made London sound like a war zone. But it was home, too. It wasn't just the job she'd chosen, it was walking through parks where the dew was diamonds on the grass, standing on the street when the first warm day arrived, in shirt-sleeves with frosty bottles of beer. London was soft green fuzz on the trees in spring, and hot orange neon at night. It was birdsong and the beat of music from clubs, pavements fizzing under your feet. She loved the city for its colour and diversity, the shared smiles with random strangers, friendship and anonymity rolled into one. It was in her blood, and under her skin. She could no more walk away from London than she could leave a job half done.

Raffa Belsham and Sam Haile . . . Lorna Ferguson wanted both cases closed, and quickly. Felix Amos would be charged and released, before reoffending. It was becoming harder and harder to break the cycles. London was made of wheels that wouldn't stop turning, not even for a minute. Matilda Reece's face came to her as she sat in the car, hearing the fading wail of ambulances. Matilda, who'd told the press, 'Let him be an example. My Frank. Of how to live best, and to stop all this *death*. Let them put down their knives, stop being ruled by fear. They're all so fearful, that's why my boy died. Not because another child was showing off, like the papers said, not muscles being flexed. Because of *fear*. That's what we must stop, not the knives and guns alone but the things that make them reach for weapons and go that way. *Fear*. Of being the one without a blade when the fight starts. Children, put down your fear. Please. Let my Frank be the last of London's dead.'

The final leg of Marnie's route home bypassed Bloomsbury, where the British Museum cast its elegant shadow as far as Russell Square. Then onwards to the threadbare charms of Shoreditch, whose art galleries outnumbered the strip clubs but not by a conspicuous margin. All along the road, plane trees were shedding the city's poisons from their bark. A handy trick, if you could manage it.

Her phone rang, hands-free. 'Harry, hello.'

'How's it going?'

'Slowly. I was late getting away, and the traffic's one long jam.'

'It gets worse, doesn't it? I was hoping you might fancy a drink, but if you're not home yet . . .'

'A drink sounds great. Where were you thinking?'

'Anywhere that suits you,' Harry said. 'I'm in Spitalfields.'

'Uncanny. I'm about ten minutes away.'

The venue Harry suggested was one Marnie would've chosen, tucked away from the main drag of bars and clubs, dimly lit despite the late hour, looking more like an all-night coffee place than licensed premises.

Harry had ordered Negronis, the drinks sitting like two small fiery sunsets on the table he'd chosen at the back of the bar. He'd stripped off his jacket and tie, rolled back the cuffs of his shirt. He looked like she felt, beaten down by the day's work.

'My hero . . .' She reached for the drink before she sat. 'How did you know?'

'It's been one of those days.' He smiled, lifting his glass. '*Saluti.*'

Marnie touched her glass to his, sliding into the curved banquette at his side. They drank in silence, just the bitter-red scent of the Negroni and its bitter-orange taste, ice knocking in their glasses. She broke the silence by saying, 'I've been stood down from the Belsham case.'

'Me too. We're officially celebrating the demise of Terrance Malig.' Harry pressed his thumb to the corner of his mouth. 'I'm told we should be grateful Guy isn't pursuing a charge of police negligence for failing to arrest Malig before Raffa's murder.'

'He was furious when Noah and I visited. It's hard to imagine anger like that going away overnight.'

Harry held his glass in the curved palm of his hand. He

waited a beat before asking, 'How's Noah? Seeing Samantha Haile fall like that . . . I can't think what it did to him.'

'He's shaken up. Finding it hard to stop working, you know how it goes.' She drank a mouthful. 'Part of me thinks I should sign him off sick and force him to rest. But I'm afraid of what it would do to him. At least while he's coming into work we can look out for him.'

'He's not forgiven me.' Harry kept his eyes on his glass. 'I don't mean that in a self-pitying way; this isn't about me. But I thought you should know. Because he's more than just shaken up. He's very, very angry.'

'No, Harry . . .'

'It's okay. Like I said, I'm not after sympathy. He has a right to be angry. I just don't want you thinking . . .' He moved his fingers. 'You know him better than anyone. But the way he's been with me? He says we're good, but we're not. He hates my guts right now, and that's okay, I get it and I can take it. But I thought you should know. Anger like that . . . I'm worried for him.'

'I'm sorry.' She reached for his hand. 'For Noah, and about Sol. Sorry you're on the receiving end of his pain. It won't last, I have to believe that. I hope you do too.'

He turned her hand in his, pressing his thumb to the heart of her palm. She met his gaze for a moment, smiling, then freed her hand by reaching for her glass. 'I charged a thirteen-year-old with possession this evening. Felix Amos. He had a blade on him, and more front than Brighton.'

'Sounds familiar.' Harry sat back. 'But I don't know the name.'

'He lives in Erskine Tower. I suspect he knew Sam Haile. And Raffa.' She swirled the ice in her glass. 'I spoke to him like an adult. I'm not proud of it. He's a kid, and a frightened kid at that.'

'Frightened by what?'

'I'm not sure. He clammed up when he heard about Sam. It's possible he was dealing to her, but where he's getting the drugs is another matter. The Bellamys, I imagine. He wouldn't name anyone. His social worker was reluctant to let him answer my questions until the morning, so he's in a detention unit for the night. I couldn't get hold of his mum to let her know. He said she wouldn't care in any case. He's rarely at home, but he was in the flats often enough to have met Raffa there. I think they were friends.' Princess and her Flea. 'Hopefully we'll find out more tomorrow.'

They finished their drinks. 'My round. Same again, with less work-related angst. Okay?'

Harry smiled at her, propping his head on his hand. What was it Lorna Ferguson had said? *He's a handsome bugger. Doesn't seem to know it either . . .*

Marnie turned away, towards the queue at the bar. She took out her phone as she waited, texting Ed to say she hoped his evening was going according to plan. He was fighting to avert a catastrophe in Harlow, where women and children were being turned away because of new funding restrictions. No matter how hard they fought to make the streets safer, there'd always be violence behind closed doors. And the city's refuges were shrinking at an alarming rate. Ed refused to be daunted by the fact that his work was becoming more difficult and less rewarding. Every week another of the victims he'd helped was back on the streets, or in fear of being deported, or lost from the system. She didn't know how he did it, but he carried on, his energy and optimism undented.

'Two Negronis, please.' She watched the barman work his magic, glancing back to where Harry was sitting, his elbow on the table, next to their empty glasses. He'd resisted the urge to check his phone, although she knew he must be worrying about his mum. There was so much pain doing the rounds. It was hard to carve out moments like these, for simply stopping and being. London discouraged it. Except on those rare occasions when it put out a frail flower between paving stones, or sent down a sudden froth of birdsong to stop your heart at the end of an evening like this one.

As she paid for the drinks, her phone buzzed. 'Noah?'

'I've screwed up.' He sounded wired. 'I've been—'

The line broke, editing his words.

'Where are you?' She carried the drinks to the table where Harry was waiting. 'Noah?'

Harry took the glasses, freeing her hand for the phone. She checked the display, saw the call was still connected.

'Noah, what's happening?'

On the other end of the line, Noah gave a laugh, hard and breathless.

Then he said, 'I've been arrested.'

14

Lorna Ferguson was not amused. On a good day, she wasn't amused. And today was not that day.

'Just what the bloody hell were you thinking?'

It was a great question, but Noah had no idea how to answer it to his own satisfaction let alone hers. 'I made a mistake.'

'I'll tell you what, DS Jake, that does not improve on repetition. It sticks out a ruddy mile that you *made a mistake*. It's a bloody bat signal in the sky: "I made a mistake!" Everyone from here to Slough can see you did that. What I need to know is why.'

Marnie came back into the interview room with a bottle of mineral water. 'Here.' She reached across the table, blocking Ferguson's line of vision for the time it took her to send Noah a look of unconditional sympathy and support.

'Thanks.' He wrapped his fingers around the bottle.

'Retrocide.' Ferguson pointed at the inked logo on the back of his hand. 'What's that when it's at home? Nostalgic ways to top yourself? Slicing your wrists in a bath of Badedas to an easy-listening LP by the Carpenters?'

'It's the name of a club.'

'This club where you got yourself arrested.'

'Where . . . Yes.'

'And you were there why, exactly?' She dusted the shoulders of her fleece. 'Words of one syllable, if you could. It's getting towards my bedtime.'

It was past midnight. Marnie had done what she could, but it'd required DCS Ferguson to get Noah out of trouble following his arrest at the Retrocide club. Not that he was exactly out of trouble now. More like a realignment.

'I met this woman at Erskine Tower, earlier today. Terri.'

'Terri what?'

'I don't know her surname.' He paused, measuring that particular failure, before continuing: 'She was a neighbour of Sam Haile's. We got talking, and she invited me to this club.'

'You got talking,' Ferguson repeated with heavy irony. 'Is that slang for mucking up an investigation into a suspicious death? Only DS Prowse is bound to ask.'

'It's not suspicious, though, is it? Sam's death. They've ruled out arson. They let her dad into her flat to collect her stuff. It's not a crime scene.'

'But you couldn't keep away. You were told to rest. Instead of which, you got yourself dolled up and went out clubbing with the dead girl's neighbour.'

Noah rolled the bottle between his hands, trying to find a way to explain what had happened without digging himself deeper into the hole he was currently inhabiting. 'I was having difficulty resting. I went for a walk, ended up at Erskine Tower. I met Terri by chance, and she invited me to her flat . . .' He stopped, since the look on Lorna's face was not improving.

'Go on, Casanova. You went up to her flat. Then what happened?'

'She made a cup of tea. We talked a bit, about the fire. And Sam.'

'Did you caution her before this chat?'

He shook his head.

'I didn't think so. Since she went on to invite you to this rave where you got yourself arrested.'

'It wasn't a rave—'

'Don't you get semantical with me, Detective Retrocide. I'm not here in my house pyjamas for the privilege of listening to you explain the hierarchy of unlicensed night-clubs.' She folded her arms, fixing him with a gimlet stare. 'You were arrested at Erskine Tower. Trespassing in the "plant room". Perhaps you'd like to explain what that is. Actually, no, park that. Let's rewind to the start of your evening.' She straightened, turning to Marnie. 'DI Rome, perhaps you'd like to tell me how your night was going before DS Jake's bat signal ruined your plans?'

'I was at work,' Marnie said peaceably. 'Questioning a boy we'd arrested for possession. Felix Amos. He needed an appropriate adult, so DS Pembroke and I waited for his social worker, who recommended we postpone the interview until the morning.' She smiled at Noah, her solidarity undiminished by his misadventures. 'All of that took a while. I was late leaving the station, and then the traffic was particularly bad.'

'Riveting,' Ferguson said drily. 'DS Jake, let's hear your story. Start at the beginning. I'm assuming you didn't set out to spend the night in handcuffs. But feel free to enlighten me.'

Noah drank a mouthful of water, considering the best way to proceed. He ought to have been grateful Sol was staying away on this particular occasion, but the skin at the back of his neck nagged and he had to stop himself twisting in the chair to see if his brother was here, enjoying the spectacle of Noah squirming on Sol's side of the law for a change.

'I got a phone call,' he began. 'Just after eight p.m. . . .'

'Is that you?' It was a girl's voice. 'The guy I met at the flats earlier?'

'Sorry, who is this?'

'Terri. You puked in the gutter. I made you a cup of tea.'

'Oh . . . hello.' Noah mouthed an apology at Dan, taking the phone call into the hallway.

'I was thinking about what we talked about. Me seeing Sam.'

When Noah didn't speak, Terri said, 'I read in the paper about her being happy. It's not true, not all of it anyway.'

'It's not true Sam Haile was happy?'

'Yeah. So I'm thinking that's why I'm seeing her. The ghost. Hallucination, whatever. Because I know it's not true. What if she wants it putting right, what they're saying about her? What if that's why . . .' She sucked a breath. 'Look, I dunno, are you free tonight?'

'Tonight,' he repeated.

'There's something you should see. A place here, like a club.'

'At the tower?'

'Yeah. We went there a couple of times, me and her. If the papers'd seen this place, they wouldn't be writing crap about her being in love with life. That made me gag when I read it.'

'There's a club inside the tower block.' Noah was stalling for time. 'Sam used to go there.'

'Starts soon,' Terri said. 'Nine-ish. Dress down, yeah?'

By 9 p.m., Erskine Tower was a slice of grey stone socketed against the night sky by windows of electric light.

Dan had work of his own to get done; he hadn't objected to Noah's departure, just told him to take care. He'd thought Noah was going to his mum's house.

On the twenty-eighth floor, Terri answered the door in a silver string vest over a sleeveless black top, fishnet tights and torn jeans, black Doc Martens with the laces pulled out. Lots of smoky make-up masked her eyes, silver bracelets armouring her wrists. She was unrecognisable.

'Show me your watch.' She shut the door once he was inside the flat, looking him over.

'What?'

'Take it off.' She dug her hand in the pocket of her jeans.

'Why?'

'Wear this.' She offered up an Omega. 'It's a fake, but a good one. They'll need to think you've got money. You're way too straight to get in otherwise.'

Noah didn't correct her. 'Where exactly is this club?'

'In the plant room.' She turned to the mirror, checking her reflection before facing him again. 'What else've you got on you?'

'The plant room. You mean where the power comes from to heat this place?'

'Where it *used* to come from. They cut the gas off years ago.'

The plant room. He'd seen it from outside, a rectangle protruding from the main shaft of the building, right at the top of the tower.

'Reckoned they'd make it into a penthouse. Never happened, of course. It's locked up but these guys have keys. We have to get there in the lift 'cos they've blocked off the stairs.' She looked him over, feet to face. 'Seriously, what've you got?' She closed in, started frisking him.

213

'Hey. *Hey.*' He held her off. 'Phone and wallet. Keys. That's it.'

'You'll have to leave them here.'

Noah shook his head, but she said, '*Yes*. You'll get robbed up there. My place's empty, it's safer. Here.' She pulled a fob from a shelf under the hall mirror. 'Spare key, if you don't trust me.'

The key was printed with a pattern of purple flowers. He didn't take it. He didn't recognise her as the same woman who'd made tea for him, in her gypsy skirt and fraying sandals.

'D'you want to go to this party or not?' she demanded.

'I really don't. Can't you tell me about it?'

'I'm crap at descriptions. See for yourself. C'mon.' She held out the key, grinning when he took it. 'It's good you're kinda hot, because you're way too straight for this place.'

Noah caught sight of his reflection in the lift's greasy mirror. He was gaunt and muddy-eyed, his skin bruised by lack of sleep. Wearing an ink-blue T-shirt he'd not worn in years, long-sleeved, with loose-fitting Levis. He looked younger than he did in a suit, might've passed for twenty-four in a bad light. 'Did Sam go to these parties with you?'

'Couple of times. But they're not really parties. You'll see.' Terri fixed him with a look. 'Don't say too much, okay? You'll get in 'cos you're with me, but don't ask questions. They hate that.' She put her eyes over him again. 'Roll up your sleeves. They'll want to see the watch.'

He rolled up his left sleeve, showing off the ugly Omega. He'd put his own watch into his pocket. It was a present from Dan and he didn't want to lose it.

Terri was different, all trace of the hippy-sandalled girl

214

gone, replaced by this grim party creature. Only the dreadlocks were the same, ratted-blonde, slung over her
shoulders. He didn't trust her, doubted her motives for
bringing him here, her story about the haunting, Sam's
ghost. He didn't believe it. She wanted something from
him. Drugs? Sex? No, it was more than that. She kept
her distance in the lift. Did she think he had money; was
he about to be robbed? None of these questions needed
an answer as badly as the question of why he was here
at all. Off duty, unofficially undercover. Misleading a
member of the public, bringing the Metropolitan Police
into disrepute. Sol lolled inside the lift, laughing at him.
'Blad! You are *bad*.'

The lift shuddered to a stop, doors hissing open. In the
dim light from the corridor, Terri's silver vest gleamed like
a breastplate. The skin under her eyes had a matching
sheen that might've been make-up, or drugs. He hoped it
wasn't drugs. Each of her ears was pierced four times. Her
square nails were painted purple and she wore a dozen
rings, different to those she'd worn earlier, one a skull and
crossbones. Each time he looked at her, he noticed something new. They reached a closed door pinned with a *Keep
Out* notice. Terri knocked twice in quick succession. A
murmur came from the other side, wary. 'Hey.' She put
a drawl into her voice, like gravel on velvet. 'It's me.'

Silence from inside. Then a key chucked in the lock
and the door opened. A slice of face was put out towards
them, backlit by blue. Pale eyes moved past Terri, to Noah.
'Who's this?' He had an eastern European accent.

'This's Noah. He's okay. Pete said I could bring someone.'

Terri was nervous. Noah could smell her skin heating.
A muted pulse of music came from the plant room, no
tune he recognised, a deadened beat. The bouncer pulled
the door wide open.

The place was lit like a fridge, blue. Boards covered the windows, blocking out the night. Someone had painted curtains in black paint that'd dried in slugs. No furniture, just bodies. Maybe as many as twenty people, men and women, most of them closer to Terri's age than Noah's. The bouncer was five foot six, upper body solid with muscle, Bench sweatshirt, grey jeans, sneakers. His face was composed of flints, his profile an axe blade, its nose shaping the letter S as if it'd been broken twice, first to the left and then again to the right. 'Hand,' he said.

Noah put his hand out to be stamped above his thumb joint with the word *Retrocide* in orange ink. He hoped it would wash off. Sol ducked past the man, pushing into the crowd of bodies.

Terri grabbed Noah's arm. 'Let's get a drink.'

On a shelf against the far wall, drinks were lined up in narrow glasses like the test tubes in the schoolroom where they'd interviewed Neville Peters. How long ago was that? It felt like years. Terri handed him a glass, its swamp-green contents quivering. Jellied vodka? He took it, with no intention of adding its insult to his already squeaky stomach lining.

'Sorry . . .' He'd nearly tripped over a girl seated cross-legged on the floor. She looked up, the light putting stars where her eyes should've been. An oval face, chameleonic, with the savage glassy beauty seen on catwalks. Dark hair cut with an asymmetric fringe that parted in bat's wings, eyebrows plucked and redrawn until it was like seeing someone else's version of her face, an e-fit. Dressed like Lara Croft's skinny sister in a vest and combat trousers with more pockets than he could count. Nothing about her was recognisable, not the old-young face, not the tight clothes or the androgynous body underneath. He'd expected some likeness somewhere in the room to Sam

Haile, or to Raffa. Instead, everyone had the same outsized skull and truncated body, as if they'd been here forever, grown in the fetid dark, in air abbreviated by the rusty reek of bodies perspiring chemicals. The smell reminded Noah of another place. He fished for the memory, but it eluded him.

'Hey, Milla.' Terri grinned down at the girl on the floor.

Milla grinned back. Something passed between the pair like the connection between loose electrical leads, random and unreliable. A heaviness rose in Noah's throat.

Milla said, 'Hey.' Same accent as the man at the door. Were they Russians? She was taking the skin off an apple with a penknife, peeling it precisely, the skin coming away in a coil that made a red bracelet around her wrist.

'This's Noah. It's his first time here.'

'Hey, Noah.' Milla bent her head and licked apple juice from her knuckles. No Retrocide stamp on either of her hands.

Noah said, 'Hello.'

'We're going to chill for a bit, okay? Catch you later.' Terri walked him away, into a tighter clutch of people. 'This is Pete. Pete, this's Noah.'

Pete was taller than most of the men in the room, the only one who didn't make Noah feel like a giant. Six foot three, about a hundred and eighty-five pounds, leanly built with a hungry edge. Dark face and pale eyes, white hair buzzed back to scalp. The hand he offered to Noah was mapped with calluses. 'You met Milla.' He grinned in the direction of the girl with the apple. 'Ten years ago she's selling cabbages at the side of the road to support her family. Russia's a dump. Now Moscow's one of the world's richest cities and she wants to get back. Over a hundred home grown billionaires, Bentleys, Land Rovers. I keep telling her, give it another decade and Vietnam'll be next, or Shanghai. But Milla's a Muscovite at heart. She wants to eat sushi and drink champagne. Why not?'

At Noah's side, Terri's smile rose like smoke, weaving up from her mouth. He was dreaming, was that it? Or hallucinating. He was home with Dan, and this was just a mad nightmare courtesy of his subconscious, Sol in the mix, keeping out of sight. It couldn't be real. London wasn't this – displaced young people with taut, hungry faces and Russian paymasters. It was *his* city, and Dan's. London belonged to Matilda Reece, Frank's mum. But Frank was dead, and so was Sol, and women in heels screamed abuse at young men leaving nightclubs arm in arm.

'Muscovites love sushi, d'you know that?' Pete yawned. 'Milla wants to make it all the way to Zhukovka village, Moscow's Bel Air. She wants private boats, a jet. Why not? She's worth it.' He gave Noah a last look, then moved away, Terri following as if she was on his leash.

Noah tried to imagine Milla at the roadside selling vegetables to support her family. She looked like razor wire ran through her veins, so wasted she resembled a negative of herself. No one in the room looked healthy. Noah had been in worse places, but not recently.

'You seen Razor?' The man with the S-shaped nose nudged his elbow.

'Who?'

'Forget it.' The man moved on.

Noah leaned into the window, watching the room. In one corner, a couple with multiple piercings were groping audibly. The man had a row of steel spikes embedded across his forehead. The woman's tongue was forked and scarred, silver tears studding her cheeks. Noah told himself to wake up. But he wasn't dreaming. He was here in the plant room, trespassing. He turned to the window, the way Luke Corey had in the flat below. *What did you look like to her all the way down there?* The sudden lurch of sky made him queasy. His vision tunnelled, a sick pitch of vertigo forcing him to shut his eyes. What was he doing here? What was anyone doing?

Under the metallic smell was the post-operative stench of life leaching out of ruined skin. The stench of the morgue – that was what he'd recognised, seeing the slab in the dead eyes of the other trespassers. The plant room felt acutely empty, as welcoming as a wall stuck with broken glass. He looked out into the night, seeing again the ghosts from that morning. Sam Haile at the window, curtained by light. Sam Haile falling towards him, bringing down the day. The plant room partygoers moved like bodies under murky water. He swallowed the bile at the back of his throat and found Terri, handing back the untouched drink. 'I'm leaving. I'll get my things from your flat, with the key you gave me.'

'You'd have a hard job. It's the key to my locker at work.'

The deadened pulse in the room pressed at Noah from all sides. He was giddy with nausea. 'Then will you come back with me so I can get my wallet and phone?'

'Sure,' she shrugged. Her stare was opaque, drugged.

In the lift, he handed back the Omega watch. She took it without speaking.

Her flat was in darkness, exactly as they'd left it. She returned his wallet and phone, holding the blonde dreadlocks from her face with a fist.

'How often did Sam go to that place?' Noah asked.

'Dunno. I only went with her a couple of times.' She sucked a sigh into her mouth. 'See what I mean, though? Not the place to go when you're in love with life.'

'You seemed to like it.' He strapped his watch back onto

his wrist, thinking of Dan waiting for him at home. 'What goes on there really? Why did Pete tell me about Milla? Was I supposed to give her money? Is he her pimp?' He was asking too many questions; had she been sober, Terri would have been suspicious of that.

'What goes on there?' She toed off her boots, stumbling, then flexed each foot in turn. 'Nothing. It's a black hole, headspace. I like it because you can stop thinking up there. Shit-all happens. You get off your face, wipe clean, come home and sleep.'

Is that why Sam went there, he wanted to ask. *To get drunk, or high? To escape?*

When Terri moved towards the balcony, he followed her. The sky was wounded with stars, pollution packing its own peculiar darkness around the tower. The chimneys of Battersea Power Station were floodlit to yellow, the Thames bisecting the city in a series of glassy scars. *London's all layers.* Someone had said that to him recently. Who?

Terri scratched a foot at the grit on the balcony. 'Know what I'd like? Just once to be on holiday somewhere hot. With a proper balcony to myself where I'd be barefoot and naked, all day.'

The wistful speech was reassuring; she wouldn't jump. Not like Sam. Then she turned her opaque gaze on Noah and said, 'So what d'you take? Coke? Xans? H?'

He blinked and she grinned, shoving her hands into the tight pockets of her jeans. 'C'mon. It's okay. It's why you chose this place, right? You're looking at one of the new flats, the ones they're clearing out. Pete's got a plan he can show you. Two bedrooms, great views, easy supply. Girls, too. You liked Milla? Pete's got new girls coming all the time. Younger ones, if that's your thing.' She swayed closer to him. 'You've got money, I saw that straight off. Pete needs a bit of help, 's why I gave you the Omega.

He doesn't always see stuff straight away, but that's what I'm for.' She reached to touch the cuff of his T-shirt. 'Is it H? I can get you H. Or crack.' She looked at him through her lashes. 'Coke. You've got that shine . . . Whatever you need, seeing as we'll be neighbours.'

'I'm not buying a flat here,' Noah said. 'And I'm not an addict.'

'Course you're not,' she soothed. 'You've got it under control. Money keeps everything under control. But you're sad.' She looked into his eyes. 'I can see that. You're lonely.'

'You're wrong.'

'Hey, it's okay.' She pinched at the cuff of his shirt. 'That's what I'm saying. You're in the right place. Pete'll sort you out. Even if you're not moving in – if you just want takeout. He's careful, keeps it dialled down. No one gets into the plant room unless I've vetted them. No one even knows about it.' She stroked the knuckle of her thumb at the bone in his wrist. 'Soon's I saw you, I knew. You've got that look. That lovely, lonely shine.'

A cokehead with money to burn, that was what she saw when she looked at Noah. She'd summed him up the second she'd seen him in the street. He'd been suspicious of her kindness, before berating himself for being overly cynical. But his instinct had been right – she'd been after something from him from the start. Seeing a black man in decent clothes, gaunt-faced, liable to puke at your feet if you weren't careful, but well-spoken, polite. Someone you could invite into your home without worrying too much. An addict, an easy mark.

'You're wrong,' he repeated.

She turned back to the view. 'That's Notting Hill over there.' She pointed, as if the conversation about drugs had never happened. 'Where the famous people live.'

Luke Corey. It was Luke who'd said London was all layers.

'Did you meet her bereavement counsellor? Sam's.'

'Luke?' Terri poked her foot at the grit again. 'I met him, soppy fucker.'

Noah waited, to see what else she'd say about Corey.

'Sam had fun with him.' She stretched an arm under the stain of the city's light, letting it catch the dazzle from her cheap bracelets. 'Dirtied him up, that's what she said. He had a thing for her. A *crush*. So she crushed him. It's what she liked to do.'

Noah's pulse slowed. 'She liked to crush people?'

'The cleaner the better.' Turning her wrist, light striking the silver. 'Respectable. She liked to scratch it all away, see what was underneath. Said it was fun.'

'She had fun.' He watched her face for every flicker that crossed it, needing to know if she was telling the truth. 'With Luke Corey.'

'She looked nice.' Terri's expression hardened. 'She *was* nice, to start with. Everyone fell for it, for her. But it was a game she played, just part of her game.'

'What was the rest of the game?'

A car blared its horn in the street below, tyres screeching until the traffic moved on.

'I'll tell you one thing.' Terri turned her back on the city, facing Noah. 'She hated that brother of hers, the soldier. She was *glad* when he died.'

'That can't be true.'

'It's what she said. She told it to everyone in that room.'

'Everyone in the plant room?'

Terri shrugged. 'I was drinking. She was going from person to person saying how much she'd hated his guts, how glad she was he'd died so she didn't have to lick his boots any longer.'

Bereavement as anger.

'She was unhappy,' Noah said. 'That's what you're saying.'

'Then?' Terri widened her eyes at him. 'That was the one time I saw her happy. When she was telling all those strangers how much she'd hated him. How she really felt, inside. Guess that's why she tried to hook up with Princess Bel Sham. The pair of them were sick of pretending.'

'Princess . . .' Noah's neck prickled. 'Who?'

'The other girl,' Terri said. 'The one who died the day before Sam.'

DCS Ferguson listened to Noah's account in silence. 'So this young woman who set you up to be arrested just happened to drop a huge clue in your lap beforehand?'

'She wasn't dropping a clue. She didn't know I was a detective.'

'Easy mistake to make, under the circumstances.' Eggs could have pickled in Ferguson's voice. 'You weren't exactly behaving like one, were you?'

Marnie said, 'Terri confirmed that Raffa and Sam Haile knew one another?'

'Yes.' Noah looked at her gratefully. 'That's why I went back up to the plant room, to see what I could find out. That's when I got arrested. Someone had reported the party to the police.'

'Someone who *was* behaving like a detective,' Ferguson put in.

'Terri didn't know the details, but she confirmed that Raffa met Sam in Erskine Tower. Raffa had been to the plant room on at least one occasion. I'm betting Pete was grooming her.'

'All bets are off,' Ferguson snapped. 'Your opportunity for placing them came and went. Right now you're lucky not to be locked up facing a disciplinary.'

'I know that, ma'am.' Noah held hard to his temper. 'But this's more important, isn't it? This is about the death of two young women, one of them just a child.'

'Two investigations.' Ferguson climbed to her feet. 'Which *you* have royally screwed up. So you sit and think about that for a while. DI Rome? Outside.'

'Pete and his pals were talking about money,' Noah said. 'And Guy's an investment banker with Russian clients and a property portfolio. Are we calling that a coincidence?'

'We're calling it *police disciplinary*. Stand down!'

'Wait a minute, please.' His hands clenched into fists on the table, knuckles taut. 'What if *Guy* hid that bullet in her bedroom? It would explain why he's so keen to close the case, and why the bullet was wiped clean. If he knew there was a link between him and Erskine Tower, and if Raffa found out about it—'

Lorna Ferguson leaned in his direction, looking furious. 'Your fantasy life's already cost me a quiet night in. I appreciate you're under a lot of stress, but *my God*, if you don't get a grip right this minute and stand down, I'll put you back in handcuffs myself. Is that clear?'

'Noah?' Marnie met his eyes and nodded. 'You need to stop talking now.'

In the corridor, Marnie caught up with Lorna. 'Are you going to charge him?'

Ferguson put her hands on her hips, pulling her face back into shape. 'This isn't just on him, lady. You were in charge of seeing he was fit for work. You're the one they'll be questioning.'

'It reflects badly on my judgement,' Marnie agreed. She paused before adding, 'On both of us.'

She met Lorna's stare, unflinching.

'I'm covering my arse, is that what you're getting at? Too ruddy right I am. And yours too, if I can manage it. You're up for promotion, in case you've forgotten. Except *matey* in there just drove a truck through your chances. So yes, excuse me if I'm furious on your behalf.'

'Let me talk to him. It's salvageable, I'm sure. He was off duty, signed off sick. But if he's uncovered a connection between the two girls—'

'Oh, we'd better hope not! Because I can see the steam coming out of Lenny Prowse's ears from here.' Lorna stopped at last, looking back towards the interview room. 'He's worse than we thought, isn't he? Is it a job for Karie Matthews, or do we need bigger guns?'

Marnie didn't have the answer to that. She'd never seen Noah like this before. His fitness for work had been her responsibility, and she'd failed him, miserably. For weeks he must've been on the brink of collapse, but she'd carried on regardless. Her own blindness shook her. How many opportunities had she missed to prevent this? His health, his career? How many?

'I'll call Karie,' she said. 'She'll know what to do.'

'Ma'am?' The duty officer beckoned from the other end of the corridor. 'We've got Daniel Noys in reception asking for you.'

'The boyfriend.' Lorna heaved a sigh. 'I'll leave that to you, shall I?'

'Can he take Noah home?' She didn't want the woman returning to the interview room in her current mood, or Noah's current mood. 'As you've dealt with the charges?'

'And risk getting further up Kilburn's nose? No, he can't. And the idea of charges hasn't gone away; it's been shelved until we've all had some sleep and can talk about it without shouting.'

The arresting officer had been especially keen on putting Noah in handcuffs. It had taken DCS Ferguson at her most phlegmatic to convince the man he was a detective sergeant.

'Then can he come home with me? You can swing that as a form of custody, I'm sure.'

Lorna inspected Marnie's face as if she expected to find weakness there, something Noah might exploit. 'Fine, take him home and put him to bed. But no conferring on this nonsense about Guy Belsham and the bullet.' She drew herself up, as intimidating in her house pyjamas as she was in her power suits and Louboutins. 'Understood?'

Marnie nodded, and went to find Dan at the front desk. He was wearing a hi-vis cycle jacket, one hand holding his helmet, the other shoved in his fair hair as he scanned the posters in the waiting area. His eyes went to Marnie when she came to the desk. She could see how worried he was. 'Noah's here.' She held the door so he could come into the corridor, where they'd be able to talk in private. 'He's safe.'

Dan nodded, letting out a breath he'd been holding. 'He said he was going to his mum's. But when it got late, I called there and his dad said he'd not seen Noah in days. His phone's off, but I guessed he was working. It's what he does, lately. All he does.'

'He wasn't working.' She paused. 'I'm afraid he's been arrested.'

'What?' Dan lost what little colour he'd had. 'Where, and why?'

'At Erskine Tower, for trespass. He was with a group of people at an illegal party. It's unclear whether he'll be charged, but I've been advised not to send him home just yet. We need to smooth things with the team at Kilburn. He's ruffled some feathers over the investigation there.'

'Samantha Haile.' Dan's voice was hollow. 'The girl who jumped.'

Marnie nodded. 'I'm sorry.'

'Will he . . . You're not keeping him in a cell, are you? Only he's not well. He's pretending he is, but he's not. Since Sol. And it's worse just lately.' He searched her face. 'You must've noticed.'

'He's not in a cell. I'm taking him home with me; it's the best way to keep everyone happy. I'll make sure he gets some sleep, and tomorrow he'll see Dr Matthews. After that, hopefully he'll agree to go home and get some proper rest.'

'Thanks.' Dan linked his hands at the back of his head, blinking tiredness from his eyes. 'I don't know how to help him, that's the trouble. He won't let me near. Won't talk about Sol, not even in passing. It's like he's still around and Noah's . . . *hiding* him, somehow. Whenever I've tried to talk to him about Sol, he's flipped. It's not like him to be angry, not like this.'

Harry had said the same thing. That Noah was very, very angry.

'I'll take care of him,' Marnie promised. 'I'm sorry he can't go home with you. I'll sort that as soon as I can. Let's hope he won't face any charges, but we have to cover ourselves.'

'I understand. Can I see him, at least?'

'Of course. Come on.'

Noah was sitting with his head down and his hands on the table, fingers locked into fists. He looked up when Marnie came back into the room, his eyes heating with tears when he saw Dan was with her. 'Shit, I'm sorry. I had one phone call . . .'

Dan crossed the room to crouch at the side of his chair. 'Shut up, that doesn't matter.' He leaned close enough to rest his forehead against Noah's, gripping at his clenched fists.

Noah opened his fingers stiffly. Dan's hands were cold, but Noah's were colder. He'd started to shiver, and couldn't stop. The long-sleeved T-shirt stank of weed and candle wax. He couldn't even remember seeing candles in the plant room.

'I've screwed up,' he said into Dan's neck. 'I've really screwed up. I don't think they're going to let me go home with you.'

'You're going home with Marnie.' Dan straightened, and smiled. 'That's what she says.'

Marnie must have done a deal with Ferguson. Noah knew he should be glad he wasn't looking at a night in the cells, but he'd wanted to go home with Dan. He'd hoped to start making things right. 'I'm sorry,' he said again. 'You're putting up with a lot of crap from me lately.'

'You're going through a lot of crap,' Dan said simply. 'I wish you'd offload more of it my way.'

'We'll talk,' Noah promised. 'When I get home. Properly. There's a lot I've not been saying, but it's so messed up in my head, I've not known where to start.'

Dan pressed the ball of his thumb to Noah's eyebrow, not speaking.

Behind him, leaning against the wall of the interview room, Sol said, 'You're not t'inking 'bout giving me up again are you, bredda? Because that'd be sick.'

Noah ignored him, concentrating on Dan, keeping him near.

'You'd better not, blad. All I'm saying. You'd better not be giving me up.'

Dan's skin smelled of traffic fumes, of London. Noah breathed it in, shutting his eyes. For the first time, he was afraid of his brother's ghost, properly afraid. The way he should have been, he saw that now. The way he should've been afraid right from the start.

15

It was after 1 a.m. by the time they reached Marnie's flat. She showed Noah to the spare room, bringing a clean towel and a new toothbrush. 'Tea?' she offered. 'Or are you ready to sleep?'

'I need to, but I'm too wired. Sorry. About tonight, all of this.'

'I'm sorry, too. I should have been there for you. That was my responsibility.' She set the towel on the foot of the bed. 'I'll put the kettle on.'

After she'd gone, Noah stood with his head bowed, trying not to think too hard about what he'd done. He was aware of a sensation under his skin as if something had torn and was starting a slow bleed. He turned his hands over, expecting to find a bruise coming up. There was nothing to see, but it stayed with him – the sensation of blood escaping inside, a small cloud of it unfurling, paling to pink at the edges, a dark knot at its core binding the red stain to him in the way an egg was bound to its shell by a delicate, complex cord.

In the kitchen, he sat with Marnie, listening to the tick of the kettle as it cooled. She'd made herbal tea, liquorice and peppermint, surprisingly good. She didn't ask questions or offer advice, sitting in companionable silence. Sol had stayed away. Noah wondered what would happen when he started to tell the truth about the strange shape his grief was taking, whether his brother would appear and shout him down, or stay away for good this time. Hard to believe it was less than three days since he'd argued with Sol about his choice of tie. Three days since Raffa's death.

'Guy Belsham,' he said instead. 'I know we're not talking about him, but he has a property portfolio that includes Erskine Tower. I found it online. The council's looking to offload some of its more expensive social housing and the flats are being offered as an investment opportunity to private landlords and companies. "Skyline living units", they're calling it. From what I saw of the plant room, some of those investors are more interested in rinsing their drug money than admiring the skyline.'

Marnie listened, but didn't speak. It served the purpose of obeying DCS Ferguson's instructions, without stopping Noah from sharing what he'd learned.

'These Russians, whoever they are . . . they're bringing guns and drugs into the country. Girls, too. Everything in the plant room is a microcosm of what Trident's trying to fight. No wonder they've been making so many arrests in the flats, finding so many weapons caches. The plant room's rotten. The smell and feel of the place, the *people* up there.' He turned the mug on the table until its handle was facing away from him. 'Terri thought I might be interested in one of their skyline living units, or else looking to score. She introduced me to Pete and Milla, but they didn't offer me anything. I suppose they were checking me out. If they're dealing, you'd think their security would be better. But I'm guessing it's as simple as this: I'm the right colour. They assumed I was up for whatever business they were pushing.'

Marnie sipped at her tea, staying silent.

'I'm not going off the rails, although I appreciate it must look like that after tonight.' He tried a smile, too tight on his face. 'Guy's connected to Erskine Tower, his portfolio proves it. The bullet in Raffa's room was a match for ammunition found in those flats. We assumed she hid the bullet, but what if it was Guy? He knew we'd investigate what she got up to in that place, given the reputation it has. It was always going to be a big focus for our investigation, there was no getting around that. If he could've deflected our attention away from the tower, he'd have done it. Deflecting it towards Raffa – maybe that was the next best thing. If she was murdered by the people he's involved with there, as a warning or punishment of some kind, he might've put the bullet in her room so we'd look into *her* connection to the place rather than his.'

'That's cold. Guy didn't strike me as cold. And he was furious about the bullet.'

'Oh, I believe his fury at the people who killed her. He's outraged. But he's also a pragmatist, very focused. Those phone calls when we first arrived at the house? He was working, even with everything that'd happened. If he's involved in something shady and it resulted in his daughter's murder, he'd want to cover his tracks. He'd see no sense in going to jail when she was already dead. He'd rationalise it, tell himself he needs to be at home for Lynne.'

Marnie sipped at her tea. 'Part of his rage could be guilt, you think.'

'Exactly. Yes. The bullet was wiped clean. Why would Raffa have done that? And remember what Guy said about making sure she was safe at the flats, for the school project? What if he was talking about the Russians in the plant room? What if he imagined he was pulling their strings rather than the other way around? He's arrogant enough to have misread that situation.'

'But cruel enough to implicate his dead daughter? That's another level, and I'm not sure I can square it with what we know of him. Don't get me wrong, I'm no fan. He's a bully and a bigot. But his daughter's reputation matters to him. I believed that much of what he told us.'

Noah nodded his acceptance of this. 'It's a theory, maybe it doesn't hold up.'

'And Samantha Haile?' Marnie said. 'Where does she fit into all this?'

'Terri said Sam had visited the plant room parties with Raffa. Sam took a shine to her because they both came from difficult families. But Sam wasn't a good person. Manipulative, Terri said, a game player.' He rubbed the heel of his hand at his eyes. 'It's possible the drugs they found in her flat weren't for personal use.'

'Noah. You need to sleep.'

'Yes, soon.' He traced a triangle on the table with the ball of his thumb. 'Raffa was a dreamer, wasn't she? The sketches, stories of princesses and goblins. Swords, Eric said, and sorcery. I think she saw Erskine as one of her games, a fortress to be conquered. She escaped there, maybe she made friends there, but I don't think they were necessarily bad. Princess and Flea . . . She was a good kid, I believe that.' He frowned. 'That morning I saw Sam fall, the tower looked like a battlement. That's when I thought of Raffa's stories, all the ways she was escaping from her life – *that's* the connection I saw. Because Sam was escaping too. We could say she had no choice, because of the fire. But I'm not so sure. I know they've ruled out arson, but from the way Terri described her, Sam wasn't the kind of person given to panic.'

'So . . . you think it was suicide?'

'Sometimes suicide's an act of aggression . . .' He stopped, on the brink of saying more.

The Audi's roof crushed into the jagged shape of a grin. Sam buried in its bottom teeth, joined to the pavement by the long hang of her hair. He could smell the smoke she'd brought down with her, his skin itching with distress. The thought crossed his mind, borne on a wave of fatigue, that he'd imagined it – stripping off his shirt and fighting to stop the blood, save her life. Was it possible he'd stood there doing nothing while she lay dying, the car steeled shut around her?

'They're doing a post-mortem, aren't they?'

Marnie nodded. 'It might help us make sense of whether or not it was an accident. Ferguson thinks she was high when it happened, hallucinating maybe. That could account for the panic.'

'They ruled out arson, but what if Sam started the fire to make her death look less desperate? An easier thing for her family to process, fewer questions to be asked and answered.'

'Disguised suicide?'

'A way out, if she needed one. Suicide can feel like a double death. You don't just lose the person you loved, you lose your vision of them. All your trust and hopes and truths. It's all gone.' He shook his head, trying to clear the fog. 'I'm probably overthinking it.'

'Thinking is good,' Marnie said gently.

'I told Ed I wasn't so sure about that. Less empathy, more action, that's the new skills set. You care too much, it slows you down. Maybe that's where I've been going wrong.' He crooked his mouth. 'One of the ways I've been going wrong.'

Searching too deeply instead of casting a wide net to catch the scum floating at the city's surface. He saw the whiteboard faces, dead kids as young as eight and nine. They should be the focus of his attention. Not Sam Haile, however tragic her death. He should be concentrating on Frank and the others robbed of their childhoods. Trident was working the cases, it wasn't all on his shoulders, but he owed those kids his attention. If what he'd witnessed was suicide, then Sam had thrown her life away. The thought was too quick for him to snatch back. It shamed him, and he knew why. He felt about suicide the way Sam must've felt about fire, seeing the remains of Grenfell Tower outside her window each day. He'd buried the memory – from Sol and everyone else – of their mother's suicide attempts. Successfully buried it, until now. *Don't dig the dead.*

'Does Samantha's dad know about the drugs?' he asked Marnie.

'Yes. DS Prowse told him.'

Howard with the *Bananas* box tight to his chest, the new version of his daughter fresh in his head. Drugs, death. Luke loitering nearby. *Please let me help you with that, Howie.*

'I met their bereavement counsellor. Luke Corey.'

'At Kilburn station?'

'Yes, but at Sam's flat, too. Just after I met Terri.' He paused, conscious of trying Marnie's patience. 'When I was at home resting, allegedly.'

She sipped at her tea.

'Bad move, I know. But I think Prowse might want to take a closer look at Corey.'

A siren bled out streets away, filling the silence he'd carved with this statement.

'That's a complicated allegation,' Marnie said. 'I'm not sure I can pursue it under the current circumstances.'

'I'll be lucky to have a job in the morning, let alone a career. That's why I need to do this now. Download the content of my brain for whatever it's worth, before I'm pulled off the case.'

'Explain Luke Corey to me.' Her eyes were very clear and blue, fixed on his face. 'He was helping the Hailes after their son's death?'

'Yes. He said Sam visited her brother when he was dying in hospital, from burns. He'd been inside a tank when it was shelled. Luke implied her fear of fire may've come from seeing that.' Noah remembered something else. 'He called her Samantha, not Sam. Her dad was "Howie" but it was *Samantha*. That struck me as odd, formal. He wanted to help the whole family, that's what he said. He was desperate to help, in fact, saw Sam as the victim of her parents' grief for her brother, spoke about families closing ranks. He wanted to protect her from that. But he was . . . *off*. I can't explain it, but you'd feel it if you met him. There's something not right.' He needed to provide facts, not feelings. 'Terri said Luke had a crush on Sam, and Sam exploited that. She crushed him. Sam liked breaking people. She could be nice when she needed to be. Everyone fell for her act, Terri said. Luke did.'

And I did, he thought. Her final act. I believed she was tragic, innocent, a victim.

He should stop talking and start sleeping. He was clinging to the case by his fingernails, afraid to let it go. 'I was the last person to see her alive, and the first person to see her dead.'

236

A thing like that, Corey had told him, *can feel very personal.*

'Her dad couldn't look at me. He was there at the flats with Luke, but he wouldn't look at me. Because he knew I saw her die. He was afraid that if he looked, he'd see her ghost.' Noah clenched his hands on the table. 'Should I tell you the truth? About Sam. I'm angry with her. For choosing death, choosing me. I'm even angry about the car and the paperwork, that interrogation by Prowse, the crap cup of coffee while he asked his questions. I'm just . . . so angry.'

'I know.' Marnie didn't move her gaze from his face. 'And it's okay. You should be.'

'I can't . . .' His throat clenched shut. 'Can we make this about Sam? It's about Sam, not . . . Sol.' Just saying his brother's name was hard. He had to push it past his teeth. Panic crowded his chest, as if he was down in the dark of the Underground. 'Can we talk about Sam?'

'DS Prowse is heading a very thorough investigation,' Marnie said. 'So far the findings point to accidental death.'

'Is that what you think?'

'I think the fire is odd.' She pushed the curls from her forehead. 'Disguised suicides do happen, of course. But a fire is a lot of trouble to go to, and frightening. Traffic accidents are more usual if you're trying to do that. And there's no evidence she was suicidal, or depressed. There's her brother's death, but that was five years ago.'

'And Terri said she hated Dylan. She told that to people in the plant room, anyone who'd listen. She was glad he was dead.'

Noah could see Sam passing through a clutch of strangers, talking about the war hero whose boots she no longer had to lick. How had she felt, sober the following morning, remembering what she'd said and how she'd smiled as she said it? Guilt wasn't always a rational reaction. It could be a reflex, like gagging. Noah saw tears all the time in the eyes of people he questioned at the station, but it was rarely an indication of grief. Sometimes the body couldn't help itself. Even if it was true – the real Sam, party girl with a nasty streak – who was mourning her? And why did he feel such responsibility for that truth, caustic and unpalatable as it was? Because Sol's truth had died with him, no one to bear witness to his brother's final moments. There should always be a witness, even one as reluctant as Noah felt right now. It was a basic tenet of his work: you didn't look away simply because what you were seeing was ugly.

Marnie said, 'Karie Matthews will want to talk to you tomorrow.'

'I've seen worse.' He rubbed at his scalp. 'We both have.'

'I'm not sure that's true. I can't imagine what you're going through.'

He fell silent, aware of the space between them where Sol was sitting, even though he wasn't here in the room. He'd stayed away since the warning he'd hissed back at the station. But he'd carved a space between Noah and Marnie, between Noah and everything.

'You should do something about the anger.' Marnie put a hand on his wrist. 'Even if you do nothing about the rest of it, that's your choice. Anger won't go away by itself.'

'You don't think it's healthy to be angry with whoever drove her to that? Suicide, or fear, whatever it was?'

'I'm not talking about how it happened. I'm talking about how you witnessed it, how it must have felt to see that.'

He wouldn't look at her, clenching his teeth until his jaw ached.

'Noah,' she said sadly.

'I saw a documentary.' He touched the ends of his fingers to the table. 'About the Twin Towers, those people who jumped from the World Trade Center on 9/11. They interviewed witnesses; so many of them were angry. Mass suicide, that's how it was seen, not mass murder. Some of the jumpers landed on people on the ground, and I understand how traumatising that was.' He himself could've died that way, if Sam had landed on him. 'But the idea that the jumpers committed a mortal sin and couldn't be forgiven . . . Plenty of people believed that. One of them described a man who jumped as a "piece of shit". He was *murdered*. By any measure, the people who died that day were murdered.'

'By any measure,' Marnie agreed.

'They covered up how many jumped, did you know that? At least two hundred people. They edited the audio tapes to remove the sound of them hitting the ground, stopped newspapers from carrying their photographs. Actually, that's not true. No one stopped them; it was an act of self-censorship. The pictures were too difficult to look at, that's what they decided. The planes going into the towers, the towers coming down. But not the people who jumped, no one wanted to see them. It's what they said: "No one wants to see that." And I keep wondering why *I* didn't look away when I saw her falling. "You didn't have to watch", that's what I was thinking. But *someone* did. There had to be a witness.'

It was quiet in the kitchen, just the fridge humming, the city slipping into that short spell of silence just before dawn. The words he'd spoken crackled in the quiet, refusing to settle.

Marnie said, 'She would be dead whether you saw it

or not. How she died, and why she died, none of that is altered by what you saw, or think you saw.'

'Someone should tell the truth,' he insisted. 'She wasn't happy. Why do we have to pretend she was? There should be *someone* . . .'

He stopped, because he didn't know where he was going with this. He'd thought everything he felt began and ended with the anger. With Sol. But it was more complicated than that.

'There should be someone to defend her?' Marnie turned the cup in her hand. 'Is that what you think you should be doing? Defending the truth about her, no matter the cost to anyone else, including yourself?'

'You don't think she deserves that?'

'I don't think *you* do. Noah, this is survivor guilt. You're punishing yourself. That's how it looks from here. And I don't believe you deserve to be punished.'

'Maybe she didn't deserve it either. Sam Haile. If it was suicide, she was unhappy. To do that, she must've been deeply unhappy. That *matters*. For all we know, she was driven to it. By someone in the plant room, or a neighbour.'

'Or it was no one's fault. Just one of those things. Inexplicable.'

'Then what about the plant room? It's *toxic*. If she went there when she was low, perhaps someone preyed on that. Pete, maybe. That's more than suicide. And what about Guy and his Russian investors? These cases are *linked*.' He drove his thumb at the table. 'I'm sure of it.'

'I'm not saying you're wrong. In fact I'm hoping Felix Amos will be able to help us establish a connection when I interview him tomorrow. He met Raffa in Erskine Tower, and he knew Sam.' Marnie's voice was calm, almost hypnotic, talking Noah down from the summit of his frustration. 'He's Flea, did I tell you that? Princess plus Flea. Raffa and Felix.'

'The kid with the deal bags? Eric's friend?'

'Yes.'

'Is he black?'

She hesitated before saying, 'Yes.'

'Sorry, it's just . . .' He spread his hands, showing their empty shape. 'You've no idea what it's like to be black in London right now. Every day I'm told to fuck off home, and not just by builders or skinheads. By women in Armani, by kids.' He closed his hands slowly. 'Right at the start of our sessions, Karie Matthews said Brexit brought London closer. She spoke about solidarity, because so many of us voted the right way, but she has no idea. None. And it's not a coincidence, this new violence. Young black men killing one another. It's not a coincidence, it's a *response*. To the hostility. London's full of it. It's . . . an infection.'

Marnie heard him out, not interrupting. He was conscious of the distance he was putting between them by speaking about this, but he couldn't help it. Perhaps Sol was right and there'd always been a distance – always would be – because of the amount of melanin in his skin.

'I'm interviewing Felix,' Marnie said, 'in about six hours. I need some sleep, and so do you.' She stood, holding out her hand to him. 'Come on.'

16

By eight o'clock the following morning, Lorna Ferguson's mood had improved exponentially. She called Marnie's number positively purring with saved face. 'Erskine Tower was famous in the seventies for drugs and people-trafficking. That's right, isn't it?'

'Yes.' Marnie checked the car's mirrors, taking the call hands-free since she was driving to the station. 'Colin's research bore it out.'

'Well, it didn't end in the seventies. Or else it was on extended leave, and came back eighteen months ago with a nice tan and an expensive appetite. Last night's raid was the culmination of a lot of hard work by a lot of people, including a couple of undercover lovelies who took a shine to DS Jake. They were delighted when he delivered Teresa Shaw into their safe keeping.' Purring with saved face, and reflected glory. 'I said I'd pass on their thanks. We don't want to steal anyone's thunder, but I've let it be known in certain circles that we did our bit to make last night's raid a roaring success. What the young people call an Instagram moment.'

'And Noah's arrest?' Marnie asked. 'I'm assuming that's not for Instagram.'

'Our dashing DS Jake is off the hook. All charges dropped, and an apology on its way. This is a big win for your team. A *big* win. Right when we needed one. Congratulations.'

'I'll let Noah know the good news.' Marnie caught her own eye in the mirror, and looked away. 'I'm assuming he's allowed to return to work, when he's ready?'

'As soon as he's ready,' Lorna agreed.

'And the officer who arrested him last night?'

'An apology's in the post. I did point out that we're none too happy about the zeal of the arresting officer. DS Jake hardly looks like a thug, unless of course you're colour-blind.'

'You accused the arresting officer of racism?'

'Whatever fits, don't you think?' She hadn't forgiven Noah, in other words. Once the headlines were chip papers, it would be business as usual. 'Let's talk when you get here.'

Marnie sat in traffic, seeing Raffa's face pinned alongside Sam's on the evidence board. Had Lorna already added the faces of the girls arrested with their traffickers during last night's raid? Milla and the others, all those lost lives. A vicious trade in hard-faced, lean-limbed young women who wanted to make enough money to return home in style. Terri Shaw's face would be on the board. She'd told Noah she liked the dead air in the plant room, the place Sam Haile whispered her secrets to strangers, confession without consequences. It wasn't a club. A club was for people who wanted to congregate, participate. The plant room was for those who'd opted out. A place to get lost, not found. Rotten, just as Noah had said.

Erskine Tower was waiting when she turned the corner, the plant room a bolt in the building's neck. It was an architect's eye-catcher, gravity-defying. But by night it transformed the block into Frankenstein's monster, man-made, no mother involved. She shut her eyes, imagining the violence of Sam's fall, Noah's act of witness: *Sometimes suicide's an act of aggression.* Other people had said the same to Marnie, families torn apart by suicide. It paralysed those you left behind, made a sick joke of their outstretched hands, stuck two fingers up at their comfort and love, and their loss. If Sam had killed herself, perhaps it wasn't to escape, or not only that. Perhaps she wanted to punish those left behind. Terri had said she liked to play games, to crush people. She'd crushed Noah under the weight of his act of witness.

Her phone was ringing. 'DI Rome.'

'Your leaper.' It was Fran Lennox, from the morgue. 'Samantha Haile. She was clean. No drugs in her system, not even a trace. And no injuries other than those consistent with the manner of her death. No track marks, no torque marks. Whatever drugs were in her flat, she wasn't using them.'

So much for Lorna's theory of why Sam had died. She wasn't high or hallucinating; she was sober when she jumped. Was Noah right, then? Was it suicide? An ultimate act of aggression.

'Did you finish with Raffa Belsham?'

'Yes.' A thread of sadness in Fran's voice. 'If you're asking whether *she* was clean, it's the same answer. Not a trace.'

Marnie ended the call, releasing the handbrake to inch the car across the gap in the tailback. No drugs involved in the deaths of either girl. But drugs were found in Sam's flat, a lot of drugs. If she was dealing, it would fit with what Noah was told by Terri. Had Sam used her law credentials to act as a go-between? How had the Bellamy brothers felt about a nice white girl moving in on their turf? Her phone rang for a third time. 'DI Rome.'

'We've got trouble.' It was Ron. 'Felix Amos.'

'I'm on my way to question him. He's in the detention centre, isn't he? What's happened?'

'He absconded in the early hours,' Ron said. 'Took a night bus to Muswell Hill. Where he just did his best to murder Guy Belsham.'

17

Guy Belsham was the colour of bad bacon, propped by pillows, a blood pressure cuff strapped to his right arm, bloodstained shirt kicked to the foot of the bed. His eyes were shut, his feet bare, their soles black. Marnie observed him from a distance, listening to Oz explaining what was known about the incident in Muswell Hill.

'Mr Belsham called the police at 5.43 a.m. to report a disturbance outside his property.' Oz tongued the inside of his cheek. '"Some little shit's smashing up my Merc!" Along those lines. He was told to stay indoors, but his temper got the better of him. Stormed out to have a word; that's when he got a knife between the ribs.'

'And it was Felix Amos. We're certain about that?'

'Oh yeah. He was shouting his name up and down the street, seemed to want everyone to know who was trying to top Belsham, and why.'

Marnie didn't take her eyes off the man in the hospital bed. 'Tell me the why?'

'For Raffa, that's what he was shouting. "For what you did to Raffa, you sick fuck."'

'Along those lines, or is that an exact quote?'

Oz referred to his notes. '"For Raffa, you *evil* fuck." Close enough.'

Marnie wished she had Noah with her. He would never dismiss a distinction like that. 'Sick' was a hundred miles from 'evil' to a kid like Felix. 'What was Mr Belsham's explanation for how Felix knew his daughter, and his address?'

'Oh, that's our fault.' Oz rocked on his heels. 'We failed in our duty to protect and serve, only found his daughter's killer because he drove himself under a truck, couldn't locate our own arses with both hands. All the usual stuff, hence the blood pressure obs.'

'What's the prognosis?' She considered the black soles of Guy's feet.

'He'll be up and about in no time, that's what I've been told. Couple of shallow punctures, but most of it's shock. Bet he couldn't believe it when the little bastard managed to ching him.'

'And Felix is in custody. Any eyewitnesses?'

'A neighbour, Beatrice Farrow. We're taking her statement.'

'Where was Lynne Belsham?'

'In bed. Paramedics looked her over at the scene, advised her to take it easy.'

Marnie turned to Oz in surprise. 'She's not here in the hospital?'

'Nope.'

'But she was questioned at the scene. She gave a statement.'

'She was asleep at the top of the house. Said she'd taken a pill, didn't hear anything until the paramedics came. Slept straight through her husband's stabbing.'

The room at the top of the house was Raffa's, not Lynne's. Marnie remembered the woman's face blinded by horror when she saw the bullet they'd found in her daughter's bookshelves. The first time her husband lost his temper, Lynne had defused the situation. But she didn't even attempt to defuse it after they found the bullet. 'The car alarm didn't wake her? I'm assuming it went off when Felix did whatever he did to the Mercedes.'

'Keyed it up both sides, kicked dents in the doors. Yeah, the alarm went off. That's what alerted Belsham. But his wife slept through it. If she'd taken a Valium, that makes sense.'

'The paramedics advised her to take it easy. Is she safe to be left on her own?'

'They seemed to think so.' Oz nodded towards the hospital bed. 'This'll be a nice break for her. The way he went for the kid . . . Mrs Farrow said she thought he'd kill him. Not the first time she'd seen Belsham in a rage by the sounds of it.'

Guy heaved himself up against the pillows then went still, muttering.

'They've doped him for the pain. But look at the size of him. Can you imagine that barrelling at you?' Oz shook his head. 'Little git's got some balls.'

'Did we recover the knife?' Marnie asked.

'Yep. Bigger than the one we took off him last night. Basic kitchen knife according to the surgeon, but it managed to miss all the vital bits. Belsham got lucky.'

They considered the man in the bed. A kitchen knife. Marnie wondered whether Felix had stolen it from the detention unit where she'd sent him for the night. 'What else did Beatrice Farrow say?'

'Just that her husband wouldn't mess with Guy on a good day, let alone this week. He came out of the house in a full rugby tackle, head down, steaming nostrils. A miracle he didn't kill the kid.'

248

'Is he hurt? Felix.' Marnie thought of the boy's skinny frame, those big eyes burning in his face. 'Presumably not, if he's at the station instead of here.'

'He needed a couple of plasters for nicks on his fingers, but he's fine. His mum's calling him all the names under the sun. He'll get a thick ear when he's allowed back home. *If* he is.'

'He doesn't think of her place as home. Hasn't in a long time.'

Her phone rang. 'Noah? You should be sleeping.'

'I heard about Guy, from Ron . . . Is he okay?'

'He will be. I'm at the hospital now.' She walked a short distance from Oz. 'DCS Ferguson has good news. No charges. She's having you fitted for a halo, in fact. For your part in the arrests at the plant room. A big win for the team.' She let him hear her cynicism, knowing he would share it.

'No charges?' Noah sounded dazed. 'Are you sure?'

'It's complicated. I'll explain later. You'll want to get home. I'm heading back to the station to interview Felix about why he tried to commit murder this morning.'

'I can go home?'

'I've made an appointment for you with Dr Matthews. She's working here this morning, at the hospital. Call a taxi, charge it to the station. Then yes, go home. Get some real rest.'

At the station, Felix Amos was unrepentant. Sitting in the same chair as last night, wearing someone else's grey sweats, his own clothes taken for forensics. Elastoplast on his fingers, sweat on his upper lip, fury in his eyes. 'I stabbed him because he's a fucking loser. He lost her and he couldn't stand it. Tried to make it my fault because I'm scum, but I never gave her *anything*. No drugs, no bullets. *He's* the one who pushed her away.' He scrubbed his hand under his nose. 'He got her killed.'

'He lost her,' Marnie echoed. 'Can you explain what you mean by that?'

'He thought he could tell her what to do, where to go.' Felix kicked the leg of the table. 'He'd been telling her shit her whole life. House rules, school rules, *his* rules. Then one day she realised he wasn't God, that he got stuff wrong. Loads of it, all of the time. That's when she started arguing with him. She told me. Not fights. *Debating*. Like they taught her at school, asking questions instead of taking shit at face value. But she was meant to be his angel, his baby doll. Wasn't supposed to talk back or have opinions of her own.'

He looked at his fingers, then shook himself as if he wanted to be free of whatever emotion was hiding behind his hostility. Fear? Guilt? He cocked his head the way he had last night when he was arrested for possession, curling his mouth to match. His social worker sat at his side, her hair crimped, face pillow-scarred. She listened to what Felix said, looking as if she'd heard the same story so many times it hardly mattered. It wasn't that she didn't care, just that she knew the story and its ending, and had no expectation of being able to alter any of it.

'When did you first meet Raffa?' Marnie asked the boy.

'Weeks ago, when she started coming to the flats. A bunch of them getting off the bus, looking disgusted. Well, it's a toilet.' He studied the plasters on his fingers. 'I wouldn't want to go on a school trip to a toilet. *She* wasn't disgusted, though. She was into new places, that's what she said. You could see it in the way she looked at stuff, even arseholes like me.' He picked at the corner of the Elastoplast, his lower lip turning out. 'She didn't think I was scum.'

'You became friends. Princess and Flea.'

'You think you know shit.' He scowled at Marnie. 'But you don't. I wasn't giving her drugs, or stealing from her. Her laptop went missing, she told me about it. And other stuff – missing off the bus. But it wasn't me. You can write that down, for starters. I didn't steal shit from her.'

'Raffa told you about her missing laptop.'

'I know who it was.' Felix half shut his eyes. 'I'll tell you, if you drop the charges.'

'You can tell us now,' Lorna Ferguson said. 'Unless you want us to write down that you're withholding evidence from the police.'

Felix ignored her, focusing on Marnie. 'I'll tell you who nicked the laptop, and why. If you drop the charges.'

'You don't want to be charged with the attempted murder of Guy Belsham? That wasn't the impression you gave the officers who arrested you in Muswell Hill.'

Felix had climbed onto the bonnet of Guy's Mercedes with his arms flung wide, shouting to be heard above the racket of the car alarm: 'I *chinged* him! Me! Come and get me!'

'He was asking for it.' The boy pointed his face towards the door. 'Where were his rules when she was getting shot? All those lectures about staying home, staying safe, and she's shot on his doorstep. She'd have been safer in that dump, with me. I'd have kept her safe.'

He looked fierce for a second, ready to take on the world. He and Raffa could have done it, too. A dreamer and a doer. Marnie could picture them together, invincible, until the bullets came.

'Did you know Terrance Malig?' Lorna asked.

'No.' Felix threw her a look. 'Did you?'

Lorna rolled her eyes at Marnie as if she wished she'd stayed away from this interview. Guy Belsham's connections had brought her here, not wanting any further blowback. She hadn't expected a thirteen-year-old with a glare like a flame-thrower.

'You don't know shit about that place,' Felix said. 'Or shit about us.'

'Erskine Tower, you're talking about.' Lorna clicked her tongue. 'We know a fair amount from the number of arrests in recent weeks. Terrance Malig didn't live there, but it's where he got the ammunition that killed your friend. Your princess. I'd have thought you'd want to help with that, instead of hiding behind whatever grudges you're holding against the police.'

Felix looked her over as if deciding where he'd like to stick a knife. 'She was the one good thing – the one *clean* thing – in my life. And he got her killed. Him and that bitch who jumped.'

Now they were approaching the truth: a connection between the girls. If Marnie could prove Noah's instinct had been right, it would go a long way to restoring Lorna's faith in him.

'Samantha Haile, is that who you mean? You knew her, then.'

'That bitch.' Felix shrugged off his social worker's bid to advise him. 'Shut up. I don't care, okay? I'll answer their questions if I feel like it.' He chewed his lip.

'You knew Sam Haile, but you didn't know about the fire in her flat. You were surprised when I told you about it last night. Surprised to hear she was dead. But not sorry to hear it.'

Felix stared at her in silence. What secrets was he keeping, and why?

Lorna said, 'Two deaths in two days. And you were keen to make it three. How did you know Mr Belsham's address?'

'Raffa told me.' He shrugged. 'Said I could crash there sometimes, if I needed to.'

'Oh, I'll bet Mr Belsham would be delighted to have you as a house guest.'

'Who cares what he wants?' Felix shot back. 'He wasn't doing shit about Raffa. *She* was doing more.' He pointed at Marnie. 'Only you had to start making it about that bitch and the fire.'

'You keep calling her that,' Lorna said. 'A bitch. Putting aside your conspicuous love of humanity, what did you have against Samantha Haile?'

'Same thing you would if you'd known her.' He slunk down in his seat, plucking at the Elastoplast. 'She was dealing, right? To anyone, even little kids, even . . .' He caught himself, editing whatever he'd been about to say. 'Ask anyone who lives there, they'll tell you. They all knew what she was doing. She was *evil*.'

'Like Mr Belsham.' Lorna folded her arms. 'You need some new adjectives, Felix. Because the way this is looking, anyone who crosses you is "evil". It makes our job very difficult.'

'Oh, your job's difficult.' He mimed tears. 'Least you're not dead, in the gutter.'

Marnie watched his face twist out of shape, as furious in his own way over Raffa's death as Guy was. She looked at his hands, the way he fretted at the plasters covering the nicks on his fingers. After he'd stood on the bonnet of the Merc and yelled for the police, he'd slid down, sitting in the road for the time it took officers to reach the scene. Sitting next to the man he'd stabbed, waiting for the police to come. All the bravado gone, ripped out of him. He'd been shaking when they arrested him, hardly seemed to know his own name. It wasn't until he found himself back at the police station that he'd recovered his swagger. But it was a different brand to last night's, under-scored by this nervous picking at his fingers. How much worse would it've been if he'd succeeded in killing Guy? A thirteen-year-old murderer. Locked up for life.

Marnie placed one of the little deal bags on the table. 'What's this?'

'What's it look like?' Cocking his head. 'It's pills.'

'Does it belong to you?'

'No.'

'So where did you get it?'

Felix stuck his tongue in his cheek.

'The logo. Flames and a bullet. Raffa drew this in the stairwell at Erskine Tower. She signed it too. Princess and Flea. Your nicknames.'

He looked at the deal bag, not speaking. One foot jumped under the table, not quite kicking.

Marnie added a second bag, larger, marked with an evidence stamp. 'Raffa had this in her bedroom. Do you know where it came from?'

He leaned in, looking. She smoothed the bag so the bullet was unmistakable. His face closed, lips tightening over his teeth, eyelids slitting. 'No way . . . No *fucking* way.'

'Hidden in her bedroom. We found it the morning she was killed.'

His eyes jumped to her face. 'Fuck off.' He sounded out of breath, as if she'd punched him. 'Raffa didn't . . . No *way* is that hers. Ask anyone! Ask that old bastard she was always talking to.'

'Eric Martineau?'

'Ask him! No way Raffa was anywhere near any guns!' He balled his fists on the table. Here was the boy who'd brought down Guy Belsham. 'You think I'd have let that happen?'

'But she was in contact with Sam Haile. You had no control over that. Sam took her to parties in the plant room. Did you go with her?'

'One party! Once.' Felix lowered his head, eyes blazing. 'We fought about it, okay? I told her it was sick, that bitch was evil and she should stay away. So she did.'

'Following *your* rules,' Ferguson said. 'Even if she wouldn't follow her dad's.'

'I know that dump! It's a shithole and I'm a scumbag so she trusted me to tell her straight . . .' He broke off, looking for a second as if he might cry. 'She trusted me when I told her to stay away.'

'From the plant room. And Samantha Haile.'

'Yes!' He thumped the heels of his hands to his eyes, hard. 'Fucking yes.'

His social worker said, 'I really don't think this is a fair interview. Felix is clearly distressed, and exhausted—'

'Shut up, I've got this.' He dropped his hands and pointed at Marnie. 'You found her killer, yeah? Under a truck. So why're you still stirring it? Why're you saying shit like this?' He shook the table, making the evidence bag bounce. 'Trying to make out like she deserved it.'

'Her dad accused us of the same thing. You have that in common. But he didn't know about the parties or the graffiti or whatever was going on with you two and Sam Haile.'

Felix glared at her, breath panting behind his teeth. 'This's a stitch-up. You're taking that evil fuck's side because he's paying your wages and I'm nothing. Nobody.'

'You're wrong.' Marnie held him steady with her stare. 'You're the most important person in this police station. Because you're the one who can solve this case. By telling us exactly what Sam Haile was doing in Erskine Tower, and why Raffa had to die because of it.'

Felix raised his gaze to the ceiling, then dropped it to the table. He shook himself roughly, wrestling with his instinct to refuse help to the police. 'She was messing with us, okay? Like she messed with everyone. Soon as she saw Raffa, she wanted a piece. Fresh meat, that's what she saw. Razor was the same.'

'Razor . . . Teresa Shaw?'

Felix nodded. 'She's not as bad as that bitch but she's deep with Pete, dealing his shit, getting him girls. You should ask *her* about Sam, she'll tell you.'

'We'll do that.' Marnie removed the bullet from the table, leaving the deal bag where it was. 'Did Raffa draw the graffiti in the stairwell?'

'Princess and Flea.' He nodded, looking miserable. 'That was us. And it was good. *Clean*. We weren't hurting anyone, just hanging out. Whenever she came on the bus from the school . . . She brought biscuits for him, Mr Martineau. We ate biscuits together. It wasn't anything, but it wasn't nothing.'

'Then she met Samantha Haile,' Lorna said. 'And went to the plant room.'

He shoved his stare at her. 'It was one time, yeah? *One*. I thought it'd be okay because it wasn't even night.' His face thinned, adding years to his age. 'I'd never have let her go up there at night.'

'They have parties in the plant room during the day?'

'Different ones, for us. Sweets and shit.' He pushed a finger at the deal bag. 'Pills.'

'Parties for kids? In the plant room. Is that what you're saying?'

Marnie tried to imagine the rotten place Noah had described, strung with balloons and banners, bowls of sweets and jelly. Party bags filled with pills – and what else? Bullets?

'They held parties for you,' she repeated.

'They need us.' Felix tucked in his chin. 'To run the stuff out of London. Because most of us don't have records, not yet. Because we're clean. What you lot call *county lines*, innit?' He swiped at his eyes angrily. 'I didn't know Raffa was going, I'd have stopped her if I knew. She said it was stupid, the party. She hated it up there, the stink, the people. She didn't stay. We should've reported it, that's what she wanted. Only I talked her out of it because I had to live up there with that bitch.' His voice was full of tears unwept. 'She wanted to report it, but I said no.'

His social worker shook her head at Marnie hopelessly. Had there been a time when she'd tried to comfort Felix? A time when she could've reached out and rescued him from this path? Or had it always been impossible? Because Felix armoured his fear in assertion and aggression.

'Who organised these parties?'

'Razor, mostly. For Pete, but he didn't hang around the kids. He was too scary, that's what Razor said. The kids didn't trust him, not like they trust the Bellamys.'

'Were the Bellamys involved with Pete and Razor?'

Felix shook his head. 'But they left them alone. Guess there's enough kids to go round. Pete and the Russians weren't into the same shit anyway. Just girls and drugs.'

'The Bellamys aren't into girls and drugs?'

'Not like that.' He shrugged his narrow shoulders. 'It was only the kids who were too scared to run stuff for the Bellamys that got invited to the parties. That's why they had Razor and *her* – the little kids liked her. She was good at hiding how bad she was. Loads of us fell for it.' From the sound of it, Felix himself had fallen for Sam Haile's act at one time.

'Did Raffa fall for it?'

'I told you, *no.*' He wrapped his skinny arms around his torso. 'She just went to see what was up because she loved new stuff, new places. But she saw straight through that evil cow's act.' He lifted his chin with pride. 'She was *smart*, and clean.' His chin quivered. 'And she's gone.'

'What do you know,' Lorna asked the boy, 'about Sam Haile's death?'

Fear moved lightly across his face like the last ripple from a pebble dropped in water. But he leaned into the question, enunciating his words: 'That bitch got what she deserved. There's not a kid in that dump she didn't mess with. We were running errands to stay in her good books. Drugs, knives sometimes. But *not* bullets. They didn't trust us with that. We did what she asked because it was easier that way. And we were the lucky ones. The rest got their heads fucked, or Social Services got a call. She had kids taken away and put into care. Pushed down the stairs, burned with cigarettes. *Raped*. She didn't care how much damage she did.' His face stayed fierce, but his hands shook. 'I'm *glad* she's dead. I wish she'd died slower. She was an evil, evil bitch. When she started on Raffa . . . I wish I'd killed her. I *wish* that was down to me. But it wasn't. Okay? It wasn't.'

18

'Felix Amos.' Marnie pinned the boy's photo to the evidence board, turning to face the team. 'He had the motive to kill Sam, but he denies starting the fire and I'm inclined to believe him. The news of the fire, like the news of her death, came as a shock to him last night.'

'Yeah?' Oz objected. 'Well this morning he tried to kill Guy Belsham.'

'He's admitted that. He wanted Guy dead. He blames Guy and Sam for Raffa's death. As I say, he had a clear motive to kill her. But that's not enough to charge him.'

'For all we know he's telling lies about Raffa's dad, and about Sam. He can say what he likes about her, can't he? She's dead, so she's got no right of reply.'

'We need to ask questions,' Marnie agreed, 'about Sam's reputation in Erskine Tower. Let's ask Eric Martineau what he knows about her, and about Felix.' She wrote Eric's name on the board, adding Guy's alongside it. 'We need to look into Guy's property dealings. He failed to tell us he's involved in the sale of flats inside Erskine Tower, and that a number of his keenest investors are Russians. Which brings us to last night's arrests.' She began writing the new names on the board. 'Peter Ruslan. Milla Bukin. Teresa Shaw. There are others – the reports are on my desk. Colin, I need you to look into possible connections between these people and Guy Belsham. And the same for Sam Haile. Any connection. See what you can find.'

'More suspects?' Oz groaned. 'I thought her death wasn't suspicious? They ruled out arson, didn't they? She freaked out and jumped. She was a crackhead—'

'The post-mortem found no trace of alcohol or drugs in her system. We've no evidence she was a user.' Marnie stood back from the board. 'She was sober when she jumped . . . *if* she jumped. I've asked DS Prowse to reopen the crime scene. Until I say otherwise, this is a suspicious death. DCS Ferguson agrees.'

The team fell silent, digesting this development.

Ron asked, 'How's Noah?'

'He's resting.' Marnie added another name to the board. 'Luke Corey. Samantha's bereavement counsellor. Terri Shaw claims he had an unhealthy obsession with Sam.'

'I can save us some time.' Oz cracked his knuckles. 'Felix Amos was a suspect in an arson attack a couple of years back. He likes starting fires, and he hated her guts. How's that?'

'Let's look into it, but her death came as a shock to Felix. Given how readily he's admitted to everything else, I can't see a reason for him to hold back his involvement in her death.'

'Actual murder versus attempted?' Oz argued. 'I'd call that a reason. And we're seriously looking at Belsham as a suspect? Because Felix is saying Sam messed with Raffa, took her to these parties where they made the arrests last night, introduced her to God knows how many traffickers and perverts. If her dad found out about that, he could've done something. No, wait.' He fake-rolled his eyes. 'Because Guy Belsham has an alibi for the time of the fire. A breakfast meeting at work.'

'On the morning after his kid died?' Debbie Tanner raised her eyebrows.

'We all cope in our own ways.' Oz shrugged. 'The alibi checks out. I did a bit of digging as soon as it looked like we might fancy him for this.'

'In any case, the fire was accidental.' Colin cleaned his spectacles. 'Highly unusual for the fire investigation team to rule out suspicious death unless they're certain. Far more likely they'd err on the side of caution.'

'Dodgy electrics, isn't that what they said?' Oz bounced on his heels. 'Well, electrics can be *made* dodgy. What if someone tampered with a fuse box?'

'Let's get hold of their report. Ron, can you contact Lenny Prowse? See if we're able to speak with the team who went into the flat after the fire was out.' Marnie underlined Guy's name. 'I'm aware we need to treat Mr Belsham as a victim at this point in time, so let's be discreet. But we know he has a violent temper. Beatrice Farrow says she's seen him confronting people in the street, threatening violence over parking spaces, shouting racist slurs. She and other neighbours are intimidated by him. She had concerns over Lynne's safety, and for Raffa. She told us she was shocked by Raffa's death but not surprised that the family was "visited by violence". That's an unusual statement, to say the least. So . . . I want details of Guy's financial connections to Erskine Tower. Colin, you're on that.'

'I am. And I've already found something. Allegations of financial misconduct dating back eighteen years. No charges, but there was a suspicion of money laundering at a couple of the businesses he was advising. The company he worked for went into liquidation. He bounced back, as we know. For the past twelve years, he's been doing very nicely making money from empty properties in Kensington with absentee landlords in Russia and the Far East.' He handed round a report. 'All that's coming to an end with Brexit looming. He's having to diversify.'

'Erskine Tower is diverse,' Oz said. 'If you want to put it that way.'

'There's also the matter of a police caution for chanting at a rugby match.' Colin referred to his notes. 'I think we can be fairly confident he's a racist.'

'Yeah,' Oz conceded. 'The team who arrested Felix said they nearly cautioned Belsham for the language he was using. They cut him slack on account of the stomach wound, but he was calling the kid names that'd make Bernard Manning blush. That said, being an arsehole racist doesn't give him a motive for topping Sam Haile.'

'Could he be money laundering for the gang in the plant room?' Ron suggested. 'Lots of Russians arrested there last night.' He nodded at the names on the board. 'Raffa's death could've been a warning, or a punishment. If she found out what he was up to and challenged him, threatened to take it to the police. We know she liked to ask questions, and that she fell out with her dad.'

'According to Felix Amos.' Oz looked sceptical. 'It's in his interests to stir things in that direction, so we don't go looking too closely at him for this.'

'Mrs Farrow confirmed it.' Marnie capped the marker pen. 'She's witnessed numerous arguments between them. Guy wanting to escort Raffa to school. Raffa refusing to get into the car.'

'Normal teenage stuff,' Oz complained. 'You can't leap from that to blaming him for her death.'

'No one's leaping anywhere. Or blaming anyone. But

we need to look into Guy's connection to Erskine Tower, and to Sam Haile.'

'Is this because of Noah?' Oz sucked at his teeth. 'Only I get it. He was right there when she jumped, and Belsham's been gunning for him from the start, but the bloke's just lost his kid. He's in hospital because that little git stuck a knife in him. Now we're digging for dirt?'

'We're doing our job,' Marnie corrected.

'Long as it's for the right reasons. And we're not just after a scapegoat.'

'Any kind of goat,' Colin said, 'would be good. There's still the mystery of Raffa's missing laptop, and where exactly she found that bullet.' He looked at Marnie. 'Felix didn't know?'

'He claims to know about the laptop, but he's keeping quiet.' He'd clammed up after seeing how much Lorna liked him as a suspect in Sam's death. 'About the bullet, he has no idea.'

'He says,' Oz stuck in.

'Thank you, yes.' Marnie put down the marker pen. 'Anyone in need of an extra shot of cynicism to start the day, DS Pembroke has more than enough to go round. Otherwise, let's get on.'

Ron climbed to his feet. 'Mind if I come with you, boss? To chat with Mr Martineau, and to see Sam's flat? I can get Lenny Prowse to okay that.'

Marnie nodded. 'Let's go.'

19

Noah lit the cigarette with his head down, one eye shut against the sting of smoke.

'You quit,' he heard Dan's voice saying in his head.

'I did,' he said aloud to the empty car park.

He may as well have spent last night drinking jellied shots of vodka, since this morning his skin was too small for his skull, and stiff. He'd avoided his reflection in Marnie's bathroom, showering with his eyes shut. Every inch of his skin felt gritty, baked dry with dirt. Keeping his eyes shut, he smoked, emptying his head of the last twenty-four hours. The plant room party, the handcuffs, his dressing-down by DCS Ferguson. He should've known better. He did know better. Stirring at the past, even the recent past, just brought all the junk to the surface. *Don't dig the dead.*

He finished the cigarette, crouching to rub out the filter before straightening to study his hand. It wasn't possible to read *Retrocide*, but its orange stain on his skin hadn't shifted when he'd scrubbed at it in the shower, the way he'd scrubbed at his head in a bid to dislodge the detritus of last night's dream. In ten minutes, he'd be sharing the dream with Karie Matthews. His penance. And a way back, or so he hoped. Above everything else, he needed a way back.

He gathered a breath and turned to face the hospital, its new wing rising like a totem above an original building so old it carried the scars of centuries of pollution. London was full of similar structures, the past in uneasy alliance with the present, city planners torn between tradition and innovation, the need to appease tourists never far from their minds; too many came to London expecting a Dickensian stage set. He followed the old bricks around to the new entrance, moving cautiously to contain the hammering in his head.

'DS Jake?' Dead eyes, a hood of hair like steel wool worn at the back of his balding skull.

Noah struggled to put a name to the man's face. He could smell bananas and knew it was a sensory trick, his memory serving the mental image of a box in this man's arms. It was Sam's father. He put out his hand. 'Mr Haile.'

'Howard.' His hand was bony, the handshake limp. He was dressed in the same tan suit and polished black shoes. 'I saw you at the flats when I collected her things.'

'Yes.' Noah glanced towards the hospital entrance. 'Is everything all right? You're not waiting to see a doctor?'

'Patsy, my wife.' He wetted his lips. 'She's been having these sweats. The bed's soaking most nights. She's on pills for it.' His eyelids were pruned, as if he'd been weeping for days. He searched for something more to say, the effort stark on his face. 'It's hardest on the mothers.'

'Hard on you both,' Noah said. 'I should have thought.'

'Yes . . .' Howard put his hands together, easing the loose skin back and forth across his knuckles. 'D'you know where they let you smoke round here?'

Noah went with him back out into the car park. Karie Matthews would wait. Just at this minute, Sam's dad needed him more. Howard took a packet of Silk Cut from his breast pocket and removed a cigarette with his thumb and forefinger, offering the pack to Noah.

'No, thanks.' He shook his head. 'I'm quitting.'

Howard scratched a match at the wall and propped his elbow in the palm of his hand as he smoked, a curiously effete gesture.

A sudden din from inside the hospital made them turn their heads. It died almost instantly, but left Noah's pulse racing; too much cortisol in his system.

'Dylan would've hit the deck at that.' Howard sucked at the cigarette. 'After Helmand, he couldn't stand loud noises. Not that he was nervous; just a reflex. Lots of his mates had it worse.'

'It's hard to imagine how anyone does that job.'

'They'd these warnings, Dylan said, on the barrack doors. About tarantulas, infection . . . I told Patsy, that'll be the least of it. Think about the boiling metal, bloody sand burrowing everywhere.' He looked at the red end of his cigarette. 'Turns to glass in the jet engines, does sand. Dylan had nosebleeds all the time, said it was nothing compared with some of the things he saw. Wouldn't talk about it, not at first. Never, in front of his mum. Then he started telling me bits. Trivia, you'd call it.' He checked Noah's expression. 'Nothing critical. No official secrets, none of that. He was a smart lad and he loved his job.' His face buckled as he said it. 'Some of the things he'd seen, I don't know how he stood it. And it changed him. We knew it would. They tell you how it'll be, or try to. He'd never taken to civilian life, but he was downright sick of it when he got back.' The cigarette shushed between his fingers. 'Patsy took him to the garden centre this one time. He couldn't stand seeing the crowds milling about as if bedding plants mattered one way or the other. Everything should have a purpose, that's what he felt. Fair enough. He'd been fighting for us, for everyone here, and it made him sick to see folk queuing up to buy azaleas. His mates died out there, some of them. Too many. It was hard for him to see life going on as usual, like nothing'd changed.'

Noah kept still, taking careful custody of the man's words.

'He was fed up with Sammy.' Howard sucked at the cigarette, pushing his foot at the dropped ash. His shoes had Velcro fastenings. 'She didn't seem to care enough, about anything. Dylan hated her living in those flats, said it was a pit of thieves, she'd end up making the wrong sort of friends.' He narrowed his eyes at the cigarette, measuring how much remained. 'They fought about it, cat and dog. Seems like decades ago now. I told him the place was different once you got inside. It looks bad, but some of the flats are decent enough. Hers was.' He blinked twice, smoked for a second or two. 'People her age, it looked like it might be all right. You get bad wiring everywhere.'

'Mr Haile.' Noah tried to stop him, knowing he couldn't risk another unofficial interview. 'I'm not sure I should hear this. If you have details about your daughter's death, you should go to the station. Please. Make a statement. I can put you in touch with Detective Inspector Rome . . .'

Howard didn't seem to hear him. 'Bad wiring. That kind of thing goes on all over the place, immigrant labour to save money. Poles, people from the Ukraine. I said to Patsy, how're they to know about British wiring? I reckon they send them all on the same course, but it stands to reason some of them aren't legit. Not their fault, we've all got to make a living. It's the bloody landlords I blame, using cheap labour so they can take bigger bonuses. They're the ones I'd arrest.' He stopped, out of breath. 'Dylan said it'd do her no good living there, but I couldn't see how it'd make much difference where she was. She needed a purpose, he said, but he said that about everyone. And she wasn't bothered. Nothing ever bothered her, even as a kid. Not like Dylan.'

An older brother, decorated war hero. Had Dylan put her under pressure to perform a function worthy of the sacrifices he and his comrades were making overseas? He'd made the ultimate sacrifice. How had his sister felt about that? Noah was groping after the truth again, unable to leave it alone. 'Please, Mr Haile, go to the police. Make a statement . . .'

'Her and Dylan couldn't've been more different.' Howard dropped his voice, shrugging off Noah's objection. 'She saw the burns, back in the hospital. It wasn't the seeing, so much. It was the smell of him, burned up . . . My boy, my brave boy.' He sucked another breath from the filter. 'They shouldn't let you near that. It's wrong. They shouldn't let you, not near that.'

Noah had seen burns victims. Sam had every reason to be afraid of fire if she'd witnessed her brother's injuries up close. Every reason to jump if the alternative was burning. He watched her father, pity adding its quota of pain to his chest. How did it feel to be Howard, to wake every morning and feed his wife a coloured pill, walk past two empty bedrooms, Dylan's and Samantha's, sensing the ghosts in the house, of which his wife had become one?

'I'm so sorry your wife's unwell. And for what I said at the station . . . I didn't mean to offend you.'

Howard shook his head at the apology. 'We knew that.'

'From what Luke said, my statement made it worse.'

'Didn't bother us.' He moved past Noah, heading to the main entrance as if he wanted to put distance between them. 'Corey shouldn't've made a meal out of it.'

'He implied I'd upset you. I can see I might've done that.'

'He makes a meal out of everything. Feasting on scraps, we used to call it. Made a meal out of there being no flowers at her funeral, as if we're made of money. As if *flowers* could put anything right.'

The anger in his voice might have been directed at Luke, or at Noah. Because Noah had reminded him of a good reason why he shouldn't be standing around talking about his children to the man who'd raised questions he couldn't answer and should not have been asked. *Feasting on scraps.* Luke wore the watch given to him by a grieving mother, craving recognition from the broken families he helped. How many others had given him gifts like the diver's watch? Or was the real prize the chance to feel needed? How hard had Luke tried to be needed by the Hailes?

'Do you think he feels he let Samantha down? As her counsellor, I mean.'

Howard stopped and stood for a second with his back to Noah, the hood of grey hair raised at the nape of his neck. 'You'd have to ask him about that.' He turned, stuck out his hand. 'You were the last one to see her alive.' It didn't sound like an accusation but it sounded as if he was stating an unpalatable truth. One that offended him deeply. 'The last one.' He shook Noah's hand – a brief, bony pressure – then went through the sliding doors of the hospital in search of his sick wife.

*   *   *

269

'Noah, hello. Please take a seat.' Karie Matthews wore a purple dress, the colour of the heather on Eric Martineau's balcony. She poured two glasses of water, handing one to Noah. 'I'm glad you decided to come.'

'I wasn't given a choice.' He leavened it with a smile. 'You heard about the arrest, I'm sure.'

She shook her head, taking a sip of water before setting her glass down on the low table between them. 'Which arrest?'

'Mine. I was arrested last night, for trespass. It's been resolved, from a legal point of view. But I'd be lying if I said it wasn't a wake-up call.'

Karie waited, her expression unchanging.

'I half believed I was dreaming the whole thing. It didn't feel real, even when they put me in handcuffs. That's the scariest part, if I'm honest. That I was able to imagine I was dreaming, the whole time it was happening.' He rubbed at the stain on his skin where the bouncer had stamped the name of the club. 'I've been having a lot of odd . . . dreams. Lately.'

'Would you like to tell me about one of them? Your dreams.'

Noah considered his options before offering: 'I'm driving, in the Audi. The one she landed on when she fell. I'm driving too fast, but it's okay because the road's one-way. We're headed for the beach. I can hear the sea off to the west, there're high hedges on either side. It's a narrow road and I'm driving too fast but it's okay.' He shut his eyes, concentrating on the memory. 'Dan's in the passenger seat, I think he's sleeping. Sol . . . Sol's in the back seat.' An accusing presence Noah can see without looking, like a gun pressed to the base of his skull. 'But it's not only Sol. It's Sam, too. She's next to Sol and she's smiling.' A bigger smile than the one she wore in the photo with her own brother, Dylan. 'The really weird thing is how I'm feeling in the dream. I'm satisfied, proud. I'm with my family, driving us to the beach. Everyone's happy. That's . . . odd. Right?'

'Does it feel odd, in the dream?'

'No.' In the dream, the feeling was uncomplicated, childlike and absurd. He had the peripheral vision of a fly and could see consecutively the road ahead and Dan, and Sol and Sam side by side on the back seat like siblings strapped in safely for a long trip. 'No, it feels right in the dream.'

'Anything else?' Karie asked after a short silence.

'Oh, just the usual stuff in the last couple of days. Sam Haile, falling.'

Always the same thing. The sky emptying her out at him. Or him rushing up to meet her, the ground and sky like moving parts of the same escalator, one he can never step off. He grabs for her hair but it runs like water from his hands, or else it catches on the buttons of his shirt, snagging him to her, the pair of them free-falling together, turning and turning until it's unclear whose skull will hit the ground first. Or he's right up outside her flat, standing in empty air, shutting the window from the outside and holding it shut. Keeping her from jumping, forcing her to be safe. But when he does this, the smoke snakes up behind her, a flame catching the yellow hem of her T-shirt, leaping to light her hair. He puts his weight against the window regardless, shutting her in there until the glass heats under his hands and splinters, the cracks racing one another to the centre of the pane, a place where it can shatter, the logical breaking point.

He didn't tell any of this to Karie. Only, 'The usual thing. What you'd expect. She's falling. I'm trying to save her. I can't.'

He reached for the glass of water, tasting the cigarette's poison on his tongue. Heat shivered behind his eyes, but he was past the point of weeping. He was very tired, wanted to sleep. He had to let it go, move on, whatever the popular platitude might be. If not Sol, then Sam. Obsessing about her death wasn't healthy, and there was an even chance he was doing it because of the memories her death provoked, the way it made the scars on his ribs itch. The marks on his mum's wrists had been shallow, but he saw them very precisely, even now. Thin, pale threads that never tanned.

'How do you feel Sam's death has affected you, in terms of your recovery?'

'It's been a setback, of course.' He had to fight to loosen his tongue, too used to lying to Karie, or keeping quiet. He'd forgotten why he'd fought her so hard in the first place. Other than for Sol.

'This sense last night that you were dreaming when you weren't, it sounds frightening. I think you're right to take it as a warning that you need to reconsider things. A wake-up call, you said.'

'There's something else I should probably have shared with you.' Noah leaned forward to set his glass down on the table between them. 'Two things, in fact.'

He straightened, searching behind her for Sol, every nerve ending attuned for a trace of his brother in the room. He could smell the white scent Karie was wearing, and the soil from the pot plant on her windowsill. The air was very still, but it was fresh in the room, as if she'd kept the window propped open all night. Fresh, like the sky after rain, and empty. Sol wasn't here.

Karie was waiting, her patience like a pillow he could lean into, fall asleep on. He wanted so much to be able to sleep.

'The first thing's about my mum.' He locked his hands. 'When I was thirteen . . . she attempted suicide. I'm pretty sure that's skewing my feelings about what happened with Sam Haile.'

'I'm so sorry you had to go through that. Especially as a child.'

'And the second thing,' Noah said, 'is about my brother, Sol.'

20

Eric Martineau looked pleased to find Marnie at his door. 'But where's that nice Jamaican lad?'

'DS Jake's off duty today. This is DS Carling.'

'Delighted to meet you.' Eric reached to shake Ron's hand, ushering them to the living room where the ceremonial sword hung over the fireplace. 'Is there news at all, about little Raffa?'

'Our chief suspect died,' Ron said, 'in a traffic accident.'

'Perhaps that's for the best?' Eric's brow beetled. 'No trial for her poor parents to sit through.'

'We wanted to ask you about Samantha Haile,' Marnie said. 'And Felix Amos.'

'That young rascal. What's he been up to?'

'He stabbed Raffa's dad,' Ron said. 'With a kitchen knife.'

'Felix?' Eric huffed a breath, looking to Marnie. 'Why, for pity's sake?'

'He blames Mr Belsham for Raffa's death. Mr Belsham and Samantha Haile.'

Eric was silent, his face settling into a frown. Eventually he said, 'The lass from upstairs.' He chafed his hands together as if chilled. 'The fire?'

'Yes.' Marnie watched him closely. 'So I was wondering whether there was anything you might have forgotten to mention when we were last here. Anything pertinent to our inquiries.'

'Me?' Her question took him by surprise. 'What're you imagining I might know?'

'Shall we sit down?'

'Oh dear, that sounds ominous.' He lowered himself into an armchair, waiting until Ron and Marnie were seated. 'Now then. What's this about?'

Marnie held his gaze, waiting to see if he would falter or look away. He didn't, his expression of surprise deepening to one of puzzlement. 'What is it you think I'm up to, Detective Inspector? Starting fires, keeping secrets?'

'I think you know a little more than you're sharing with us. Raffa's friendship with Felix, for instance. And their dealings with Samantha Haile.'

He pulled at his left ear. 'Why on earth would I hamper your investigation if I could be of any help at all? I loved that girl like my granddaughter.'

'Do you have a granddaughter?' Ron nodded at the walls. 'No photos.'

'Well spotted. You have me there.' Eric put up his hands, wry amusement in his eyes. 'I suppose you've arrested him, young Felix?'

'And charged him with attempted murder.' Ron was admiring the ceremonial sword.

'Then I hope you'll look into the extenuating circumstances.' Eric eyed Marnie. 'His mother's a drunk and a bully; the boy doesn't get a moment's peace at home. Like Raffa, or so she said. Not that I've any reason to suspect Mrs Belsham of being on the bottle.'

'We asked you if she'd made any friends here, and you said no.'

'Because I knew you'd draw the wrong conclusions about our Felix. He's a rascal, and rude with it. But he's no monster. Raffa asked me to be kind to him. It wouldn't have been kind to put the police onto him, least of all when he's grieving.'

'You might, however, have helped us to avert the current situation. The assault, and the charges.'

Eric accepted this with a nod. 'Is Belsham going to make it?' He looked afraid of the answer.

Marnie checked her watch. 'He's being discharged from hospital around now, in fact. But that doesn't alter the fact of it being attempted murder.'

'I've known Felix since he was a nipper, like I said. I hoped he'd dodge the Bellamy boys, and maybe he did. But I reckoned without her.' Eric raised his eyes to the ceiling.

'Samantha Haile.'

'That's the one. If anything, I should've told you about her when you called round before. Too late, the day after.' He sighed, scratching at his cheek. 'I'd the radio on, making myself a bit of breakfast, when the sirens started. You learn not to listen after a while. I tuned out the car alarm, had no idea what she'd done until Elsie came round. Her flat's on the other side; she'd made the mistake of looking out of the window.' He grimaced.

'How did you think it'd happened?' Marnie asked. 'When you heard she'd died?'

'Oh, I thought murder, of course I did. And a bit of me was glad, though I'm not proud to admit it. Lives she'd ruined in here. Harder not to be glad . . . Excuse me, but I need to walk. This knee's seizing up.' He climbed to his feet, moving towards the balcony, pulling at his left leg with both hands. 'You're wanting to know about the sort of young woman she was. You'd not have believed it to look at her, but she was hard as nails. No evidence of it, nothing I could've taken to the police or I'd have done just that. I saw Felix run the other way when she was coming. Even the Bellamy brothers gave her a wide berth.'

He gathered a breath, standing with his back to the balcony where the heather was growing. 'Saw Felix with a cigarette burn once, which I'd swear was her work. I knew a lad in the war who turned out the same way. Bitter about everything, and sly with it. Elsie'll tell you. "She's not got a heart, that one. She's got a swinging brick!" We were afraid of her, the lot of us.' He turned and made his way back to the armchair. 'You might think the war zone round here's down to the Bellamys and their gangs, bringing in knives and what have you. But *she* was the worst of it. There's no spite in those boys, not really. Not like there was in her.'

Marnie sat under the hanging sword, listening to Eric confirm all their worst fears about Samantha Haile. Drugs, weapons, blackmail. The list of people with a motive to kill her grew longer with every sentence he uttered.

When it was time to go, she thanked him for his assistance, standing for a second by the balcony with its sunlounger and shallow garden, trying to imagine this flat made over into one of Guy Belsham's skyline living units. It would happen, if the Russian investors had any say in it. Pete Ruslan and his friends. Vertical living was the answer to the city's overcrowding. What became of the displaced families, pensioners like Eric and Elsie, was someone else's problem.

'One last question, before we go.'

'Yes?' Eric stood to attention in his tartan slippers.

'Neville Peters, Raffa's teacher. How many times would you say you met him altogether?'

'Oh, six or seven, I expect. Whenever he dropped her off and picked her up.'

Marnie considered his poker stance. Knowing Eric, he'd have shaken Neville by the hand each time they met. 'Remind me of your impression of Mr Peters?'

'Nice enough chap. Sweaty hands, though.' Eric wrung his own hands as if in imitation, making a grimace of distaste. 'I always thought he liked it here a lot less than Raffa. Seemed more nervous, if you catch my drift, but I expect he was feeling the weight of being in charge, responsible for their safety.' His face clouded over. 'Strange to think she was safer here than she was at home. She came from a nice neighbourhood, but of course it travels, does trouble. You can take all the precautions you please, but it'll find you in the end.'

Ron and Marnie took the stairs to the twenty-eighth floor of Erskine Tower.

'What was that about Neville Peters?' Ron asked. 'You and Noah interviewed him, didn't you?'

'At the school, yes. Where his hands were the opposite of sweaty. Bone dry, in fact. I'm thinking he may've had a good reason to be nervous here, more than his professional duty to his students.'

'Such as?'

'Let's try and find out.'

When they reached Sam's flat, they found it sealed with fresh crime-scene tape, more of which trailed the corridor and the stairwell leading up to the plant room. Terri's flat was taped off in the same way, being searched by a unit of trafficking specialists from the National Crime Agency.

'You'll have it in hand, I know.' Marnie showed her badge. 'But might I make a suggestion?'

The NCA officer nodded. 'Go ahead.'

'Dig up the garden, out on the balcony. There's a garden, yes?'

'Not much of one. See for yourself.'

Marnie and Ron followed him through the flat. The balcony was a match for Eric's, nine floors down. Except Eric had tended the strip of soil in the shallow balcony wall, planting heather and hyacinths. Terri had neglected the same strip: upended plastic buckets and a windmill that turned half-heartedly in the breeze drifting over the concrete lip. At the far end, protected from the rain by a piece of corrugated polytunnel, two shop-bought sunflowers were dying dramatically, shaggy heads hanging in a welter of petals.

'I'd start at that end,' Marnie said. 'Since it looks like she was trying to keep the rain off.'

'You want a hand?' Ron offered the NCA man.

'No, you're all right. I've got this.'

They watched as he removed the polytunnel from the concrete trough before uprooting the sunflowers by their necks. They came easily, still inside their supermarket pots. The NCA man leaned down, digging a gloved hand under the surface of the compacted soil, grunting a little as he searched. Two of his companions stopped what they were doing in the living room to join Marnie and Ron on the balcony.

'Okay, this is . . . Nice.' He straightened, holding a black bin bag wound tight with parcel tape around an object the size of a slim phone directory. 'Laptop.' He dusted soil from the find. 'I'd put money on it.' He handed it to one of the others, reaching back into the trough, whistling between his teeth. 'And there's more!' He nodded in Marnie's general direction. 'Good call.'

Back at the station, DCS Ferguson agreed. 'It wouldn't make the Chelsea Flower Show, but I'd call that a decent crop for a balcony garden. One laptop, four phone chargers and an iPod Touch. DS Carling, you can make the light-fingered-not-green-fingered joke. My gift to you.'

'It's Raffa's laptop. And its webcam was switched on,' Marnie told Lorna. 'Our gift to you.'

'You'll want to see this,' Ron agreed. 'It's better than *Gardeners' World*.'

They gathered around Colin's desk to watch the webcam footage. It began with a blurred close-up of a bookcase, then a table, white light cutting across the camera from a window or possibly a lamp. The picture settled as the laptop was set on a steady surface. A torso loomed into view, wide, wearing a white shirt under a dark jacket, coming close to the camera before retreating, as if the person caught on the webcam was uncomfortable, shifting position.

'Is there sound to accompany this?' Lorna asked. 'Or is that a greedy question?'

'Sadly not,' Colin said. 'But if we wait a while . . . There.' He reached to freeze-frame the image caught on camera.

It was a hand, too wide to be a woman's. Square nails, thick fingers. The back of the hand was red and shining.

'Wait.' Lorna leaned in. 'Is that blood?'

'It's a burn,' Marnie said. 'A chemical burn. This is Neville Peters.' She nodded at Colin, who ran the footage on, stopping it a moment later as the laptop was lifted, its camera capturing the detail of a wall with a beech wardrobe. 'And he's in Sam Haile's flat.'

21

'It's November, not long after Bonfire Night. We don't do fireworks, as my mum isn't a fan. But Dad's building a fire in the garden, to bake potatoes. He says Sol and I can eat potatoes for Britain.'

'How old are you?' Karie asked.

'Nine, ten? We moved here when Sol was still a baby.'

Noah remembered the garden putting up a wall of cold that reached into the house. 'I'm wrapping the potatoes in foil and handing them to Dad. They'll bake in the fire until they're ready.' Papery skins stretched thin, then burst by the tip of a knife, filled with yellow butter, frothing under a fork. 'Sol always wants to eat his too soon. It's my job to make sure he doesn't burn his mouth.' Swapping the potatoes from hand to hand until they're cool enough, helping Sol with the skins.

'Dad's taking the old glass out of the greenhouse, demolishing it so we can have a shed. Sol wants to keep comics in there, but Dad's worried the damp'll get to them. He's being careful with the glass. It's my job to keep Sol away until all the glass is out.' The previous owners had left the greenhouse to rot until its roof sagged and all the tacks curled out. Dad had considered replacing the roof with corrugated plastic, reinforcing the sides. But in the end it made more sense to knock it down and start again. 'He got rid of the bigger panes while we were inside the house, watching from the bedroom window while he stripped out the putty. He's tapping the outer edges of the panes, knowing where to put pressure so the glass will fall inwards.' Safety first, that was his Dad.

'After a bit, Sol gets bored and wanders off to find Mum. In bed, I expect. She was in bed a lot back then. I'm waiting for the potatoes to bake, and for the glass to be gone so we can go back outside. When Dad gets down to the smaller panes, I join him in the garden. He's missed a bit, so I point it out.' A square of glass lodged at a right angle to the house. 'I can see the back window reflected there. It never occurred to me that was Dad's way of keeping watch over her. She had to have her privacy, she was always saying that, but he was afraid of what she'd do if she was left alone for too long. I didn't know that, not then. "You missed a bit," that's what I tell him.'

'Noah, take a moment. Just breathe.'

He struggled to follow her instructions, wound too tight to stop straight away. He breathed, listening to the murmur of the hospital at their backs. He needed to tell Marnie about Howard Haile, the things he'd said about his daughter. About Sam.

'Just . . . breathe.' A cool hand on his wrist. Karie's hand.

He was so tired he could weep. He chased down the memory of the November garden, soil steaming at his feet. 'The potatoes taste better for being baked in the ground. Sometimes Dad lights a barbecue, cooks sausages.'

A charred purple taste he loved. 'I remember . . . turning circles on the grass with Sol until we lose our balance.' Lying on the grass, dizzy with laughter. 'Sol cried sometimes, said he'd bumped his knee, ran indoors for Mum. I used to think he wanted her attention, but it wasn't that. It gave her a role in the game, that's why he did it. So she wouldn't feel left out.' His brother, bringing her back from the brink with his baby talk, his tears.

'Dad never fools around. He's careful with the fires. For the barbecue, or to burn leaves. "A lot of grief comes from fires." And he's always listening, his ears on the house. I don't listen, because I hate the sound of her crying, or being sick.' The memory crowded him, bringing a sweat of shame to his neck. 'She's sick after meals sometimes. I can't stand the sound of it, or the smell.' A sharp, sloppy stink, yellow. 'She looks all right when she comes out of the bathroom with her face washed, fresh lipstick on, spearmint breath. But I know she's not. She's not all right.' He learned to shut his ears to the noises she made, to look but not hear. Later, when she made it too hard, he stopped looking too. But Sol hadn't. Sol stayed in the house long after he'd left, playing the baby for Rosa, shouldering that on his own. No wonder she was broken now, with Sol gone and Noah to blame.

'Noah? I need you to take it slowly. There's plenty of time.'

But there wasn't. Not for Sol, and not for him. There was work to be done, killers to be found. Raffa and Sam's deaths to explain. Frank, whose mother was planning her son's vigil. He wished Mum had someone like Matilda Reece in her life, a good woman. He should speak with Dad, find proper help for her. He needed Marnie to tell him the traffickers in the plant room had been rounded up, no more kids being exploited, no more bullets in the bedrooms of thirteen-year-olds. He needed to explain himself to Dan. And if he could manage it, after all that, there was his career to salvage.

22

Neville Peters sweated freely in the interview room. Not just his hands, the whole of him, a collapsed mountain of a man with rivers of sweat running down his red face.

'It was for my brother.' He wiped at his head. 'For Adrian. That's why I did it.'

Marnie held out a bottle of water. 'Tell us about Adrian.'

'He's epileptic, has been since he was a baby. I've done my best to look after him since our parents passed on. I'm his carer, but it's more than that. He's my brother.' He gulped water. 'He's on medication, but they took his benefits away, so I pay for his prescriptions. Only of course I lost my carer's allowance when he lost his benefits, so none of it's easy.' His chest heaved, the chemical burn on his hand shining under the fluorescent light. 'I was managing, just about. Took on some private tutoring, that helped. But the medication changed *again*, they wanted to try a different dosage. I told them it was a mistake. I'm a chemist, I do know how these things work. He was having seizures twenty, thirty times a day. At night, too. Nocturnal seizures can be deadly. I wasn't sleeping, for fear of it. Adrian was sleep-deprived, and getting sicker.

No one was listening, no matter how loud I shouted.' He mopped sweat from his eyes. 'It's not just the epilepsy. He's in chronic pain from rheumatoid arthritis. If you knew how many times I'd had to talk him out of giving up, how often he's begged me to help him end it. If you knew that, you'd understand.'

'You were buying cannabis.' Lorna Ferguson cut to the chase. 'From Samantha Haile.'

'I . . . Yes. For Adrian. It was the only thing that helped.' He looked away from Lorna to Marnie. 'He'll need someone with him. When I don't go home tonight. You'll arrange that, yes?'

'Yes, of course.'

'You stole Raffa Belsham's laptop,' Lorna said, 'and her phone chargers. An iPod Touch. To pay for the drugs from Sam Haile.'

'I should have a solicitor.' Neville's eyes watered. 'I'm his carer, I can't afford to go to prison. I know I said I didn't want one, but now I think I really should have one here.'

'It was an experiment,' Lorna said shortly. 'You got away with it so you did it again. Those rich kids had parents who could replace whatever you stole. Raffa got her new phone charger in the blink of an eye. It wasn't really stealing, not when they could get it replaced so painlessly. And they didn't know the meaning of pain, did they? With their comfortable lives, lifts to school, exotic holidays. Wrapped in cotton wool until you opened their eyes to the real world, at Erskine Tower.'

'It wasn't like that. I'm not . . . I'm not a thief. I'm his carer.'

'How did you discover Samantha?' Lorna looked him over, her expression straying towards disgust. 'Or did you already know about the set-up over there? Was that why you were so keen on this project to introduce your students to the real world – of drug-dealing and stolen goods?'

Neville shook his head with force, perspiration landing on the table in damp spots that looked like insects. 'I had no idea. *None*. It was that boy Byron Jeffries who . . .'

'Go on,' Lorna prompted. 'It was Byron Jeffries who introduced you to the magical properties of cannabis as a cure-all for your brother's woes?'

'I've broken the law.' Neville gathered himself up. 'But I won't sit here and listen to you judging Adrian. I won't be the object of your contempt.'

'From where I'm sitting, you haven't a lot of say in the matter. You stole a child's laptop, sold it to a drug dealer who went on to introduce that child to people-traffickers who very likely had her killed. So yes, I find you contempt-ible. And yes, you can sit here and listen to me judging you and Samantha Haile and anyone else who needs judging, until you tell us the whole truth of what went on in those flats in the weeks leading up to Raffa Belsham's murder.'

'People-traffickers?' Neville repeated blankly. 'In Erskine Tower?'

'Oh that's too real for you, is it?' Lorna curled her lip. 'You don't mind the drug-dealing, just the people-traf-ficking.'

'My dealings with Samantha Haile—'

'Are captured on camera. In case you were thinking of inventing a sob story in that direction. We have film of you sitting in her flat, calmly discussing the price of cannabis. We happen to know she wasn't a particularly wholesome young lady, law degree notwithstanding. So I imagine she saw you as a source of income, one way or another. Did she blackmail you? Threaten to expose your little scam? Were you in her flat on the morning she died? You're no stranger to fires.' She nodded at the burn on his hand. 'Did you think you'd give her a scare, get her to back off?'

Neville turned his horrified gaze on Marnie. 'You can't suspect me of *murder*!'

'*I* can. And what's more, I do.' Lorna folded her arms. 'I've met men like you, Neville. Up north we've a name for you, but I'll spare your blushes. You told DI Rome you were fond of Raffa Belsham. But you stole from her, and you left her alone in those flats while you bought drugs. Did you buy anything else? You've said Adrian was begging you to assist his suicide. Did Samantha have any suggestions to help with that?'

'Absolutely not.' Neville dried his face with the cuff of his shirt. 'You're talking about the bullet, I imagine. The one DI Rome said you found in Raffa's bedroom. I'd never seen it before. I never discussed weapons of any kind with that young woman. Byron suggested I talk with her about the cannabis after he overheard a telephone conversation I was having with Adrian's doctor. He said he'd been offered pills by the kids in the tower block and out of curiosity he'd traced them back to their source.' He tried a weak smile, his face already wet again. 'He has the makings of a detective.'

'You've a funny idea of what detectives do, Neville.'

'Twice. That's all I did – went to her flat twice. Once to ask the question about whether she could help, and then again with the laptop and other items.'

'What was she like?' Marnie asked. 'Samantha.'

'Hard as a cat's head. There's an expression for you.' He nodded at Lorna. '*Harder* than a cat's head. She didn't even pretend to care about Adrian. Just named her price for the drugs, then put it up when I attempted to negotiate.' He shuddered. 'She frightened me, if I'm honest.'

'*If* you were honest perhaps that would be a character reference worth considering.' Lorna glanced at her notes. 'What else did you talk about during this negotiation?'

'Just the cannabis. I asked about Adrian's old meds, whether she could get hold of those, but she wasn't interested.' He eased his thumb into the collar of his shirt, wincing. 'She mentioned stronger options. Xanax. Then cocaine, heroin. I could tell she didn't think much of me as a customer. Why was I bothering with weed when she could give me smack, that was the impression I got.'

'Did you see anyone else in her flat?' Marnie asked. 'On either occasion.'

'No one. She lived alone, she made that very clear.'

'She didn't mention anyone else?'

He shook his head.

'But she was happy to have you there, knowing her address and her name. That didn't strike you as odd?'

'It did, but then I thought, she enjoys this. The danger, the risk. It was a game to her. *I* was a game. She made it clear how pathetic I was. She enjoyed the story about Adrian, the pain he was in, how desperate we both were. She laughed at us.' He looked at Lorna. 'You think you have contempt for me, and I'm sure that's right. But you could've taken lessons from Samantha Haile. I've never met any young person with such *loathing*. Not just for me and the law – for everything. For life itself.' He shuddered. 'I'd never met anyone with such utter contempt for life.'

'Someone else with a motive to murder Sam Haile.' Ferguson addressed the team, pinning Neville Peters' picture to the evidence board. 'And only an angry denial. No alibi other than his brother. I'd say it's a toss-up between Neville and Felix Amos. But if I had to pick one?

My money's on Felix. He has more guts than Neville, for starters.'

'And we know he's capable of killing,' Oz agreed. 'Look what he did to Guy Belsham.'

'Felix knew about Neville and the laptop,' Ron added. 'That's the bargaining chip he tried to use in his interview. He knew all about the cannabis – was prepared to sell Neville out for immunity, if he could get it.'

'I've spoken with the district nurse.' Marnie returned to the room, pocketing her phone. 'Adrian Peters will have someone with him while his brother's here. DC Tanner, would you let Mr Peters know that's been arranged?' She turned to Colin. 'Anything else from the electronics in Terri's flat?'

'Nothing yet. But you asked me to look into Luke Corey.' Colin approached the evidence board, glancing at Ferguson for her approval before adding the man's name in marker pen. 'He's thirty-one, lives in Islington, works as a grief counsellor. And he has a sideline business, on eBay.' He pinned up a series of screen grabs: jewellery, enamel boxes, games consoles. 'From what I can tell, most of this comes from the families he's counselling.'

'He's profiting from people's grief?' Oz sucked at his teeth. 'Jesus. Is there anyone in this case who isn't a first-class bastard?'

'He has a number of fund-raising sites online, for charities nominated by the families he's working with.' Colin added further sheets to the board. 'I expect he'll claim it's for their own good, to help them move on, put the past behind them. All the proceeds from sales go to charity, or so he claims in his comments online. But if Sam found out what he was doing?' He tapped a finger at the final sheet. 'These were added to his eBay shop three weeks ago. Medals. The Military Cross, and the Conspicuous Gallantry Cross. They're a match for Dylan Haile's distinguished service awards.'

Oz whistled. 'Luke's selling her dead brother's medals?'

'That's how it looks.'

Ferguson made a noise of disgust. 'Scratch Neville and Felix. This's the scumbag we should be looking for. Let's get an arrest warrant for Luke Corey.' She nodded at Colin. 'Good work.'

After Lorna left the room, Marnie said, 'Luke may be a suspect in Sam's death. But there's no connection between him and Raffa, or none that we know of. Let's not lose sight of Raffa in all this. Did Sam introduce her to someone in the plant room? Terrance Malig, perhaps? We're expecting confirmation that he was connected to the trafficking ring. If Raffa died because of something she saw or heard there, it gives both Guy and Felix a motive for Sam's murder.'

Colin nodded. 'I'm looking into Guy's business dealings with the Russians, and checking his alibi for the morning of the fire.'

'What about Terri Shaw?' Ron asked. 'Are we going to be allowed to interview her? She said all sorts to Noah at the party she took him to.'

'She's being interviewed by the NCA. We don't have access to her at the moment.' Marnie nodded to the team. 'Let's concentrate on what we do have.'

Marnie called Noah on her way out of the station. 'How was Karie?'

'Good. Tiring.' He sounded spacey with exhaustion. 'I'm heading home in a bit.'

'We're getting an arrest warrant for Luke Corey.' She filled him in on the eBay enterprise, Dylan Haile's medals being offered to the highest bidder. 'Ferguson fancies him as Sam's killer.'

She listened to Noah digesting this before he said, 'He told me he was helping her to sell things on eBay . . . I saw Howard here at the hospital. He was waiting for his wife, Patsy. I got the impression he didn't think much of Luke. And Luke said something else: Sam didn't let him help her, just "shopping or changing a fuse". The fire started because of faulty wiring, isn't that what we think?'

Oz Pembroke's theory: that someone had tampered with the wiring in Sam's kitchen.

'And with the medals,' Marnie said, 'we have a motive. If he was stealing from her and she found out . . . But Luke liked her, isn't that what Terri said?'

'Maybe he wasn't trying to kill her.' Noah paused. 'Maybe he even planned on riding to the rescue. I can see him doing that. He's convinced he's a white knight, a hero.'

'From what I've been hearing about Sam, she'd have welcomed a heroic rescue about as much as I'd welcome another close encounter with Guy Belsham.'

'How is Guy?' Noah asked.

'Up and about, so I'm told. We'll be interviewing him if Colin keeps finding evidence of his financial misconduct. I'll keep you posted. Right now, we're going after Luke. Any tips?'

'I wouldn't trust much that comes out of his mouth. He's a con man with a sob story. Twin sisters, stillborn. His mother never recovered, made a shrine of the house, kept him out of the big bedroom. Luke said she couldn't love him because of it.'

'That's a good sob story.' Marnie waited a beat. 'Is there any truth in it, do you know?'

'I've no proof, but I'd say so.' There was an edge in

Noah's voice, sharpening his exhaustion. 'The self-pity part was real enough.'

'You really don't like him, do you?'

'I really don't. But my instinct's misfiring right now. I could have it wrong.'

'Assuming you haven't, do you think it's possible Luke killed Sam?'

'To be honest? I don't think he has the stomach for it. He's too much of a boy scout, wedded to the idea of his own decency. That said, he sees grief as a sickness, some-thing to be avoided at all costs. He's wrong, you and I know that. But he's convinced he's right.'

'That's a dangerous combination,' Marnie agreed. 'Let's see what he has to say about the fire, and these eBay auctions. Howard didn't mention Dylan's missing medals?'

'Nothing like that. He talked about the fire, and Luke. He would've said more, but I steered him wide. Said he should contact you to make a statement.' Noah sounded as if his session with Karie had wrung him dry. 'I didn't want to dig myself any deeper into last night's hole. Will DCS Ferguson be sitting in on Luke's interview?'

'Try and stop her.'

'Good,' Noah said emphatically. 'Luke's in need of a reality check.'

'I'll let you know how he handles it.'

23

'What you need to understand about grief,' Luke Corey said, 'is that it can be an affliction. It drains the life from you, stunts a family's growth. To heal, you have to get past the pain. Put it away.'

'Or stick it on eBay,' Lorna retorted, 'and flog it to the highest bidder. I'd say your compassion's out of control, but that'd be underselling it.'

The interview room was hot, still branded by Neville Peters' body odour. Marnie had spent too much time in here over the last thirty-six hours. Her eyelids throbbed from the fluorescent lighting, and there was an ache in her temple like a bruise coming up.

'How's DS Jake?' Luke leaned towards her, his face twisted with concern. 'I want to apologise for the way I was with him when we met at Samantha's flat. He must've thought I was being pushy, but I really feel for him after everything he's been through. He and I have a lot in common.'

'Less than you think,' Marnie said shortly. Before meeting Luke, she'd wondered at Noah's dislike for the man, but she wasn't wondering any longer.

'I read about your parents, too.' Luke's face slid into sympathy, his habitual expression from the ease with which he found it, every feature slotting into place. 'And I'm so sorry. That's what I meant about wanting to help.'

No, there was absolutely nothing wrong with Noah's instinct when it came to Luke Corey.

'We're not here to talk about DI Rome,' Lorna snapped at him. 'We're here so you can explain your eBay empire. Did Samantha Haile know you were selling her brother's medals?'

'Of course!' He spread his hands. 'It was at her request.' His face flickered. 'One of the few ways she let me help.'

'Really,' Lorna said flatly. 'So Howard Haile knew you were selling his dead son's medals.'

Luke looked troubled by the question, but as if the trouble belonged to someone else and not to him. 'I found out something about Howie,' he confided. 'And Samantha. She wasn't the nice girl I thought she was. Not remotely.' His mouth turned down, hurt. 'I went there day after day. Trying to talk to her, to make it better. But as far as she was concerned, it got better when Dylan died. Can you imagine how it felt finding that out?'

'You tell us,' Lorna said. 'Starting with this fuse you replaced for her. In the kitchen, was it?'

'In the bedroom.' He blushed. 'Actually.'

'Spend much time in the bedroom, did you?' Lorna saw the blush, and recognised it as a way to get the man's guard down. 'Helping her deal with her grief.'

'Whatever you're suggesting, you're wrong.' The pores showed in his soap-and-water skin. 'I was trying to help, but she shut me out.'

'She crushed you,' Marnie said. 'That's what we heard.'

Luke stared at her, straightening his shoulders inside the baby-blue sweater he wore over a white polo shirt, pale khakis. Strip off the sweater and he was dressed in the new uniform of white supremacy. 'I don't know who told you that, but they're lying.'

'Teresa Shaw told us. Do you know Teresa? She also goes by Terri, and Razor.'

'I don't know her.' He was lying, tight-lipped since the question about the bedroom. 'I'm sorry.'

Marnie considered him, remembering Noah's verdict on Luke's pathological need to help. He'd shared the story about his twin sisters so readily, handing it out like sweets, what should have been a private sorrow reduced to a shortcut, bartering his tragic past with strangers the way he was bartering Dylan's medals. Why go after information about Noah's family, and hers? Digging under that untrustworthy rubble, with what purpose? Marnie could think of two reasons to dig: either Luke was trying to find something, or he was trying to hide something.

'Raffa Belsham,' she said. 'Did you know her?'

'I heard about her, of course. Her poor parents.' Turning on sympathy like a tap, as if he'd been taught that this was normal human behaviour. As if he'd *had* to be taught, because normal human behaviour didn't come naturally to him.

'Samantha never mentioned her?'

'No. Did she know her?' Genuine curiosity. He couldn't fake the emotion.

'Did Samantha ever take you to the plant room?'

'I'm sorry – where?' Bafflement now.

'At the top of the tower block,' Lorna said. 'She liked to party there.'

He shook his head. 'I don't . . . No.'

'Did you see much of that side of her?' Marnie asked. 'The party girl.'

He pressed his lips together. 'We all deal with death in our own way.'

'But it wasn't the way you'd have chosen for her,' Lorna deduced. 'You'd have preferred something more whole-some. Prayer, maybe. Or an eBay auction.'

Luke didn't like her contempt any more than Neville Peters had. He scowled. 'I've already told you she wasn't the nice girl I imagined her to be. I don't know what more I can say about that.'

A knock on the door interrupted the interview. An important phone call for DCS Ferguson. She nodded at Marnie to continue without her.

When she was gone, Luke smiled hopefully. 'I didn't mean to upset you earlier. I just wanted to tell you that I understand, I really do. Growing up, there were things in my childhood that weren't a million miles away from what you went through.'

'I'm sorry for that, but it's none of my business. Just as my family is none of yours.' Marnie referred to her notes. 'You say Samantha gave you permission to sell her brother's medals. Were you also planning to sell his knives?'

Luke sighed. 'I waived my right to a solicitor because I wanted to help. Was that naïve of me?'

She looked at him. 'Only if you have something to hide.'

'It's not illegal to sell medals. Unless the soldier's still serving, in which case the medals officially belong to the government. But Dylan is dead, so . . .' He shrugged.

'And the knives?'

'Sam wanted me to sell various things of Dylan's. She may've mentioned knives, I can't remember. But you've seen my eBay shop, that's obvious. There are no knives on there.'

'All right, let's focus on the medals. Let's assume you're telling the truth and that Sam was the one selling the medals, using you as the facilitator. You withheld that information after she died.'

'I couldn't see how it was pertinent.' His nose wrinkled in confusion. 'Howie's in enough pain without me exposing the truth about her.'

'The truth? I thought you were arguing for the wholesale auctioning of family heirlooms as a form of therapy, a good thing.'

'It can be. It should be.'

'But you hadn't persuaded Howard of that. You knew it would cause him pain to hear his daughter was selling his son's medals. With your help.'

Luke tried a smile, adjusted it, lowered the wattage. 'It's not the way I usually do things.'

'And the medals didn't belong to Samantha, did they? You must have known that.'

'Poor Howie.' He switched off the smile. 'And poor Samantha, too. She must've felt remorse, to do what she did. To jump . . .'

Footsteps in the corridor, but the door stayed shut.

'You're saying her death was suicide. A convenient new theory, given that you're sitting here.'

'I'm here voluntarily.' His fair skin flushed with colour. 'I'm not a suspect, or you'd have charged me. And I discussed the possibility of suicide with DS Jake, the day after she died.' He flicked the sympathy switch again, relaxing his face. 'How is he, really? DS Jake.'

'He's not why you're here. But since you ask, he warned me not to trust a word you say.'

'He's upset, of course. Because of his brother. Perhaps it was wrong of me to go digging, I put my hands up to that.' He did put his hands up, palms facing outward. 'But *he* went digging, too. And you know what I think? It was *guilt* that made him dig for the truth about Samantha. After everything he went through with Sol. When I read about the drugs, the guns? Then prison, the stabbing, I thought, that poor guy, some lives are so hard. And you've kept him at work this whole time.' Watching her. 'I wonder how he keeps going.'

'Shall I tell you what I think, Luke?' She took her time, wanting her words to sink in. 'You're a con man. A psycho-babbling bully, and a con man. You never cared about Sam or her brother, or her parents. You were exploiting the family for whatever you could get out of them. What were you hoping for? Dylan's car, a share of the compensation money? Only you couldn't get close to them, could you? The Hailes. They didn't buy your act.'

A short flare of anger edited the last of the boy scout from Corey's face. 'This was *never* about money. It's about moving on and letting go.'

'Really? I don't see you letting go of that watch from Jeanie, whose son died.' Luke had shown her the watch while she was signing him into the station. 'How many people have you persuaded to *let go* of things in your direction? Is it a good business, profiting from other people's grief?'

'The watch isn't worth anything, you can see that.' Luke's neck was pink. 'Any money I've raised has gone to charity. Every penny. I can prove it!'

'You'll need to.' She glanced at her notes. 'I take it you're admitting to selling the heirlooms of bereaved families on eBay.' She looked up. 'They didn't teach you that during those long hours of training to become a bereavement counsellor.'

'You have to get rid of the reminders. You can't hold onto grief, or it'll take over.'

'So you sell it. A trade in other people's misery. Dylan's medals, was that your idea?'

'No.' His face squirmed. 'I told you.' He bit his lip to stop it moving. 'It's what she wanted.'

'Samantha wanted to sell his medals.'

'I *told* you. She wasn't a nice girl. She spent too much time online. That's how she found out I was auctioning, raising money for charity. And she laughed at me, said I was pathetic. I told her it wasn't about money, but she threatened to report me unless I helped her sell some of Dylan's things and split the proceeds.' He lifted his shoulders, frowning with his whole face. 'People *need* me, that's what you've got to understand. The charity needs me. I do *good*. Go ahead and laugh, but it's true.' He touched the diver's watch.

'She threatened you,' Marnie repeated.

'I was meant to be selling whatever she'd taken from Dylan's room. Military awards, she said those would make the most money. But she had clothes and books, too. And, yes, she had knives.'

'And she threatened you.'

'Oh *God*!' He widened his eyes. 'If you're thinking I had a motive to get rid of her, I didn't do it. I have an alibi for the morning she died.'

'You had access to her flat, you'd changed a fuse for her. You could have started a fire.'

'I didn't.' He placed his hands flat on the table. 'I swear to God, that's the truth.'

'But you didn't go to the police with what you knew about her. Or to report her threats. Instead you stayed close to Howard, helped to clear out her things – were you hoping to find something saleable? And you tried to get close to DS Jake, so you could follow the progress of our investigation.'

'Because I knew how he must've felt seeing her die like that.' Luke wrung a smile from his mouth. 'Think what you like but I wanted to help Noah, I really did. Shall I tell you the worst part?'

This, Marnie thought, is the worst part. That you can sit and talk about Noah as if you have the smallest understanding of what he's going through.

'He knew.' Luke brought his hands together in the shape of a prayer. 'Howie. He *knew* what she was like. He said she was sly, she didn't get on with Dylan even when they were kids. Perhaps it should've made me feel better hearing that, because I never stood a chance of helping her. If she didn't care about Dylan – and from what Howie says she really didn't – that explains why I failed. But at least I *tried*. I tried to help her, and Howie too.'

'Don't dress this up as compassion on your part. You were covering your back. Why? Was it just about selling Dylan's things, or were you trying to cover up something worse?' She put her stare over him. 'You had access to her flat. You could have started a fire.'

'I didn't.' He rubbed his cheek as if she'd hit him. 'I went there to help.'

'But it's not about helping, is it? Be honest. It's about control.' The repulsion she felt for Corey had no edges, filling her from head to feet. 'You had no control over your own family, couldn't force your mum out of her grief into loving you. So you control other parents. It's a way of punishing her, isn't it? Paying back your mum for failing to deliver the childhood you think you deserved. This is about the big bedroom, the shrine to your poor sisters. You bully everyone about loss, getting rid of memories, but you've not learned the first lesson about grieving. You don't *get rid* of grief. You certainly don't auction it off on eBay. You find a place for it and you keep it close. Because that's the way it is with loss. You give it the big bedroom, Luke, is what you do.'

'What about DS Jake's brother?' He marshalled his face into a smile, nine parts scowl. 'He's clearly not over that death, but you're allowing him to be at work, putting people in danger because he's not over it . . .' He moved back, recoiling from her expression. 'It's a matter of public record where and when his brother died. And it's a matter of public interest that you're allowing him to continue working when he should be on compassionate leave.'

'Just so we're clear,' Marnie said rigidly. 'You had a motive for Sam's murder. You sold Dylan's medals for money while pretending to help her family recover from their grief.'

'Their grief?' His eyes widened. 'Howie *hated* her. Every time I tried to find something nice to say about her life, he'd look at me as if I was polishing a turd. If you'll excuse the expression.' He wiped his mouth with his fingers. 'Look, you and I both know it wasn't suicide. Because we know the kind of person she was. But I wonder how much Howie really knew about what she was up to. If he knew she was stealing Dylan's things, his medals? I don't think he'd've let that go.'

'Now you're saying her father's responsible for her death?' Marnie wanted to hit Luke, had been wanting to hit him for the last ten minutes. Her whole arm ached with not doing it. 'Is that it?'

'I'm saying I don't think he'd have let it go. Not the way he was grieving for Dylan. If he found out she was stealing his medals, his memories?' Luke's voice cracked. 'My mum's got these handprints, plaster of Paris. Lily and Pearl's little handprints. Howie's the same about Dylan's medals. If he found out Samantha took them, tried to sell them? I'm not sure what he'd do.'

The tears could have been faked, but they looked real. Blurring his face, making it hard to get a fix on the truth about him. Unloved child. Boy scout. Counsellor. Profiteer.

Marnie considered his accusation against Howard Haile. Both his children gone, his son while serving in a war. His daughter lost to violence of another kind.

Had Sam shown her father the same contempt she'd shown Raffa and Felix? If so, was Howard able to love her in spite of it? Or did he take refuge in loving his son, a child he could be proud of? An unblemished record, with honours to prove it. If then he'd discovered his daughter was selling Dylan's medals to strangers for whatever small price she could get – what had that knowledge cost Howard, and Sam?

24

The hospital car park ended abruptly in a makeshift barrier erected by workmen extending the parking spaces at the rear of the building. An unmanned excavator stood guard, its big jaws slack to the ground. The spot was popular with smokers, butt ends littering the trench where work had stalled. Noah made his way through the empty ranks of parked cars, head ringing, his confession to Karie Matthews raw as a freshly scraped knee. He hadn't intended to share his mother's suicide attempts, but it'd come down to this: Mum, or Sol. He hadn't been lying about the wake-up call – he needed Karie's help, he knew that. He'd meant to tell her about Sol, the delusions he was having, but in the final instance he'd offered up memories of his mum's illness in place of that bigger truth. He wasn't proud of it; in fact he was sick. Sick and tired of himself, the mistakes he'd made, and kept making. And the choices. To arrest Sol, to join the police. Sol was right: he'd picked a side and it was the wrong one. If not then, now. Everything was lines, all the choices stark. You stood on one side, or the other. He'd picked the wrong side, and nothing had been right since.

'Sol?' He didn't need the prop of his phone in the car park's dead end. 'Can we talk? About Mum. I'm sorry. I didn't want you to find out that way. Please, can we talk?'

It was madness, but different now, after Karie. He'd made a follow-up appointment because he owed it to Dan and Marnie, and to himself. Not only an explanation for what'd gone wrong these last ten weeks, but a marker in the sand to say, 'This much and no more.'

'Sol? Can I put this right? I'd like to put it right.'

He didn't expect a response, but as he turned to look for his brother, he caught a flash of pink, heard Sol shout, 'Tek weh yuself!' but too late, as the back of his head burst blackly open.

25

Everything stank of petrol, rubber, sand. Impossible to breathe. Panic crowded him into a corner, had him clawing at his eyes. Trying to claw . . .

'Lidung. Nothing you can do right now.'

He was a body in the boot of a car, blindfolded. 'Sol?'

'I'm here, bredda. Lidung.'

Lie down. As if he had a choice.

'Tried to warn you,' Sol said. 'Back there.'

Tek weh yuself. Get away, never come back.

'You did . . .' Noah didn't speak the words out loud, partly because his mouth wouldn't cooperate but mostly because he didn't need to. Sol was inside his head, along with the pain planted by whatever had hit him. A hammer, by the feel of it; his skull was screaming. He concentrated on not vomiting, afraid he'd choke on it. His wrists were tied behind his back with smooth cord. Thick cloth had been fastened across his eyes. 'Talk to me, Sol.'

'We in trouble, bruv.'

'I worked that much out for myself . . .' He rolled onto his hip to see if his phone was with him, but it was gone.

Taken by whoever hit him. His subconscious had tried to warn him in the shape of Sol, but he'd not been paying attention. Story of his life, these last ten weeks.

Wake up, he told himself savagely. *Pay attention.*

The car was moving. He'd thought it was concussion, that he was imagining the sensation of tipping forwards. But he was being driven away from the hospital. He listened for sounds of traffic, a clue to where they were headed, but the noise in his head got in the way.

'Did you see who it was?'

'Her dad,' Sol said shortly. 'Angry man.'

'Sam's dad? Or—' The car turned a corner and Noah slid in the boot, his head finding a box filled with hot white stars. Sol cursed under his breath, gripping at Noah's fingers. Noah felt his brother's breath on his cheek. Sol had been eating Chippie's banana chips, his favourite snack as a little kid. A sob rose in his throat.

'Easy nuh.' His brother's fingers held his.

Under the petrol and rubber and the Chippie's, Noah could smell cool linen air freshener. He was in the boot of a car with a head injury making the collar of his shirt tacky. He'd been hit hard enough to split the skin at the base of his skull. Whoever was driving was doing it fast, but not fast enough to get stopped or snapped by a speed camera. On a mission, with a purpose.

The car took another corner, thumping his shoulders as he slid again. He fought to wedge his body so it was less at the mercy of the steering. Another corner. *God*, it felt like the top of his skull was coming loose. He tried for the cord at his wrists. Nylon. He couldn't get purchase, fingers slippery with sweat and teeth-achingly numb. He worked them furiously to get the blood back. Sol stayed at his side the whole time.

'Thanks, for not . . .'

The car was stopping. *Traffic lights. Let it be lights.*

He was afraid of the destination, of what would happen when he was no longer in the boot. He needed more time to get his head straight, to figure out a way to reason with the driver at the wheel.

The engine cut. The car went quiet.

Wherever they'd been headed, they were here.

26

'That was Beatrice Farrow on the phone,' Lorna told Marnie. 'She's increasingly concerned about the safety of her neighbour, Lynne Belsham. She's been knocking on the Belshams' door with no joy. It occurs to me we should send someone round, if only to appease Mr Belsham when he gets home from the hospital. The last thing we need is him finding his wife has upped and left him.'

'Was she seen leaving the house?' Marnie checked her phone for messages. 'According to DS Pembroke, the paramedics left her sleeping in bed this morning.'

'She slept through his attempted murder?'

'She took a sleeping pill.' In Raffa's room at the top of the house.

'Pills?' Lorna's face darkened. 'In that case, we should definitely get a team around there. In fact, let's you and I go. Given Guy's connections and our track record in keeping his family safe.'

'He might see this as interference,' Marnie warned as they headed for the stairs.

'Well, that'll make a change from his usual charge of negligence.' Lorna glanced back in the direction of the interview room. 'Any joy with our crooked grief counsellor in there?'

'He wants us to suspect Howard Haile of killing his own daughter.'

'Do we have grounds for that?'

'He lost his son.' Marnie didn't share the fact that Noah had bumped into Sam's father at the hospital, but it had been eating at her since Luke's statement about Howard's possible state of mind. 'Luke wants us to consider the possibility that Mr Haile may have reacted violently to the discovery that Sam was selling Dylan's medals for profit.'

'Is that likely? What do we know about Howard Haile?'

'Not enough,' Marnie admitted grimly. 'Nothing like enough.'

27

The petrol fumes were a giveaway even before the driver sprang the boot; they'd stopped in an underground car park. Dank air wafted into the car. Metal was shoved in Noah's face, below the cloth covering his eyes, twin studs icy against his skin. The studs were pressed to his lips before he could speak, or shout for help.

He felt for his brother's hand but Sol was gone, vanishing when the boot opened. Blood bumped in his temples. The driver took a fistful of his shirt, hauling him out, turning him to face the car. The shove of studs at the base of his spine, blindfold dragged from his eyes. Not much light down here; what there was swam in and out of his vision, a sickening shade of orange. His body pitched forward as if it wanted to get back inside the boot. He'd felt safe there. A shard of memory – hiding in the airing cupboard listening to his mum putting on her make-up, little noises of dislike pouting into the mirror. How old was he then, four, five?

'Stand still!'

He managed to do as he was told. The cord at his wrists made it tricky to get his balance, his body cramping from the crushed journey, a hard hammering in his skull. Pain percussion. *Easy nuh*. He tried to calculate how much time had elapsed since he was hit on the head, how far they'd driven from the hospital. Not far, he guessed. There was CCTV at the hospital, had to be. Marnie knew he'd been going there for the appointment with Karie. She'd told him to stay in touch. When he didn't get home, she'd know what to do. As long as the kidnapper had kept Noah's phone . . .

'You're going to walk.' A jab to his vertebrae supplied the threat. 'And keep quiet.'

Walk? If he could. Staying upright was a challenge.

Sol? Stay with me.

The car park was empty. Not a hotel; private parking for an office block? High-rise, judging by the echoes thrown back from their feet. A tower. Not Erskine, too clean for that, but they were going up, climbing to the top. Walking was easier than he'd anticipated, the dizziness subsiding as soon as he was moving. Regardless, he maintained the sideways lurch. Let the man with the weapon think he was badly concussed.

Where were they? Up a flight of concrete steps. No stink of urine; that ruled out a public car park. Scuff marks on the walls, but no graffiti. His shoulders ached and his fingers burned, blood flow restricted by the nylon knots. The bondage was excessive. Overkill.

On the third floor, a fire door led into the main body of the building. Smoke detectors on the ceiling. Sprinkler system, looking new. A hand pushed him face first into the frame of a second door, shoving with the metal studs at the base of his skull where the pain began. He pressed his forehead into the frame, keeping a curse inside, just.

The *chuck* of a key in a lock. He was thrust into an empty office, open-plan, unfinished. The ceiling showed

exposed pipework, structural support beams. A single chair
and a stepladder stood in the middle of the room, grey
tarpaulin huddled on the floor. No other furniture. A little
light came through the tinted glass, pinwheeling with
dust, but the windows were sealed shut to facilitate
air-conditioning, heavy-duty panes. He wasn't going to
be made to jump. They'd only climbed to the third floor,
not high enough to make it look like suicide.

'Get on your knees.'

Not suicide. An execution. He shrank from the sharp
stink of his own fear.

'On your knees!'

He got on his knees because there wasn't another
option. 'Please . . .'

'Shut up!'

He shut up.

Dan, he thought. *Sol.*

The room stank of recent paint. He breathed it, wanting
a solid sense of the place. The carpet pricked his knees.
He listened for the hum of a generator, or any sound
beyond the immediate span of the room. Nothing. The
wall in front of him was beige, climbing to the blank face
of the window. No view, just another wall, this one of
whitewashed bricks. He wished there was a view – a slice
of blue sky, clouds; anything but these bricks. He rubbed
with his tongue at a raw spot on the inside of his cheek,
bringing a ripe taste into his mouth. He didn't think their
names again. It wasn't right. They didn't belong in this
place with him. He didn't want them here when he died.

'You're not scared. Why aren't you scared?'

'I am.' His voice sounded scooped out. 'I am scared.'

'There's a chair. Sit on it. Don't get up. Crawl.'

It was impossible to crawl with his arms tied behind
his back. He shuffled on his knees in the direction of the

chair, trying to keep his balance, afraid if he fell he'd knock himself out. He needed to stay conscious. He reached the chair and straightened, swaying when he found his feet. Turning to face the man for the first time before sitting. The chair had metal legs and a stiff plastic seat. A sting of static raised the hairs on his arms, scar tissue tightening across his ribs.

The driver of the car came to stand in front of him, six feet away. The room's dead air was charged with his rage, the meat of his face like a mask, eyes and mouth soured with hate. His earlier anger was nothing, a polite sap to the investigation into his daughter's death. This was what he really looked like, as if everything toxic in the city had crawled under his skin, poisoning his grief.

Raffa's father. Guy Belsham. Noah hadn't been certain before, half expecting another grieving father, Samantha Haile's. But it was Guy Belsham. Of course it was.

His vision wavered. He held onto the spine of the chair with the ends of his fingers and tried to control his breathing, taking small sips of air, remembering to breathe out, hoping to steady the sick pitching in his stomach. He wanted his brother's fingers back, gripping at his. But he didn't want Sol to see this, didn't want his brother bearing witness to whatever shape Guy's revenge was about to take. He could smell the hospital on the man, yet there was no evidence of the knife attack, unless it was the old blood on his shirt, hectic colour under his eyes.

Guy shifted his weight from one foot to the other, watching Noah. The thing in his hand wasn't a gun. It wasn't even metal except at its pronged tip, and in thin stripes up its sides. A black baton, rubber. Shorter than a police truncheon and broader, its blunt nose sporting twin steel studs. He moved his fist and a spark jumped between the studs, crackling into a blue arc. 'Stun baton,' he said.

Noah was dry-mouthed. He forced himself to sit still.

'Banned in the UK, but I've worked with some nasty bastards. This was a gift from a Latvian . . . gangster, I suppose you'd call him. I kept it in case it came in handy.'

'You don't . . . need to do this.'

'What?'

'This.' Noah swallowed to get shot of the dryness in his mouth. 'You didn't need to hit me, back at the hospital. I'd have come with you if you'd asked. I'd no reason to suspect you.'

'You're lying.' A narrowing of both eyes. 'You *knew*. You always knew.'

'Knew what?'

'This.' Guy swept his arms wide of his body. 'All of it.'

Noah followed the path of the baton, not looking at the fury in the man's eyes.

'You've always known. Right from the start. The bullet in her bedroom, that crap about gangs. Look at you! *You* of all people know about bullets, about violence. Your brother was in a gang and I'll bet you're the same. You're all the same. *Blacks*.' He packed so much hate into the word it warped, the sibilant hissing long after he'd stopped speaking. He dropped his arms to his sides. The baton struck his thigh and he looked at it in surprise, before wiping the emotion from his face. 'Your ball-breaker of a boss guessed it too. The pair of you in my daughter's room, nosing at her things, drawing your nasty conclusions. Suspecting me, right from the start. *She* should be here. DI Rome.'

'She's coming. With backup.' Noah swallowed. 'Met Police . . . we work as a team.'

'You stitch people up! That's what you're trying to do

to me. Saying my girl was in a gang, making her mum so ill she doesn't trust herself, letting that thug attack me with a knife!'

'If you'd told us the truth at the start—'

That was a mistake. Guy cut him short with a thrust of the baton.

Pain punched a hole through Noah's shoulder. It came from a mile away, swinging in like a concrete ball to demolish a condemned building, its momentum sufficient to pile-drive him halfway across the room despite the fact that the chair didn't move from its spot on the floor. The muscles in his neck and shoulder contracted until he thought they'd snap. Sound, sight, smell – everything tossed, out of reach.

When he could breathe again, he gasped, hauling air into his lungs until they burned. Guy switched the baton off and stuck it under Noah's chin, forcing his head up. Around him, the light spread in a thin, unforgiving glaze. His throat convulsed. He tried to speak, but words wouldn't form. He knew, in any case, that words wouldn't stop this. Guy stroked the studded nose of the baton at Noah's face. Cold and heavy, snagging at his skin, smelling of rubber. When it reached his cheekbone, he stopped, pressing with the studs until Noah was forced to drop his head to the right. He made himself look up, saw a scowl flatlining the man's mouth.

'Don't,' Guy warned, 'lecture me about the fucking truth.'

Sweat ran coldly between Noah's shoulder blades, his skin crawling from the baton's brutish caress. He'd forgotten all about the blow to the head. It was nothing, a friendly pat. He saw the glaze of bloodlust heating the man's eyes and knew Belsham wasn't able to stop, not now, not ever. In that split second, time was suspended, dust motes frozen, a nerve at the side of Noah's mouth ticking without release. Then he slammed forward in the chair, the baton kicking, stuffing his head with so much pain he was sure his skull would split wide open, spilling his brain like a stone. When it stopped, his body sagged, the cord biting at his wrists, a pressure in his chest the only thing keeping him from tipping to the floor: Guy's fist in the front of his shirt. A keening sound struggled up from his sternum, leaking between his lips in a sequence of unsteady sobs. *Sol . . . please . . .*

Static crackled from the baton. The air fried, crisp.

He couldn't move, exhausted beyond belief, shaking like he'd run a marathon, balance shot to pieces. His teeth felt as if they'd been loosened, wanting to rattle free from his skull. He shut his mouth as a precaution against this happening. Where was . . . where was Guy? *Here.* Right in front of him. He flinched, feeling his pupils expand. Aftershocks made his fingers twitch in spite of the circulation-stopping tightness of the cord.

Guy took his fist from Noah's chest and replaced it with the baton, shocking him a third time.

He could hear screaming, but it was a long way off. In another building, miles away. No – it was here, it was him. He was on the floor. Lying on his side, the whole of his head filled with the bright sound of shattering glass. Guy was over him, talking at him, but he couldn't make sense of the words until his brain unscrambled sufficiently to give him the truth.

'You fucking blacks think you own this city! Violence, that's the only language you understand. You've polluted our city – *our* city – made it impossible to live here without watching our backs every second of every day. You know how many investors I've lost because they're counting the knife crimes? How many properties I can't sell because the neighbourhood's full of you? We can't move for it! I told Lynne it would ruin us. *You*. You're ruining us!'

It wasn't true, but that didn't matter. The truth didn't matter. Only whatever excuse Guy needed to justify doing this – taking his pain out on Noah because Noah was nearest. Because he had too much melanin and was stupid enough to wander around an empty car park after he'd been told this man was in the hospital. Whatever Felix had done to Guy, it wasn't enough. Not enough to stop him. Senseless . . . just another senseless death for the city to swallow.

Noah blinked at the ceiling through a slow slide of syrupy light, his heart beating irregular time, body wasted, all the energy slammed out of it. Footsteps circled him. The toe of Guy's shoe was blonde, the rest of the shoe black. He blinked at the blonde toe, willing a degree of coordination back into his body. When Guy squatted, he tried not to scream. The baton was right next to his face. Another hit so soon would kill him. Would it? Yes. *Grief does terrible things to people.*

'What's that?' Guy leaned in. 'Laughing? Are you fucking *laughing*?'

Noah shook his head, but it was shaking anyway, like the rest of him. He had no control over any of it. Guy did. Guy had control. Sudden pressure crushed his chest, as if he was being buried under bricks. Fingers found the pulse in his throat.

The air crackled, his skin scalding where the volts had hit. The light wasn't orange any longer. It was red. The crushing pain moved from his chest to his neck, Guy's fingers pressing the air from his throat, sending it back down into his lungs.

Belsham breathed thinly through his nose, punishing Noah's throat until his body danced under the pressure of the man's fist, the light bleeding out, turning everything the colour of bone.

28

The Belshams' house stood in darkness, blinds drawn at its windows. At the kerbside, the ruined Merc was marked with a police notice warning the public to stay away.

'Police!' Lorna Ferguson tried knocking. 'Mrs Belsham!'

Beatrice Farrow, the neighbour, watched from across the street. Marnie saw the shadows in the woman's face – regret at not calling them sooner, worry for this family visited by violence.

'Big red key.' Lorna nodded at the officer with the battering ram.

The door gave under the first blow, splinters of wood and glass skittering across the expensive hardwood floor. 'Mrs Belsham! Lynne! It's the police.'

Lorna moved towards the sitting room. Marnie took the stairs, heading for the converted loft. Raffa's room.

Under the swag of fairy lights, her fair hair ratted on the pillow, face tugged sideways by pain and pills, Lynne Belsham lay motionless.

29

'Noah . . . wake up!' Sol's voice from a long way away. Too far.

Easier to listen to his body, the way Fran Lennox would listen, listing the damage done, assigning cause and effect. The stun baton had seared his skin, branding his shoulder and chest. Electrical burns were distinctive; they didn't look like fire damage. There'd be blood in his urine. The post-mortem would record ocular irregularities. Electrical shock could cause acute bilateral iritis, cataracts even; facts from old cases squirrelled away in his subconscious, shuffled to the top of his skull by the baton. They'd know it was murder. His body, his eyes would tell them that. No need for anyone else to bear witness.

'Too much t'inking, bredda!'

'Get up!' Guy tried to sit Noah in the chair, but his body wouldn't cooperate, poleaxed by trauma and exhaustion, so Belsham dragged him by one elbow, propping him against the wall under the sealed window.

Blood had glued shut the lashes of Noah's right eye. When he succeeded in opening it, a red film clouded his vision. More blood was in his ears and mouth. He tried to swallow, but his throat felt crushed, as if Guy's fingers were still around it. Everything was worse when he moved, threatening to drop him back down into the black hole he'd clawed his way up from. The injury to his temple felt like a steel pin implanted above his right eye. He was hurting in places the baton hadn't touched, his ribs and lower back. Guy must've put his boots in when Noah was unconscious. The man was out of control, no coming back from here. He'd have to kill Noah, he'd have to.

Not the first time he'd killed someone; that was what Noah's brain wanted him to believe. Sam Haile, who'd hurt Raffa, tried to exploit her. Was it Guy who'd set the fire in her flat? He was a property developer, wanted the tenants out so he could . . . No. No more questions. Noah would happily never ask another question in his life, if only he could live. If Guy would only grant him the time to make peace with his monsters. To see Dan again, and to say goodbye to Sol.

Belsham was turning tight circles, pacing as he waited for Noah to be awake enough to hear what he had to say, whatever speech he wanted to deliver before he ended this. Like that first day, the morning Raffa was gunned down in the street, on the phone, talking, doing deals. It was what he did, who he was. Nothing would ever change that. Noah moved his hands behind his back. His fingers would be dead by the time he was in the morgue. Torque marks around his wrists. Proof he'd been tied up, tortured. None of this could be written off as anything other than murder.

Why wasn't Guy finishing it? The circle he was turning . . . like he was tracking prey, except there wasn't room in the circle for anyone but himself. Noah regretted every second he'd spent not looking at the evidence properly, every second spent chasing ghosts . . .

322

'Hey.' Sounding offended. 'I'm right here.'

Sol. Thank God.

'Please . . .' He didn't say the word out loud, didn't need to. 'Sol, help me.'

Guy kept circling, shoes chafing at the carpet. He had his phone out, or was it Noah's phone, punching at the screen. Trying to reach someone. Marnie? Belsham blamed her too, for the chaos that'd engulfed his family. He blamed everyone but himself.

'Sol . . .' Noah was greying out, giving in to the slow suck of pain. 'Help me.' A foot stirred at him. He opened his eyes on Guy's face. He could smell his blood on the man's toecap.

'This job you do is *shit*. You know that? You don't make a difference, just more mess. Pretending to be a policeman when you're no better than the garbage running round with guns and knives. Least *she's* the right colour to be that side of the law. Bet you're wishing you'd stayed with your own kind now. You could've knifed me like that thug. If you weren't pretending to be a hero. I hope you're learning your lesson now.'

Guy expected an answer of some kind. Noah's agreement. Well, he'd wait a long time for that. Because he was wrong. It mattered, this job he did. He'd made a difference. To Ayana Mirza, and not just to her. He wouldn't die believing it had all been for nothing. He wouldn't give Guy the satisfaction.

The man stepped away, the carpet eating the sound of his feet. Noah tried to stand, using the wall for leverage. A swarm of black sucked at him from all sides. 'Sol! Talk to me. Don't let me pass out.' He needed to be conscious, to not make this easy for Belsham. He wanted to look the man in the eye when he did it.

But Guy wasn't in the room, not any longer. Just Noah

and the voice in his head that fell silent as if his brother had followed his killer from the room. Leaving him to die as Sol had died in that prison yard, bleeding out beside a brick wall, alone.

30

Lynne Belsham was carried down from her daughter's bedroom on a stretcher, the paramedics negotiating the stairwell with skill and patience, one of them repeating the lie to her: 'It's fine, you're doing fine. It's all good.'

Marnie stood for a moment in the empty room, seeing Raffa's shape kicked from the bedding by her mother's feet. Lynne hadn't wanted them to find her like this, in time. She'd wept when they tried to wake her, beating at them weakly with her fists, telling them to leave her alone.

Lorna looked around the room. 'This is where you found it?' She scanned the stuffed toys and snow globes. 'The bullet.'

'In the bookcase, yes.' Marnie scrolled through her phone for the hospital's number. 'This is Detective Inspector Rome with the Metropolitan Police. You have a patient, Guy Belsham? I need to get a message to him, please.' She waited while the call was put through to the nursing station, repeated her request to speak with Lynne's husband, listening to what was said. 'When was this? Thank you.' She ended the call, looking at Lorna. 'Guy was discharged two hours ago.'

'But he didn't come home?' Lorna frowned.

Panic, out of nowhere, froze the ends of Marnie's fingers.

Are we there yet? Are we done?

'This doesn't feel right.' She speed-dialled Noah's number. 'Voicemail,' she told Lorna, waiting for the recorded message to end. 'Noah, I need you to call me back when you get this.'

'You're imagining what?' Lorna asked. 'A rampage? I can't see Mr Belsham running amok.'

'Can't you? I can.' She dialled another number. 'Harry, I need your help. When your team searched Guy's house, did you find sleeping pills? Lynne took an overdose . . . No, we got here in time. What about car keys? The Merc's here but they have two cars, yes? . . . Where? Text me the address . . . Got it. Thanks.'

'Well?' Lorna quizzed her with a look. 'Where's the second car?'

'Guy keeps it in a car park at work. Two blocks from the hospital.'

'Why the hell would he make a run for it after Amos stabbed him?'

'Because he's panicking,' Marnie said. 'And because he doesn't know what else to do.'

She rang Colin at the station. 'We need to find Guy Belsham. I'll text a registration number and a property address where he keeps the car. Free parking, apparently. Take a look at the address, will you? We may need CCTV from the hospital. And I need to get hold of Noah, urgently. He's not answering his phone. Can you find out if he's home? Thanks. We're on our way back to the station, but Colin? Call me as soon as you hear anything.'

31

Everything was curling in and out of focus. Greying the gap between floor and ceiling, bringing the walls closer, silking under the door to sit on his chest like a slab. Noah could taste it at the top of his lungs. *Smoke.* He swung his eyes to the ceiling, too fast, seeing a swarm of spots. The sprinkler system looked new. Please God let it be wired up, working.

'Best get up, bredda.' He couldn't see Sol, but he could hear him. 'Noah. Get up!'

More smoke slunk into the room, coming from the direction of the stairwell. No response from the sprinkler system. He blinked wetness from his eyes, willing his legs to work.

Guy came back into the room with an empty plastic bottle in his hand, viscous dregs inside. Accelerant. He upended it over the huddle of tarpaulin, a last dribble *swishing* as it hit. He dropped the empty bottle to the floor beside Noah.

'Get up, blad!'

Where was the baton? In Guy's pocket, a phallic bulge. He squatted next to Noah, too far to be reached without an effort. The sort of effort he'd made sure Noah couldn't manage thanks to the baton and the beating he'd dealt out. He reached for Noah's shoulder, pushing him into the wall.

'Noah!' Sol yelled his name hotly into his ear.

He must've blacked out for a second. When he next heard Guy's voice, it had a whine in it. He wanted Noah to take note, kicking with the toe of his shoe at his shin. 'This's your fault.' He stank of diesel. His clothes were freckled with it. He'd been clumsy, letting it spill on his clothes. What did that mean? Noah's throat closed in fear.

'Means he's going to burn! Means you need to get the fuck up!'

'I wasn't going to walk away from this,' Guy said. 'Ever. Because of *you* and that bitch.' A red smell reached Noah from outside the room, white at the surface like candles in church. 'Why couldn't you stop when Malig died? Why'd you have to keep digging? I could've held it together if you kept away from us. Lynne would've got over it, in time. She'd have been okay. Maybe even another kid, another baby, in a few years. We'd have moved away, we could've afforded it. But you had to bring the whole thing crashing down. The money, the deals. Everything.'

Noah's teeth shut tight together. The smell lifting from Guy was terrorising. Diesel fumes, frustration and fear – the kind an animal emitted as musk.

'While you get to play happy families! I saw your phone, the filthy texts from your boyfriend. The pair of you – *perverts*. You should be down!' He gestured at the floor, violence clawing at his face. 'Down *here*, with the rest of us. Lynne and me. You belong with *us*.'

'Noah,' Sol said softly in his ear. 'You need to get up. Now. You need to make this stop.'

'I can't. My legs won't work.'

'Fuck that. Get up.'

He tried, he really did. But his body wouldn't cooperate, as if it belonged to Belsham now. When did Guy stop being just another angry bigot and become a killer, soaked in sweat and diesel with a baton that prodded blindly in all directions like the rhino . . . what was its name? Dan's rhino, smashing the side of the truck, making the banker weep actual tears. He couldn't remember its name; the shocks had scattered his memory in six directions like cheap beads from a broken string. He fought to put the memories back in place. It felt new, this change in Guy. But perhaps he'd always been soaked to the skin like this, flammable. It was about much more than hate, or revenge. It was about Guy's failure as a father and husband. A man took care of his family, took charge. Guy wasn't in charge any more, of anything other than this. Fire, death . . .

Bella. That was the rhino's name. Bella.

'That's right,' Sol said. 'And now you're going to get up and fight this fucker. Because you're the police and that's your job. *Do your job*. Put him down.'

Smoke rose, on all sides. The smell of the fire was hot and inhuman, hanging like a solid thing between them and the door. They were going to burn, him and Guy. Noah was going to burn. No one to say what really happened, to tell the whole truth of how Raffa died, and what her father did. He pushed his fists into the wall. *Get up*. No, not up. He should stay down, because of the smoke. *Crawl, then*. Where was Belsham?

'Do your job, bredda!'

He tried. Lay on his side and used his elbows and feet to inch away from the wall, towards the door. He thought of Dan being asked to identify his corpse, and that got him as far as the chair. But smoke was crowding his chest; he didn't have the strength to cough, let alone crawl.

This, he thought, this is why she jumped.

Samantha Haile. To be in the clean air one last time. Because anything was better than dying under a stone wall of smoke, all the colour gone, your lungs crushed to nothing in your chest. He would've jumped if he could, gulping air on the way down. No breath to waste on screaming, a better way to die than this. He curled on his side, covering his face. He could hear the blaze now, eating its way from the staircase outside. Why hadn't Guy set fire to everything in the room? He couldn't have meant Noah to escape. Unless he couldn't help himself, all control gone after he took that first step towards this finish.

The fire had a different sound now, like sirens. He wished he could see its shape, flames licking, anything but this wall of grey. Hands reached for him, Belsham holding him down, pressing him into more of the smoke. He twisted, kicking out.

'Down,' Guy thundered. 'You belong down here!'

'No . . .' He thrust against the man's weight, using him as ballast to be upright, on his feet. He couldn't use his fists, but he could use his head, and he did, breaking the man's nose savagely.

'Rain a fall, rasshole!'

Guy punched at him. Noah wasn't fast enough to dodge, would've taken the full force of the blow had Guy not dropped to the floor, felled by someone else's fist.

Sol's? No, that made no sense. Even through the smoke and pain, Noah knew it wasn't his brother who'd brought Belsham down. He fell with the man, collapsing under the weight of the last three hours, finding the floor with his shoulder and blacking out.

The smoke was still thick when he came to, in his eyes and chest, around his feet.

'Noah? Hang in there, an ambulance is coming. The fire's out, it's out. I'm going to wash some of this dirt off so I can see where you're hurt. Keep your eyes closed, that's it. You're doing good.'

He doubted it was real, afraid to believe in the idea of a rescue. But he recognised Marnie's voice. When she pressed a wet cloth to his eyelids, he sobbed.

'That's good. You're good.'

He couldn't stop the tears once they started, his chest convulsing, synapses blazing. His body overwhelmingly alien, flaring with sobs. Sol was gone, but he was here. He was still here.

'It's all right. Lie still. I'm not going anywhere. I'm right here. Paramedics are coming. It's going to be okay, you're just . . . Yes. Noah. Come here.'

She let him cling to her until the panic gave way to exhaustion. Relief, disproportionate to everything, washed him up at last, like storm wreckage. He was still here.

'That's good. Hang in there.'

He did as he was told.

32

'I wanted it to be suicide.' Sam's father sat stooped at the table. 'When I saw your lad's statement, I was glad. I thought if she was capable of being sorry, it'd be something.' He looked at the soot stains on Marnie's shirt, frowning. 'Better than doing what she did and getting away with it.'

Marnie gave the man her full attention, although her mind was on Noah, shocked and broken in the hospital. No permanent damage, the paramedics had said. But they'd said the same about Lynne Belsham, whose child was dead and whose husband was locked up, charged with attempted murder.

'I was a good dad to Dylan.' Howard Haile clenched his fists on the table where Felix Amos had clenched his. The interview room was fetid with the scent of fear and confusion, denial and misery. All the things they were fighting, all the things that'd overtaken Noah. 'It was *her* – there was no doing anything for her. She didn't care. Laughed in my face, called me a fool.' His features creased. 'Then I found she'd stolen things of Dylan's from his bedroom back home. She was going to sell them. Medals, clothes. All we had left of him. All we had.'

'You could have come to the police,' Marnie said. 'When you made that discovery.'

'I've Patsy to think of. She's been through enough and she won't cope, not with that. What Sammy did, what she *stole* . . .' He swallowed a laugh. 'Reckoned without the pills, though, didn't I? She's not my Patsy any more. It's all cotton wool up here,' tapping the side of his head. 'Can't feel a thing, can't even dress herself. I've tried cutting down the dose, but she gets mad. She needs the pills. *Needs* them.'

Marnie wished Luke Corey was here to see the anguish in Howard's eyes. Perhaps then he'd understand what grief did to families. He was being charged with withholding evidence, but she feared the lesson wouldn't be enough to change him. Unlike Neville Peters, who was facing drugs charges and the prospect of his brother being moved into a care home. In the wake of Guy's arrest, Marnie was hopeful of a re-evaluation of the charges against Felix Amos.

'Maybe Sammy should've been on pills . . . she was that scared of fire.' Howard blinked. 'Only time I ever saw her afraid was when she came with us to see Dylan at the hospital. Didn't want to come, of course, but I made her. Said she'd not get the money she was after if she didn't. We gave her some each month, not much, but it helped her afford that place. She'd wanted her own place since she was thirteen. That flat was her idea of heaven but she couldn't meet the rent, so we helped out.' He moved nicotine-stained fingers. 'She said she wouldn't come to the hospital, not even with the chance he was dying. Patsy never knew the extent of it, just that they didn't get on, her and Dylan. Kids, she thought, it was just them being kids. She never knew the half of what Sammy said about her brother. "You're dishonouring a

333

hero," that's what I told her. "He was fighting a war for you." "Not for me," she said. She wouldn't even give him that much.'

He wiped at his eyes. 'I didn't want Patsy finding out how bad it was between them, not by Sammy refusing to see her own brother when he was dying. So I made her come. And she was scared, seeing him like that, burned.' He swallowed, hard. 'I thought: "*I* did that, got through to her at last." I was proud of it. Only it must've stayed with her, mustn't it? That fire in her flat. I think . . .' He squeezed his hands. 'She was thinking of Dylan, when she jumped. Your lad saw her, said she didn't look scared. But she must've been, mustn't she?'

'Yes,' Marnie answered. 'She must have been scared.' Like Noah in the empty office where Guy tortured him before starting a fire, making Noah believe he would burn. She'd seen the panic in his eyes, the gut-wrenching fear.

Sam Haile's death had been an accident, they were certain of that now. No foul play in the fuse box, no one else in the flat at the time. She'd seen the smoke and flames, and she'd panicked.

'I did that,' Howard said in a hollow voice. 'Got through to her at the hospital, me and Dylan. She was thinking of her brother when she jumped, of how he died a hero. I wanted it, you see. I know you've decided otherwise, but I wanted it to be suicide. Horrible, *horrible* . . . I didn't know I was capable of it, not of hate like that. Of my own flesh and blood.' His chest caved. 'I knew who she was, what she was capable of.' The grey hood of his hair bristled, as if he were carrying someone on his back. Someone small, grey and profoundly heavy. 'I needed to believe she was sorry.'

*   *   *

'Well?' Lorna looked as tired as Marnie felt. 'Did he confess?'

'He didn't kill her. No one did. It was an accident.'

'Just as the fire investigation crew said. Are you certain?'

'As certain as I can be. The thought of burning, the memory of her brother's injuries – all the evidence says she panicked.'

'DS Kennedy's waiting for you,' Lorna said. 'I was glad of the chance to shake his hand, the one he used to punch Belsham's lights out. Good job you called him when you did, and that he wasted no time riding to the rescue. Teeth-shaped bruises on his knuckles, but as dishy as ever. I like him even better now.'

'Any news of Lynne?'

'She's recovering. Seeing a counsellor, and her sister's flying home to be with her.'

Marnie knotted her hair away from her face. 'How did she take the news of Guy's arrest?'

'Surprisingly well. She was sorry about Noah, said if she'd known the full picture of what was going on with Guy she'd have alerted us. I believe her, for what it's worth. His business was going down the drain, all sorts of debt piled up that he'd not told her about. The Russians were bailing him out but they didn't like his rate of return, hence the warning shots fired into that poor child. Belsham must've planted the bullet in her bedroom to mess with the investigation.'

'It's such a strange thing to have done.' Marnie couldn't quite believe it. Even now, with the proof of Belsham's character stamped all over Noah.

'Arrogant, contemptible, foolhardy. Just some of the better words I'd use to describe him. And gutless, at the end of the day. Giving in to his racism, like the revolting animal he is.' Lorna looked her over. 'Get some rest, lady, you've earned it.'

'I'll do that,' Marnie promised.

Lorna had forgotten her plans for the weekend, and Marnie was glad. She didn't want to fight with this woman, or with anyone. Least of all over Stephen Keele.

33

Sol was gone. Noah felt his brother's absence acutely, as if someone had reached inside him and carved out the space where Sol had been living these past ten weeks. Of all the wounds they'd treated, this one hurt the worst. But Dan was here, and so was Dad. Sitting either side of the hospital bed. 'Hey . . .' he managed.

Dan squeezed his fingers.

'That's better.' Dad wrapped his hands around Noah's. 'That's more like my boy.'

'Is Mum okay?'

'She's with your Aunt Marcia. She's going to be fine.'

'There's someone I want her to meet.' Noah tested the Sol-shaped space inside him, its rawness, its depth. What could fill it? Only time, and love. 'Matilda Reece. She's organising a vigil for her son. I thought if Mum could meet her . . .'

'I'll do that.' Dad held Noah's hand between his. 'My own boy. You're safe now.' He climbed to his feet, nodding at Dan. 'I'll be outside.'

'I'm sorry,' Noah said when it was just the two of them. 'Forgive me?'

'Depends.' Dan smoothed his thumb lightly at Noah's frown. 'If you'll forgive yourself.'

'It was . . . Sol. I couldn't let him go.'

'You don't need to. We can talk. I'd like to talk about him. I miss him too.'

And there he was – his brother. In Dan's eyes, and the warmth of his touch. Not a ghost, but a memory, alive. They'd keep Sol alive, like this, between them. Dad, too, and Mum when she was better. It wasn't down to Noah, not alone. He was here, but he wasn't alone.

34

HMP Cloverton had new doors and windows, freshly whitewashed corridors. Twelve weeks ago, a deadly fire had ripped through this wing, leaving bodies behind. It'd taken a long time for the soot to clear. Even now the walls were spotted with it, a constellation of distant black stars in the white paint. Marnie had attended too many crime scenes where fire had been the killer. Old Albie Crane sleeping in a doorway down by London's docks, his cardboard mattress set alight by kids. Knives were sharp and guns were worse, but fire was a terrible weapon. The kids who killed Albie wept when they were finally caught; they hadn't considered how bad it would be to watch a body burn.

'Marnie Rome,' she told the guard. 'Visiting Stephen Keele.'

Stephen knew she was coming. He'd been asking for her, filing visitor requests on a weekly basis since he was discharged from hospital. But Marnie had been busy with work, and there'd been Sol's funeral to attend. She'd had no interest in seeing Stephen, still less in explaining to Noah that while his brother was dead, she was intent on visiting hers in the prison where he was serving time for the murder of her parents. Stephen was her foster brother, brought into the family as she was leaving to pursue her career, but she'd trained herself to stop calling him that – her 'foster brother' – since her parents wanted them to be brother and sister and felt the distinction didn't help. It certainly hadn't lessened her feelings of guilt and grief.

He had killed her parents savagely, stabbing them to death in the kitchen where for years she'd sliced bread for toast, sneaked drinks from the fridge and cupboards. Where she'd crept in and out, breaking the rules when she was fourteen, the age at which Stephen had taken the bread knife and turned it on the couple who'd fostered him. Feeling betrayed, he'd said, because they'd brought his birth mother Stella back into his life, a fatal attempt at reconciliation. Cornered and powerless, remembering the abuse he'd suffered at Stella's hands. Perhaps. Perhaps that was the reason he did it.

'Turn around, please.' The female officer completed the pat-down.

Marnie had considered every angle of the case. She'd researched reactive attachment disorder, PTSD – anything and everything to explain Stephen's actions. And her own. Because she'd been a detective when he'd picked up that knife. For six years she'd seen him at close quarters, but she'd missed all the clues. Unless, subconsciously, she'd known and failed to act. The subconscious was a strange thing. The longer she was a detective, the more she appreciated how very strange it could be. She'd met psychiatric nurses who in their personal lives inadvertently channelled their most challenging patients' behaviours . . .

Enough thinking. She tied her hair back from her face. The guard was finished. It was time to go.

*   *   *

Stephen sat under the light, his hands linked on the metal table, his head bowed. She'd last seen him in a hospital bed, wired to a ventilator. He'd looked so small there, but she hadn't forgotten how tall he was, or the broad sweep of his shoulders. He raised his head when the door closed behind her, dark eyes seeking hers across the expanse of empty tables and chairs. The one concession to her status as a detective inspector: a private visit.

She walked to where he was sitting, seating herself on the opposite side of the table, linking her hands as his were linked. He didn't speak, or move his stare from her face. His hair had grown back from a buzz cut, looking like thick black velvet over the shape of his skull. Otherwise, he was the same. High cheekbones, a curved crimson mouth. Dressed in the grey sweats all prisoners wore, the cuffs rolled back from his wrists. No bruises on his knuckles, no puffiness either. She didn't need to look directly at his hands to know this. Her peripheral vision had always been excellent when it came to Stephen.

'How are you?' she asked.

'I'm here.' His voice was a little deeper, grainier, as if the fire had woven its way into his throat. Into his eyes too, their dark stare more opaque than ever. 'I've been here for ten weeks.'

'Since the hospital discharged you, yes.'

He studied her composure, searching for cracks. 'You've been busy.' He spoke as if supplying her with an excuse for not responding sooner to his visitor requests. 'Busy with knives, and guns.'

'It never stops,' she agreed.

'You chose it, this life. You chose knives. Long before I did.'

She let this go. It was time to let it all go.

'I came to say goodbye, in fact. You and I have been

playing this game for seven years. That's a good number, a good place to stop.' She offered a smile. 'You're right to say I'm busy, but you should be too. Getting better, getting well. I want you to get well.'

'Because I'm sick?' His stare moved over her like a hot shadow. 'Your sick little brother. *Foster* brother. Your pet psychopath.' He shoved back in the chair, keeping his hands on the table. 'You're not saying goodbye, because you can't. You're not ready to quit, you're just starting a new game.'

'I'm saying goodbye.' She didn't move, sitting peaceably. 'I'm not coming again, so please stop putting in requests. This is the last time.'

'If you meant that, you wouldn't be here now. Wouldn't be sitting smiling at me. Stopping means staying away. You couldn't stay away if your life depended on it.'

'Well, I wanted to say goodbye. And to ask you to stop putting in visitor requests. I knew you wouldn't stop doing that unless I told you – like this – that it's finished.'

'You're breaking up with me?' His mouth curled. 'Fuck you. What about the photos, that bitch sitting on their sofa? I know you've seen the photos.'

'Because your mother told you.' She could see it clearly now, the damage the fire had done. It was under his skin and in his lungs, running its red riot through his blood. Physical weakness, the doctors said, exhaustion, reduced resistance to infection. He'd been on a ventilator for days. The damage would stay with him forever. 'I know you're in touch with Stella. I met her at the hospital, the day before you were discharged.'

His eyes filled with flames. A trick of the light; he'd moved his head. But he was made of rage. She saw its shape in his shoulders, the fists he'd made of his hands. She'd never been afraid of him, not in a simple physical sense, had never feared he'd attack her during one of these visits. She'd only ever been afraid of the power he had to summon her guilt, snapping his fingers as if it were a dog he could bring to heel whenever he chose. She'd been afraid of how easily he could pull her past into the present, flavouring it with death and grief. She hadn't been able to see a young man in grey sweats with new muscles from the prison gymnasium, badly brushed teeth and tinned food breath, cheap soap under his fingernails. She'd only ever seen a phantom, her tormentor. Not this Stephen Keele, but another. One who didn't exist now, if he ever had.

'You bitch,' he said slowly, his voice low under the lights.

She turned her head a fraction towards the guard standing in the doorway. Twenty, thirty feet away. 'Don't be stupid,' she instructed Stephen. 'You have a chance at parole. But not if you do something stupid.'

'Worth it, to see you lose that fucking smile.'

'And to see your true colours.' She nodded. 'This game we've been playing? You pretending you have answers. Me insisting on my questions. It's doing neither of us any good.'

'You mean you've lost.' He took his hands off the table, folding his arms. 'And now you want to run away. Because of the photos.' He stared her down. 'Because of what you saw in the photos. You know I wasn't alone in that house.'

'Do you really want me believing it wasn't you who killed them? After all this time. Do you want me to start seeing you as the victim? Falsely accused, falsely imprisoned. Innocent. Is that the Stephen you want me to see?'

Something rippled across his face. Pleasure? She knew he relished these meetings, the chance to refill her head with doubt. To bait her.

'You're a shit detective if you think photographic evidence doesn't matter.'

'You killed them.' She didn't break eye contact. 'And you don't know why.'

She waited a beat before she said, 'But that's okay. It's not unusual. Most murders have no real reason. Most are senseless.'

'Not theirs!' He spat the words into the space between them, his whole body clenched.

Relief flooded in from a distance, like seeing the city lights after a long drive through darkness, coming home. His rage meant one thing: she was right. He didn't know why he'd killed them. Her parents. *Their* parents. Two more senseless deaths to add to London's tally.

'It's okay,' she repeated. 'I understand.'

That trapped him right on the edge of his rage – the idea of her understanding; her empathy, although he'd never use that word. She saw Felix Amos's face, transformed by fear. Felix who was unrepentant after stabbing Guy Belsham, but she'd seen his fear, how he'd fretted it into something bigger, buying into the legend of his own badness.

'You slept in my room,' she told Stephen, 'never changing it. You knew I was unhappy there, just as you were. You wanted me to understand. One person who did. And I do, I understand.'

The ghost of the boy was there, hiding behind the man's mask. The boy who'd trusted her to lift him onto the garden swing when he was eight and wouldn't let anyone else touch him. Who'd liked her police uniform when their mother had been afraid it would scare him.

'It must've been frightening to do what you did, without knowing why. And then I came with my questions, demanding an explanation. Needing it to make sense. It

344

must've been easier to start believing there *was* a reason. Better than accepting you'd made a terrible mistake.'

'No mistake,' he hissed through the clench of his teeth. 'I wanted them dead.'

'In that moment, perhaps.' She nodded. 'But it's exhausting, isn't it? Killing people. You couldn't even run after you'd done it. Just sat on the stairs and waited for the police to come.'

The way Felix had sat by the side of Guy's ruined Merc.

'I was waiting for *you*!' Stephen spat.

'I believe you. Because you were scared, and confused. Because nothing made sense.'

'I killed them for you.' He leaned forward, eyes slanting. 'You're the one who's scared. You don't want your share of the blame, won't admit how much you wanted them gone. Dead.'

'I never wanted that. But I don't believe you did either. You were angry, yes. You were confused and scared and you felt betrayed because they'd brought your mother back into your life when it was the last thing you wanted. You were meant to be safe in their house. They made a mistake, but they didn't deserve to die for it.' She held him still with her stare. 'I think you knew that, the second you finished killing them. Maybe even while you were doing it. I've seen a lot of scared kids in the last seven years. They all look like you did in the photos they took at the station, just after the murders. You looked lost.'

Right now, Stephen looked carved from stone. 'Fuck you,' he breathed. '*Fuck* you.'

She let a moment pass, the relief washing a little closer with each word they exchanged. Again she thought of Felix, how the police interview gave him the chance to show off, all their attention focused on him, Oz's and Lorna's and hers. Making him believe in his badness.

'Remember that day I came home in my uniform for the first time? You were sitting on the stairs; you liked to sit on the bottom step. I expect you were watching the door. I wanted to surprise them with the uniform. You smiled at me, kept my secret. I didn't appreciate the significance of that until I remembered it recently. We were sharing a secret, you and I. There weren't many secrets allowed in that house.' She could hear the breath churning in his chest. 'You sat on the same step after you killed them. Waiting for the police to come, waiting for me. You didn't run, or hide. You sat and waited. Did you think I'd understand?'

'I could've killed you, too.' His face fought for its mask. 'I *should* have killed you.'

'You did your best, over the last seven years. Making me doubt myself, and them. Making me search for a reason why you did what you did. As if there could be a motive for killing the two people who loved you best in the world.'

'They didn't love anyone! Not me, not you . . .'

'They loved us. You know it's true. But you panicked. And then I kept pushing. Asking the same question over and over until it must've felt so huge in your head there wasn't room for anything else. Anything better. Like remorse, or regret. That's why I'm putting an end to it. An end to us.'

'You're wrong.' He hissed the words. 'There was a reason. You just never knew the right fucking questions.'

'I'll take that much of the blame,' she agreed. 'For asking questions, making you search for answers when there were none. You killed them, and you don't know why. You've invented reasons over the years, to keep me coming. But you never pretended to have a reason back in the beginning. I should have accepted that, but I couldn't. Then I wouldn't stop coming, or asking. You must have started hating me for that, for never giving you a moment's peace to think about what you did. The senselessness of it, the waste. Their lives, and yours.'

'You think you can walk away from this?' Stephen sucked a breath until it rattled in his throat. 'From us? I'll find you. I'll fucking *haunt* you.'

'I'm sure you'll try. But I wish you wouldn't. I mean it when I say I want you to get well.'

'I'm a psychopath. We don't fucking *get well*.'

Carefully, slowly, she stood up from the table. 'I'm going now, but I want you to know I'm sorry for the part I've played in the mess we've made over the last seven years.'

'Fuck you.' His eyes were wet. 'Bitch.'

'They did love you, Stephen. They made me promise to take care of you after they were gone.'

'So do it!' He gripped the lip of the table. 'Fucking do it. You *owe* me.'

'I forgive you.'

He stared at her.

She nodded. 'I do.'

'You can't . . .' His voice broke.

She turned and walked towards the guard.

Stephen slammed his hands at the table, the room ringing with the noise of it. She heard the chair scrape under him, saw his shadow shrink as he stood.

'I'll fucking *haunt* you!' he shouted after her, kept shouting as she walked away, but the fire had frayed his voice and the shout didn't carry, cut off by the door between them, leaving her in the deep, empty silence of the corridor.

35

A thin rain was coming down, so slowly it could almost have been falling upwards, clear beads of water seeming to lift from leaves and branches, roofs and railings, upwards into a white sky.

Noah climbed from the car and straightened, his body protesting, blazing with tiredness. But he was okay, he was good. Everyone he loved was here.

Matilda Reece wore a dress so rainbow bright it dazzled. Her smile was dazzling, too. She greeted everyone with the same smile and soft words, welcoming Noah's mum as if they'd been friends all their lives. Mum shrank a little, but Dad had his arm around her, solid. It would come good. Noah was able to believe that now.

'Let my boy be the last,' Matilda told the gathered crowd. 'Let London know peace.'

Noah reached for Dan's hand, twisting their fingers together. The park was lined with people, umbrellas in a long arch over their heads. Flowers were everywhere, bouquets and wreaths, simple bunches tied with string. Tulips and roses, peonies and daisies. Beneath umbrellas, the Bellamy brothers stood shoulder to shoulder with mothers and grandmothers, fathers, uncles and grandchildren. Eric Martineau bowed his head like Oz Pembroke and Ron Carling. Marnie stood with Ed at her side, Harry Kennedy a little further back. Noah lifted a hand in greeting and Harry returned the gesture, warmly. The Bellamys carried an elaborate wreath of lilies and bronze chrysanthemums to the foot of the bandstand where Matilda was speaking into a police microphone.

'No more boys gone, no more children lost. Where there was emptiness, let us be *filled*. Put away the knives! Stand tall. Be proud of your empty fists and full hearts. Lift up London on your shoulders, carry our city forward . . . Remember Frank.'

The wreath smouldering at her feet sparked a distant memory in Noah's head. He looked to where Marnie was watching, her eyes moving from the flowers to the crowd of mourners. Working, because that was what she did. What *they* did. Marnie and Noah, and Harry and Ed, always working even when they were mourning, or remembering. What had she seen? The bronze chrysanthemums, the Bellamys shoulder to shoulder with the crowd, their heads held high. Free, for once, from the scrutiny of the police. Never mind the fact that they were Trident's chief suspects in the murder of this child they had come to mourn. The vigil, like a funeral, afforded them immunity.

'Remember Frank, and all our lost children. Let them be the last.'

Noah tipped his face to meet the rain. The exhaustion heightened the colours everywhere he looked, as if a lens had been lifted. All the shadows and soft focus stripped away, and *this* – razored edges, acid colours bright on his tongue – was the world as it really was, somewhere he was seeing for the first time. London, a place he had to learn all over again. Home.

36

In her florist's shop, Lynne Belsham was sitting at a table crowded white with flowers, arranging lilies into a wreath like the one laid by the Bellamys at the vigil for Frank Reece. Her fingers twisted the stems, pollen staining the collar of her dress.

'Mrs Belsham, may I have a word?'

Lynne looked up at Marnie, then down, at the wreath. A sigh left her, sounding almost like relief. 'You've come about the bullet.'

'Yes.' She hadn't expected it to be so easy.

'It wasn't Matilda. It wasn't anything to do with her or the other mothers, so you know.'

Marnie accepted this with a nod. She watched Raffa's mother gather a handful of green stems, holding the flowers with their fluted heads turning like living things away from her. The scent was crushing, densely funereal, a stark reminder of the service commemorating the life of Matilda's murdered child. The wreath laid by the Bellamys, with its lilies and chrysanthemums, had come from this shop. Marnie had suspected as much when she'd seen the striking choice of colours, such a close match to the floral arrangement in the Belshams' fireplace. As the crowd dispersed, she was able to study the wreath, finding a small card stapled to the foam support bearing the name of this shop, *Canterbury Belle*. A tiny florist's tucked away on the high street, four miles from Erskine Tower, blue window boxes above a pale yellow door.

'Matilda was magnificent, wasn't she?' Lynne watched the stems turning in her hands. 'So brave. Like all the mothers . . .' She laid the lilies down, inspecting the tarnished tips of her fingers. 'It was Raffa who persuaded me to send the first wreath, months ago. Ashley Benjamin, do you remember him?'

Marnie remembered. Ashley's face was on the evidence board, his head cocked, a careful crop of stubble on his chin – one of the faces haunting her and Noah. Another victim of the Bellamys, if only they could find the evidence to convict.

'Raffa was following the news stories; she'd met so many children at the tower. The school project, that's where it all began, Mr Martineau filling her head with stories, telling her about the boys lost to gangs . . . She wanted to meet them.' Lynne's face faltered in confusion. 'She *hated* boys, had nothing to do with those at her school. But the ones being arrested for possession, those she wanted to know. She tried to explain it to me, how she understood them because they were broken . . . I told her she should speak to me, or her father.' Her fingers strayed to the lilies, touching their waxen heads. 'She couldn't speak with Guy, of course. He'd adored her when she was small, but as soon as she started having opinions of her own, he lost patience with her. They were forever fighting and I was always stepping in to try and keep the peace. It was *exhausting*.' She put her hands over her face. 'I'm not looking for sympathy, I don't deserve that. I tried to put this right with the pills, but you found me.' She spoke bitterly. '*Saved* me.'

When she lifted her hands, the imprints of her fingers were on her face. 'I hid the bullet in her room because I wanted you to know. *Everything*. I had no other evidence; it was Guy's word against mine and I'm afraid of him, I'm a *coward*.' Her face tightened. 'I tried to put it right. I deserved to die, I still do. You should have let me die.'

'You were concealing drugs and weapons in the flowers at the funerals and vigils.'

'*They* were concealing them! The Bellamys. I had no idea. *None*. Not at the beginning. I delivered the wreaths in good faith. How they were using them was . . . horrible. But by the time I found out, it was too late, that's what they said.'

'How did you find out?'

'They told me!' She gave an incredulous laugh. 'They could have kept ordering the wreaths, they said, never saying what they were doing with them. But it was simpler if I knew.' Her mouth twisted out of shape. 'I was making them too shallow, when they needed more room for whatever it was they were hiding. Not every wreath, that would be too risky. But they placed lots of orders, became my best customers.' She sounded nauseated. 'It was easier, they said, if I knew what I was doing. And too late by then for me to report it. The evidence led right back to my business. They threatened me too, of course. Have you ever been threatened by a gangster?' The red stains darkened on her face. 'I was *terrified*.'

'But you didn't go to the police.'

'Because they threatened Raffa! They knew she was going into those flats, that she'd made friends with a boy there. They knew all about her, how she wore her hair, the pictures she drew. They said she wouldn't stop asking questions . . . So I did what they asked and they killed her anyway. Because they were fighting over who should get the bigger cut of whatever was being sold out of that place, the gangs in there like *rats* turning on one another. And my girl – my Raffa died.' Her eyes heated with tears but she fought against them, setting the flowers aside and stiffening in her chair. 'So you've come to arrest me for putting that bullet in her bedroom, perverting the course of justice. As if it's not perverse enough all on its own.'

'I've come to help you,' Marnie said, 'if you'll let me.'

'No.' Lynne shook her head. 'Arrest me, please. You saved me once, when I didn't want it. Guy's gone now. He'll be in prison a long time. He deserves to be, but so do I.'

She'd made friends with pain, deep in its pit, no desire to climb out. No hope of escape.

'Did you know the young woman who died the day after Raffa was killed? Samantha Haile.'

'No,' Lynne said wearily. 'I heard about her on the news, of course.'

'The Bellamys never mentioned her?'

Lynne shook her head.

'And you didn't ask about the trafficking or the young people affected by it. The lives being lost and ruined. You didn't ask questions. It was only Raffa who did that.'

'What good is asking questions? It could only make it worse. It *did* make it worse, for Raffa.' She smoothed her hands at her dress. 'I heard Matilda speak about peace, but I can never have that, I don't deserve it. I let them hide their knives and bullets because I was scared, but also because I was weak. Guy's business was doing so badly, we were going bankrupt and I was *scared*. Of him and of them, what they'd do if I stood up to them. Haven't you ever been scared?' She shut her eyes. 'They made it so easy. As if . . . All of London is knives now, and guns. You may as well try and live with it, because it's everywhere. I didn't have to *do* anything, I just delivered the wreaths and they did the rest. It was so . . . easy.' As if the city's violence was irresistible, a tide that would sweep you away if only you'd take that first small, passive step.

'Tell me about the bullet.'

'I wanted you to find out who we really were, Guy and me. Living in that house, lying to each other and everyone else. Lying to Raffa.'

'So you let us suspect her of being part of the violence in the tower block. You let us imagine she might be guilty of the weapons-smuggling she hated so much.'

'I couldn't just hand you the bullet – he'd have killed me! He was doing his own deals, with Russians, although I didn't know that until the Bellamys told me. They said it was how they knew I'd help them, because our family was corrupt. That's the word they used. *Corrupt*. They wanted to even the score between them and the Russians, like rats fighting over scraps. Guy kept saying he'd made sure we'd be all right, that money wasn't going to be a problem any longer, that he had *connections*. Russian people-traffickers!

'I'd wanted to move out of that house for a long time, downsize, but he said the city was overrun with . . .' She edited herself. 'If he'd found out about the Bellamys, he'd have killed me, I honestly believe that. And yes, I wanted to go to the police. That's why I stole the bullet. I thought as soon as I could be sure Raffa was safe – the way he kept saying she would be – I'd take it to the police and tell you everything.' She shut her eyes. 'But I left it too late. And I'd no evidence against Guy of whatever he was doing with the Russians. I didn't know enough, only that we deserved to be punished, the pair of us. I wanted us to be punished. It's what we deserve.' She fell silent, her hands lying between the fallen flowers.

Had she made the wreath for Frank in colours she knew Marnie would recognise? Or was it subconscious, a silent shout for rescue from this pit into which she'd fallen? Marnie wanted to believe that she'd meant the bullet to lead them here, to a place where she'd be arrested and persuaded to give evidence against the Bellamys. Evidence that would convict Frank's killer, and Ashley's. Justice, finally, for all the children caught in the Bellamys' cross-fire. Trident kept a respectful distance at the funerals, which meant the brothers were able to move among the crowd free from suspicion for those scant hours when families gathered to mourn their dead, using the opportunity to put weapons into new hands, more young lives in danger. Lynne's testimony, together with the bullet she'd hidden in her daughter's bedroom, could help to bring an end to that.

'I'd like you to arrest me, please.' Lynne climbed to her feet. 'I'd rather you did that than pretended there was a way out. My family's gone, my daughter's dead. *My* fault. And Matilda was right, it needs to end. That's your job, it's what you do, you *end* things. So please.' She held out her hands, their red-scaled wrists together. 'End this for me. I want it to be over.'

'Lynne Belsham, I am arresting you on suspicion of attempting to pervert the course of justice, and participating in the activities of organised criminals. You do not have to say anything . . .'

Marnie stayed behind after the squad car took Raffa's mother to the station, wanting a moment longer in the fresh air outside the florist's shop. Jasmine had been planted in the blue window boxes, its flowers in hoops, strung with heavy raindrops. Jasmine had been her mother's favourite flower. She stood and breathed its scent, so familiar, watching as the petals straightened under the weight of the rain, growing towards the light the way flowers did.

Her phone rang, a number she recognised: HMP Cloverton. Stephen, calling to curse her. Or the prison staff needing to contact her, perhaps urgently.

She declined the call and returned the phone to her pocket, reaching her empty hand to touch the frail petals of the jasmine as it faltered, trembling, for the sun.

Acknowledgements

Rhyhiem Ainsworth Barton was seventeen years old when he was killed in London on Saturday 5 May 2018, just after 6 p.m. He was one of three teenagers shot in the city on the same day. Rhyhiem was not in a gang. He was an aspiring architect who was learning to work with children because he wanted to make a difference. His mother, Pretana Morgan, said, 'Let my son be the last and be an example to everyone. Just let it stop. It's not about race, it's not about nation, it's not about culture. Nothing. It's just a human race. Just one human race. So children, please let my son be the last.'

This book is dedicated to Pretana, and her wish for Rhyhiem to be the last of London's children killed in this way.

I'd like to thank my fellow panellists at the Killer Women 'Changing Crimescape' event at the Bath Festival of Literature, for a fascinating discussion that informed a lot of the political detail in this book: Leye Adenle, Winnie Li and Mel McGrath.

Both Imogen Taylor and Stephanie Glencross helped to make this a better book. I'm grateful to Clare Mackintosh for her advice on bereavement counselling within the police force; any errors are entirely my own. My thanks to Mick Herron for the loan of the Russians.

My happiest thanks to the readers, bloggers and reviewers who've supported Marnie and Noah on this journey. It's possible I could've done this without you, but it wouldn't have been nearly as much fun.

And lastly, thank you to Karie Matthews, who won the Get in Character auction in support of the CLIC Sargent charity. I hope you approve of your role in the story.

NEVER BE BROKEN

Bonus Material

London's lost children

On a recent trip to Japan, I was struck by the sight of a small child taking the subway by herself. No older than five, with a rucksack strapped to her back (containing a pair of ice skates), she was unfazed by the crowds, slipping into spaces between the salarymen and tourists with a solemn expression on her face. Our guide for the day explained how it is common for kids of her age to be independent and, evidently, Tokyo is a safe city.

Initially chilled at the thought of infants travelling alone, I came to see how positively it affected the children in question, and the adults around them. We felt safer, on our first trip to Tokyo, after witnessing the confidence with which this little girl navigated her city. The usual state of affairs in Japan is only shocking to tourists like ourselves, who have come to view our own cities as such perilous places.

How many parents in London would allow their infants to travel alone on the tube? How many children would feel safe doing so? We proclaim child safety to be an essential feature of any civilised society, but even a casual study of statistics for knife crime fatalities among our young people give the lie to this ideal.

Lost children haunt my DI Marnie Rome series. Those

who have fallen through the cracks in the system, becoming killers like Marnie's foster brother Stephen, or those who are simply battling to stay alive. We may not think it a good idea to allow our five-year-olds to travel alone but in too many other ways, we are failing to keep them safe.

Never Be Broken, at its heart, is about the care we take of our children, and the carelessness which typifies too many violent and senseless deaths.

Where is the protection we owe to our young people, not just in terms of policing, but youth support workers, education, mental health services? Child poverty has hit a record high, and is set to rise over the next four years. Over half of these children are under the age of five. How is it that we are failing them so badly?

If our primary duty is the protection of our children, we also have a responsibility to raise strong and independent young people. Increasingly, it seems to me, these two duties are in conflict. We cannot keep our children safe simply by shutting them away, although it is not hard to understand the temptation to do exactly that, when our cities and towns are fraught with threat and danger.

While writing this book, I thought often of the little Japanese girl on her way to ice skating class, standing so steadily in the crowded subway car. And I wished the same freedoms for our children. Which is not to say that Japanese society does not have its own problems, but such confidence and independence at such a young age is a rare gift.

The children in *Never Be Broken* have been dying in London at an alarming rate by the time Marnie and Noah find themselves face to face with the grieving parents of Raffa Belsham. Her brutal death appears to be a tragic accident, but is it any less tragic or appalling than the deaths which have come before, or will follow? Marnie and Noah must keep faith with all of London's lost children if they are to do their jobs properly, and well.

Never Be Broken is dedicated to Pretana Morgan whose son, Rhyhiem Ainsworth Barton, was seventeen years old when he was needlessly murdered in London on Saturday 5 May 2018. Hearing his mother speak on the BBC so movingly of her loss drove home to me not only the scale of our collective failure, but the absolute need to cherish and celebrate each life.

All the evidence suggests we are becoming inured to violence, that the rising tide of knife crime is sweeping away our shock and outrage. We are in danger of committing a new betrayal of our young people: a passive acceptance that their deaths are no more than the price to be paid in our cities.

I wrote *Never Be Broken* as a battle cry against this acceptance, and as a tribute to the courage of Pretana Morgan and every mother who, despite her overwhelming grief and loss, is fighting on behalf of London's lost children.

August 2019

A Short (Mostly True) History of The Scala

London has changed a lot since I lived there in the 1990s (hell, it's changed a lot since I started writing my DI Marnie Rome series, six years ago). One of the themes of *Never Be Broken* is how much it's changed, feeling so newly alien and dangerous to men like DS Noah Jake, who was born in London and is struggling to police his home city.

In this piece, I wanted to write about one of my favourite places, from all those long years ago, when I was new to London and still learning its secrets.

Noah's favourite nightclub, where he and Dan drink tequila, is loosely based on the Scala in King's Cross. Like so many of the characters in my books, the Scala has a chequered past. Beneath its brash, newly neon surface, is a building that's been home to drunks, lovers, zombies, hooligans, a cat called Roy, countless lonely hearts and caged apes.

Yes, really. Apes.

I knew the Scala when it was a cinema. For me, all cinemas are magical places. Like books, they open doors into other worlds. As a teenager, I'd spend hours watching double-bills in a pokey auditorium in Manchester, emerging like a newborn blinking into the dazzle of late afternoon, giddy on adrenalin.

What made the Scala special was its all-nighters. From pm on Saturday night until 9am on Sunday morning, for the price of a good cup of coffee in today's money, you could watch film after film after film, in the company of anyone and everyone who wanted a warm home for the night.

All-Night George A. Romero. All-Night Alien-Blob-type-Things. All-Night Woody Allen. (That last one was a mistake; a little Woody Allen goes a long way.)

The Scala was my idea of heaven. With just a flavour of hell.

Because – what was that strange smell haunting the auditorium? Probably whatever the person in the row behind you was smoking. And the heavy-breathing soundtrack from the stalls? Couples who found Woody Allen inexplicably arousing (or just possibly they hadn't come to watch the films). And what brushed against your leg at all the scariest moments onscreen? That was Roy, the Scala's resident cat. His timing was terrifying.

Downstairs, things got even stranger.

If you wandered off piste, you'd find cages in the basement. Green paint slashed up the walls, peeling to bare plaster in places, but emphatically green. Were those . . . trees painted on the walls? And vines? Creepers?

Yes, yes, and yes.

At one time, circa 1971, the Scala was a blue movie venue, to use the old-fashioned vernacular. King's Cross was notorious for that sort of thing but the business wasn't lucrative, and new owners moved in. How to make money out of premises this size, in such a prime location? Where blue movies had failed, what might succeed? Apes, apparently.

In 1979, London's first (and to date its last) ape-house opened its doors. With walls painted to resemble a jungle, the London Primatorium lasted only months before it went the way of its predecessors. The cages however remained, together with the fossilised droppings of the poor primates. Years later, film-lovers like me would wonder at that strange, warm, earthy scent that seemed to come up from under our feet. Forget surround-sound; the Scala had surround-smell.

(There was a glorious period in the 80s, sadly before my time, when the cinema's clientele included Andy Warhol, Pasolini, Fassbinder and Derek Jarman, and the Scala acquired the nickname, 'The Sodom Odeon'.)

The Scala cinema closed its doors in 1993. Rumours say it was sued into the ground by Stanley Kubrick for showing *A Clockwork Orange* once too often, and always in contravention of his ban on UK screenings of the film. An anarchic ending for a home to the strangest heroes. Like many, I was sad to see it go. When, years later, I was wondering where DS Noah Jake might unwind, dust the day's work from his feet and get frisky with his boyfriend, the Scala sprang to mind.

Luckily for me (and Noah) the Scala had reinvented itself, again. Cleaned out the cages, whitewashed the creepers from the walls, banished the zombies. But it still has its arms wide open for drunks, lovers, lonely hearts and the coolest of cool cats.

Sarah Hilary's Top Ten Strange Tastes in Fiction

It's a special kind of alchemy when a writer lets you taste the words on the page – not black ink on white wood pulp, but the waxy acid-yellow of lemons, or an iron-rich tang of blood. Visceral writing is my favourite kind. I want to see and hear and smell and taste the world I'm reading about. These books will grab you by the tonsils and never let you go.

1. *The Siege* by Helen Dunmore

Leningrad, September 1941. The dead of winter. Snow in the streets, ice inside the houses. No food for weeks. Resourceful Anna feeds her starving family first on wallpaper paste, before boiling leather to make soup. A tribute to Dunmore's skill that, after pages of feeling the taut hunger in the house, you smack your lips at the prospect.

2. *Serenade* by James M. Cain

Surely the greatest meal in one of the greatest crime novels of all time. As our hero says, 'Well, brother, you can have your Terrapin Maryland. It's a noble dish, but it's not Iguana John Howard Sharp.' Caught by the woman he's just assaulted, cooked alive in a pot in a desecrated Mexican church, this iguana should leave a nasty taste in your mouth, but that sticky, tender soup is something else.

3. *Lolita* by Vladimir Nabokov

I suspect Humbert's Pin, a blend of gin and pineapple juice, has a sweet, stern flavour. A tang of forbidden fruit, a splash of mother's ruin; the weeper's drink. He writes, 'A reek of sap mingled with the pineapple . . . the gin and Lolita were dancing in me.' And there, in a single buzz on your tastebuds, is the whole thirsty rotten core of the story, so expertly wrought.

4. *American Psycho* by Bret Easton Ellis

Peanut butter soup, 'a playful but mysterious little dish,' is followed by red snapper with violets and pine nuts. A step up from leather soup, but not by much. It's one of my chief regrets that Patrick Bateman isn't dining out in this day and age; I'd love to listen to him laying into quinoa and kale.

5. *Chocolat* by Joanne Harris

Better than any cookbook (no cooking required) this is a story steeped in scents and flavours. Bittersweet, piquant and delicious. Not only the chocolate, but every meal is brought to your tongue by well-chosen words.

6. *The Road* by Cormac McCarthy

What do I taste when I think of this book? Black tar, scorched earth, and the parched inside of my own mouth.

And – for one miraculous, syrup-slippery, golden moment – tinned peaches. Eaten in a bunker, in the book's only breathing space. A bright burst of taste that sustains you through to the bitter end.

7. *The Metamorphosis* by Franz Kafka

I'm still trying to get the taste of this one from between my teeth: 'Bones from the evening meal, covered in white sauce that had gone hard'. Something about that sauce stays with me; like eating someone else's dental plaque.

8. *The Hitchhiker's Guide to the Galaxy* by Douglas Adams

Four words. Pan-Galactic Gargle Blaster. Say it out loud. You can taste it, can't you?

9. *Hannibal* by Thomas Harris

Not the best of Harris's books by a long stretch, but I have a weakness for 'a portion of Krendler's brain – from the prefrontal lobe – sautéed in a pan with shallots and white wine.' Way to cleanse our palates of the fava beans, Thomas.

10. *Lamb to the Slaughter* by Roald Dahl

Mary Maloney cooked her leg of lamb straight from the freezer. I've often wondered whether it tasted as good as fresh lamb, or if the policemen who belched as they ate it, ended up with food poisoning, on top of everything else. It's terrible the way a crime writer's mind works.

THRILLINGLY GOOD BOOKS
FROM CRIMINALLY
GOOD WRITERS

CRIME FILES BRINGS YOU THE LATEST RELEASES FROM
TOP CRIME AND THRILLER AUTHORS.

SIGN UP ONLINE FOR OUR MONTHLY NEWSLETTER AND BE THE FIRST
TO KNOW ABOUT OUR COMPETITIONS, NEW BOOKS AND MORE.